Toby

Book One of a Trilogy:

Toby
Toby Seizes the day
Toby's Fight

By

Charlie Loughman

Published by New Generation Publishing in 2014

Copyright © Charlie Loughman 2014

First Edition

www.newgeneration-publishing.com

New Generation **Publishing**

To my wife Angela who has put up with me for nearly 55 years and to my wonderful former PA, secretary, carer and general gofer Gabriella who has been with me for over 12 years and become almost one of the family; she transcribed my long hand scroll into type, all 700 pages. Also all my thanks to my son Piers and daughter Claire and for their support!

I am grateful to Angela's cousin Suzi and her husband Simon for their help with checking the typescript.

Characters

Toby Cooper-Sneyd, also known as Toby Cooper: Leaves the Army to carve out a new career in Yorkshire

Mother: Angela killed in a hunting accident when he was 8

Father: Charles was a corn merchant auctioneer and a bon viveur, raconteur, gambler, brilliant golfer, shot, fishing

Claire: Toby's mistress in the Army, her husband Peregrine

Liam Reilly: Irish, ex life guards, rough riding instructor at Aldershot Saddle Club

Kath: Liam's wife

Joe Smith: Toby's batman, good mechanic working in a garage in North Yorkshire

Christine: Joe's girlfriend, working at the garage as a secretary

Silas Rigby: Reclusive farmer, ex SAS, Toby's mentor

Colin Parker: Garage owner

Jenny: His wife, died a few years ago of breast cancer

Penny: Their daughter, pretty girl with long auburn hair, keeps men at bay, went to grammar school, then college studying interior design and antiques, works for Hugo

Hugo: Runs an antique shop, in his 50's

Carol: Hugo's wife, snob, fridgid, no time for Hugo

Liz: Elizabeth Mellor, ex debutante, moved up with old friends Freddy and Bobbie, her Labrador dog Bess, has on-off affair with Lord Thomas Middleham

Freddy: Late 60's, landlord, old retired Guards Major, very smart, a drinker, gambler, little work shy

Bobbie: Early 40's, Freddy's long term partner

Lord Thomas Middleham: Eton, The Blues, his wife Catherine Woodhouse was killed in a carcrash

Harry: Thomas's son, 23 years old, The Hon.Harry, only son, Eton, Royal Agricultural College Cirencester, looks a bit simple but really very bright

Jill: Harry's girlfriend, is the daughter of a landowner/farmer, met Harry at Cirencester

Harold Farrar: Bank manager, Barclay's, Masham

Joyce: his assistant

Millie: Little girl, clerk

'Lino' Moore: owns carpet shops in Masham, Bedale, Ripon, Harrogate, Knaresborough, he sells more lino than carpet

Pub Locals:

Major Murphy: 'Spud' called by everyone The Major

Walter: Very good builder

Arthur: Walter's right-hand man

Harry: Builder-carpenter

Bert: Old stone mason who taught Walter his skills

Paul: Young apprentice builder

Major Holgate: head of the waterboard

Maggie Williams: His secretary

Basil Mortimer: The local Doctor

Eunice: his wife

JeremyWoodhouse MP: Lord Thomas's brother in law

Felicity: Mark's wife

Gerald Woodhouse: Marks's younger brother, merchant banker

Miranda: His wife

Mark Thompson: Area director for William Hill
Sylvia his wife

Ernest Simpson: Local lawyer

Simon: His son becomes Toby's lawyer/friend

Mike Mortimer: friend of Ernest retired surveyor

Myles Jackson: waterboard surveyor

Karen Bateson: Assistant planning officer

CHAPTER ONE

The pale, late April sun, that afternoon in the early nineteen sixties, struggled through the chink in the cheap curtains to land in a golden splash down her long, naked thigh. She was lying on her back, her thick, auburn hair spreading across the pillow.

Toby, on his side, gazed at her wonderful body: her long, slender aristocratic nose, the full, slightly pouting mouth and superb full breasts with their still excited nipples, down to the flat stomach and mass of thick auburn hair.

She slowly opened her eyes to look at Toby, who had always thought they were her greatest asset, being large, green and oval.

They had been lovers for over a year. As she ran a finger over his lips she said huskily, 'that was one of best ever Toby, but how long will it be before we can be together again.'

She adoringly took him in for what might be a long time. How could she let him go? He kissed her full on her mouth and stood by her side.

His blond hair was parted down the middle, and swept back over his ears. She traced a finger down his broken nose as he smiled in that 'little boy lost' way of his, showing his even, perfectly white teeth.

He was just under 6 feet tall without a spare bit of fat on his athletic body. She couldn't stop looking and touching his larger-than-life penis, who he called Tom.

She had once got her tape measure from her needlework box and giggled as she had recorded 7 1/2 inches.

She adored his wit, humour, cleanliness and total care for a woman. She still wondered why the hell she wasn't going with him.

Claire was married to a major, some 10 years her senior, dedicated to become a Brigadier like his father.

She wondered why she had married him. He was all that Toby wasn't. He was cold, unemotional, very tight with money and had no sense of humour.

She at least had some 'standing'. The adjutant's wife, destined for good postings to exotic places. All she yearned for was love and having children, which, regretfully for Peregrine's low sperm count, seemed unlikely.

'Look luvvie,' said Toby, 'I will have to shove off as I leave the army tomorrow. God knows where I'll end up. Give me the telephone number of your sister so we can post letters through her.

'I feel so awful about leaving you, but as you know, I'm virtually penniless, and will have to bring in some real money before I could even think about asking you to join me.'

'I know my love,' she said. 'We are a bit like Romeo and Juliet'.

'Or Abelard and Heloise,' pondered Toby.

'No, I don't think I'm cut out to be a Monk.'

'Nor me a nun,' replied Claire.

'I can think of nun nicer,' quipped Toby in the old gag.

He slipped on his boxer shorts and tracksuit before his trainers and taking a sobbing, naked Claire in his arms to give her a long, deep kiss.

He turned and as he opened the bedroom door he blew her a kiss, saying 'I'll see you tonight in the mess.'

**** **** ****

He nipped into the front room and quickly scanned the empty road outside, before going into the kitchen, sliding out of the back door and vaulting the low fence into the empty sports field.

He ran a couple of fast circuits round the cinder track before running onto the road leading to the officer's mess. The brightly lit windows cast a bright pool of light onto the gravel drive outside.

He could see uniformed bandsmen carrying their instruments in the large, open double front doors.

Glancing at his watch, he realised he had about half an hour to shower, shave, get into his mess kit for the last time and be present in the mess. Drink in hand he would wait for the colonels' arrival with all the senior officers and their ladies.

Ladies' Night was looked forward to for months by the ladies, as an occasion to glam up to wear their best dress, get their hair done to look their best to support their husbands. It was a great opportunity to gossip and pass on the latest scandals.

Toby ran into the single officer's block opposite and let himself into his small, single-bedded room.

The room was lit by the bright glow from a coal fire in the small, round pot-bellied iron stove. Its black chimney pipe went up through the roof.

He grinned to see that Joe had filled a full skip of coal and laid out on his bed his mess kit jacket and trousers, a white shirt with his grandfather's gold cufflinks in the cuffs and his highly polished boots and spurs under the bed.

He whispered a 'thank God' for Joe, his Batman, and taking off his wet track suit, hung it over the back of a wooden chair, putting it at a safe distance from the fire.

He slipped on his old leather mules, a towel round his waist and, grabbing his plastic wash bag, sprinted up the cold corridor to the washroom at the end of the block.

After briskly towelling, he ran back to his room, the damp towel round his waist.

He rotated like a joint of meat on a spit in front of the fire. He clambered quickly into his uniform, stoked up the fire and strolled over to the mess. All done in 15 minutes, he thought.

**** **** ****

There were two guards in their best uniforms who quickly snapped to attention. Toby returning their salutes, addressed them by name and hoped they wouldn't be there too long.

After Toby had gone inside, they muttered to each other how bloody good he was to remember their names, as they were both from another company. What a bloody shame he was going 'cos he was a really good bloke, the sort you trusted to get you out of shit.

It was a glittering affair. The Corps Band played military music in the lobby, and Toby joined all the other junior officers, gathered like gannets, to make sure they had more than their fair share of drinks and canapés, which were served by soldiers that had quickly been turned into waiters.

The president of the mess announced 'Dinner is served'.

The band struck up with the Regimental March, and all the junior officers lined up to shake hands with a line of senior officers and their ladies. They then went in to take their places at the table.

The senior officers and wives went into the now-empty ante-room, and guzzled a rather good rose champagne and canapés.

On their eventual appearance in the dining room, the young officers stood up and slow hand-clapped them into their seats. The padre said Grace and they tucked in what was the first of seven courses, if you counted the sorbet in the middle and the savouries at the end!

After a truly sumptuous dinner well-washed down with copious glasses of sherry, wine and port, came the tedious speeches. Acknowledging Toby's service, the colonel presented him with an initialled pewter beer mug.

Toby had prepared a quick speech and couple of good stories, which to him seemed to go down quite well.

The senior officers and their ladies, followed by the rest, trouped into the ante-room and lobby, where the lights were dimmed and the band was playing dance music. The rules were you had to queue up for a quick dance with the colonel's wife, than move down from the old major's wives to the more junior wives.

There was a definite hold-up of young bucks not wanting to leave Claire, who looked sensational.

Toby eventually got to her, and they were a little too close for the ferret-like Peregrine, who stayed within an arm's length, dancing with some ancient old major's wife.

'That was the best ever today,' she murmured as they whisked away into a far corner. 'You'll write, won't you?' she asked. 'Course,' Toby replied.

'Come and join me when I can afford to keep you.' They managed one last kiss unnoticed by Peregrine!

**** **** ****

Toby's alarm had gone off at 07:00. He was immediately awake and swung his legs onto the bedside mat. God, he felt grotty and stuck two alka-seltzers into a water glass and groaned as even the bubbles seemed too loud!

After a quick shower and shave he quickly dressed in an old check shirt, blue slip over, old light-coloured cord trousers, wearing his highly polished brown Brogues.

He fished out a large cardboard box labelled Alkits, and added his mess kit, boots and spurs to the service dress, cap, and Sam-Browne belt.

Everything else was crammed into an old leather suitcase. He took out a large A4 brown envelope, and, sitting, on the bed checked his final bank statement from Williams & Glynn's.

His £500 bounty from the MOD for his five years short service commission (called National Service Bounty Hunters Bonus), and the £1000 he received from his late father's estate for the year.

At least, I'll get £20 a week, thought Toby. The rest had gone on mess bills, keeping his old TR3A on the road and generally having a good time.

Now he realised that he had to make his own way, and had decided to go north with Joe, his Batman, who was also leaving the army today.

They got on well. Joe was a straight-talking, Yorkshire countryman. He was engaged to a pretty girl, working at the same family run country garage in Masham.

Toby, Lincolnshire born and bred, had no longer any ties and decided to go along to see what he could do to make some money and settle down.

The one thing he had really got from his late, gorgeous, young mother had been her love and skill with horses, though not skilled enough or just bloody unlucky to have been killed in some freak riding accident when Toby was just eight.

A natural horseman, Toby had wrangled himself onto the advanced riding course at the saddle club run by an old cavalry colonel.

The Army Cross Country Team trained there, and it was where Toby had met Liam Reilly, a former rough-riding sergeant from the Life Guards.

Liam was hard on his pupils, and even harder on himself, seeking perfection and dedication from his pupils, staff and even the horses. He would look after a horse before a man.

He had been used to having all the problems or 'head bangers' of horses left to him to 'sort out'. Sort them out, he did. Toby supposed he was one of those original breed of horse whisperers, because he would be on his own in an enclosed riding school when the groom brought in the horse. He was told to take off the head-collar and bugger off.

No sightseers were allowed until after about forty minutes to an hour, when Liam would give a couple of light taps on the stable door.

When the groom entered with the head collar and lead, Liam would walk up to the calm horse standing alone in the middle of the empty arena. He would give it a piece of carrot from his pocket and walk back to the groom, the horse calmly walking by his side.

Many have said that whenever in the future one of these former 'naughty' horses got within 20 yards of Liam they would snicker to get near to him.

Liam had seen a kindred spirit in Toby, although they were from entirely different backgrounds. They would tack up a horse early in the morning and go over the cross-country course and end with a good gallop near the tank training grounds. A mutual respect and friendship developed and Toby was often asked back to Liam's married quarters that he shared with his wife Kath, who he always called Mavourneen. They had two bright little boys, both the spitting image of Liam and both could nearly ride as well as their doting father. 'Sure they will both wearing the Hunting Green of the Irish Team before they are out of their teens.'

Liam's dream was to buy a small farm near Kildare and set up training horses, maybe even for the flat, because, 'Jesus,' said Liam, 'That's where the money is.'

'How on earth can you scrape the money together?' asked Toby. 'Believe me Liam, I'd help if I could, because I believe in you and you have a lovely family with Kath to keep your feet on the ground.'

'That's kind of you lad,' said Liam laying a gnarled hand on Toby's arm. His brown eyes narrowed and bored straight into Toby's trusting blue eyes. Liam quickly looked at Kath who gave an imperceptible nod, before he growled 'I'm going to give you the key to Pandora's Box, the secret of how I'm quietly starting stocking up a lot of cash.

'It sounds a bit like the Mafia,' muttered Toby.

'Well, it is a bit,' joined in Kath, 'But Liam trusts you, Toby and knows you won't let us down.'

'You will have realised,' said Liam in an unnaturally low, soft voice, 'that I've had hundreds of young riders pass through my hands over the years. Well, a handful have become trainers, Head lads in top yards, even owners, bloodstock agents, you name it, I have had them. Well, out of all that I have now got eight or ten who give the nod when a certain horse will win. We are not talking about short odds here, but real touches at around 10/1 even 25/1.

'I know it's daft, but they do win about 80% of the time at huge prices. Okay, there might only be one or two a week or occasionally two or three in one day. Now, that's when I wet myself because even a small bet on say three horses at odds of perhaps 8/1 gives a 576 treble.

'I have been doing very well. With Kath, we have just about got the money to buy a farm in Kildare that I have had my eye on. One more year will stock it and leave plenty in the bank.'

'I don't know what to say, Liam.'

'Simple. Ring Kath and she will tell you the course time and name of ones we are backing. She will tell you when next to ring. I have found it best to use two or three bookies 'cos they will soon be onto you if you keep winning.'

With that Liam spat into his huge upturned hand. Toby did the same and they slapped their hands together before they all drank the bottle of Jameson's Irish Whiskey he had brought for Liam.

CHAPTER TWO

That had been several months ago, which allowed Toby to pay off his bank overdraft, several gambling debts, expensive mess bill and living life to the full. Now he'd got to build up a good asset base and a bank big enough to tide him over the bad times.

He remembered he had to ring Kath today around 8.00. She excitedly gave him three horses, saying, 'they are all at long odds, but each from a really reliable source. Liam says, put them in an each way patent. That's fourteen bets of course! Liam also says, be brave as it could be our best day yet!'

There were sharp three taps on the door and then it crashed open. Joe, his Batman dressed in jeans, trainers and a faded red T-shirt launched into the room. He was about 6'4 tall. A shock of black hair topped his brown, tanned, round face. The face of a solid, dependable countryman, with the huge hands of a boxer.

'Are you about ready, sir,' he asked, snapping to attention. 'You can call me Toby from now on, Joe. I've just got to grab some breakfast. If you will pack the kit in the car, my shotgun, old leather case and that big cardboard box for Alkits. They will want to drum me out after breakfast, so will you wait with TR just outside the gates?'

'Done boss,' replied Joe. 'I'll just clear up here, hand my own kit in and be waiting for you.'

Toby slapped the gentle giant on his back, saying, 'See you soon'.

He walked slowly up to the Mess for the last time, loving the crisp spring sunshine turning the stone a mellow gold.

He took his silver napkin ring with his initials on and slipped it into his pocket. The long table was still filled with silver as he went to join the queue of officers. Grabbing a plate, he quickly lifted a solid silver tureen top and scooped out two generous spoonfuls of fishy-smelling kedgeree. Topping up a tumbler with freshly squeezed orange juice, he took his place at the long mess table.

There were various comments about civvies not being allowed in the mess. He quickly downed the excellent Kedgeree before returning to the sideboard filled with silver tureens. He decided on a full English breakfast of two fried eggs, bacon, mushrooms, and tomato. After all, he thought, he was travelling north and it might be a while before his next meal.

'When are you leaving dear boy?' asked an older major. 'I've just to take a quick look at the papers and down a coffee in the anteroom,' said Toby, 'And I'll be off and out of your hair chaps.'

He took his coffee into the ante-room, picked up a copy of Sporting Life and sat in one of the dark brown leather chairs in the corner. With trembling fingers he found the first horse on his list in the 1:15 at Haydock. Checking the forecast odds, he couldn't believe it was 12/1.

The next horse in the 2:00 at Catterick was forecasted at 20/1, with the final horse in the 3.00 at Catterick at 8/1. Only a fool would think they could have a chance, but knowing they very rarely failed, he calculated the best bet with the £30 he had available would be a £2ew Patent (3 wins, 3 doubles, 1 trebles) costing £28.

A big sum, but with a big pay-out if even three horses were second or third.

He pulled a blank William Hill betting slip from his wallet and wrote down the bet. Finishing his coffee he carefully refolded the new paper and stuffed it under the Times.

At the door he was grabbed by both arms, legs, hoisted aloft by a group of young officers and run down to the Main Gate. The military police and their sergeant lined the barrier, rifles at the ready.

'Having trouble, sir?' enquired the sergeant to the senior officer.

'No sergeant, we've just found a civvy in the mess and we are running him out of camp.'

The guard moved, the heavy barrier was raised and Toby dropped into the passenger seat of the waiting TR3A driven by Joe. Toby's old platoon and many from the other units cheered and wished him well. One wag yelled out, 'If you find it too hard in Civvy Street, sir, you are always welcome back here.' Praise indeed from an ordinary squaddie for a popular officer.

With a roar, they were off, and on turning the corner they saw a single auburn-haired young woman, Claire, who waved a handkerchief shouting, 'Promise you will write.'

Toby blew a kiss. 'You know I will.'

**** **** ****

'Right boss,' said Joe. 'Where now?'

'First stop Alkits, Joe.' They sped down Queen's Parade, turning left at the traffic lights. 'Look at that Joe, one space bang outside! I think it's going to be a lucky day,' hastily crossing both fingers.

He staggered out of the car, cradling the large cardboard box in his arms, like a baby. As he reached the door, it was swung open by a small, dapper little man.

Later Toby would think that Mr. Humphrey's in "Are You Being Served" was based on him. Sydney took the box from Toby and minced over to the counter.

'Mr. Turner and I have been expecting you.' Mr. Turner came out of his cubby-hole office with the name "D.D. Turner Manager" on the door. Toby thought how un-thoughtful the parents had been to saddle him with the initials DDT.

A bald, very thin, worried-looking Mr. Turner put out a limp, well-manicured hand to Toby, who gave it a good shake, making Sydney wince.

Sydney pushed open the lid and started gently lifting out the contents.

'One blue cap, one service cap. Oh,' he exclaimed, 'you haven't got the badge. Never mind.'

He laid everything, closely checking for marks. His hand travelled softly over the trousers, remembering with excitement when he had taken Toby's inside leg measurement. He just couldn't believe anyone could have such a whopper. He had almost broken out in what his aged mother called palpitations.

'That all looks as we agree sir,' broke in Mr. Turner. 'We agreed on £25.'

'That's fine then,' said Toby. 'I've closed my bank account, rather than a cheque may I be paid in cash?'

'Of course sir,' replied Mr. Turner, opening the till with a key from his pocket. 'Sydney, please make out a receipt, oh and good day sir, it's been a pleasure of being assistance.' He swept off to his 'cubicle'.

Sydney handed over five crisp £5 notes saying, 'If ever you are in need of a nice new suit sir, I would personally assist you,' and in a half whisper said, 'I'm sure I could work out a little discount.'

'That's very kind of you and if I'm ever back, might well take you up on it.' Sydney giggled all the way to the door. For a ghastly minute Toby thought he was going to blow him a kiss.

Climbing back into the car, Toby told Joe to go round the corner, where they parked up near William Hill.

'Won't be a tick, Joe.' The betting shop was fairly small, dark and smelled a stale cigarette smoke even this early in the morning. Toby handed over the betting slip to the clerk behind the counter asking, 'Can I take the prices on these?'

The clerk quickly entered the current prices from his ledger and passed it back for Toby to check. He couldn't believe it, just the same as the prices in the paper in the morning as he handed over £30, getting 2 £1 notes back.

'Just say I was lucky with any of them. As I'm going north, can I collect it at any branch of William Hill?'

'Of course.'

12

'What is the nearest to Ripon?'

'We have one at Ripon and one in Harrogate, both close at 5.30,' replied the clerk with the condescending look from a parent to his misguided child. Not missed by Toby who thought, I'll show you, you bugger.

'Right, home, Joe and don't spare the horses.' Very apt, he thought as they set off.

**** **** ****

Leaving Aldershot they travelled north to get to the A1. It was a pleasant, bright morning with fairly light traffic, so with the hood down and the warm sun they made good progress. 'Tell me about the garage you work at, Joe.'

'Oh, it's a small country garage with a couple of petrol and diesel pumps with the Roots Group Agency. Colin, my boss, inherited it from his father, who was the local blacksmith. Colin did well at Ripon Grammar and went on to do a motor mechanics apprenticeship at a big dealer's in Leeds.

'He is always full of new ideas and smart ways to make work more efficient. He's wasted on a small garage. I reckon he should be M.D of a right big company. I know he could do it.'

'What's stopping him?'

'Well, I think he had a good offer to sell up and join a big outfit, but that was before.' Joe tailed off.

'Before what?' asked Toby.

'Before his wife got cancer. It was right quick. She was a lovely woman and so sad to leave a little girl, Penny who was about 15.

It's been hard on Colin, raising her single-handed these last 10 years, but he loves her so much. She is the spitting image of her mum, who was a right head turner. Penny was brighter even than Colin at school, but didn't want to leave Colin and go to university. She studied interior design and antiques at a local college, and went on to be an antiques and fine arts dealer with an old pal of Colin's in

Harrogate. She runs his shop in Harrogate and goes all over with him, buying stock and giving important valuations to some of the biggest country houses. She is right well respected, is our Penny.'

'What age is the bloke she works for?'

'Oh, about mid-fifties, I'd say. Bit too neat for me, some say he's AC/DC, you know, likes to bat for both sides,' chuckled Joe.

'Surely Penny, with her looks must attract a lot of young blokes?'

'You'd think so, but some says she is frigid, one of those ice maidens, maybe a bit of a prick teaser who eggs 'em on then that's it, just gets rid of them.'

'How fascinating,' muttered Toby, privately thinking that Penny certainly needed the attention of a younger man and he could not help a quick grin.

'What are you so pleased at?' asked Joe.

'Only that we were doing bloody well and I think we ought to stop for a pint, pie and a piss.'

'In that order?'

'Well, piss, pint, pie and another piss for the road. Talking of the road, we ought to fill Fiona up.'

'Why do you call your car Fiona?'

'After a headstrong, reckless, gorgeous ex-girlfriend, who was just as headstrong and difficult. She was a brigadier's daughter I met in the officer's club, when I was an officer cadet at Mons.

'I'd arranged to meet her at the weekend. The whole platoon was given a rare 48 hour pass out of the blue. Gerald and I took off like bats out of hell to London, where his mother Lady Killarney had a flat.

'She was away for the weekend. We went on to South Kensington Young Conservatives, where all the bright and footloose daddy's girls in London used to go on the prowl.

'Well, Gerald and I took four home and never moved out of the flat for nearly two days. Lady Killarney's cellar was totally drunk dry, while two of the girls, both cordon bleu trained cooks, fed us all between romps in bed.

'I completely forgot about poor Fiona. It was only when the CSM called me into his office after the parade. He told me I was a complete disgrace, and the brigadier had chewed his balls off and I had to make amends.'

'What did you do?' asked Joe.

'I lent my car to the CSM for the weekend so he could take his missus shopping. Then I rang the local florist to deliver a large bouquet to Fiona. I never heard from her again. I knew I'd been a complete shit and deserved it.'

**** **** ****

They pulled into the Ram Jam Inn near Stretton, where Toby first filled Fiona up to the brim.

'That should be enough to get us to Masham.' They pulled into an empty spot near the pub and they noticed that the car park was nearly full of Rovers, Jags and salesmen's Ford Zodiacs, a promising sight as they obviously reckoned the pub was worth the stop.

They pulled the tonneau cover over to cover the open cockpit, and went into the dark, beamed pub. A log fire cracked in the grate and they both went into the Gents. Seeing a pay phone by the door Toby told Joe to grab a table and join him after he made a call.

'Is that the first?'

'Yes, at 12/1.'

'Do you say the second was at 20/1?' asked Joe. 'I will just sit and work out our possible returns, though I think you've lost it Boss.'

Toby rang the nearest Wm Hill from the list in his wallet, explaining he had placed a bet earlier and he was travelling. 'Do you have the result of the 1.15 at Haydock?' He crossed his fingers while the clerk checked the result. It was about 30 seconds, which seemed a lifetime. The line crackled.

Toby asked him to repeat himself, than sharply replaced the phone. Muttering a prayer, he went to join Joe.

'Don't tell me, we've blown it, haven't we.'

'Au contraire, mon brave, it's just won at 12/1, that's £26 for a win and £7 for the place making £33 and two more to go!'

'Bloody hell, Boss. When does the next run?'

'In about 45 minutes. Here is a pound note Joe, get us 2 pints of bitter and let's have a ploughman's each.'

When Joe had gone, he quickly calculated on the back of the menu, that if the next won at 20/1, they would get £42 for the win and £10 for the place. He daren't work out the double but it could be around £520.

They drank their beer, nibbling their excellent ploughmans, whilst nervously looking at the clock behind the bar. Toby paid the waitress, giving her a generous tip.

They both got up together, Joe saying, 'I'm coming with you this time.' A chap was just leaving the telephone box as they both wedged in. Toby dialled and asked again about the result. Another eternal delay before the phone crackled again. He held it between them, so both could hear that their horse had just won by a short head on a photo finish at 20/1.

'How long to Harrogate, Joe?'

'We should be there about 4.30 to 5.00.'

'Well, let's cabby on mate, as they close at 5.30!'

They passed through Newark and the outskirts of a fairly busy Doncaster around 3.30. By-passing Leeds, they pulled off the A1 at Wetherby going through Kirkdeighton and Spofforth into Harrogate arriving around 4.20.

Driving down Leeds Road into the centre, Toby saw a Coral Bookies and pulled in. 'I thought you were after Wm Hill.'

'I am, but haven't a clue where to start looking. I bet one of those downbeat blokes over there with his britches arse hanging out will know,' muttered Toby.

After a quick chat with a sad-looking figure in ripped jeans and two days growth of stubble on his chin, Toby was back in the car. Whilst just keeping to the speed limit they sped through town, turning right at the war memorial

16

in front of Allen's Gents Tailor's. They parked at the post office to find a small Wm Hill discreetly behind blacked out windows.

They both jumped out of the car, Joe staying in the doorway to keep an eye on the car, whilst Toby dived into the dimly lit room, almost impenetrable by the blue haze of cigarette smoke which lay at eye level.

There were discarded betting slips covering the lino floor, with about 6 sad looking men who looked up from their racing paper. They didn't see 'Toffs' like Toby very often, and wondered what his hurry was about.

Toby went up to the results board, covering the day's races and checked on the first two. Yes, what the lad had told him on the phone was correct. He turned to his last race. He had just been beaten into second at 8/1.

He felt a tap on his shoulder, an equally ashen-faced Joe said, 'Bloody Hell, you have done it! How much do you think?' 'Correction Joe, we have done it! You've got a £100 coming, a little gift from me.'

Toby checking the odds calculator sheet in his diary scribbled away and showed Joe the final figure of about £687, saying 'Don't forget, your cut is about £100.'

They both went up to the clerk and handing in the betting slip they had got in Aldershot, Toby said 'They told me in Aldershot that any branch would pay out.'

'That's quite correct sir,' said the clerk, But first I'll have to check with my manager.'

'I'll keep the ticket' said Toby, remembering reading about a bookie who swallowed a slip on which he would have had to pay out a lot of money, and then denied ever having it.

His old father had always said 'never trust a bookie'. The manager appeared and on seeing the ticket noted down the serial number and put a call through to Aldershot, who were just closing. After many nods and yesses and obviously describing Toby, he put the phone down and said, 'How would you like paying, sir?'

Toby checked the calculations and said. 'In two amounts please. £100 for this gentleman,' indicating Joe, And the balance to me.'

'Very good, sir,' said the manager as he disappeared into the office returning in a couple of minutes with the cash which Toby counted.

**** **** ****

They went through the villages of Killinghall and Ripley, before swinging right onto the Ripon Road. There were some wide sweeping bends with huge grassy banks at the side. Toby, taking a racing driver's line, flung the car expertly from the nearside to the far corner to give maximum visibility to round the next bend.

'They call those the Daffodil bends,' stated Joe, adding, 'A lot of people had been killed by taking them too fast,' but adding quickly that he'd never felt safer in Toby's expert hands.

They wended their way through the narrow streets of the market town of Ripon, whose beautiful cathedral they could just make out to their right. It had been market day, and the stalls which had filled the square were being taken down.

As they crawled through traffic wending its way home, Toby counted the pubs around the square. He counted five with four on the way in.

'How can they keep going? The citizens must be permanently pissed.'

'Pretty much so,' said Joe. 'Look at the end of this street, you will see a clock tower in the middle of the road. We turn left to Masham.'

Toby topped the car up at a little garage with two pumps at North Stainley. It was getting dark as they crossed the River Ure. Joe joked that his uncle, a keen fly-fisher, had once fallen in and loved to tell everyone how he'd be urinated on. They re-crossed the Ure at Masham climbing the hill into the Town.

18

'That pretty ivy-clad stone house on the right is the doctor's,' Joe pointed out. 'Look, here is the post office, run by a Mrs. Draper, a large, gossipy woman, who they reckon listens into all long distance telephone calls, which all have to be routed through her. Be warned, boss, any scandal and the whole of Masham will know in 5 minutes!'

Again Toby noted, pubs sprouted up everywhere and the end of the road led into a large square with the church at one end and a solid, stone branch of Barclays Bank at the other. 'God not quite meeting mammon!' said Toby thoughtfully to a slightly puzzled Joe.

'There you are,' said Joe, pointing to the Kings Head. 'That's your new home.' The King's Head lay in the middle between the church and the bank. How appropriate, thought Toby.

CHAPTER THREE

It was a large, stone, ivy clad building, with a high stone arch in the middle, showing it must have been a coaching inn way back. It had a flight of stone steps leading up to the wide-open front door. Lights sparkled out of the many windows, casting pools of yellow light onto the cobbled square.

Joe swung the car through the arch and parked in one of three empty places. Toby grabbed his bag whilst Joe took out his old kitbag.

They went into the lobby of the hotel to find a chap who looked a bit like an old colonel with his Guards Tie, country suit, polished brown shoes, grey moustache. He was checking in what looked like a rep in a creased, shiny suit with a very battered old suitcase.

What caught Toby's eye was the girl who popped up from the counter where she had bent down to check a book. She had long, dark hair piled up on her head, large, dark brown eyes with high cheekbones. Her long, aquiline nose had a slight bump, obviously a break.

He quickly took in the pearls over her navy blue jumper with rolled up sleeves, revealing thin but strong tanned arms, her smallish, pert breasts and neat trim waist. They stood for a moment taking each other in.

'I'm Liz,' she said.

'Toby,' he replied gently shaking her hand.

'I believe you have a booking for me,' said Toby. Jabbing a thumb at Joe, he explained 'My friend's girlfriend, Christine had booked me in. Sorry,' said Toby. 'You will have to put up with me for a week or so.'

The girl, with direct eye contact gave a tolerant but taunting look, opened her full lips to reveal the whitest teeth he thought he had ever seen as she said, 'We will do what we can to make your stay as pleasant and comfortable as we can.'

She turned to reach for a key from the board behind her, Toby getting a view of her nicely rounded little bottom in a pencil skirt and gorgeous long legs in black court shoes. Meanwhile Tom gave a second and third throb, which meant he was getting ready for action.

Toby stooped and clutching his old suitcase in front of him to cover any embarrassment from Tom.

Liz handed him a key, asking him to sign the book. 'As you are here for at least a week, I've given you one of our best doubles at single rate.' She hastily added, 'It's overlooking the garden and is quiet and peaceful. I do hope it's OK.'

An elegant older woman in twin-set and pearls had appeared. 'Oh, Bobbie,' said Liz, 'Can I introduce Toby, who is staying with us for a while.'

'I do hope you enjoy your stay,' said Bobbie in a cut-glass, very aristocratic voice. Smiling broadly she added, 'I will rely on Liz to look after you.'

Two more guests had come in, and Bobbie told Liz to show Toby up to his room whilst she dealt with these gentlemen.

Toby shook Joe's hand, saying he would pop into the garage tomorrow. Still clutching his case and gun case, he followed Liz up the wide flight of stairs to the first floor.

He was sure he glimpsed what looked like stocking tops as she turned right at the top. They went down a corridor with about four doors either side with brass numbers, and door knobs all highly polished.

The good quality red carpet had now faded to deep pink, which looked good against the white walls, covered in sporting prints. At the end, Liz opened No5 and held the door open for Toby to go in.

Chintz curtains covered a bay window with a matching covered window seat. The oak double bed was covered in a patchwork quilt, and on a bedside table stood a "teasmaid" with two cups and saucers and all the bits.

Liz airily waved at a door in the corner, saying 'voila' as she opened it to reveal a washbasin, loo and shower cubicle. 'Apart from Bobbie's, Freddie's and my room of course, your room is one of only 4 en-suites.'

'It's absolutely fab, thanks so much Liz. By the way, what time is dinner served?'

'Seven. Oh cripes,' said Liz 'I'd better go down and help out in the bar, as Bobbie always likes to check out the dining room and flit between reception and the bar keeping an eye on Freddie, in case he drinks the profits.

'You will like Freddie, everyone does. He's an ex-guards major, whose wife was killed in air raid. He met up with Bobbie, who's an old flame. I think she's got the money, and took over the hotel about 5 years ago. Got to dash, see you in the bar, when you've sorted yourself out.' With that, she went.

Toby unpacked and put his toilet kit in the bathroom, then checked the room out. He moved a large wardrobe away from the wall, propped the shotgun behind, with the £1000 of money on top, then slid the wardrobe back so they were wedged in tight. Should be safe until the morning, he thought.

He took a quick shower and put on a clean shirt before going down to the bar. It gleamed with well-polished horse brasses. There was a small log fire with bench seats either side. Two or three men were drinking on their own at the bar, with a group of three farmer types at one end, several groups of couples sitting at little brass topped tables.

An elderly man was sitting in the corner with what looked like a whiskey, reading the evening paper. Behind the bar, Liz was single handedly keeping everyone served. As she said 'Hello Toby, what can I get you?' the locals turned to look as did the elderly man.

'A pint of the local bitter, please, Liz and a drink for yourself.'

'Thanks, I haven't time now, but can I have it later? Oh, by the way Toby can I introduce you to Major Rankin, who is also staying with us.'

The elderly man with the Royal Artillery tie, blazer and a very red face, got to his feet as Toby strode over to shake his hand, saying, 'Well, if Liz can't have a drink with me, will you do me the honour, Major?'

The old boy beamed, folded up his paper and grabbing his glass followed Toby back to the bar, where Liz had poured a frothy pint and was just filling a glass from the Famous Grouse optic.

The major quickly downed his glass, which he had been eking out until dinner.

'There we are. I'll put it on your slate Toby,' said a smiling Liz. God, she is gorgeous thought Toby, but also thinking that probably the whole bar thought so too.

'Cheers Major,' said Toby, 'I see you were a Gunner,' pointing to the Major's tie.

'Cheers my boy,' he replied. 'Jolly decent of you. Yes, I saw the last year out of the 1st world war, then dammit the second! A staff job, driving a desk,' he chortled.

The locals were chatting again, as they had obviously heard of the major's war before. 'Were you a military man?' asked the major. All heads turned as Toby answered.

'I did 3 years in the Paras and 2 years in the RASC.'

'Did you see any action?' persisted the Major.

'I was in 3 Para and we were the only Para Battalion to drop at Suez.' All ears were cocked as Toby went on.

'It didn't last as long as yours, Major, all over in a few days. Anthony Eden bowed to the Yanks and pulled us out. We lost about 9 and suffered 20 odd serious casualties.'

At this moment a pretty, plump young blonde in a black top and skirt came in with menus for dinner. The lone drinkers all took one, as did the Major and two lots of couples.

Toby looked one over and catching Liz's eye she mouthed 'wait'. So he ordered another pint, as the Major and the rest scuttled off to the dining room.

The farmers departed, wishing everyone a cheery goodnight. Liz leaned over and said 'Look, we are fairly quiet tonight, I am nearly finished. Would you like me to join you for dinner?'

'That's fantastic,' exclaimed Toby. 'You can choose. I can and do eat everything!'

'Very well, follow me sir,' she grinned, leading the way to the dining room which was beamed, and the walls covered with more sporting prints. Another log fire blazed in the inglenook fireplace.

There must have been about 15 people seated at round tables, covered in red & white checked tablecloths.

Liz led the way to a corner table with a reserved sign on it. Toby couldn't help wondering how long the reserved sign had been on, or whether it was Liz's permanent table. She chatted with everyone on their progress to the table, introducing Toby with a flip of her hand.

The waitress came in loaded with plates, which she deftly set down in front of very happy looking customers. She came over to Liz who quickly jabbed at the wine list with her finger and asked 'Toby, I suppose you prefer a red with your steak?'

'Rather,' replied Toby. 'I'll be idle and let you choose.'

'In that case, Lucy we will have a bottle of house red. It's fab,' she said as Lucy hurried away.

'Freddie, who I will introduce you to later, has some fantastic wine contacts, who let him have the Bin ends from big restaurant orders at knockdown prices.'

'He sounds an interesting character. Tell me a bit about him.'

'Well,' said Liz, 'He came from quite a well-to-do family, second son of a lord. Eton and the guards, but couldn't make any more than a major and left to run the family estate. I think he was gassed in the first war and suffered badly from his chest. I think he hit the bottle, fell out with his brother and went off with a pretty girl from the village. Family didn't approve. They went somewhere in London where he put virtually all of his inheritance into a very good wine merchants. He was a director, dealing with all the London clubs and golf clubs, because he was a bloody good natural golfer. Things were perfect for quite a few years until the depression hit hard. His wife took off with a younger man, and he was hospitalised.

That's where he met Bobbie who was a staff nurse. He's a great pal of Thomas, Lord Middleham who arranged for him to take this pub, which he absolutely adores and runs really well. He still plays a couple of rounds a week at the local golf club, guest guns and fishes the Ure, a great trout river. So you see we are all a happy family.'

'It sounds idyllic,' said Toby. 'And what about you? You seem wasted just running a pub.' At that point, Lucy placed two large oval Portmeirion designed plates in front of them. A large fillet steak surrounded with garden peas, tomato, mushroom and thin golden chips.

'English or French mustard?' asked Lucy. 'French for me please, I seem to always prefer it with a super steak like this and English for everything else,' said Toby. Lucy poured out two large glasses of red wine from the bottle wrapped in a white napkin. She looked at Toby, with slightly narrowing eyes as she said 'Bon Appetit' and quickly whisked away.

Liz grinned back, saying, 'She's quite a girl, our Lucy. A great fun and grafts like a good un.'

They touched glasses and Toby said, 'To happy days!'

The steak was pink and tender, and between mouthfuls Toby told Liz of his early life, when his adored, wild beautiful mother had been killed in a freak riding accident when he was eight. As he was an only one, his father Charles couldn't cope and sent him off to prep school, which he hated. Being sent in the middle of the school year he was mercilessly bullied and tried to run away twice.

His father ran a very good family business of corn merchants and had ruthlessly taken over smaller competitors to eventually own what was one of the big four in the country. Like Freddie, he loved golf, wine, women and horse racing. The latter was to be his downfall.

25

As he once ruefully contemplated, 'If only my horses had been fast and my women slow, I might have stood a chance!'

CHAPTER FOUR

'Father had met Claudia, twice divorced, at the races in the glory days. After a whirlwind romance they were married within the month. She was a slim, elegant blonde with large green/brown eyes, long legs and a very ample bosom almost revealed by her huge cleavage.'

I remember Dad once saying, 'It was like looking down the Nile Delta,' grinned Toby. At which, Liz spluttered in her wine saying, 'He wouldn't have thought much of mine,' pointing to her smallish, but uplifted breast. 'As an old soldier once said to me,' went on Toby, 'Any more than a handful is being greedy!'

Liz broke out in a husky giggle and said to Toby, 'It's weird, but I feel I have known you for yonks and not just a few hours. I like your sense of humour, and you seem to have hidden depths, which is sort of compelling and making me want to find out more. What happened when Claudia married your Dad?'

'I was about 12 and didn't really think much of it. I remember her coming for an exeat or a weekend break, when I was in my last year at prep school.

'They arrived in a new white Jag XK120, with the rear wheel arches removed. It looked like a real racer and had all the boys, masters, and dads crawling all over it. She openly flirted with the young, unmarried masters, who were falling over themselves to bring her coffee and biscuits.

'Some of the fathers started pulling in their tums and straightening their ties whilst trying to catch her eye.' He looked thoughtful as though recalling his schooldays.

'I was suddenly very popular, and several parents asked Dad if he and his lovely wife would like to join them for lunch. Claudia trilled out, 'Love to boys, but maybe next time' as they had already made plans. I wedged in between Claudia and Dad as we flew down the school drive.

'It was a gorgeous sunny day and we drove on for about half an hour, before we came to a super old pub, with a full car-park of very classy cars, but nothing to compare to the Jag.

'Claudia and I stayed in the car, keeping guard as Dad went into the pub. He was back in a couple of minutes with an opened bottle of Claret, water and two or three bottles of my favourite ginger beer. Seeing my surprise, he said, 'Too sunny a day to be in, we will have a picnic.'

'We drove off down a twisty little lane with high hedgerows to a gate. He drove through, and always one to obey the country code, clicked the five-barred gate in place. Driving between two large bushes we came out on a flat, sandy riverbank.

'It was absolutely quiet, the only sound being the gurgle of the broad blue river.' Liz squeezed his arm.

''Over there I think,' said Dad opening the car boot, pulling out a chrome wire oven rack and four builder's bricks, a bag of charcoal and various Tupperware baskets. He went off to a tree, I watched as he dropped the bits and bobs and started building an oven with the bricks and grill.

''I'll just change,' said Claudia, disappearing behind a tree unseen by dad but in full view of me. Honestly Liz, it was the first time I'd seen anything like it. An actual naked woman in the flesh. As schoolboys, we always looked at our father's naughty magazines, usually kept under his bed or we bought Spic and Span which had all girls' details airbrushed out.

'Claudia just whipped everything off and put on a very tight white bikini. I went terribly red, looked away but couldn't help getting visibly excited. She looked and smiled that seductive look that had obviously got dad.

'Well, dad got the charcoal going with fillet steaks and a lovely salad, followed by strawberries and cream. Claudia boiled some water and made coffee.

'Dad lay back in a folding sun lounger and smoked his pipe, while Claudia said, 'Come on let's have a dip,' and ran off to the water. I had stripped to my underpants, which were a bit tight as I was a growing boy. We swam and floated in the river, which was really warm and silky.'

'I can just imagine it,' said Liz.

'She was as good a swimmer as I was, and we raced from one side to the other. As we climbed out, the water had made her bikini almost transparent, she wobbled and I grabbed her hand.

'She said 'We are going to get on, aren't we?' I blushed and mumbled 'I am sure we are,' She threw a towel at me before going to the bush she had used earlier. Glancing at Dad, I saw he was fast asleep.

'Turning back I saw she was stark naked, towelling herself. I was embarrassed but thrilled at the same time. After all I had nothing to be ashamed about, as it was reckoned by all the boys that I had the biggest one in the whole school.

'I dropped my trunks, looking at her. Her eyes opened when Tom, as I call him, was free. I couldn't help it, he just grew to his full length. Her eyes were wide open, as she just stared her mouth half open.

'I turned and dried off quickly, got into my school wear and went back to Dad, opening a ginger beer. I felt very grown up.

'Nothing was ever said about that time, she only said if ever I need help in anything, she was there for me. 'I can never replace your Mum' she said, 'But I'll do my level best to help.'

'She did too, getting Dad to take me away from that horrid school with the snobbiest parents. I think by pulling strings with the head master of the best grammar School in the area, she saved on expensive school fees and had me living at home!'

'How did you take the change?' asked Liz.

'Like a duck to water, almost literally, as I was in the school swimming team, travelling all over to away matches. An education in itself I suppose. I really enjoyed the work which I now found easy in getting my O and A levels. I loved acting in the school plays where we

29

sometimes joined the girls' grammar school. Another education!'

****   ****   ****

Lucy came and took away their empty plates, asking if they'd enjoyed it. 'Absolutely splendid, thank you,' said Toby. 'I'm afraid if I stay here and eat like this I will put on a vast amount of weight and end up like a Michelin Man!'

Liz, looking at him with a knowing smile, her eyes wide open said 'We can't have that! We will have to keep you trim. Look Toby, I've got to do a bit of bar work for a bit, but do you want to walk Bess with me when I've finished?'

'That's a great idea' said Toby, leaning down to stroke Bess's ear, where she lay at his feet.

'That's quite amazing,' smiled Liz. 'She doesn't normally take to men, as I got her from a gamekeeper who was hard on his dogs. As he thought she was too soft and timid for a gundog, I bought her very reasonably.'

'I hope he wasn't called Mellors,' chuckled Toby.

They thanked Lucy, and headed to the bar. There were two or three of the men who had been drinking alone perched at the bar nursing their drinks and chatting to Bobbie.

A group of what looked like local farmers were laughing at the other end, with several tables of couples having a night out. Toby spotted the major alone at a corner table doing a crossword with a nearly empty whisky glass in front of him. Turning to Bobbie, Toby asked for a pint of the local bitter, and lowering his voice, softly asked, 'What would the Major like?'

'Oh, the Famous Grouse is his favourite, with just a wee splash of water.'

'That's fine' stated Toby, handing over a pound note, pocketing the change. He took both glasses over to the major's table saying, 'I hope I'm not interrupting the brain power, Sir' indicating the half-done crossword.

'I thought this might help,' he added as he put the whisky in front of the old boy, whose eyes lit up as he thanked Toby.

'Slangevar,' Toby toasted, clinking glasses, to which the major replied, 'Slange'.

'God, it was good to meet someone civilized,' he pronounced, wondering how long his small army pension would allow him to have the odd drink after paying his weekly board.

'How long will you be staying, my boy?' he questioned taking a tentative sip.

'I'm not really sure, I thought I'd give it a week or two to get my bearings and find a job. I don't know what, as I've just left the army with no real qualifications.'

'You will find something, I'm sure. A bright, young chap like you. But tell me about your service life, I'm always interested, lost touch now,' muttered the Major.

'I was in the CCF at school, where we had a regular CSM from the Para's as our permanent staff instructor. He persuaded me to join the TA Paras, whilst I was still at school. I was hard up and he allowed me to help him over the long summer holidays on a full regular private rates! An absolute fortune to a hard up schoolboy! I really revelled in it.

'He got me to teach weapon training to a group of ten to fifteen hardened Paras, who soon realised that I was as good or better than them. They adopted me as one of their own and looked out for me like a baby. I was one of the youngest to get my wings at just 17 and three months. Quite a training. I did 2 years and realised that National Service was looming, so I resigned. I was determined to pack in as much living as I could. I acted in one or two good productions at our local amateur theatre, raced my Austin-Healey and partied like crazy. Then the dreaded envelope dropped on the doormat, instructing me to report to Strensall near York.

'After basic training I passed my WOSB (War Office Selection Board) and went on to Mons Officer Cadet School. Everyone was going into the Guards, The Green Howards and other good regiments. One of the instructors, a Para said, that as no-one has opted for the Para's, who normally only took regular officers from Sandhurst. To make up numbers, they would make me an exception, having already got my wings.'

'You must have been absolutely thrilled,' exclaimed the major.

'It was a doddle as I flew round 'P' company (the hard Paras selection course) for the second time, before joining 3 Para.'

'Wasn't 3 Para the first Para Battalion to drop after Arnhem at Suez?' quizzed the major.

'Yes, with a platoon we created a diversion at the Airfield. The rest of the battallion encircled the airfield, ready to attack, when we made our diversion.

'I asked the adjutant why we had been singled out, to be told that we were the fastest runners in the battalion but he clammed up when I said it was an odd co-incidence that we were all national servicemen,' laughed Toby. 'I reckon they thought we were expendable.

'We lay in a defensive position, outside the main gates whilst the battalion got in position. I sent a section to cut the wire so we could wriggle through.

'Amazingly, not a sound, and we were within 100 yards of a couple of a pill box. A couple of scruffy guards were having a smoke. My sergeant had a rocket-launcher to his shoulder waiting, when a pair of boots came crashing on to us from above one of our last boys landing. His weapons container was about 20 yards from him. The gyppos woke up and put their rifles to their shoulders. Our lad with no weapon, stood up, and reaching into his smock pulled out an imaginary grenade.

'He pulled out an imaginary pin and then threw the imaginary grenade at the two soldiers. They flung their rifles down and dived back behind the bunker. Laughter broke out from all the blokes and after such a performance, he was forever called Oscar.'

The major giggled like a schoolgirl, wiping tears from his eyes. The three at the bar had joined them at the table, saying, 'Do you mind us joining you, major?'

'Not a bit, let me introduce to you Toby.

'This is Walter,' nodding at the older, balding, thin man. 'He is one of the best builders in Yorkshire.'

Walter, shaking his head with an exasperated look, firmly shook Toby's hand, saying 'Good to see some young blood around. The old farmers will have to lock up their daughters when they see you,' with a wink.

'And this is Jack,' continued the major, 'the local travelling blacksmith, who covers the Dale in more ways than one that's so isn't it Jack?' he said, digging him in the ribs. Jack, well over 6 feet in height, had a shock of black hair, huge forearms and biceps almost bursting out of his rolled up, faded denim shirt.

He had the large brown eyes of a trusting Labrador and grinning lop-sidedly he thrust out a huge hand the size of a table tennis bat to grasp Toby's hand firmly, yet gently, for such a large man. Jack turning jerked his thumb at a middle-aged, ginger haired man with freckles saying, 'This is Arthur, Walter's right-hand man and the best chippy (carpenter) for miles around.'

Paul, his young apprentice, shyly stuck out his hand and grasped Toby's, saying 'Pleased to meet you'.

'There you are,' said the Major, 'the finest builders. Trouble is, they are so much in demand, they've got a waiting list longer than the doctors.'

'Look chaps,' said Toby. 'I've had a little win on the horses today, very rare for me–' he lied '-and I would like to top you up, as I seem to be in the chair,' and before they could resist he downed his pint and nipped over to the bar and waited patiently to be served by Bobbie.

'4 pints of bitter and a double for the Major, oh and please take one for yourself, Liz and Lucy.'

'Do you want me to put them on your tab,' asked Bobbie with a smiling thank you. 'Kind of you' replied Toby, 'but I'd rather pay as I go,' putting two pounds down.

'I'll get Lucy to bring them over' as Toby was glancing at Liz bending over revealing a bit of black panty in the gap between her tight jeans and her top. She turned quickly and saw him looking at her. Smilingly thanked him for the drink and said 'After I closed the bar, in half an hour, I was going to walk Bess, if you would like to join us.'

'How could I turn down such an invitation from two gorgeous brunettes?' He was sure he saw a faint, pinkish blush come to Liz's cheek.

He expertly picked up the 4 pints and the whisky in two hands and returned to the table. 'Bloody hell,' said Walter. 'That was damned clever,' indicating Toby's full hands and not a drop spilled. 'I bet you've done that before.'

'I once worked in a working men's club as a bar assistant to earn a bit of cash when I was at college. I would have been lynched if I'd spilled any,' grinned Toby.

'Cheers Gents, it's good to meet you!'

'And you too Toby, cheers,' they all replied, clinking their glasses, even the major joined in.

Walter said, 'The major's been telling us you've just left the army and were with the Paras that dropped at Suez.'

'Yes,' admitted Toby, 'But as I ended up with a gammy leg, which left me with a bit of limp when tired, I went in the RASC for the last two years.'

'I did my national service in the RASC,' chirped in Jack.

'No horses left, so I ended up driving a tank transporter,' continued Jack. 'Quite enjoyed it, made me feel right powerful crawling on main roads, holding all the traffic up. I had police motor cyclists buzzing round like bloody flies.'

They all laughed. 'But why the RASC Toby?' asked the major. 'Well, after my leg problems, coming up to two years left of my short service commission, there were only regulars being kept so they transferred me to the only airborne unit available.

'I hadn't trained as a gunner, medic, engineer or signaller. Then the Airborne RASC company decided they too were only accepting regulars, and that's how I ended up in the training wing at Buller Barracks for the last two years of service,' not telling them that he was made assistant adjutant, carrying the same rank of captain. Not bad for originally a National Serviceman. 'Bit of a come down what?' quizzed the major.

'I wasn't really bothered by then, as I couldn't carry on doing my dream job in the Paras, I just wanted out.' Toby quietly said. 'I thought I would pack everything I could into that time. I drove tanks, got my motorcycle and HGV licences. The best time was the 6 months I spent at the riding school. I had a pony as a boy and could do most things, but those riding instructors were something else.

'We did a lot of show jumping, dressage and cross-country. They naturally gave me the worst horses and made me work, but it was a hell of a training.'

'I see our Liz keeps looking over here,' said Jack. 'What a fit bird. If I hadn't my old lady, I would be there.'

'You wouldn't have a chance' chipped in Walter, 'A rough bugger like you. No, it's our young Toby she is after, mark my words.'

'I think so,' chirmed in a normally quiet Diesel, a farming contractor. 'I'd love to chat her up,' he finished, blushing.

'You're as daft as a brush,' exclaimed Walter, gently cuffing him saying, 'She wants real experience, like a fine filly needs a delicate rider.'

The bar had thinned out, as Bobbie called 'Time, gentlemen, please.' Walter thanked Toby again, saying next time the drinks were on them, and then everyone left, the major included.

35

CHAPTER FIVE

Toby took the empty glasses to the bar.

'Let me give you a hand,' saying to Liz and Bobbie, he nipped off to collect all the empty glasses, ashtrays and crisp packets, straightened the chairs as he did so. Bobbie turned and looked at Liz as she said, 'You lucky girl, for God's sake hang on to him, they don't come much better than that.'

'Do you want to wait for me by the rear door Toby?' asked Liz. 'I'll get Bess.'

She was quickly back with an excited Bess, whose wagging tail could only beat double-time like every Labrador. 'Do you need a lead?' asked Toby.

'I always have one in my pocket, but she follows me everywhere, and has never gone for sheep or game.' It was a fine, warm night, with a very near full moon, casting its soft light, which lit up the cobbles of the huge square in front of the pub.

They turned right passing a couple of stone, three story Georgian houses, then past a large detached house which hid behind large beech trees lining a long pebble covered drive. 'Who lives there?' asked Toby.

'Oh, that's the home of Mark Woodhouse, the brother-in law of Lord Thomas Middleham' replied Liz. 'Between you and me, he's a bit of a shit. Even his own brother Thomas, who is an absolute sweetie and one of the finest blokes I've ever met, told me that Mark was a shit, saying if you can shit for Eton you can shit for anywhere.'

Toby couldn't stop laughing as he stole a quick glance at Liz. The moon lit up her pale face with her broad cheekbones, fine nose framed by her dark long hair. Like a silhouette, Toby thought.

He pointed to the moon 'Ah, the moon, that great circumambulation aphrodisiac,' adding 'Christopher Fry.' The lady's not for burning.'

'Oh, Bess, we have a literary gent with us' squeaked Liz. 'I thought you rough soldiers weren't bright enough for the arts.'

'Quite right,' replied Toby. 'I only did it for A levels, hoping to go to Kings Cambridge, but I buggered up the interviews, so the queen got me instead.'

They turned into the churchyard, tip toeing past the faintly lit ancient gravestones, where Bess took off like a bat out of hell, sniffing here dashing off into the distance after a scent she picked up. 'Is she ok?' asked Toby. 'I mean, she won't take off?'

'No, she never leaves me and always come back when I whistle.'

'I wonder if I could get used to that,' pondered Toby and turning, putting his hand gently on her shoulders, as if he had done it many times before. He stooped down and kissed her wide, full mouth. His mouth still covering hers, he traced her lips with his tongue.

She gently pushed her tongue into his mouth, pulling him closer. He could feel her tight breasts pushing into him. There was no way he could stop old Tom, as he affectingly called his penis, from quickly thickening and starting to rise. To see her reaction he pulled slightly tighter. She broke off the kiss and wide-eyed said,

'God, what have you got there? I don't think I've ever felt anything like it. Let's finish off walking Bess and go back, I want to see more of you.'

**** **** ****

She skipped away down the path after Bess, Toby chased after them. As she reached the side of the church, she tripped over a stone flag. Toby quickly gathered her up, which raised her skirt, to reveal a ladder to her black stockings.

Toby bent down and licked the ladder, saying 'Kisses will make it better.' Bess came running to her mistress. Toby gently stroke her back saying, 'It's ok old girl, your mistress had a little slip, but she is fine now.' Bess looked at them both, her tail thumping the floor.

'You know, she approves of you and likes you. Just like me.' Toby put an arm around her waist, and they went quietly back to the pub. Bess running away from them and skipping back for an affectionate pat from Toby.

They let themselves in by the back door and started up the back stairs. Liz stopped, and with a finger to her lips, whispered 'watch'. Holding Toby back, she went up the stairs her feet spread widely, to avoid any creaks from the ancient old oak stairs.

She stopped at the top, looking down on Toby, who looking up saw a glimpse of two long slender legs, clad in black, grip-top nylons and an expanse of white thigh.

He nipped up the stairs, copying exactly where she had gone, without even a squeak. Grinning broadly he whispered, 'How was that?'

'Come on you,' she whispered back, leading him to his door, saying 'you sort yourself out, while I go and grab a few things. By the way do you mind if Bess comes with me, as I don't like leaving her alone?'

'As long as it's only the three of us, don't want to make it a party' grunted Toby. He washed quickly cleaning his teeth and gargled. He scrubbed his hands and fingernails, finishing off by giving Tom a thorough cleaning. He had on a singlet, which half covered a long, but relaxed Tom. The door opened by a black paw, as Bess busied into the room sniffing in delight to find the two polo mints Toby had put on an old rug at the bottom of the double bed.

Liz appeared in an old shirt, just reaching her knee. Her long dark hair tumbled down to her shoulders. 'God, you look fantastic,' he said, stroking her cheek.

Her eyes were fixed on his penis, which as she looked, started inflating like a huge sausage. He gently pulled her shirt over her head. She brushed the hair from her eyes. They stood about two inches apart, and as his eyes took in the full pointed breasts with the nipples slightly stiffening, her flat stomach and mass of soft black hair.

38

He slowly moved his head from side to side, saying, 'You are truly beautiful, and I've seen many girls, but you are something else.'

'So is that' she uttered looking at Tom, who had risen to his full length and girth. 'I've never seen or dreamed of anything like it.'

She looked in horror at the huge hole in his right thigh with a white jagged stitch.

'Before you ask,' muttered Toby 'it's a bullet wound I picked up at Suez it hit the back of my thigh and took a lump out of the front. I left it somewhere on the airfield!'

'How did it happened?' enquired Liz

'I was zig-zagging away, and must have zigged when I should have zagged!'

She giggled.

He carried on, 'the bullet missed the bone by half an inch. If it had hit and smashed, could have lost my leg. Two inches to the left it could have castrated me, or God forbid another inch left and it would have gone through my arse, which could have be fatal. So by and large, I am a lucky boy.'

'Does it give you any trouble?'

'Only when I stand for too long or jog too far. Then my limp comes back.'

Dropping to her knees, the lovely dark hair falling between them, she gripped his cock one hand on top of the other and slowly kissed, licked and took it in her mouth. Slowly more went in, Tom throbbed and Toby moaned. She quickly stood up leading him by the hand to the bed. She climbed on and lying on her back in the middle, spread her long legs.

Toby climbed on, kneeling, bent down to kiss and lick her wet pussy. His finger gently found her firm clitoris, before exploring inside her to find her G spot. By now her stomach was rising rapidly, and her breath came in gasps. Now he straddled her, sliding Tom in a little more each time, until he had to hold his hand over her mouth to stop the whole pub from hearing her.

It seemed to go on forever, until they both collapsed into each other's arms and fell into a deep sleep. Something sharp was on Toby's toe, hanging over the bed. Something was shaking him. He awoke instantly from his army training to find Bess tugging him.

Looking at his watch he saw it was 7.00am. The time that Liz had told him she had to start breakfast. He gently shook Liz awake saying, 'What a clever old Bess.' Liz said, 'Fuck, I should have started half an hour ago,' and grabbing Bess fled to her room to put her day clothes on, pausing at the door to say, 'Thank you for the best night for a long, long time. See you at breakfast sir,' and with a cheeky salute she closed the door.

**** **** ****

Toby lay naked on his back. Old Tom now nearly it's normal size throbbed and was quite tender when he touched the end. He smiled, as the sudden thought struck him that he had been to bed with two of the most gorgeous girls he had ever met within thirty hours and over 200 miles apart.

He showered and shaved quickly and stood at the small wardrobe looking at his worldly possessions neatly hung up.

His old Savile Row pinstripe suit in charcoal grey, his father's perfectly fitting dinner jacket, trousers and blazer, a couple of pairs of grey trousers, his old British warm overcoat, a light brown covert coat with a brown suede collar, an ancient Barbour waxed jacket and his old corduroys.

Well, he thought that should see me covered for most events and stashing yesterday's winnings, the William's and Glynn's cheque into the pocket of the old Barbour, slung it over his arm, and went down to breakfast.

There must have been about a dozen in the dining room. Several he had seen the night before. The major at his corner table bellowed out a hearty, 'Good morning.

40

What are your plans today Toby?' who sitting in his 'reserved' table in the windows, replied, 'Just going on a tour Major, want to see the village.' Liz had served the next table and stopped at Toby, saying, 'Good morning sir. I hope you slept well. What would you like to order?'

'Like a log, thank you' replied Toby. 'May I have orange juice, a kipper, well done brown toast, and coffee please?'

Toby quickly checked the race cards for the day in the paper. It looked a very interesting day, but thought he would have breakfast and then give Kath a ring to see if anything had come up. Liz reappeared with his order on a tray.

As she took everything from it, she leaned closer, whispering 'Bobbie has given me the day off until the bar opens at 6,' her large brown eyes anxiously searched his face as she added 'I could show you round if you like'.

'That's absolutely fab,' said Toby, 'I couldn't wish for a more fantastic guide.' She grinned from ear to ear and he couldn't keep his eyes off her neat round bottom as she wiggled away.

He waited for her in the Resident's Lounge until eventually she appeared in a navy husky jacket over a pink check shirt, tight jeans and a flat loafer shoes. She looked stunning, and Tom started to take appreciative notice. Toby quickly rose up and grabbed his old jacket from the back of his chair.

'Where to, my Lord?' she started, as they stood at the front door. Toby said, 'Last night we went right, past a couple of terraced houses and the one that the MP chappie lives. Then the church. Next to the church you see that large, detached house with a wide driveway.'

She waved her hand. That rather grand house with pillars is where Archie, one of the twins, who owns the brewery lives.

Then in the eight other terrace houses there are local shopkeepers and retired people. You see the one with the blue door? Well, that's where the Miss's Brown live. Two old spinsters, who Walter, the builder you met last night, reckons are a pair of lesbians.

'After supper and Coronation Street they pop up to their front bedroom and watch the bedroom windows in our pub for anyone leaving the curtains open with a pair of tripod mounted binoculars.

'He once saw them when he was doing a job for them. You'd better keep your curtains carefully closed my dear.'

'Au contraire' said Toby. 'I'll put a display tonight, enough to give them a heart attack!

'That reminds me of an army pal, called Roger. Very apt really 'cos he not only had a true whopper, but would go to bed with anyone he could.

'He and his pal had time off during an army exercise in Devon and found an isolated cove. Only just an old biddy in a pink swim cap was swimming out to sea. Her ample bra, big enough to launch a jet from an aircraft carrier, huge knickers and the rest of her clothes in a neat pile on the beach with an old box brownie camera perched on top.

'Roger took the camera behind a rock, and after a few flicks and shakes, produced his ginormous erection. After his pal had taken a shot of it, he wound the film to the next photo and carefully replaced the camera.

'Checking she was still swimming with her back to them, they quickly went back up to the cliff-top laughing at what her local branch of Boots the chemist would say to her when she collected her holiday snaps.'

Liz burst out in giggles, as she steered him left, pointing out a row of neat terrace houses owned by locals, a couple of holiday lets. Another solid stone detached was owned by the chemist. 'That's what you were wanting' she said pointing to a branch of Barclays Bank. 'I'll bet you are the first customer today. Old Harold Farrar, the manager, will be having his coffee, reading the Financial Times, pretending he understands it. The pompous little prick!'

'I take it you don't approve of him,' asked Toby.

'Dead right,' exploded Liz. 'The bald headed, little bugger turned me down for a small overdraft, to cover my horse's training and vets bills. It was only till the cheque came in. I was so annoyed, I nearly told him to stuff his account, but really couldn't go to next branch which is in Ripon. I'll come with you and grab a cup of coffee from Joyce, his assistant.'

Sure enough Joyce, large bosomed, her dark hair piled into a bun above her cheerful, round face welcomed Liz, who explained that Toby wanted to open an account and see Mr. Farrar.

Joyce offered Liz a coffee and picking up the intercom arranged an appointment. She introduced Millie, her assistant, a pretty young girl with long fair hair, a pale oval face, large, expressive eyes. She had full lips and even bigger breasts forcing their way out of the thin, navy cardigan. As Toby gently shook her hand, saying 'what a lovely name' she blushed and hurried off to the little kitchen with much clattering. Joyce smiled saying, 'She is such a sweet little thing. I wish I were her age again!'

**** **** ****

Toby was ushered into Mr. Farrar's office. Sitting at an enormous partner's desk, was a tiny little man, completely bald apart from two little tufts of grey hair at the sides and four or five long grey/black hair combed over his bold pate.

His cherubic face was almost hidden by a pair of thick, black spectacles with the thickest pair of lenses Toby had seen. Rising to his full 5'3", his wainscoted chest thrust out like a little robin, he took Toby's hand in the limpest, wettest handshake ever. A little tap at the door, to which Farrar spoke, 'Come in,' a surprisingly deep voice. Millie plonked two nearly full cups of coffee on a tray, with a little jug of milk and two Bourbon creams, onto the huge desk.

After pouring Toby a black only, and serving her boss, she stole a quick glance at Toby, who thanked her saying, 'That's perfect Millie.' She tried to beat the blush as she hastily left.

'I didn't know you were staying at the hotel. A wise choice. Now I believe you would like to open an account,' reaching for a large journal. He entered Toby's name, date of birth, and address at the pub.

When Toby handed over the Williams and Glyn's cheque he smiled 'Ah, I see you must have been in the Army like me.' Toby politely asked 'what unit, sir, the Guards or Cavalry perhaps?'

'No, taking the Mickey,' replied Farrar, 'but something almost as important. The Royal Army Pay Corps,'

'Gosh,' said Toby, 'Who would have guessed it!'

He then handed over his pile of winnings, and Farrar called Joyce in to count. 'Nothing illegal?' quizzed Farrar as Toby carefully explained he was something of a pro gambler, to which Farrar turned puce, as he had never taken a chance on anything.

Toby also handed over a copy of the £1000 pa to be paid into his account from his late father's trust. Toby reckoned it was the gross salary of a middle manager and would keep him going until he could get established.

He opened a current account into which the trust would be paid monthly, and a saving account depositing the cheque, the trust mandate and his £500 winnings. He kept £200 in cash for betting. Farrar told Toby that if he popped in next week he would be able to pick up his cheque books and paying in slips and asked if there was anything else? Toby quickly rose and giving the little man a true extra firm handshake, took a little pleasure in seeing him wince.

Collecting Liz, they strolled out into the warm September sunshine.

'And now, my Lord?' she enquired. 'How did you get on?'

'Just as you said, a smug little prick, but I think I'll be able to use him if I cosy up to him. I think I might need him on my side, sooner or later.

They turned left to find the road bent at right angles, with several cottages and lock-up garages on the left. Then a very small baker's with a fruit and a veg shop doing a fair amount of business by the customers coming and going. She led him across the road to a large double fronted shop with huge windows selling rugs, carpets and piles and piles of rolls of lino. Liz whispered, 'This is Moore's carpet emporium, known throughout the Dales for selling the most amount of lino to farmer's wives who replace it annually. Hence his nickname 'Lino More'.

'That's clever,' said Toby as they were met by a tall stooping figure with the fixed, mournful face of an undertaker Toby thought, especially with his huge, sunken dark eyes. Toby judged him 6ft 2" and about 10 stone. But the most noticeable feature was his huge hands. Useful for lino laying.

Lionel wound himself through two rolls of upright carpet and, taking Liz's little hands in his great shovels, he pecked her on both cheeks asking if he could be of service.

Liz airily waved at Toby and Lionel, introducing them and said, 'Not today, Lionel. I'm just showing our latest resident the metropolis of Masham.'

'I wish it was,' muttered Lionel. 'Then I could put another van on the road. Anyway I'll be glad to help whenever I can.'

Toby thought there was something of the reptile about him, but time will tell. They carried on down Main Street, visiting the grocers, post office, a fishmonger and a hardware shop which Liz said stocked everything from birds-eyes to bees-knees. Toby had developed a thirst as they passed the fourth pub and suggested they pop in. 'Just a bit further,' she said, 'is the White Swan. It's built right on to the brewery, known as the Brewery Tap.'

The bar was cool, dark and smelled of freshly drawn ale mixed with polish. The little wooden tables sparkled,

45

the walls covered with hunting prints and horse brasses. There were five or six locals happily chatting and smoking.

Behind the bar stood a big, red bearded chap who was expertly pulling a frothing pint. Looking up he grinned at Liz, saying 'I see you are doing a bit of that market research Liz. Checking how the experts do it.' The rest all joined with a good-natured laughter. Liz introduced everyone, but the only name that stuck was Bob the barman. They exchanged a firm handshake. So unlike the limp one of the bank manager, Liz explained that Bob, an ex-builder often helped Walter out, but had given up his old job to be a landlord after an accident a few years ago.

Toby asked Liz what was her tipple she said, 'I'll just have a half of shandy please.' Toby asked Bob what he recommended, wondering if the very strong traditional beer was worth a try. 'Oh God,' said one of the regulars.

'It's great, but we call it lunatic's broth, and you need to sip it over a while. Taking it steady like, otherwise it'll come back and nip you in the arse.'

They all nodded wisely at this piece of wisdom. Bob said, 'Try a pint of bitter, I put a new barrel on today and it's in right grand fettle.'

'By God, it is,' said Toby, after a first sip of the delicious hoppy, malty balance. 'That's one of the most delicious brews I've ever had,' to much applause and appreciative knowing nods. Toby ordered a ploughman for himself and a Yorkshire ham in brown for Liz.

CHAPTER SIX

They headed back to the hotel and climbed into the TR still parked in the stable yard. Hood down, side screens off as they went gently out of the square, turning past the post office out towards Middleham, to the race horse centre of the Dales' where Liz kept her horsey.

At the junction of the Masham-Bedale road stood a neat, low, single-story car garage, with five pumps on the forecourt. There were three cars in the showroom. A Singer Gazelle, a Sunbeam Rapier and a basic Hillman Minx. All new and very shiny.

To the side was a large services sign, with a Land Rover on the ramp and several other cars in front. Very neat, tidy and professional, thought Toby. The sort of garage that exuded confidence. The place where Joe worked.

Toby pulled the TR3A up under the canopy beside the Shell plus pump, climbed out and went to open the wide filler up at the back.

An elderly, smart, tanned man with a shock of white hair emerged from the office, loudly greeting Liz, 'How are you my lovely? And who is the lucky man?' She cheerfully introduced Toby to Colin, the proprietor. Colin stood back admiring the TR, saying, 'we don't see many of these around here. Had her long?' whilst running his hands along the wings and peeking at the speedo showing 50000 odd miles.

'Bought her about 5 years ago from Sid Hurrells, who worked on her. He entered and won many sport racing events. I followed on and took a few pots before using her as a road car.'

'Some car! What did the legendary Sid do?' asked Colin. 'He skimmed a few thou off the cylinder head, bored out the pots, drilled the con rods and fitted harder dampers, racing brakes and straight through exhaust. He turned her into a pigeon catcher,' said Toby undoing the bonnet to reveal the spotlessly cleaned engine bay with the squat Webers twin carburettors.

'That's something,' Colin uttered in revered tones. 'Who looks after her now?'

'Well, I do my best,' said Toby, 'But your Joe has spent a lot of his spare time keeping everything ticking. I was hoping to see him, so long as I wasn't taking him off doing his job. I'd like to put a fiver's worth in.'

Colin quickly filled the car, saying 'you two had better pop and see Joe and his fiancée Christine, who is our secretary. By the way,' he said to Toby, 'I've just made him works manager, so you'd better congratulate him,' he said laughingly.

They trooped into the small office, where Toby paid for the petrol, and on to Colin's inner sanctum with a big desk and high backed old leather chair. A bank of three metal filing cabinets was in one corner across from a hand-wash basin. Sitting at a smaller desk with an ancient Imperial typewriter and Intelcom telephone was a pretty, red haired girl. Her oval face was covered in freckles, with wide green/brown eyes.

'This is Christine,' proudly announced Colin. 'The brains in the organisation.'

'Pleased to meet you,' she said, shyly extending her hand to Toby, who straight away lifted up her left hand, admiring her engagement ring and exclaimed, 'How lovely, it really looks good on you. I hope you will both be very happy. Joe is such a good man.' On the cue, Joe appeared in smart overalls, with general manager embroidered on his left breast pocket.

'Hello again boss,' he said pumping Toby's hand.

'You sly old devil,' said Toby. 'You never told me you had become engaged, and also been promoted,' pointing at his chest.

Colin called for tea all round, and as a special occasion, Christine would dish out the bourbon creams, kept for important or awkward clients.

Toby turned to Colin, giving him the TR keys jokingly saying, 'Give her a quick trip round the block, Colin. I suppose your motor trader policy covers you.'

An ecstatic Colin went out with Toby to see him off and explained it was a stiff clutch. Colin, as he eased himself in and blipped the throttle to a lovely deep burble asked what that familiar smell was. 'Oh,' said Toby. 'I filled the engine with Castrol R.'

**** **** ****

They were on their second cuppa, and had caught up on all the latest goings-on when an exuberant Colin re-appeared. As he got out of the car, an old Land Rover pulled into the forecourt.

A tall, gangling young chap in his early twenties got out.

'God, what a car! Colin, have you just taken it in?' As Colin filled the Land Rover, Liz explained to Toby that this was the Honourable Harry, Lord Middleham's son.

They came into the office together and Harry was introduced to Toby. 'I wonder how you ever get any work done Colin, with trespassers like us.'

He declined a cuppa saying he had to catch Graham, his head keeper, about Saturday's partridge shoot.

Christine returned to her desk, Joe telling Toby he would pop down to the pub to have a jar together.

As Toby and Liz thanked Colin and were preparing to leave Harry asked, 'I don't suppose you ever considered selling your car?' To which Toby replied, 'Harry, everything is for sale, it's just a question of price, a willing buyer, and a willing seller.'

Collin was trying to keep a straight face as Toby turned to him saying, 'May I?' as he grabbed a copy of Glass's Guide (the car dealers' price bible) from Colin's desk.

He expertly flicked open the TR page. Colin thought, he has done that before, as Toby ran his finger along the columns. He showed the page to Colin saying, 'I think with the car's age, relatively low mileage, good condition, the extras, my thought would be about £650. Would you agree Colin?'

Colin swallowing hard, as it was about £150 over price said. 'I think that's fair, considering the extras you have.'

'What is more useful to me now would be a Land Rover like yours,' Toby indicated to Harry. Harry beamingly said, 'Pa has put his name down for one of those new Range Rovers. The Land Rover is going in as a part exchange. I think he said he was being offered £250 quid for it.'

'There you are then,' confirmed Toby. 'If you can persuade him to let you have it, the TR will only cost you £400.'

'Gosh, yes,' stuttered Harry excitedly. 'I am sure that would be fine. May I give you a ring when I've spoken to Pa?'

'Of course,' replied Toby.

'May I suggest you book it into Colin's for a really good going over before we swap?'

'Will do,' stated Harry as he skipped off to the Land Rover, stealing a long last look across at the dark blue TR gleaming in the sunshine.

'That was one of the neatest bits of selling I've seen for a long time,' came from a tall, willowy blond with large blue eyes and a full, luscious mouth. She had legs up to her armpits.

Thrusting out her hand she announced, 'I'm Penny, Colin's only daughter.'

Toby thought, there was something of the ice maiden about her. Very upfront, self-assured, yet possibly fragile beneath the veneer.

'I agree love, very well done Toby. I don't suppose you would like a job here selling cars? I used to enjoy it, but since my Jenny died of cancer a few years back, I've lost the appetite,'

'What a good idea dad,' said Penny. 'You could take a bit more time off playing golf, and spending time with

Margot,' who turned out to be Colin's new lady friend. Penny approved of her, as it made him so much more cheerful and more like his old self.

Both she and Colin had taken it badly when Jenny had died. Colin had to bring up an independent and outspoken only girl all by himself.

He had thrown himself into his job and built up a very successful, profitable business, allowing him to send Penny away to board at Harrogate Ladies College.

He is really quite dishy, thought Penny, gazing at Toby.

She'd had short affairs with a couple of young students at Art College, where she'd studied Fine art and antiques. She had not had a long-lasting relationship, nor trusting herself and always telling herself she would know when Mr. Right came long.

She worked for a very upmarket antiques dealer in Harrogate. Hugo, her boss, was in his mid-fifties, with a frigid wife.

He always took the glamorous Penny away on antique trips or to fairs. Plump little Hugo with his silver, swept-back hair, bow ties and pink shirts was light years away from this tough, masculine man called Toby.

It was love at first sight and her heart thumped as Colin said, 'I've got a leg in a horse running at Catterick next week. If I wangle a couple of extra badges to the Owners & Trainers, would you and Liz like to join us?' he waved at Penny.

'How very kind of you Colin. We would love to, wouldn't we Toby?' Penny inwardly flinched at Liz's we, but was relieved when Liz added, 'we are not an item, it's just that Toby is a pub guest and we occasionally have a meal and a drink. You'd never know how boring it can sometimes be, Penny. The same old stale jokes from the same boring people. Honestly, I think villagers are positively incestuous sometimes.'

Colin said he'd drop the badges off with Liz and they all shook hands before leaving.

Toby thanked Christine for tea and the scrumptious bourbons. They climbed into the TR. Toby blipped the throttle which gave a deep, burbling exhaust note. Colin standing close behind again smelled the Castrol R smelling like methanol. It brought nearly as broad a smile to his face as Penny's, but for an entirely different reason.

**** **** ****

Back at the hotel, Liz dashed off to change and open the bar. Toby took a lead, and put a few bickies in his Barbour pocket, strictly for good behaviour. He took Bess for a walk along the riverbank. It was blissfully quiet as Bess busied herself chasing scents and occasionally having a wee to mark some lucky dog's card.

They wandered along for the best part of three quarters of an hour before Toby turned round and retraced their tracks. Bess, spotting a water vole on the other bank, dived in splashing around in the slow moving brownish river, well-known for its good trout fishing.

Toby jumped as someone tapped his shoulder saying 'That's Liz's dog, Bess, isn't it?' The craggy face above the old sweater and even older Barbour broke into a grin as he pointed to the sign proclaiming "Non Permit Holders strictly forbidden".

'Geoff Barraclough. I am the water bailiff to his lordship. Don't worry, you haven't disturbed anyone fishing, and I promise not to tell Liz.'

'Many thanks,' said Toby sheepishly. 'I would really like to take up fishing again. I haven't fished since my schooldays.'

'Well, get in touch when you are good and ready,' said Geoff.

Bess crept guiltily out of the river, shaking herself like something demented until she was dry. Sitting at his feet she looked pensively at Toby who relented, saying to her, 'You've been a naughty girl, but thank God you came back.'

As he reached for a couple of biscuits in his pocket, she put her head on one side, and he was sure she grinned at him. She was dry and angelically trotting at his heels when they entered the hotel.

'You seem to have been ages,' said Liz. 'I thought you might have both fallen in the river.'

'Not us, eh Bess? It looked a bit too chilly,' patting Bess and giving her another biscuit.

'You'd better stop that before she gets too fat!'

'I'll just go and freshen up before dinner,' said Toby.

'You've got my company, if you like, as we haven't many bookings.'

He quickly showered and changed before grabbing a pint and popping into the residents lounge as he hadn't read a paper all day. The major hailed him from a corner where he had the telegraph crossword spread out on a low coffee table. 'Just the man I want,' he said, 'can you help? I'm stuck on the last word.' By more luck than management, Toby was quickly able to fill it in.

'I'll tell you a tale, major,' he said. 'There was a chap, working in the city and commuting by train every day, in the same carriage with the same chinless dull commuters. They would all nod at each other then get out the Telegraph crossword, working on it all the way to London. There they would nod. Might even say good day, see you tomorrow.

'Now, our chap got bored, and to liven things up, he cut yesterday's crossword out, pasting it over today's with the answers. The train left. Telegraph out, everyone thinking hard. Our man quickly filled in the whole crossword in 5 minutes, and carefully turning the page started to read. Complete silence ensued. Papers were put down and conscious of them all staring at him, he laughingly explained to the incredulous faces what he had done. Their stony looks soon gave way to laughter and conversation. Their journey was for ever afterwards of pleasant humour and anecdotes. They all became good friends,' said Toby.

'What a lovely tale,' laughed the major. 'They will love to hear that at the bridge club.'

Toby went into the dining room, where Liz quickly joined him over a fine fish pie, which had seen a lot of fish. They discussed the day's events, with Liz confirming she'd got the Saturday off to go to Catterick Races the following week.

'You don't let the grass grow under your feet,' exclaimed Toby. 'By the way, I've been in touch with my contact re tips and they think one is ready for Monday, with two possibly three for either Friday or Saturday. I'm really praying for it to be Catterick on Saturday.'

**** **** ****

The weekend passed uneventfully,Mondays tip winning comfortably at 8/1, returning nearly £50 profit for the £5 each way (ew) stake.

Kath told Toby to ring on Friday, but pretty sure it would be Saturday.

Toby was in a state of excitement all week, as rarely had he felt the excitement and anticipation held back in Kath's voice as she had said, 'If these come up, Liam will be debt free at last.'

Colin popped into the bar for a quick pint and just confirmed that Toby and Liz could pick up their owners' badges at the Owners and Trainers entrance. He gave Toby a large windscreen sticker for the Owners and Trainers car park. Toby thought, if he stuck it on the smallish TR windscreen he would never see through, so he told Liz they would hold it up for inspection when needed.

After a light early supper, Toby retired with a pint to the Residents' Lounge with today's Sporting Life to check all the Catterick declared runners.

He nodded to Liz as he went up to his room, and had a quick wink in return.

The bar was nearly empty so she wouldn't be long. He pulled out his old but super quality Huntsman of Savile

Row charcoal pin-stripe suit, his best blue striped Jermyn Street shirt, and quickly gave a polish to his black brogues. He dithered when choosing a tie, but thought, 'bugger it', he'd earned it, and chose his old Parachute Regiment maroon tie with its distinctive wings.

He had to stop himself humming 'Wagner's Ride of the Valkyries', the Regimental March.

He also smiled when he remembered the army's old saying of six P's. Perfect Planning Prevents Piss Poor Performance!

He was smiling as the door opened, a black paw, and then a black head wiggled through and bounced over to slobber over his hand. Bess's tail was thumping his leg as Liz slipped in, quietly closing the door. 'Goodness,' she said. 'I pong like a barmaid. Stale ale and bacon. Can I shower?' She quickly stripped off.

Toby slipped off his boxer shorts and led her to the shower over the bath. Taking the showerhead, he played it over her then himself before reaching for the Badedas shower gel, and gently massaged it in all over her. Turning, he held it out for her. By now Tom had risen to his full glory as she caressingly washed him.

Handing the shower to Toby, she bent down, holding Tom with one hand clenched on top of the other. She was amazed to see 2" of Tom's huge head still appearing. She was just able to take it in her mouth and proceeded slowly, then quicker to bring him to ejaculation.

He was still hard, and lifting her by her thighs, Toby carefully positioned her over Tom before sliding gently up and down until she started to moan louder and louder. He wedged her right foot on the bath, and released his hand to cover her mouth as she convulsed into a series of orgasms.

She became quiet. Toby lifted her up and dried her with a large fluffy bath sheet, before laying her in bed. He quickly dried himself and climbed in beside a sleeping Liz. Checked, that his alarm was set before turning off the light.

He spooned up to Liz's bare back, with a now sleeping and contented Tom lying between them. Even Bess was quietly snoring beside the bed.

**** **** ****

The alarm went off at 7am, quickly awakening Toby, who stretching out his hand stopped button. As Liz was still snoozing, he quietly slipped out of bed, putting his finger to his lips as he patted an awakening Bess. He went into the bathroom and the loo before shaving under the shower. As he finished dressing, Liz awoke. The most beautiful beaming smile lighting her face as she said, 'What a fantastic night, I've got the whole day off'.

'Look poppet! I have got to get a Sporting Life from the newsagents, make a call and do some studying. I'll see you at breakfast at half eight.' Chucking a biscuit for Bess to catch, he was gone.

It was a bright, crisp, sunny day as he strode to the phone box on the corner. He fed the coins in, dialled Kath and immediately pressed the button. She must have been waiting for the call. 'Hello,' started Toby. 'Top of the morning, what's cooking'

'We're on at the best prices we've seen. I'll be quick. Are you ready?' she asked breathlessly.

'Yup' replied Toby, his diary open, pen ready.

'As I said yesterday,' she continued 'All at Catterick. In the 12.20 Larsare should open around 12/1. Then in the 1.20 Dame Wain around 25/1, and finally in the 2.20 Maria Carmen trading about 10/1.

'Best of Irish. Toby, we going big. Liam says, do the same,' and the line went dead.

Bloody hell, thought Toby. What prices, surely they've no chance, but knowing what his tried and trusted friend had said, he'd be a fool not to follow.

He quickly dialled Sylvia, giving her the information before buying his copy of the Sporting Life. He hurried back to the hotel, where he scrounged a cup of very black coffee from Lucy and retired to the lounge to check the horses and work out his strategy. They were at such good prices that each way bet on the same horse would give good returns.

The new patent bet, which was seven bets on three horses giving three wins, three win doubles and a treble. With such long odds, he decided to place an each way patent which was 14 bets. So a £1ew patent would cost him £14. He quickly calculated the returns, and he thought he could afford to risk a £5ew patent costing him £70. About a month's wage in those days!

He wrote out his bets on a spare Wm Hill slip, and nipping up to his bedroom, took out £150 from his secret stash and went down to join Liz.

Over bacon and eggs he briefly told her that he was going to Ripon to put some bets on. He would be back to pick her up in her glad rags at 10.30, so they could meet Colin and Penny as planned for 11.30.

'The first race is at 12.20,' he reminded her. Quickly squeezing her hand, he said, 'I think today is going to be very special, and don't worry, I'll put on a bet for you. Hopefully you can collect some loot too.' With that, he was gone. What a man, she thought, you are a lucky girl.

Toby nipped down to Ripon, finding Wm Hill on North Street squeezed in between a solicitor and insurance broker. Rather apt he thought, as he went in to the gloom and usual layer of cigarette smoke. He checked the prices he could find on the board displaying the papers. Walking over to the clerk behind his glass screen, he handed over his slip and asked for the current prices. Larsare was 12/1, Dame Wain was 25/1 and Maria Carmen 20/1.

The clerk said he would have to check with his boss before taking the £70 and returned the slip to Toby. The other old codgers were craning their ears to listen in, but fortunately the clerk was softly spoken. Toby put the slip in the inner pocket of his suit and set off to meet Liz.

He patted the pocket in his father's old suit, thinking how good life was and the old man would've been proud of him. Liz tied a blue polka dot design head square, which went well with the smart navy suit, pencil skirt and sensible flat shoes. They went through Bedale and out onto the A1 north to Catterick.

The traffic was busy but they found their way to the Owners and Trainers car park, Liz waving the big car park sticker. They found an empty space near the veterinary office. Toby hoped that the vet wouldn't be required today, always feeling a wrench in his stomach when the green screens were placed round a badly injured horse that the poor vet had to despatch with a shot to the head.

They went through an entrance with a smart commissionaire on the door. They collected the Ladies and Gents owner's badges from a very stern, horsey-faced lady who handed them over without so much as a smile. Probably reserved for the nobs and not for the like of us, thought Toby.

Hovering outside was an excited and gorgeous-looking Penny, dressed in a tight fitting blue dress which really showed her ample cleavage. Like looking the Nile delta, Toby thought. Even Tom gave a twitch of appreciation as Toby said 'Thanks for waiting for us Penny. You look absolutely fab,' Penny took Liz's arm and lead the way to the Owners and Trainers box overlooking the parade ring.

Colin had a table for four in the corner with a view of a cctv monitor showing the action. A small Tote window was on the other wall, run by a sour faced woman dressed in the Tote red. Just like the last one, thought Toby. They must clone them round here.

'Pull up a chair, I've taken the liberty to start us off with a bottle of house pink champagne,' said Colin.

'How delightfully decadent,' said Liz, holding out her flute to Colin, who quickly filled the four glasses with a froth of pink bursting bubbles. Toby raising his glass thanked Colin, and toasted them all by saying, 'To confusion,' at which they all laughed.

Colin then asked Toby if he had any pointers and shot an enquiring glance at Toby, who thought what the hell, we have got our money on, why not share it.

**** **** ****

'A friend of mine, who is quite good, reckons these three horses might be worth a small each way bet.' He quickly marked them on Colin's race card. 'They are huge prices!' exclaimed Colin. 'If anyone got those up, they would seriously make money. If they dared to put them in a combination, well,' he shook his head. Toby received a kick under the table from Liz, who gazed at him innocently.

Toby ordered and paid for another bottle and asked if he could pay for a round of those delicious looking smoked salmon sandwiches. Giving Liz a fiver, he excused himself saying, 'I just want to see Larsare in the parade ring.'

It was an amateur riders' handicap, and the gelding had won a couple of point-to-point seasons. He was fairly short but well-muscled with a gloss coat that his stable girl had brushed until it shone. Despite having put his patent on, Toby thought he would try to win a bit of cash, so on the way back he put £5ew on the Tote.

He just got back to the table when they were off. Every eye was glued to the TV screen. Larsare was a bit slow away and lay about 6th after the first hurdle. They went at a fairly slow pace, but gradually he crept up, jumping the hurdles beautifully, and clearly. His young girl amateur jockey crouched low in the saddle. At the last hurdle he was lying a close third to the first and second favourites.

The favourite, who had led all the way round seemed to slow, whilst the second horse landed badly and caused his young rider to lose his stirrups. Larsare dived through the gap and went on to win by five lengths to a whooping Colin, Penny and Liz.

It seemed they were the only people who had bet on him. They toasted Toby and all joined the tote queue to collect their winnings. Colin collected just shy of £60 for his £5ew ticket and proclaimed he was tickled pink and just couldn't wait for Toby's next selection, running in the third race. That race was a handicap hurdle of 3 miles 1 ½ furlongs. Toby couldn't wait either and nervously quaffed his champagne whilst watching the second race.

After it ended he excused himself, saying he just wanted to look at Dame Wain, his marked selection.

Swiftly, Penny rose and grabbing his arm asked sweetly, 'May I come too?' Toby, casting an exasperated look of resignation at Liz, who raised her eyebrows and mouthed 'go'.

Actually he quite liked Penny's closeness, capturing a whiff of a really exciting perfume he couldn't quite place. Heads turned to look at this glamorous couple, wondering if they were famous. Perhaps 'off the telly'.

Penny enjoyed it whilst Toby was oblivious. He weaved his way through the crowd to gain a ring side spot, fast filling by the spectators.

The horses were being led around by stable lads and lasses. Each wore the horse's number on a disc on their upper arm. Toby showed Penny the favourite, Crowning Glory, and then the second favourite Bourne Cliffs. They both agreed they looked magnificent. Certainly, compared to their horse Dame Wain, which was smaller, had a darker coat, and had a bit of a wild look in her four-year-old eye.

Toby nearly admitted to Penny that he thought he had got it wrong. Still trusting Liam, he placed another £5ew on her and £1ew for Penny. Giving her the ticket he said 'At 25/1, I honestly don't think she has a chance, but you never know.' Thanking him she planted a big kiss on his mouth, murmuring 'I've got trust in you. Look, let's watch it from the stands.' They climbed to a spot almost opposite the finish line, from where they could see nearly all the way round.

At the off she catapulted forward, to lead by nearly 3 lengths after the second hurdle of the 3 miles 1 ½ furlongs course. The first and second favourites were line abreast behind her. At the eighth hurdle they came alongside, crashing into her on landing. She was left some two lengths between the favourite Crowning Glory, whose jockey, peeped between his legs, realised his horse had nothing left, as Dame Wain lunged past on winged hooves to overtake the favourite and win by a head. Penny dashed in to the Owners and Trainers bar tugging an embarrassed Toby. Stern looks came from some of the stuff shirts. The usually quiet and calm Colin jumped up, slapping Toby's back, shouting, 'Bloody hell, you did it, bloody marvellous.' More tut-tutting and disapproving looks followed. Penny, hugging her dad said, 'Look at the return,' indicating the prices marked up in the Tote window.

Colin couldn't believe his eyes, as he said 'My £5ew bet had brought me in nearly £160!'

'Someone winning?' asked the Hon Harry, joining them.

Liz told him of their two spectacular wins, to which he said 'bloody hell' to more tut-tutting and frowning at someone who ought to know better.

Harry quickly downed his champagne and announced 'The old man has taken a box for grandfather's memorial race and invites you all to come and join him.' To which Liz, knowing his Lordship's generous hospitality, fun company, thinking that it's not a bad thing to put yourself about a bit. Networking, she was sure the marketing men put it.

'Yes, we would love to come.' Putting his arm around an embarrassed, giggling Liz, Harry led them to Lord Middleham's private box.

**** **** ****

'Ah, there you are,' bellowed a middle-aged man in his early fifties, Toby guessed. He was about 5'11 and clad in a tweed country suit with matching waistcoat. He sported an old Etonian tie, as did several of the guests. Toby, looking down noticed he had turn-ups to his trousers and shoes nearly as polished as Toby's!

Seeing him looking, his lordship brayed out, 'Glad to see you are not wearing suede shoes. My old father drilled it into me, to never trust chappies in suede shoes. They always let you down. You know,' tapping his pudgy nose with his fingers. Seizing Liz's face in both hands he gave her a smacking kiss on her mouth. Then, pecking Penny on either cheek he murmured, 'You look stunning, my dear girl.' Pumping Colin's hand he said 'Good to see you Colin. Is this Toby I've heard so much about from Harry?'

Toby taking his hand replied 'It's a pleasure to meet you my Lord.'

To which his Lordship guffawed and returned, 'Call me Tommy. Everyone else does.'

Waving his champagne flute wildly around, he just missed several of his guests. Introductions were made quick and fast, Toby quite forgetting their names which included several earls, barons, knights, judges and generals.

One tall, gaunt, silver-haired man, wearing an old Etonian tie and an even older pin-striped suit than Toby's, fixed him with his gimlet like eyes and pointing at Toby's Para tie rasped out, 'Which battalion?'

'Three, sir,' replied Toby maintaining eye contact.

'Ah, the gungy third,' replied the brigadier. 'My son was in one Para.'

'The immaculate one, but sir, it was the third that has done the only operational drop since Arnhem.'

'Quite correct,' replied the brig. 'My son told me it was all over Pegasus, the Para Regiment's own magazine about a young subaltern winning a well-earned MC (military cross) in the action. Can't remember his name. Double barrelled I seem to remember.' Several of his cronies had gathered around, listening as he asked Toby, 'Do you know him?' He cocked his head to one side, eyes piercing into Toby's. 'Yes sir, because it was me. I am Tobias Cooper-Sneyd,' before lowering his eyes in embarrassment. Liz nodded in confirmation to Tommy's raised eyebrows. Some of the others spluttered into their champagne. The brig taking Toby's hand in both his, cried out, 'What an honour it is to meet such a brave young man,' to cheers from the others.

Penny's eyes were the size of saucers as she gazed at the first man she had really wanted to marry.

Tommy leaning over to Toby whispered, 'I understand you already had two lucky winners. Harry said you might have one in my old pa's memorial race. I have to award the cup to the winning owner. Toby, I must say it would be fun to have a bob or two on it. Toby confided in Tommy that it was at such long odds of around 20/1, that it didn't have much of a chance, telling him the 6 year old mare was Maria Carmen carrying 9-7. Could we have a pot?' Tommy yelled. 'Cheer the miserable blighters up a bit.'

Toby shrugged, saying, 'Tommy, you will probably lose your money,' Tommy banged a spoon on a champagne flute hard enough to nearly break it, shouting 'attention, attention. I've received a bit of a dubious tip for my race, now all you good people put £1 in this pot,' indicating an empty beer mug. Harry, how many are we, including our 4 guests?' A quick head count gave 30. Toby put two £1 notes in first. His own and one for Liz, who mouthed 'thank you.' The pot was quickly filled, Tommy ended it and got his brother, the merchant banker to agree the £30 total and shoved it into Harrys large hands. He instructed him to go to the tote and put on £15 each way on Maria Carmen. Harry was soon back with the ticket, which his father quickly checked and handed it over to brother Hugh for safety.

The crowds were cheering the winner of the present race as Toby slunk out unnoticed to go along to a bookmaker displaying the William Hill sign.

A thin, ginger haired young man was hurried, scribbling into a large book taking instructions from a middle-aged man in a shiny black suit. Standing at the back was a large man wearing thick glasses smoking a cigar. His grey black hair swept back over his ears like a heron. Toby approached him and reading the name badge on his left lapel Mark Thompson Area Director, Toby said, 'I wonder if you can help me Mr. Thompson.' The cigar was stuck back in his mouth as he shook hands with Toby and enquired, 'Have you a problem?' Toby, getting Liz's £1ew patent ticket showed it to Mark saying, 'I bought this at your Ripon branch and wondered should I be lucky with this last one, could you pay me out here?' Mark looked at the ticket, his lips muttering, calculations whirling in his brain. His eyebrows furrowed. The other two were consulted and Mark said, 'If your last comes in, do you realise that you would have over £4000.' Toby tried to look surprised. Mark then said, 'It would take a bit of time to get it for you, but it could be done. I'd much rather send you a cheque,' to which Toby said, 'And if I also had a £5ew patent,' showing his ticket to Mark. 'Bloody hell you'll bust the firm. No, seriously, that's worth around 20 grand, is definitely a cheque. Look, I'll take the serial code of both slips now, verify on my machine here and have cheques sent up to our Ripon office tomorrow, where the manager is called Tony. Lucky for you, he lives in Leeds where my office is. You go to your Ripon branch, hand in your two tickets and he'll have the cheques in a sealed envelope.

'Here's my card, just in case of any query. I have written my home telephone number on the back. Now I don't want to wish you good luck for the next race, 'cos it'll cost us,' patting Toby on the back he waved him a cheery bye.

Toby found Liz at the parade ring, who was complaining to him at their selection, a big chestnut mare with four white socks and a thin tail that looked half-eaten. As the mare passed Toby, he swore she looked directly at him with a rolling almost wall eyes, tossing her head so much that the poor stable girl could hardly hold her. It was a 3 mile 1 1/2 f handicap hurdle. She certainly looked strong enough. They watched as the jockeys came out and gathered round the trainer, a foxy looking little man, obviously an ex jockey. The girl pulled the horse in for the trainer to give the scrawny young jockey a leg up. Having gone about ten yards the horse reared and promptly deposited the young lad on the turf. With a murderous look in his eye he remounted and safely got to the start.

They formed a rough line, the tape dropped and Maria shot forward, passing four horses to hit rail where she stayed. It was amazing. She just ran and jumped fluently, making the rest look clumsy and won by a good eight lengths.

The favourite, Timmy Twist was second at 3/1, the second favourite was third. Glazing at the Tote window, they were paying out about 16/1 on Maria and £5 for the place. As they returned to the box after watching a beaming, flushed Tommy presenting the trophy, they were greeted by whoops of joy. 'Bloody well done Toby.' Hugh and Harry handed out the ticket and received £330, which returned £11 to each of them.

Penny hugged Toby, and planted the softest, most tender kiss. Tom started stirring, later thought Toby. He took Liz to one side, saying, 'Let's leave before the last race because it'll be bedlam.' They said their goodbyes to the host and nipping over to the Tote. Toby collected the £5ew he had had on Maria, which brought in just over £100. On reaching the car he said, 'I've booked a table at the Black Bull at Moulton, where I know the owner.'

'Do you indeed?' teased Liz.

**** **** ****

They went up to the turning off to Moulton before Scotch Corner. Archie, the bar manager showed them to a quiet corner in the restaurant, where Toby ordered for them both a dozen oysters followed by Dover Sole, washed down by a well-chilled Sancerre. As they waited for the oysters, Toby told Liz of the meeting with Mark at the William Hill pitch. Told her that she was a wealthy young lady. 'Your £1ew patent would bring in nearly £4000!'

'Fucking hell,' said Liz, then thoughtfully putting her hand on his said, 'Which makes Mr. Smarty pants here worth about five times that! Christ, that's about 20 grand! You could buy about 8 semis with that!'

'Or start a business,' mused Toby. 'If I can just find the right one.'

He ordered a large cafetiere of black coffee and a fine cigar. 'Complete indulgence,' said Toby. 'My late father's favourite. I think the old bugger would have been proud of me.'

'I didn't know you smoked,' said an astonished Liz.

'Don't normally, just on special occasions like this or mess nights in the army,' he replied. He paid the bill, tipping generously and they went to the car.

It was still warm from the Indian summer they were experiencing. Toby jerked his thumb at the hood, asking Liz 'Up or down?'

'Oh, down please, it's such a gorgeous evening.' As he opened her door he slipped on his old Barbour jacket over her shoulders, and turning her towards him, kissed her open mouth, his tongue gently tracing her soft lips before slipping it in to find hers. 'God, I'm weak at the knees, let's go home to bed.' They drove carefully and quietly along the peaceful back roads under a full moon and a sky full of stars. Liz whispered, 'what a fantastic end to such day, I wish it could last forever.'

Toby swung the car into the gateway of a newly cut hayfield. He pulled an old tartan rug from the boot and unlatched the five-barred gate. Leading Liz by the hand he slipped off the Barbour, laying it on the ground before covering it with the rug.

Taking Liz in his arms he kissed her and dropping his hands, tugged up her skirt to reveal a pair of black holds up stockings covering her lovely long legs and skimpy black see through pants which he deftly removed. Then unzipping his trousers, he pulled down his boxer shorts to reveal a rampant Tom. She giggled as Tom caste a moon shadow. Toby mounted her at waist level, Tom about two inches from her mouth. God, she thought, I'll never get it in, but slowly Tom parted her lips, and grasping the huge shaft, she slowly and gently sucked him. Toby slid down her slender body and let Tom find his way into her. She lost count of her orgasms. It just seemed like one continuous roller-coaster of a feeling.

They lay side by side holding hands, until a little shiver from Liz caused Toby to say, 'Come on my love, let's go home to a proper bed. I want to collect our cheques in Ripon early in the morning and get them into the bank before he closes at noon.'

With Toby's Barbour on and her head-square securely knotted under her chin, Liz leant her head on Toby's hefty shoulder, her right hand stroking his left thigh. They crept home on virtually empty roads. Coming into the square, Toby knocked off the headlights and quietly crept under the arch to park at the back of the hotel as usual. Liz rummaged in her bag for the back door key. Toby took off his shoes and walking wide on alternate treads reached the top without a single sound. 'That was very impressive,' whispered Liz when they were safely in Toby's room.

Liz explained that Bobbie had walked Bess and she would be asleep in Liz's room. They quickly cleaned their teeth, splashed cold water on their faces and crashed out into the large, welcoming soft bed. Liz lying on her side, her soft dark hair willowing out behind her. Toby snuggled into her warm back, smiling as he picked a bit of hay from her hair. They were soon away in a deep, contented sleep.

Toby's inner alarm clock woke him at 7.30. He slid out of bed not to disturb a deep-sleeping Liz. Showered, shaved and put on a pair of tracksuit bottoms, Trainers, a faded blue shirt and his oldest sport jacket with leather elbow patches. He didn't want to draw too much attention to himself when he went to the bookies. Checking the two winning patent tickets were in the wallet, he slipped it into the inside pocket and went down to breakfast.

Lucy was surprised to see him so early, but quickly brought him the full English Breakfast including black pudding, bacon, beans, two fried eggs observing 'You must be hungry, Mr. Toby. Toby grinned back at her saying, 'A full English, I've found to be the best hangover remedy. That, and a big cafetiere of that lovely black coffee you brew so well Lucy.'

She beamed a radiant smile, as not many people thanked her for anything, she thought. As she turned Toby eyed her pert little bottom, dying to pat it. Finishing his breakfast and glancing at his Omega Seamaster watch, he was surprised to find it was nearly nine o'clock. He blew a kiss to Lucy, saying he would be back soon if Liz wondered where he was.

He went over the river bridge past the railway station on his right and was soon in the little hamlet of Tanfield. He pulled into a parking bay by an old red telephone box and taking out Mark's card rang Leeds on his private number.

It rang a few times before being picked up with a curt 'yes'. 'Is that Mark? This is Toby, we met at Catterick yesterday.' To a much mellowed tone the voice responded, 'Bloody hell, young man. Your lucky combination has cost the firm plenty. Anyroads, I've sent young Ginger, the Ripon Manager off with two signed cheques as promised, for £3870 and £19345. Do you realise that's what one of the highest pay-outs we've made in a long time. You will soon become a marked man and be banned. We can't keep taking hits like this. Tell you what. Next time you get ideas like this, will you please take them to Joe Coral? He's got a shop just down the road from ours. Now seriously, I'd like to have a chat with you. Would you let me buy you a dinner at the Drum and Monkey in Harrogate this week? Would Thursday around seven suit you?' A puzzled and slightly excited Toby pretended to consult his diary, before saying, 'Thank you, that'll be fine, and again many thanks for your prompt and kind attention. I am just on my way to Ripon now.'

'Good, and look forward to meeting up with you on Thursday.' The phone went dead.

Toby parked up round the back of high street on some waste land and headed into the shop, which being a busy racing Saturday was already half packed by the usual non shaved, shabbily dressed punters the usual blue-grey layer of cheap cigarette smoke at eye level. Many were pouring over newspapers on Formica tables, whilst two or three were running their dirty fingers down the Sporting Life pinned to the wall. There were two punters queuing to place bets so Toby pretended to consult a paper. Seeing the clerk was free, he leant over and said he had called to collect the envelope sent up from Leeds. The clerk rung for the manager. Ginger came round from the back office, opening a locked door which read 'Staff Only. Strictly No Admittance'. Tony ushered him in saying, 'The boss said to check your tickets first,' holding out his hand. Toby took the two tickets from his wallet, hanging on to them saying 'Now, I'll just give you the serial number to prove they are correct.'

'Don't you trust me to handle them?' Ginger queried, slightly affronted. 'Well,' replied Toby, 'I once heard the tale of a chap having a big win and on handing it over to find the bookie realising its worth popped it in his mouth and swallowed it, saying, 'What ticket?'

Ginger tartly replied, 'We are one of the top bookmakers as you know, I couldn't lose my job or pension.' Toby handed over the £1 patent ticket first just in case, there was a problem. Ginger took it, checking the issue number against a list he had, nodded and opening the envelope handed over the cheque for £3870. After that came the same procedure and the cheque for £19345. Toby quickly put them in his wallet. Ginger led him out of a heavily secured back door, saying, 'The punters might get a bit two inquisitive.' Toby thanked him for his kindness, stepped into the back alley, where he could see his car about 100 yards away. Head down, not looking around he was quickly in the car and back on the way to Masham. 'Come on Fiona,' the pet name he always called his car. 'We won't be together much longer. Let's remember the old times. On the open road he opened up, exhaust barking alive, the Castrol R warming in the engine to give the smell of methanol. She squatted low on the road, almost becoming alive as swept round corners from side to side taking a perfect racing line. He clocked nearly 90 mph on the long, straight before slowing to normal speeds approaching Masham. 'There old love, that's what you were made for. Look after young Harry as well as you have done for me.'

CHAPTER SEVEN

He parked up as usual and went to find Liz, who was busy getting the bar ready for what looked to be a busy day. Taking her aside, he showed her the cheque. 'I've never had a cheque for so much' and kissing him said, 'Thanks from the bottom of my heart. You are the most marvellous man I've ever met.'

When he asked her if she wanted him to pay her cheque in when he did his, she readily agreed.

Toby jogged off to the bank before they closed. One lady was finishing off and chatting to Joyce, who caught Toby's eye saying. 'I'll be with you in a moment, sir,' as Harold Farrar popped out of his and handed over a sheet of figures to Joyce. 'Come with me sir, as we were closing any minute.'

Toby entered the holy of holy's telling Harold, 'I've just have two cheques to pay in. One for Miss Elizabeth Mellor and the other for myself,' He plonked the cheques down on the desk. Harold grabbed two receipt forms and confirmation slips and then pen poised turned quite ashen as he read the amount, he stuttered 'That's nearly my pension pot.'

'Well,' replied Toby, 'I was extremely lucky and it's never likely to happen again! It should give me a nice little cushion while I look around for a project.' Harold handing him the two receipts, shaking him warmly by the hand saying, 'If there is anything I can do, please ask as we at Barclays want to help especially our best customers.'

Toby grinned to himself as he pocketed the two receipts, warmly thanking Harold saying, 'If I come up with something, no doubt I can call you on your support for additional temporary funding? Should I require it?'

'Of course, of course,' replied Harold rubbing his podgy little hands. Toby told himself as he returned to the hotel, you can always borrow an umbrella when the sun's shining but just try it when it's pissing down!

He pinched Liz's bottom as she leaned over behind the bar, revealing the top of a black thong. Tom started twitching. He was dying to grab her and take her up to bed. Sadly, work must go on! She turned, flaring at some chancy punter, but immediately relaxed into a soft, loving smile as she took the slip from his outstretched hand. Glancing at it, she threw her arms around his neck, saying, 'you lovely, lovely man. I now have a safe buffer in my account as I always had to live from hand to mouth! Oh, by the way, Lordy rang and asked if you and I would join him and a few family friends for supper round the kitchen table next Friday. I said yes, hoping you were free. It sounded a bit mysterious, I must admit I'm quite intrigued.'

'I'm sure I can fit into my busy schedule! Especially if it involves you,' returned Toby.

The next week was a bit slow; Toby rang Kath to congratulate them both. Kath was ecstatic, saying, 'Liam had 3 big trebles with different bookies, and had paid off the mortgage on the farm, with enough left to put up more horse boxes and still a good float. Something we've never had before.'

Unfortunately the two tips on Monday and Wednesday both lost, but Toby told himself 'that was racing!' On Thursday Kath told him, that Liam had two good long priced bets to come through which should give them a decent double.

Toby quickly showered and put on an old blazer, dark grey trousers and his father's old Gucci shoes. Giving Liz a quick peck in the crowded bar, he set off for dinner with Mark at the Drum and Monkey in Harrogate. As it was drizzling, he put the hood up and squished his way through Ripon and Killinghall to arrive about fifteen minutes before Mark's suggested 7.00. He parked up a side street, and avoiding the puddles he went up the steps. The first person he saw was Mary, the middle-aged Irish head waitress, barmaid and general factotum. He'd been several times on school exeats with his father. Her hands on her hips, she looked him up and down. 'Look what the wind's blown in. My, you have grown!' Toby putting his hands on her shoulders, pecked both cheeks and looking in her staring green eyes, asked genuinely and caringly, 'How are you Mary? I hope your manager, Peter is not working you too hard,' to which she said, 'Get away wit yer, you've got the same silver tongue your father 'ad. Now, what can I do for you?'

Toby explained he was meeting Mark. 'Oh, are you indeed?' said Mary. 'You must be in the inner circle. He often comes with top trainers and some fellars off the telly.'

'Does he now?' mused Toby, wondering what was coming. Mary waved Toby over to Mark sitting on a far off dark corner at a table commanding a full view of the room and the door. He could see who was coming and going. Rising, Mark dressed in a dark suit and very sombre tie to the flashy one he had worn at the races, stretched out his hand asked, 'I see you know Mary, not many men I know dare give her a kiss like you, they'd be gelded before they reached the bar.'

'Oh,' laughed Toby. 'I think my late father and Mary go back a long time. He used to ring her when he was peddling his barley around the Yorkshire Maltsters and Brewers.'

'What will you have?' asked Mark and Toby, noticing his frothing pint of Guinness, said 'May I join you?' Catching Mary's eagle eye, Mark just pointed to his Guinness and then to Toby's place. Smiling he raised his eyebrows. Mary was over with the pint, settling it down beside Toby she nudged him and wistfully smiling at him said, 'Just like your old man. I'll be back to take your order in a tick,' dropping two menus on the table. 'What do you recommend?' asked Toby. I'm having a dozen Whitstable number fours to go with the Guinness, and then the lobster thermidor.' No wonder you keep so trim, thought Toby saying, 'what a good choice. I'll have the same.'

They chit chatted about racing generally. Toby, through avidly reading the 'Life' daily since school days, where he was the school's bookmaker impressed Mark with his in-depth knowledge. Throughout the meal, Toby wondered when the punch line was to be delivered. The restaurant was packed and Mark, knowing that the waiter would like to serve two more who were waiting suggested they have a coffee in a small snug upstairs.

A couple were just leaving and Mark again chose two chairs in the corner with small dinner table in between. He ordered coffee and asked could the waiter bring up the cigar case. Blimey, thought Toby, the second cigar within the week, I'm in danger of being addicted!

Mark offered the selection from a wooden humidor. Toby thought he might as well have a good one so he chose a Henry Clay saying, 'I think that would truly round off a memorable meal, thank you.' Mark picked out a similar cigar saying, 'For a young man, you have impeccable taste.' After the waiter had cut the cigars and leaving them with a box of Swan Vesta matches, left them to get the coffee. Mark drew gently on the cigar before exuding the smoke with a satisfied sigh before he began. 'I checked on your bets the other day and someone with your description placed a similar bet in Aldershot before collection in Harrogate.'

'Blimey,' said Toby 'Talk about the KGB, do all you bookies work like that?'

'That's how we stay in business,' said Mark.

'Are you going to stop my betting with you or slash the prices whenever I enter your shop?' asked an alarmed Toby.

'Far from it,' purred Mark. 'Look, I am a local director, but not on the main board. Little chance now as I retire in two years, on a reasonable pension, but nothing spectacular. My Missus and I want to retire to a low-maintenance bungalow by the sea. I've seen too many people go ga-ga. I've got a proposition for you. I don't want to know how or where you get your information from, but if you deal with me personally, I'll guarantee you the best prices available.

I'll put them on with our competitors, so saving my firm from paying out. You and I make the profits from other bookies. I see you have only a few bets a month, two singles in a week, sometimes a double, and rarely a treble, or even a patent all £5ew at good odds.'

Toby listened, mesmerised as Mark put forward his proposition. 'You ring my missus Sylvia on my home number when you have a bet. Just say for example 2:15 catt-4 (215 Catterick number 4) she will read the horse's name from the paper, if correct, you say correct, and go on to the second and third if you have them! I'll put on £5ew for you and £5ew for the double if there is a second horse, and a £5ew patent if there are three horses. I'll do the same for myself.

Any winnings, Sylvia will send you from her account by cheque the following morning. That way you have the bets. Useful if you can't get into a shop. Hopefully I've made it clear. Let's give it one month as a trial, if it doesn't come off, I'm the loser, and it cost you nothing!'

He sat back and looked enquiringly at Toby who said, 'you have obviously given it great thought. I think it's bloody marvellous.' They shook hands and went their separate ways.

CHAPTER EIGHT

Toby got back to the hotel in time to grab a quick drink as Liz was closing the bar. He said he would take Bess for her walk, as Liz had been busy all day. She gratefully thanked him, saying she would take a much-needed soak in the bath, wash her hair and keep the bed warm! After a good walk around the square and churchyard Bess was tiring fast as Toby led her up to the bedroom, giving her a few biscuits for being a good girl. She settled on her bed at the bottom of theirs and was gently snoozing in a minute.

After the quickest shower Toby was in bed cuddling a warm, naked Liz, as he whispered the goings-on of his night with Mark. 'Wow,' was her reaction, 'you can't lose, so long as you keep him in profit.'

'Exactly' whispered Toby, 'And I'll still put my bets on with another bookie,' dreamily as he fell asleep in her arms. He rang Kath from another phone box near to the post office, to be told there were two separate bets, both at long odds which Liam was really keen about. Toby fished Mark's card out of his wallet and rang Sylvia, who was straight on the line in a very smokey, husky, seductive voice. Toby announced himself saying Mark had asked him to give her a ring, to which Sylvia breathed, 'I've been waiting for your call, you can go ahead.' Toby gave her the two horses, which she confirmed by name and the figure 30. Toby then knew she would put 2 £5ew singles and a £5ew double. Toby drove off to Bedale for a change to put on his bets with Joe Coral. He was delighted to get 16/1 and 9/1, and prayed that Liam's feelings were right.

He spent the rest of the day looking at properties in estate agent offices in Bedale, Ripon and Harrogate taking away piles of details and prices to get his head around. On impulse he popped into the antique shop where Penny worked. The smallish rounded figure in a pink shirt and tie announced himself as Hugo. Aha, thought Toby, so this is Penny's boss. Hugo had a round, cherubic face, thinning visibly on top with silver hair swept back. His protruding eyes were made bigger by his thick pebble-lens specs. Toby noted he was wearing light suede chukka boots. Definitely one not to be introduced to Lordy. Toby asked if he could look around, and not seeing Penny, wandered into the back, where Penny had told him they kept their reclaimed large items from country houses.

To the left he saw a step ladder and a pair of legs as Penny was reaching for something from the high shelf. Glancing over his shoulder he could see Hugo's back to him talking to someone at the front door. Moving silently forward Toby looked up to see the sheer brown stockings were held up by white suspenders up shapely thighs to white lacy pants which gaped at the sides as she lent further over. Tom started to get seriously excited, so Toby slid back to the door, slightly clinking a cup and saucer before returning to see Penny coming down the ladder. 'Hello,' he said, 'Just met your boss, thought I would come and see if you really worked here.'

'Cheeky,' she said, brushing her hair back with her hand. 'What time is it?'

'About 5.00' replied Toby. 'Christ we'd better get our skates on, 'cos you and Colin are invited to Lordy's for supper as well.'

'I hadn't realised you were going too.'

'I'll shoot off then, and see you there.' 'Don't be late' advised Penny. 'Lordy's a bit like the Queen, you're just never late.'

Toby suggested by Liz put on his old charcoal grey suit, blue shirt and naturally his highly polished black brogues. She was simply dressed in a navy polka dot shift dress and wearing her mother's pearls and earrings.

**** **** ****

They arrived bang on 6.50, pulling up at the front. Liz charged up the steps and pulled on the highly polished brass doorbell. 'You've done that before,' observed Toby.

'Just a few times, when Lordy and I had a fling a while back.' Toby's mouth dropped saying, 'You never told me.'

'Not important,' she replied, 'It's over now.' At that moment, the door was opened by a tall craggy faced Scot in a kilt. 'Evening McDonald,' said Liz brightly, introducing Toby. 'McDonald is his Lordship's butler. Without whom the whole place would grind to a halt.' Toby looking at the kilt asked 'Mr. McDonald, how long were you in the Argyles?'

'I did my pontoon, twenty one years sir,' was the crisp answer. 'Were you a military man yourself sir?'

'I only did my National Service, which I extended to 5 years on a short service commission,' a knowing nod from McDonald. 'Who were you with sir?'

'I served 3 years with 3 Para before they told me they only wanted officers with regular commission so I ended up in the RASC. Getting in 'Run Away Someone's Coming' before the Argyle.'

'A fine lot, sir,' he said with a new respect in his voice. As they were ushered across the hall, Toby asked, 'Would you ever come across Capt. Fergy Grant?'

'We met up when we did some joint exercise in Scotland. Capt. Grant was the adjutant, when I was the regimental Sgt major' exhorted McDonald. And no finer officer was in the Argyles. Any friend of Capt. Grant is a friend of mine, and if ever I can be of to help you sir, just call!'

McDonald opened the door to a large airy sitting room, with a huge log fire burning in a large stone fireplace with two men sitting on the brass bum-warmer in front of it. Family portraits and original oil paintings adorned the walls. Many old leather sofas and club chairs were dotted around. Tommy bounded up, taking Liz in both arms and planting a huge kiss, without so much as a spilling a drop from the very full whisky glass clutched in his hand. Turning to Toby, he said, 'Good to see you dear boy, I think you know most people,' he waved airily.

'Perhaps you haven't yet met our splendid doctor Basil Mortimer and his lovely wife Eunice. Don't be fooled by Doc's huge hands, they are as gentle as the many babies he's brought into the world!' Doc, it turned out was a former Cambridge double Blue for rugby and boxing. 'Here's my brother Mark who lives in the square. He is an MP for Hertford. Never see much of him, always busy running the country,' he brayed, laughing at his joke, as he waved his whisky at a very tall, balding man in his fifties, who had large, sticking out ears and a large Adam's apple which mesmerizingly bobbed up and down like a tennis ball. Toby thought to himself, I bet his parents didn't know whether he was going to walk or fly until he was three. Mark pumped his hand furiously, asking for him to support the local Tory branch.

Apparently, they were all gathered for the driven rough shoot the next day. Asked if he shot, Toby replied, 'My father was a first-class shot, and bought me my first 410 when I was eight, before I graduated to my first twelve bore when I was twelve. It was an ancient Cogswell and Harrison with short barrels, which taught me to be accurate, as well as never wasting a cartridge as they cost a lot from my pocket money. To which they all laughed and Thomas said, 'If I get a non-show one day, would you care to fill in at short notice?' to which Toby gratefully replied, 'I would be delighted, as I've heard you run a really exciting shoot with good bags!' Thomas slapping him on the shoulder said, 'Well, if you are as good at shooting as you seem to be at the horses, you'll be welcome.'

McDonald banged a brass gong and announced, 'My lords, ladies and gentlemen, dinner is served. They trooped in to the dining room. Toby was placed between Liz and Penny, which suited him down to the ground. Doing a quick head count, he toted up 14. They tucked into wild smoked salmon, caught by Tommy on the Spey and smoked to perfection by McDonald. The roast beef was served pink and washed down with a fine Leoville-Barton from Thomas' extensive cellar. Tapping his Stuart crystal wine glass Thomas said, 'I have a little announcement to make,' to which all heads turned. 'A bit unconventional, but that's me,' he started.

'After Annabelle, my late wife was so tragically killed in a car crash few years ago, I've been on my own and missing her company so much, I threw myself into running the estate and trying to give Harry,' waving at him, 'A good stable home. My dear mother taught me SLAW, safe, loved and warm as a child. I've travelled a lot, meeting many people, even looked up old flames. But I've been in the company of someone local, so local she nearly ducked under my radar. She is a lot younger than me, but has a wonderful sense of fun and love of life.

'I think and hope she feels the same for me, as tonight Liz, in front of friends and family, I ask you to be my wife.' Quickly turning to face her, he dropped on one knee, producing a ring boasting one huge diamond joined by almost as large a sapphire. Liz, her eyes moist and wide–open muttered, 'Of course, my love, what's taken you so long?' to applause and laughter by everyone and intense relief on Lordy's behalf. 'After all,' he told them 'I'd have looked a bloody idiot if she'd turned me down.'

On cue, Laurent-Perrier rose and corks were soon popping like a clay pigeon shoot. Penny's hand was on Toby's thigh, and squeezing she looked at him, whispering, 'That was really romantic.'

Toby looking into her wide eyes, whispered back, 'you deserve the same. Will you let me take you home tonight?'

Looking at him, her lips breaking into a smile she said, 'To repeat a quote I've just heard, what took you so long?' to which they broke into a fit of giggles. Flushed and happy, Lordy crashed to his chair.

Like a jack-in-a-box, up popped an excited Harry and before the applause could start, turning to his Father, cried out, 'Pa, you have stolen my thunder,' dragging a blushing Jill to her feet, waved her left hand, wearing a beautiful single diamond on her ring finger in his father's face. 'I proposed to Jill last night, who could Adam & Eve-it,' to cries of laughter. 'I think we will have to have a joint wedding if you will be my best man Pa,' to a further outburst of joy and applause as Lord Thomas said, 'Yes my boy, but only if you will be my best man,' with tears in his eyes.

Thomas toasted his bride-to-be, while Harry reciprocated. Instead of the ladies retiring to 'powder their noses' and have a gossip while the men remained at the table and took port and cigars as was normal the whole table stayed and finishing the champagne, before moving on to coffee and liqueurs. Thomas insisted on bringing in all the staff to celebrate including the maids, housekeeper and cooks. The party went on until the small hours.

Toby turned to Liz and giving her a light peck on the cheek wished her all the best for a happy future, telling her she deserved it and whispering to her that what had gone on between them had been fantastic, but he would never mention it to anyone, to tearful thanks. He also told her that he had fallen head over heels for Penny.

Someone had turned on the record player in the hall so everyone packed it out, and the men swapped partners so they all had a chance to dance. It looked strangely unconventional as a very flushed cook was doing a jig with his lordship. Harry suggested everyone stayed the night or they might all wind up in the cells. There were plenty of rooms free in the huge house so Toby and Penny crept up to find a single room with a sofa at the foot of the bed. Toby kissed and hugged her before wrapping her up in a large eiderdown and tucked her into bed. She was asleep as soon as her golden head touched pillow. Toby took off his shoes and jacket and taking a spare pillow and thick blanket curled up on the sofa. Telling himself there was another time and place, as he fantasised about her before falling into a deep sleep himself. They were awakened by doors banging and the delicious smell of bacon and eggs as Toby glanced at his watch, seeing it was 8'o clock. Penny awoke to his slushing his face with cold water in the hand basin. She sat up in bed, brushing back her long fair hair saying, 'You really are a lovely man.'

'You were a bit pissed,' replied Toby.

'When we make love, I want it to be very special, something you will always remember.'

'I know I will,' she muttered huskily. They straightened their clothes and went in search of a loo before searching out the source of the mouth-watering aromas.

People in various states of dress, all nursing hangovers were devouring bacon sandwiches served by a beaming and very happy cook. Toby wondered where she had ended up and with whom. Toby and Penny parked themselves at the end of a long bench seat, munching their thick, homemade brown bread sandwiches stuffed with a pile of crispy, well-done bacon and sipped hot coffee from mugs.

Harry and Jill came in, squidging in next to them. 'Bloody marvellous party, Harry,' said Toby. 'Again many congrats to both you and your father.'

'Glad I saw you before you left,' began Harry. 'I have had a word with the old man about your TR, and he said he'd like to buy it for me as a wedding present. He also said you could have the choice of my Land Rover or his newer, diesel one. If it's ok with you I'll come down to the hotel on Monday with his cheque for £450 as agreed. We'll have both Land Rovers at Colin's garage for you to choose which one you prefer. Leave them with you for a few hours, so you and your pal Joe can check them out. Pa thought we'd pop out for lunch to meet a chap about renting two days shooting if that's okay to you.'

'Perfect,' said a grateful Toby.

'Oh, by the way,' retorted Harry, 'Pa also said you could have the TR back for a few days whilst you do any necessary work on the Land Rover.'

'That's more than generous Harry, please thank your father.'

**** **** ****

Toby and Penny climbed into the TR, burbling gently away so as not to disturb the gravel drive. On the way back he pulled into a lay by with a telephone box, telling Penny he had to urgently phone someone as promised. Jiggling the change, he put a call through to Kath apologising for being a berk. He told her that he'd been out to dinner and he hadn't seen his morning paper.

Kath grumbled, 'It's alright for some. For a berk, you did quite well, the first coming in at 9/1 and the second at 6/1. I hope you did the double?' Before he could thank her she went on, 'Oh, Liam thinks it's pretty grotty racing till Thursday, so give me a ring then love.' Before she could put the phone down Toby said, 'Kath, I do really appreciate all the help from both of you and want to make up for it to you when you say.'

Chuckling she said in her soft accent, 'Don't you worry my dear, very soon Liam will be selling you a yearling he has his eyes on and thinks will be the next Golden Miller. You pay him for his help and you in turn will have a money making machine.' She added, 'It's a win-win situation.'

'Tell Liam I'll be ready when he is, so long as I am not paying in the Queens League.' Laughing, she put the phone down.

Calculating quickly he had made around £400. He put a call through Mark's wife Sylvia who said, 'I'm glad you called. I was just popping out to post you a cheque for £451. Mark had a right go and thanks you!' Toby quickly thanked her and told her he next expected to call her on Thursday.

'You look very pleased with yourself,' smiled Penny. 'You look like the cat that's just eaten the cream.'

'Oh I am, my honey bunch,' he said pulling her to him, kissing her sensuously. 'I've just had news of a little windfall, and have the most gorgeous girl in the world beside me. I'm the luckiest bloke alive.'

Penny wanted to shower and change when they reached the garage. Greeting Colin with a resounding kiss and hug,

Penny looking at her father and waving her finger said. 'Before you ask, we stayed the night at Lordy's, in the same room, but because I was pissed, this gorgeous hunk put me to bed and slept on the sofa himself. That will be first and only time though.'

As she skipped off Colin stopped her, saying, 'I hope you don't mind but Margot, my bridge-partner stayed the night and is still in bed.' Smiling back at him Penny said, 'I'm so glad for you Dad, I hope you'll be happy. It seems such a long time since Mum died.'

As she left Colin turned to Toby and gruffly saying, 'Thank you for looking after her, lad, she is very precious to me,' a small tear appearing in the corners of his eyes. Quickly brushing it away he announced, 'I've had Lordy on the blower saying Harry will pop down with a cheque for your TR on Monday morning. After the tip you gave him at the races, he said as he had two Land Rovers, he would like to offer you the choice. Said Harry will tell you on Monday. You seem to be the blue-eyed boy around here at present.'

'Wow, that's a turn up for the books, Colin. If Penny is free would it be ok to you if I were to take her off to the coast, and maybe stay over, if she agrees of course?'

Colin, punching his arm said 'Of course, I've not seen her so happy in years. She needs a good man, and I feel you could be the one!'

Toby told Colin he'd nip back to shower and change and be back for Penny in the hour. 'By the way, Colin, do you know of a good country pub with good bedrooms and a really good menu?'

Scratching his head, suddenly Colin's face lit up and replied, 'Yes, I've been a few times to the Old Partridge. It's a lovely, thatched inn that has about eight bedrooms and two star chef. I'll give them a ring and book a room and dinner for two in your name, which I never get right!'

Toby said, 'Just say Mr. T Cooper. Forget the double-barrelled bit, as they might charge more! Can you fill the tank up for me, Colin? I rather buy it here.'

When Toby returned, he found Penny wearing a jumper and skirt, with a dark blue navy Barbour. Colin had given him a slip of paper with the pub's name, address, telephone number and directions. He'd also got them the largest and most expensive double room with en-suite. On the beautiful drive Toby told Penny he felt a bit peckish, and suggested that they tried the famous fish and chips at Whitby.

'Oh,' she gushed. 'I've not done that for years!'

I'll bet you haven't done that properly for years either, he thought to himself.

**** **** ****

It was a bright, dry day with scudding clouds and surprisingly little traffic. They were soon through Pickering and over the purple moors. As it was just after lunch there were only three or four people queuing outside the famous fish and chip shop. It only served those dining in their large lino covered floor. Giggling, Toby, pointing at the vast expanse said, 'I wonder if our Lino has been at it. Must have been a month's profit, if he has.'

They ordered two fish, one chips and a mushy peas to be accompanied with the obligatory pot of tea and slices of white bread and butter. They were sitting at a table for two, which overlooked the pretty harbour, jam-packed with boats and yachts of every description. They munched their way through the beautiful, crisp, golden batter coating the thick, white cod. In half an hour they had come to a halt. Toby paid the very reasonable bill and they decided to drive up the coast a bit and find a long stretch of beach to walk off their lunch. Driving back over the moors, they stopped again to walk along a path through the heather. With gulls calling overhead and a brisk breeze brewing up, it made them a bit chilled. They put up the TR's hood and headed for the pub about 40 minutes away.

Its long, timbered front was lit by a golden glow from spotlights standing in the grass outside. They parked at the back and went in through the heavy oak front door to a bar built in stone, with a thick oak top. To the left was a low door with a sign saying 'Residents Only' 'duck or grouse' above the low doorway.

To the right was a huge log fire in a fireplace that was open at the back to also warm the dining room beyond. A friendly-looking dark-haired man behind the bar asked, 'How can I help you?' Toby announced that he had a room booked under the name of Cooper.

Consulting a clip board behind the bar the man said 'That's correct. Mr. and Mrs. Cooper.' Penny kept her left hand in her Barbour pocket.

'No 2. Here's the key. Would you please sign the register sir? By the way, I'm Martin, the head cook and bottle-washer,' he said shrugging his shoulder. 'If you want to go and freshen up, dinner is served in about an hour.'

'Perfect,' said Toby, while thinking that should just about give us time for what I have in mind. To a hearty twitch 'Tom' agreed too!

Ducking their heads, they climbed the narrow, creaking oak stairs looking for their room. It was situated at the very end of the corridor. It had oak beams and a four-poster bed, which Toby noticed had a sofa at the bottom. Not for me Josephine, he thought. Penny squeaked, 'Look at the super bathroom.' Toby peering in saw a vast old roll-top bath, a loo and shower all in white with antique brass taps. A pair of fluffy white bathrobes hung on the door.

Penny had put a few things she had brought into the large oak wardrobe and Toby stood at the double doors of the window leading out onto a small balcony with a white metal table and two chairs. Beyond were fields leading onto the heather-clad moor.

She put her head on his shoulder, golden hair falling between them. She murmured, 'a Penny for your thoughts.' She giggled at the pun.

'I'll not give you them, but show you them, and I hope they are worth more like a tenner,' he murmured back. Toby turned her slowly around to face him. He placed both his large palms on either side of her upturned face and gently kissed her forehead. He placed a thumb under each eye and gently pressing every half an inch until he reached the end and then repeated, slowly, caringly along her eyebrows until he arrived at the point where the eyebrow meets the nose. He pressed slightly longer and harder before gently easing her face backwards. Her eyes were wide open with pleasure and anticipation. He kissed her trembling lips. He was soft, yet firm as his tongue traced the shape of her lips before plunging in to catch her tongue and push on tenderly into her mouth. Her knees felt weak, the kiss, constantly changing, seemed to last a long time. He pulled her firmly against him, she could feel the large firm thing pressing against her. She'd been to bed with two or three students at college, and there had only been Hugo, and she had to do all the work. This was something else, she thought savage yet tender.

She yearned for him and was stirred as never before. Again, he gently eased her away and facing her took off his shirt, revealing a flat v shaped muscular body with a sprinkling of fair hair around his nipples. His trousers were quickly off to reveal a pair of snowy white boxer shorts. As he tugged them down, her eyes popped really wide as she looked at his huge erection, thinking God, he'll kill me with that. He helped her take off her blouse and skirt to reveal a white lacy see-through bra and panties. Brown stockings were supported by a white suspender belt. A cluster of golden-brown pubic hair escaped either side.

Christ! She thought as she saw 'his thing' swelling and growing ever longer. Toby quickly took her by her waist and whisked her onto the big four-poster. He knelt between her wide-open legs, quickly pulling off her pants, and before she knew it, he was kissing her between her mound tenderly and in the same way as he had kissed her lips.

His tongue was everywhere, teasing her hardening clitoris and playing at her vagina. Her stomach began the same rhythmic rise and fall as when she played with herself, but this was fantastic, she couldn't help gently moaning 'yes-yes' which became a cry, as he entered her.

Softly, gently, perhaps two inches at a time. His hand gently covered her mouth as she cried out in pleasure. She didn't count, but she seemed to have orgasm after orgasm before he slid out of her, ejaculating over her taut stomach. They collapsed into each other's arms, he sinking his face between her firm breasts. 'Thank you, thank you,' she gasped. 'I'd no idea it could be like this.'

'Thank you' replied Toby. 'You are a gorgeous girl with a body to die for. The trouble is I think I'm falling in love with you.'

'What's the problem?' she said levering herself up on her elbow to gaze at him. 'The problem is, my girl, I'm a bloody vagrant at the moment. I live in a pub, have no job and can't offer you a roof over your head.'

Glancing at his watch, Toby said, 'Look, let's have a quick shower and get down to the bar. I want to have a chat over dinner.' He led her into the small shower, where he clamped on a plastic bath cap to cover her mass of golden hair. With one hand covered in gel he expertly soaped and washed her back, breasts, her long legs and her mound covered in soft golden hair. Penny leant back in the shower her eyes closed in bliss.

Softly murmuring 'keep your eyes closed' he gently hosed her off with warm water. Softly tapping her beautifully rounded bottom, he said 'There you go my love. While you dry and dress, I'll quickly get myself sorted out.'

She stood outside the cubicle, drying herself in a large, white fluffy bath sheet, watching him quickly soap and shower in the time she towelled her back. He was out, dried and dressed in a flash. Grinning at her, he said 'Old army training, you have to be quick and not lurk about! Look, you take your time and get glammed up whilst I sink a pint. Are you on G&T and if so, what is your favourite?'

She peered through the mass of towelling to say 'I love Tanqueray, if they have it.' Blowing her a kiss, he was away.

He was wearing an old but beautifully cut check sports jacket by Huntsman of Savile Row which he'd inherited from his late father. It always amazed him that they were the same shape and size. Yes, he thought his old man didn't leave me much after the bills had been settled. A few old clothes, his shotgun, fishing rod and his small annual allowance from a trust fund set up by the old man so that the banks couldn't get their grubby hands on it.

He remembered the last time he had seen his dying father and had been able to tell him that he loved him before he had died that night. His father had given him the key to his flat and told Toby to nip round in the morning and clear all personal items out before the buggers can get their hands on it. His parting words in a croaking voice had been 'Nil carborundum illegitimi est' or 'Don't let the buggers grind you down.'

Toby had taken his advice and cleared out his wardrobe of not many, but top quality bespoke shirts, jackets and coats, shoes, shotgun and Hardys fishing rods. Ha had also found several cases of vintage Veuve-Cliquot champagne, which he promised himself he would open a bottle on his birthday to drink to the old man.

**** **** ****

The bar was filling up with several couples and a group of 'tweedy' middle-aged men and their 'blue-rinsed' wives. Toby caught Martin's eye and ordered a pint of Taylors Landlord and a large Tanqueray and tonic. 'Lime and ice please Martin.'

A tall, ram-rod straight old boy in a guards tie and brown tweed suit with highly polished brown brogues caught his eye and looking at Toby's equally polished brogue said crisply 'Evening. You ever a military man?'

'Yes sir, were you Grenadier or Coldstream?'

The old boy spluttered. 'A Grenadier of course, and you?'

'3 Para,' replied Toby, sipping his beer.

One of the tweedy guests, a chubby little man with a bright red face moved closer saying, 'I heard you telling the colonel that you were in 3 Para. My lad was in that lot. He dropped at Suez,' nodding to the equally round blue rinse at his side, who added, 'Ah, it were a right mess he said.'

'It was,' replied Toby. 'I was part of it too.'

'Was you an officer?' enquired red face.

Both the colonel and red face looked searchingly at Toby, who replied, 'Yes, I headed the platoon which broke into the air field.'

The rest of the party all gathered around, when red-faced said, 'Our Graham said there was one young officer what was the bravest bloke he'd ever met. Graham made out that he rescued two badly hit lads, before getting clobbered himself. Do you know him?'

'Yes, I do. I was with him.' He just wanted to get away and not get involved. They patted his shoulder and drifted off.

Only the colonel remained and quietly spoke to Toby. 'Yes, I recall the headlines now! There was only one young second-lieutenant involved. Had a double–barrelled name Cooper something. Got awarded a well-deserved Military Cross.'

Raising his bushy eyebrows he looked beadily at Toby who said, 'Guilty as charged, Colonel, it was me. I am Toby Cooper-Sneyd, but I don't want a fuss.'

Martin was all ears behind the bar as he pretended to polish glasses whilst listening.

Penny appeared and slid in close to Toby who handed her the G&T saying, 'Colonel, this is my friend Penny.'

The col drawing himself up to his full 6'3" bowed slightly and taking her small hands in his said, 'An honour to meet your friend, Toby here, you are a fortunate young lady indeed,' and turning to re-join the group at the far end of the bar, put his finger to his lips, winked at Toby and said, 'Mum's the word,' and moved away.

'What was all that about?'

Toby muttered, 'Harmless old buffer, but he put two and two together and clocked me as the one on the airfield job.'

'Oh, not another one,' sighed Penny. Toby taking her arm whisked her quickly, past the party. Toby just smiled and nodded. They headed into the dining room which was almost full. It looked cosy, with chintz curtains at the mullioned windows, a heavily beamed ceiling in dark oak. At one end was a blazing log Inglenook fireplace. Their table was in the bay window at the opposite end, from which they could see the whole room.

The young waitress cheerfully took Penny's G&T which she was still holding and seated them at the table, saying 'you must be honoured, it's the favourite table. All the regulars fight over it. You must be friends of Martin, so I'll have to watch out!'

Penny chose the home smoked salmon and Toby the scallops as their first course, followed by roast duck for Penny and venison for Toby, who ordered two large glasses of Sancerre and a bottle of Fleurie to follow.

After an excellent meal, they went up to their bedroom and fell asleep in each other's arms.

Over dinner Penny had reminded Toby that her late mother and Colin had often come over here to the dinner-dances they used to hold, and after a light breakfast would attend a service in the lovely, old church.

Toby, sensing her loss of her mother had said, 'Well let's follow their example!'

She had excitedly replied 'Oh, could we?' just like a little girl. Toby suggested they come back to the pub for Sunday lunch before a good hike to walk it off.

As she climbed back into the TR for the journey home and looking earnestly at Toby and squeezing his hand questioned in her little girl voice. 'Do you like me a little?'

Toby, taking her hand replied. 'Like you? I think I've already fallen head over heels for you.'

'From that first kiss, I tingle every time I touch you,' she replied. 'I know you've been around and probably had many girls, but if I can just be with you, I don't care. Please be honest and tell me if I'm not good or you fall for someone else.'

'I promise I'll never hurt you or let you down,' said Toby. 'My main problem is as I've said I have no job, no home and at the moment, living by my wits. As you know, I'm looking at houses, which I want to involve you in, and several ideas I want to check out. But let's build a solid relationship and see how we get on. After all you might have horrible habits and me horrible skeletons in the cupboard.'

Gazing triumphantly at him she proclaimed, 'I know you are the man for me, I feel it here,' tapping her heart.

They chatted easily and felt at ease and comfortable with each other. They were soon back at the garage where Toby dropped her off, as they both had an early start in the morning.

Colin smiled with satisfaction and pleasure to see the passionate kiss they shared as Toby left. He hadn't seen Penny so happy in years.

CHAPTER NINE

When Toby got back to the Hotel, he found Bobbie behind the bar, with a few locals, one of whom was Walter, who greeted Toby with 'There you are! I hung on to see you, as you'd said you'd been around the Estate Agents looking for a small property to do up and not really found one.' Toby bought himself a pint and one for Walter, who waved a newspaper cutting in front of him, saying, 'Well, what about this?'

Toby putting down his pint, squinted at the quarter page cutting from the local paper of a pair of stone cottages overlooking a lake. 'It says the Water Board are selling these two semis separately, or preferably to one buyer,' explained Walter. 'The only snag is the buyer has to be an agricultural worker, who will turn it into a small holding. Look, the two together have about three acres. They have their own well. I think they will be quite cheap as finding a buyer with the cash sale will be difficult.'

Seeing Toby's crestfallen look, he continued. 'Don't worry about the agricultural bit, as Silas Riley, now he were an ex Para or SAS, he got his hands on a similar pair a few years back.'

Toby, showing interest asked Walter, 'How do I find this Silas, and get to know the ropes?'

'Well, my sister Aggie lives in the village about a mile from Silas place. Her best friend Hattie mucks Silas out once or twice a week.

He's a solitary bird, lives by himself and doesn't welcome visitors. If you want, I'll get her to have a word with Silas, and see if she can arrange a Royal appointment,' he ended laughing.

'That's damned good of you Walter. Can I keep the cutting?' And turning it over, he asked, 'How on earth do I get there?'

'Easy,' replied Walter. 'You said you knew Colin Parker's garage. Well, I've got a job around there. How about if I collect you from the garage about teatime and we have a look together?'

Toby, thumping him on the back, exclaimed, 'Walter, you are a wonder. An absolute godsend and you'll be able to give me advice and rough costs for me to fettle it up.' He felt pleased at his dropping into the local lingo.

Sharing another pint Toby started to feel a buzz of excitement as this could be just what he wanted. He would have the shell in a beautifully, unspoiled setting that he could modernise and extend to make the home that he needed to offer to Penny to share.

There was a telephone number for applicants to call to arrange to be put on the interview list and also be sent a pack containing the plans and outline planning permission for extending, complete with all the legal details. Walter said he would ring them in the morning and give the name as Mr. Toby Cooper, care of the Kings Arms.

Toby went up to an empty bedroom, no Liz or Bess. Apparently Liz had handed in her notice and would go home at nights to live in the castle. She would just help out as needed until Bobbie could get a replacement. His head was spinning as he hit his pillow. Selling his beloved old car tomorrow, choosing the best Land Rover and sorting it out. A new, loving relationship, which looked like the real thing and the possibility to create a new home to exactly his own design in a lovely part of the world.

**** **** ****

He slept the sleep of the dead, only to wake to his alarm at seven. He was in the dining room at 7.30, finishing breakfast by eight. As usual he took his coffee and the Sporting Life into the lounge, quickly scanning the four race cards for the day. Putting a quick call through to Kath who said, 'Nothing doing until Thursday.'

Whilst waiting for Harry he took a sheet of the hotel's notepaper and an envelope, and wrote a note to Claire telling her his news and asking where she was. Realising he should have phoned her sister Anita for the address he quickly rang the number that Claire had given him. The phone rang three times before it was picked up by a very husky, sexy voice announcing, 'Hello.'

'Is that Anita?' Toby squeaked.

'Who are you?'

'My name is Toby,' he replied, 'Claire asked me to call you so you could give me her new address.'

'Ah, soldier boy,' said the sexy voice. 'I wondered when you call, Claire is so besotted with you, I'd like to see you myself. Why don't you just pop down to meet me in town? My husband, as you probably know is a boring old diplomat, and is away on a boring trade mission to China. I'm so-so bloody bored, I'm frightened I'll get like him. Will you come up and take me to a show and dins after? I'll foot the bill of course,' she added quickly.

In the old days he would have gone like a flash, naturally to help a damsel in distress. Things had changed. He realised he just wanted the adorable, uncomplicated, loving Penny. 'Sorry Anita,' he heard himself saying. 'I really have so much on I can't possibly get away for a while now.' He could imagining her pouting as she gave him Claire's address, Toby promised to look her up the very next time he was in town.

He'd just finished addressing and stamping the envelope when the Hon. Harry burst in, crying, 'There you are,' holding out a cheque for Toby. 'Look,' he went on, 'You shoot off and bank it with Harmless Harold as I call him,' and gleefully rubbing his hands together said, 'I can't wait to get my hands on your, no my car again.' Toby jogged down to find Joyce opening up. 'My, oh my,' she exclaimed. 'You are an early bird.'

'I've got a lot on today, Joyce. If you could just pay in this cheque and get my receipt, I'll be out of your hair.'

'No trouble at all Mr. Toby, you are getting to be one of our best customers. Mr. Farrar and I like to look after them,' she beamed, handing over the receipt.

Harry followed Toby who drove his cherished old car on one of the last trips to the Garage. Joe and Colin were ready to check Harry's Land Rover and had it on a ramp in the air in quick time. Colin explained to Toby that his Lordship was bringing down his Land Rover, leaving both at the garage for Joe and Toby to check and decide which one was best. In the meantime his Lordship and Harry were off to lunch and an antique sale and would be back around 4.30 if that was suitable to Toby. Toby looking at Colin opened his arms saying, 'Of course, I've put the cheque in the bank. They've been good letting me chose the best Rover and allow us two or three days to really get it in A1 shape.'

'Exactly,' chimed in Harry. 'Don't worry, father is the fairest man in the world and can be trusted with your ex love.'

'That's fair enough to me,' said Toby, handing over his keys. 'Treat her well Harry, and she will never let you down.'

At that moment Thomas arrived, and looking at his watch questioned, 'All right at your end Harry? Very well then, let's get away before we are late,' with a cheery wave. Lordy squeezed his girth in, pushing the driver's seat as far back as it would go. Harry slumped dejectedly in the passenger seat as they roared off. 'I hope they don't prang her,' muttered Toby anxiously, while Joe said, 'Don't worry boss, it's not your problem. Just remember, if they bend em, we mend em,' to a sheepish smile from Toby.

They quickly had both Land Rovers up on their two ramps. Toby borrowed a pair of Joe's old overalls and with Joe, Colin and Nick the apprentice, they were over both Land Rovers like a rash. Colin announced, 'No question, Lordy's is the better machine.' He ticked off on his fingers, '3 years younger, a diesel, far better cared for,

Lordy had two new leather reclining front seats with arms and lumber support fitted. He said at the time, in no way he would get 'Land Rover back' from the original hard fixed, three seats. He was right, of course, the old ones are a killer,' and winking at Toby went on to say, 'and if my little girl is going to travel with you, it had better be in some comfort.'

Joe and Nick spotted a new nearside track rod-end was required as was the tail section of the exhaust. Colin found the two front tyres were cut and worn, but remembered he'd kept back two almost new tyres when he had sold a Land Rover at the local auction. Toby could have those, he said, 'If you buy one brand new one for the front, and we used the present unused spare on the front, you'll have four new tyres, probably enough for another 30 thousand miles. While we're at it, we'll fit new brake shoes all round, drain all the oils, flush out and refill. We'll have her ready for you tomorrow night or at the latest Wednesday lunchtime.'

'That's damned good of you Colin. May I work with Joe to help out?'

'You will be more of a hindrance than a help,' grumbled Joe. 'You officers usually are,' grinning at Toby.

'No, it's a good idea, I can show you what to do and check on you, while I work with Nick on a couple of jobs that have just come in.'

The time flew, as Toby tackled each job under Joe's critical instructions until a waft of a familiar perfume hit Toby as he was unbolting the exhaust pipe. 'Well, hello, what have we here? Not a new mechanic for me to get my teeth into,' came from a bubbling, very excited Penny. 'Hello love,' greeted Toby, wiping his dirty hands on an even dirtier rag. 'Oh, no you don't you dirty git,' exclaimed Penny. 'Don't you put your dirty paws on my clean blouse.' Teasingly she leant forward, pursing her lips saying, 'You can welcome me with a kiss,' going on she said, 'Oh by the way, there's a bloke in a builder's van outside asking for you.'

'It must be Walter, who thinks has found me a
to look at. It's not far, do you want to come?'

'Don't I just?' Penny retorted. 'Tell Walter I'll
you in two ticks. I'll just change into old clothes ıı ı ıı
travelling in that,' jerking her head at Walter's van.

**** **** ****

Toby quickly told Walter who was busy chatting with
Colin. 'No sweat,' said Walter opening up his tobacco tin.
Making a quick roll up he lit up away from the forecourt.

They went out of the village turning left at the fork and
started climbing. 'How far, Walter?' asked Toby.

'About four miles. We come to a little village with a
green and small shop, where you can get everything. We
go on for about a mile, and then turn off a little unmade
road that leads to the cottages.'

'It's certainly twisty,' observed Penny, 'But still near
enough to shop at Masham.'

'Yes, but it can be dodgy in bad weather,' stated
Walter, who had turned up a narrow track with grass
running down the middle like a green ribbon.

'That's it,' he pointed as they crested the top. There in
front of them lay a long stone house with a grey stone roof.
Divided into two it had old Yorkshire slide windows. Tall
trees rustled at either end, but what made them gasp was
the expanse of reservoir, looking like a peaceful lake in
front of them. It was totally still and tranquil.

Walter peered through the windows saying, 'they are
just like the ones Silas bought. Same design. There will be
one big room with a scullery and bathroom, and two big
bedrooms uptop.'

'That's four beds with space for a good bathroom
upstairs,' said Penny thoughtfully. 'Room for a big
kitchen/utility room, dining room and a snug if you could
get them both in.'

'What do you reckon of the state of it?' asked Toby.
'No wet rot, dry rot or nasties?'

98

'Not that I can see,' Walter replied. 'The board would never allow it to happen. The last occupiers only left a month ago. No doubt, the board wants to sell them quickly, to get the brass in their kitty. That's why they would rather sell to one cash buyer then fart about with two different buyers who would take too much time. A cash buyer would be manna from heaven!'

Toby looking quizzically at Penny, asked, 'what do you think? Worth a go or just a hellova lot of work?'

'You are right there, it would be a big slog, and cost a fair bit, but could end up with a fantastic house, especially with a woman's touch to give it it's final touch!'

'Dare I ask for your help, after all you've got the fine art and décor background!'

'Of course I'll help,' she gasped. 'It'll be a labour of love!'

Turning to Walter, Toby asked, 'what's the next step? How much do you think is involved?'

Walter, scratching his head, replied, 'First up, you'll have to send off for an application form for the interview. That's in two weeks, it says here in the paper. You'll have to take detailed plans of what you are going to do. How you aim to make a living. Proof that you are an agricultural worker, and put in a bid for one or both lots. Having a chat with Silas should be well worth it. He'll have a good idea of what to offer. Anyway, call yourself plain Toby Cooper, don't double-barrel your name or you will push the price up,' he grinned. 'I have a retired architect who owes me a favour, so if you and Penny come up with some rough sketches of what you want, I'll get detailed plans and costs drawn up for nowt!'

Waving aside Toby's protestations, he continued, 'Nah, that's what mates are for.'

It was a cheerful trip back to the garage, with Penny and Toby coming out with ideas and plans which Walter shrewdly either rejected or said 'bloody great'.

The TR was parked up and after a loving inspection from Toby who said fervently, 'Well, they've got it back in one piece.' Walter waved cheerio, saying he'd get Toby an invite to meet up with Silas, soonest.

Penny cheerfully kissed Colin, chattering at nineteen to the dozen. He gently turned her around and tapping her bottom, said, 'I'm starving and I'll bet your boyfriend is. How about rustling us all up some ham and eggs? Pulling a face, she shot off to the kitchen.

He sat Toby down with a beer and checked out their progress. With half an ear on the conversation Penny occasionally popped in to give her ideas. Finally she shouted, 'Ok, grub's up,' she had laid the kitchen table with a red and white table cloth with a vase of white Yorkshire roses, 'literally the last bunch,' she had said.

As they sat down, Colin plonked a bottle of his favourite Rioja on the table, saying, 'we rarely have guests, let's celebrate. To you both, every success in your new venture!' Toby's eyes popped as he saw the huge gammon steaks, two perfectly fried eggs, peas from their veg patch, golden brown crisp chips and a huge field mushroom each. 'She is a fair cook,' praised Colin. 'Mind she should be, after that expensive education at Harrogate Ladies' College.' Penny winked at Toby who raising his glass said, 'Cheers to you both, for being so kind and looking after me. I hope I can look after her as well,' pointing his glass at Penny.

After supper Colin retired to his office 'to catch up on some paperwork while Penny and Toby sat at the kitchen table with one of Penny's huge drawing book, busily sketching, erasing, re-drawing until Penny proudly shoved her chair back saying, 'Phew, that's about it. I really don't think we can improve or squeeze any more out of it.' Toby looked in awe and admiration at the finished sketches, all to scale showing their dream home. Gathering them carefully up in a hard board folder Toby said, 'Walter will be chuffed. I don't think his architect pal could improve on that.'

They had time for a passionate kiss and a cuddle before Colin returned, telling Toby, 'Oh, forgot to tell you, Lordy really loves your car and is going to let Harry have it. He even topped up the tank. I told him he could bring Harry down to collect it Wednesday teatime, hope that's ok Toby?'

**** **** ****

Looking at his watch, Toby realised it was half eleven. He used the back door key and was creeping up the stairs when a light came from Bobbie's door as it was quickly opened and closed to reveal a forlorn-looking Bobbie. Her tear- stained face had made her night-cream run.

Looking down at Toby who had stopped half-way up the stairs, her hand brushed her hair and caused her dressing gown to open revealing a pair of full but slightly droopy breasts, a tiny waist and a full forest of dark brown hair. Tom started to really get excited. She closed her dressing gown saying, 'I'm sorry I'm such a mess, but I've had a terrible row with Freddie, who's hit the bottle again,' Sobbing she said, 'He tried to force me to have sex with him, when he knows he can't get it up. Hasn't been able to for years. Then he gets vicious and takes it out on me.' Toby putting an arm round her shoulders said, 'I'm so-so sorry Bobbie. I had no idea. Look I'm bushed, it's been a long day, you need your sleep. Can we talk about it tomorrow?'

'I suppose so,' she sniffed. 'I haven't had sex in years, and envy all you young people. I can't exactly sleep with any of our guests, or even any of the regulars. It's like a bloody gold fish bowl this village,' Giving her more than a motherly peck on the cheek, he went on to his room and put a chair under the handle, to prevent any sleep-walker entering. He dropped off into a deep sleep.

He awoke early, quickly showering and dressing crept silently past Bobbie's door. He resolved to have a heart to heart chat with her tonight as he felt so sorry for her. Poking his head around the kitchen door and winking at Mavis the head cook from the village, he said, 'Mavis I'm in a real rush and don't haven't really have time to sit down for brekka. Can I graze here?'

'Of course you can, love. What do you want?' Toby pouring a large glass of orange juice from the jug on the serving tray asked, 'Can you make me a nice, fat bacon butty in brown bread Mavis? I'll gulp a black coffee and be away.' No sooner than he had downed his orange juice, Mavis handed him a brown bread sandwich stuffed full with lovely crisp bacon hanging out of the sides. He wolfed it down, washing it down with a large mug of freshly filtered coffee. Thanking Mavis he told her he'd asked Bobbie to put a large cream sherry (Mavis' favourite) on his slate for her.

He was quickly at the garage where he climbed into Joe's spare overalls, joining him at the Land Rover. Joe went around the complete vehicle, ticking a long list of parts or work to be done. He popped into Colin, who said most items they could raid from stock or use from the nearly new stock Colin had squirrelled away. They all had pork pies and a hot brew of tea for a quick lunch break before ploughing on until around six o'clock.

Christine and Toby were invited by Colin to join Penny and himself for a huge pile of fish, chips and mushy peas that Penny had brought from the local chippy. She'd cut slices of bread and butter as is the Yorkshire custom. Instead of tea, she placed a cold bottle of Pinot Grigio in an ice-bucket on the table, saying, 'Come on it's a damned fine change from tea!' After a bottle or two a lovely evening was spent chatting and laughing, Toby really felt for the first time for years, what a warm, comfortable feeling it was to be among true friends. One of whom he was falling in love with.

Walter appeared clutching a large envelope, which he handed to Toby saying, 'There you are, all the docs and interview form that you have to fill in pronto and get back to Otley as they close on Friday. Oh, by the way you can pop up to see Silas tomorrow night.'

'Walter, that's fantastic. How will I find my way there?'

'Easy,' replied Walter. 'I've sketched a little map and popped it in with the pack. Silas will help you fill it in proper like. I'd take you but any more late nights and the missus'll think I've got a fancy woman!' And with a wink he was away.

As Toby kissed Penny good night, she whispered, 'we have an antiques fair in Lincoln at the weekend and I'm leaving Thursday morning to set up for the show on Friday, Saturday and Sunday. I'll be back very late on Sunday. I'm so sad, but we've been doing it for years and I'm afraid Hugo has booked the usual double room,' she gushed. 'I know it's awful but I promise it'll be the last time. I'll just look at the ceiling and think of you and England.'

Despairingly searching his face for reaction she saw him smiling tenderly at her when he said, 'I know it'll be your last time before I make an honest woman out of you, and anyway I have a little unfinished business I have to attend to.'

When he got back to the hotel, seeing the bar was really busy, he quickly got up to his bedroom and climbing into bed, opened the brown envelope that Walter had given him and quickly flipped through page by page. Composing the possible answers to many of the questions, he soon fell into deep sleep.

Hell's bells, he thought it was Wednesday already. If the Land Rover was finished, he would hand over the TR to Lordy and using the Land Rover would go and seek out the mysterious Silas.

After his customary kitchen breakfast and with a heavy heart he drove his beloved 'Fiona' for the last time. He talked to her reminding himself of the many races and scrapes they had been in together. As he swung into the garage, he asked Nick to top her up, thinking he would return Lordy's kind gesture when he'd borrowed it. A smiling Joe said 'we've just about cracked it. You've

103

virtually got a new Land Rover at a helluva saving. I've drained and flushed all oils and the road tax runs for about eight months. Oh and look at this ad, I found in Autocar Magazine. It's for a second-hand supercharger. We could bolt it on and with a bit of work we could turn the old lady into a pigeon catcher.' Such was Joe's enthusiasm, Toby readily agreed as having a good turn of speed and super acceleration would make up for the loss of his beloved old TR.

They finished at lunch-time and Toby gave Harry a ring to tell him all was ready. To a whoop of joy, Harry said, 'As Pa is out, could you bring the TR up to the castle?' Joe, listening in, and giving Toby the thumbs up, Toby told Harry they would be up straight away.

Toby drove the TR, whilst Joe followed in the Land Rover. After giving Harry all the docs and getting him to sign the paperwork, they were quickly away. Joe showed Toby how to get the mirrors and drives seat adjusted exactly to suit him. 'God' exclaimed an exasperated Toby, 'How slow the old girl feels after the TR. Let's get that blower bought and fitted Joe, asap!' Joe grinned quietly to himself.

When they got back to the garage, Toby popped in to see Colin and thanked him, asking for the bill as soon as he could make it out, saying, 'I want to thank you and the boys for their work and want to pay you in cash. I just hate owing anyone. Colin, there's just one thing if I could beg from you. Do you have a bit of that lovely ham left or a bit of meat in the fridge?'

Colin, with a puzzled look said, 'I hope you haven't got worms! Just have a look in the fridge and let Penny know. It's her department.'

Toby went into the kitchen and finding a small rump steak, quickly cut it into one inch cubes, popped them into a brown paper bag and then into his old Barbour pocket. Leaving a note for Penny he checked that he'd got the application form and details from the Water Board he waved goodbye to Christine and Colin in the office, telling them that he was off to find the reclusive Silas. A slow smile of appreciation lit up Colin's face, as he realised what Toby's trip to the kitchen was all about.

**** **** ****

Using Walter's sketch he quickly found the bend in the road, and after three twisting, climbing miles he passed a gate on the right with a sign saying 'Private Property Keep Out'.

He opened the gate by the heavy metal opening lever, drove through, carefully shut it again. Driving up a steep track, identical to the one leading to the property he was set on buying, he came around a bend to find another gate with 'Keep Out. Dangerous Dog'.

Sure enough, dashing out from a kennel beside the track came a Rhodesian Ridgeback on a stout chain, which just allowed the slavering animal to come to about three feet from the gate. Toby could see a lean, grey-haired man of average height come out of the farm house door about 100 yards away and leaned on the door post, arms folded.

Toby yelled out over the yapping, slavering dog. 'Silas, I'm Toby. May I come in for a chat?'

'I'm here, you can come if you can,' returned Silas.

Right, you awkward old bugger, thought Toby, I'll show you. He quickly climbed the gate and dropped down, facing the gate. Turning slowly, to keep his back to the gate, the howling animal was about a foot away. Toby looked it straight in the eye, before quietly saying, 'There's a good boy Ben,' seeing his name on the disc hanging from the chain on its neck. Toby was perfectly still, the dog quieter now, but as Toby reached into his pocket, a new frenzy, broke out before Toby again softly said, 'There boy,' and holding out a piece of fresh steak, the dog cocked its head at Toby who now loudly and firmly commanded, 'Sit, Ben.' Ben sat. 'Good boy,' said Toby and gently lobbed a piece of steak, which Ben devoured. Starting to rise, he was firmly told to sit. He sat and received two more delicious pieces. Toby speaking softly to him inched ever closer, until he was squatting down feeding him out of his hand. He stroke his ears, tickled the top of his collar, softly talking to him the while.

Toby straightened, and patting Ben said, 'Come on Ben, let's find your boss.' So throwing the odd biscuit he'd found from his walks with Liz and Bess, they ended up at Silas's side.

Toby commanded Ben to sit. Toby looked squarely at Silas who had a weathered outdoor look about him. Close-cropped curly, grey hair and broken nose with a 3 inch long scar down his left cheek.

'Very impressive. They must be training you lads better. I'm Silas,' stretching out a large hand. 'At least you were airborne and not a crap hat.'

Toby admired the house, with its mullioned windows and a huge pile of neatly stored logs. 'Everywhere looks so neat and tidy,' praised Toby.

'It's just as easy to keep things tidy than live in a pig's muddle,' replied Silas. 'Now, you are honoured. Only a handful of people have been in here, and like I told them, no tittle tattle in pubs or we'll have their guts for garters, won't we Ben?' To a now peaceful Ben, who was keeping to Toby's side, just in case there was any more of that gorgeous steak left!

Unusually, Silas opened his front door by swinging it outwards. 'Extra safety,' he explained. Toby's eyes opened wide as he entered into what could have come out of the finest interiors in 'House and Garden' magazine.

To the right was a roaring log fire in a deep recess between this room and what looked like a kitchen-dining room, whilst to the left was a beamed sitting room with dark green leather sofas and chairs. One wall was completely covered by bookshelves. An archway to the left lead via heavy glass doors to a huge greenhouse so full it looked like a jungle. 'See over here,' said Silas as he went through the stone arch to the right leading into a very smart kitchen packed with all the latest kitchen gadget, an

Aga and set on the outside wall a huge butchers walk-in cold room. It was filled with half a cow, pig, game in feathers and smoked ham. 'Blimey,' exclaimed Toby, 'You could feed a regiment from this lot.'

'I'm totally self-sufficient,' said Silas smugly. 'I've got an old diesel powered generator to keep me going for weeks in a power cut and my own well for water. It's far purer than the Board, I do monthly purity check,' he confidentially said. 'There're hens, geese and pigs round the back. I can't be bothered with milking a bloody cow every day, so I buy milk in carton and freeze it. Now, I understand from Walter that you want to copy me! Bloody cheek!' he growled with a grim.

'Well, seeing what you've achieved,' replied Toby, 'If I can get anyway near you, I'd be a proud man.' Slapping Toby on the back, Silas said, 'If you are hungry, I've got a nice fat rabbit pie in the Aga.'

Toby laughed and said, 'you sound like Robert Carrier, that chef on the telly. Silas, I'm so very grateful, I'd love to.'

'Right,' said Silas. 'Make yourself useful and open this bottle of claret I brought up from the cellar this morning. It should be room temperature by now.'

'A cellar?' queried Toby.

'Oh, yes,' said Silas, 'I go to these wine auctions every now and again. I've got some real bargains!' As they sat at the round oak dining table, Toby spread all the docs in front of Silas, who quickly filled in all the relevant boxes after checking with Toby.

'You know, I've got to be an agricultural worker and not a Rupert,' (slang for an officer in the army).

'Well, here's what we do. First up, I'll make out a little letter of recommendation, saying you've worked for me off and on for some time, and now feel you've learned enough to set up your own smallholding. After we've had a bit of grub, we'll work out a plan to make the property viable.

'You will have to wangle more land out of them. I know they are keen to raise cash, so if you can afford it, ask for 50 acres.' Seeing Toby's jaw drop, he went on quickly to say, 'don't worry. I know up there it's only worth about £100 an acre, but you really want an extra 25 acres to the 5 you'll buy if you take the two cottages. I know they want £2500 each, but I'm sure they'll bite your hand off if you were to offer £3500 for the pair creeping up to £4000 max. Plus say £4000 for the 50 acres land.'

Toby blew through his teeth.

'They will shuffle about a bit,' said Silas. 'But if you reduce the acres downwards to 25, I reckon you can walk away with a done deal at 5 grand. Then be cheeky and say you can make it up to 50 acres for an extra grand!'

'Blimey,' said Toby, 'It would be a juicy deal if it could be done.'

'Course it can be done. Just keep your targets in your sights. Just like the army. Remember, you are in a very strong position.

'You've got cash and make sure they know it. Let's eat, my guts are rumbling,' said Silas, sweeping all the papers into a neat pile on the table.

'How can I help?' asked Toby.

'Grab a knife, fork and spoon for us and stick them on the table. Open another bottle of wine,' jabbing his thumb at an identical bottle standing near the sink. Silas opened the Aga to a fantastic rich gamey aroma from the rabbit pie. The thick crust was golden brown with steam puffing out of a little funnel in the middle.

Seizing two deep white plates, Silas quickly served two huge chunks with lots of brown, piping hot gravy. He broke a warmed French baguette into two long sections and picking up a plate returned to the table. Toby followed, also bringing the wine with him. He stood beside Silas, and, putting his left arm behind his back in an imitated sommelier or wine waiter and poured an inch into Silas' glass.

'Silly bugger,' growled Silas. 'Fill the bloody glass and stop mincing about.'

When he filled both glasses, Toby raised his, toasting the chef and thanking Silas for his invaluable help.

'Good to see you lad,' Silas had replied. 'It's not very often I can talk to someone I trust and can get on with. A bit like when two of my old mates from the regiment call round.'

'So,' said Toby. 'You were at Hereford with the SAS. One or two of my mates passed selection and were never seen again.' He told Silas their names, to nods or a narrowing of his eyes as he tried to place their names.

Toby began to tell him about his only being a National Serviceman and having to go into another unit when the Paras decided they only wanted regular officers. Silas laid a huge, powerful left hand on his arm saying

'Don't need to tell me lad, I checked you out from the army list. I think they were complete shits to you, especially after what you did at Suez. Good man,' he slapped Toby on his shoulder and went on to tell him of his service and how he eventually ended up back in Stirling lines in the training wing.

After leaving, and feeling bored, he had gone back to look up one of his old sergeants who'd taken on the job of 'quartermaster'. The name given to a retired senior sergeant who could give out jobs to old and experienced retired SAS men. He told Toby he had gone on one or two 'black jobs,' which were clandestine, highly paid operations. If anything went wrong, you were literally 'on your own'.

Silas's parting shot to Toby as he left was, 'You drop off the application form and reference letter and a wee note saying you are a cash buyer and should you grant me an interview, I will bring a detailed proposal as to how I will make the smallholding viable.

'That will certainly get your foot in the door, and I will draw up some plans and forward costings.'

'Silas, I just can't thank you enough. It seems like a dream. I just can't tell you what a buzz it gives me. My only way of showing my thanks is to phone you through the odd horse tip I'm putting my money on. I know you are sceptical, but they are 80% accurate and pull in good money at good odds. I think there could be one tomorrow.'

'I've gambled with my life all my life,' muttered Silas 'But I've never liked the idea of chucking good money at fat bookies, but maybe I'll just have a little flutter to test the water.'

Toby and Silas walked up to the gate, with a scampering Ben who kept nudging Toby for another biscuit, which Toby only did when he reached the Land Rover. With another 'Good man' from an approving Silas, who said, 'That's just the right transport to turn up to the interview in.'

CHAPTER TEN

Toby drove away elated, grinning shyly at the old boots and ripped cords Silas had given him. He'd also instructed him to have a day's stubble, and rub soil into his hands and fingernails to look as if he'd just come from a farm.

The bar was still busy when he reached the hotel. Liz was serving to help poor Bobbie who wasn't feeling too good. The locals were in good form, requesting 'a pint of bitter please, your Ladyship. And could you possibly hand over a packet of cheese and onion crisps Ma'am.'

Spotting Toby, she rolled her eyes saying, 'It's been like this all night. They just can't stop taking the piss! I only popped over to give Bobbie a hand.'

Toby told Liz about the other night. Liz slowly replied, 'She is so good and kind. Please try to look after her,' giving Toby an old-fashioned look.

Between servings, they were able to catch up with their lives. Liz finished by saying, 'you and Penny had better come up to supper soon! I'll give you a bell. Oh there you are Mac. Thomas sent him down to collect me.' Blowing Toby a kiss she left.

Toby took the Evening newspaper and Silas's old boots and trousers up to his room. Quietly letting himself in, he gasped as he switched on the light to see Bobbie stretched out on his bed in the thinnest black negligee revealing a black bra and pants.

Her shapely legs were encased in black nylons held up by long suspenders. Tom started to do a jig, as Toby murmured 'What's up love?' Bobbie burst into uncontrollable sobs and tears streamed down her cheeks.

'I'm going to leave Freddie. No, really this time. He's flat out, plastered, spending all the profits and I haven't had sex in years. I could hear you and Liz,' and the words stumbled out, 'Liz isn't around. Won't I do?' She looked pathetically at Toby.

He scooped her up in his arms, drying her tears and smothering her with kisses. He just couldn't resist helping a damsel in distress, he told himself as Tom rose up in full support. He expertly unclipped her bra with one hand pulling the straps over her arms before gently and then more strongly kissing her breasts until the nipples became hard.

He stood up at the bottom of the bed, quickly stripping off. She gazed at him in ever mounting excitement, until he finally stood upright revealing Tom. Like many before, her mouth opened in surprise and anxiety as to how she could manage to take him. Toby knelt before her and easing off her pants, buried himself in her thick bush, feeling both breasts as her stomach rose and fell quicker and quicker.

He pulled away and turned on his back, gently pulling her up and across him. She squatted as he supported her with his arms, gently lowering her onto Tom. Her initial cries subsided into moans of joy as she drove down further and faster.

They joined in a deep, penetrating kiss as she exploded again and again. She finally slid down beside Toby, who turned and allowed Tom to continue until he also exploded.

Toby turned on his side, one leg over hers Tom still in her, whilst she continued to alternately whimper and moan, 'Oh, thank you. I've waited all my life for that. I never knew it could be so good.'

They fell into a deep sleep, she awakening first, bent over to kiss the sleeping Tom, telling him she would see him tonight. She silently entered her bedroom, hiding her sexy underwear in a drawer, before putting on her tatty, old nightie and sliding in to bed beside a snoring Freddie who smelled like a distillery. She'd just turned her back in time before the sleeping Freddie let fly a loud fart.

**** **** ****

112

Toby awoke around 8.30 wondering if last night was real or a wet dream. He realised that he must breakfast quickly before ringing Kath and keep his promise to ring Silas. Lucy was serving and innocently asked him if he had slept well. 'Like the proverbial log,' Toby replied, not quite knowing if she had spoken to Bobbie, who was nowhere to be seen.

He nipped into the phone box and quickly got through to Kath, who told him there were two strong bets. After thanking Kath he enquired about Liam and the boys. She told excitedly that they'd got the money together for the small farm in Kildare and were going over tomorrow to pay the deposit to seal the deal and complete at the month's end.

She would return to see the boys through their last year at school, while Liam stayed on in Ireland to knock the place into shape. 'Congrats to you both,' Toby shouted joyfully. 'You've both worked so hard, and now you have got your dream.'

'Thank you dear, ring me again on Monday, this is my sister's number, where we'll all staying.'

Toby rang Sylvia before he rang Silas who said, 'I'll give it a go, and if the prices are decent, I'll do £5ew and a £5ew double. If I lose, I'll set Ben on you. Trouble is now you two are best mates. He'll probably lick you to death. Where is the nearest bookie?'

'Probably William Hill in Ripon,' said Toby. 'I'm shooting off to Otley to put my application in, and I'll use their shop in there. Let's hope we will give them a caning between us!'

He hung off as he wanted to get a price on quickly. He was in Otley in quick time and soon found their shop. He made out the slip and took the prices of 7/1 on the 2.30 race and 10/1 on the 3.30 putting the slip carefully into his wallet, he asked the clerk for directions to the council office.

He found the large stone building and parked at the back. Going into a large oak panelled hall-way with a

113

black and white tiled floor, he went up to the unmanned reception desk, just as an attractive, dark-haired girl around his age he guessed was walking past.

Asking her if this was the Water Board, she turned saying. 'This is the planning department, the Water Board is in the next block down there,' pointing to the left.

Noticed her name was Karen from a badge pinned to her jacket and that her eyes were red and swollen, he couldn't help saying, 'you look as if you've been crying. Can I help in any way? It's downright shame to see such an attractive girl crying.'

'No' she sniffed. 'It's personal, but thanks for asking,' and turned and went into an office with 'Karen Bateson Assistant Planning Officer' on the door.

He left and went on to find the Water Board offices where a young blonde sat at the reception desk. Telling her he'd come to drop off an application for an interview regarding the cottages. She told him to take a seat whilst she spoke to Mrs. Williams.

After about 5 minutes she told him that Mrs. Williams would see him now and directed him to her office with a similar sign displaying 'Margaret Williams - Secretary'. He gave a knock on the door and waited until it was opened by a tall, fifties something, blondish-grey woman in a pale blue cardigan which swelled tightly over her ample bosom. Behind the silver specs she had large lively brown eyes.

Waving him into a seat opposite her large desk with no modesty panel, she sat down with her quite shapely legs spread wide apart. She asked in a husky voice, 'What can I do for you?' Toby handed over the envelope and told her, 'I've come to drop off the application form. I hope I've filled it in correctly.' She opened and spread it over her desk. As she bent over looking at the form he risked a peep. Her brown stockings were held up with white suspenders on either side of her white frilly knickers gaped to reveal a forest of brown hair proving that she was never a blond.

Tom started to twitch so Toby painfully crossed his legs. Luckily, he had just looked up as she raised her head, and taking off her glasses said 'Well done! You seem just the sort of person we were looking for, and I feel sure that Major Holgate, my boss and head of the panel would agree. I see you've been working for Silas, one of our success stories. One we are looking to repeat. We will send out an official invitation for you to attend a selection to be held in two weeks' time. Have you any questions?'

'Do I address you as Miss or Mrs. Williams? And also are there many applicants?'

'Oh, you naughty boy, I shouldn't really tell you that. There might be more applicants even at this stage, but I doubt we'll have any more than four. Oh, and it's Miss Williams, although I haven't missed much,' with a chortle.

Toby deliberately let his eyes drop to the view beneath the desk, then rose to thank her. She couldn't help noting the large bulge in his trousers. Subconsciously running her tongue over her lips smiled and said. 'A pleasure to meet you Mr. Cooper.'

Toby left the building and as he got near to the planning building, he saw several figures pouring out in twos or threes, obviously their lunch break. Just like kids from school, he thought. As he reached the front door a familiar and lonely looking figure scurried out, her head bent. Toby quickly caught up with her. 'Hello again Karen. Are you heading off for lunch?' She looked up and nodded. 'Look,' said Toby, 'I don't know this town at all, would you allow me to take you out to lunch, you need cheering up, and I guess you don't want to meet up with your usual gang, especially if you feel a bit under par.' He looked searchingly at her. 'But, but,' she stammered, 'I don't know you.'

'True,' replied Toby, 'But there will be other people around, and I'll bore you to death with my boring life, so there is no harm at all.' She suddenly straightened up and with resolve said, 'Why not. I need to do something different,' a smile breaking out. 'That's better. Look, I have an appointment with a bookie around 4.0, so have you time for a proper sit-down pub lunch?'

'Well,' she said slowly, 'There is a good steak pub just out of town, and I do a lot of work from home, so I suppose I could stretch it, but as soon as you bore me, I'm away, out of it.'

'Agreed. My Land Rover is parked around the corner. Don't worry! I'll not whisk you away to sell you, though on second thoughts I could get a whole camel-train for someone as attractive as you.'

'Oh,' she giggled. 'This sounds adventurous.'

Toby ordered a pint for himself and a glass of red wine for Karen. The place was mock Tudor, with dark plastic beams and an electric log fire. It was absolutely packed out. They had to wait for a table to which they were eventually led by a young, sweating, flustered young waitress with holes in her tights. Checking the menu, Toby asked Karen to order two prawn cocktails, and two fillet steaks. 'Medium for me please,' and looking at Toby he replied, 'Rare for me.'

Karen looked much more cheerful and Toby decided she was really very attractive, especially now she'd regained some colour in her cheeks.

Toby told her about his army life and got her laughing and much more at ease. Lying, he told her he'd left some time ago and, wanting to be a farmer, had worked for a successful small holder up the Dales to learn the ropes.

A friend had shown him a newspaper cutting about the Water Board cottages for sale. He said, 'It would be a fantastic start if I could get them and a few more acres would make it viable!'

'How many?' she asked. 'Oh, I suppose 25 would work, but 50 would be really be magic,' replied Toby.

'Well,' she drawled, 'A great pal of mine is Maggie who is Major Holgate's head cook and bottle washer.' Toby said, 'Karen, that's really sweet of you, but I want to do it under my own steam, as any favour could backfire and leave me looking a real pillock'. She burst out in laughter again, realising she hadn't felt as comfortable or relaxed for a long time.

They'd enjoyed their prawns and were now tucking into their delicious, thick, perfectly cooked fillet steaks. It was then that Karen opened up and told Toby that she and her boyfriend, Brian, of three years had split up that morning.

Toby reached out his large strong hand, completely covering hers, saying, 'Oh, poor love, you are being so brave,' which brought a tear trickling down her cheek as she told him.

'Things hadn't been good in bed for some time, and I suspected him of seeing someone else, so I had secretly followed him when he left the accountants where he worked. Brian went into a bar well known for those who bat for the other side. A boys-only meeting place. It was busy and I went behind a pillar to see him meet an older, bald-headed man in a black leather jacket. I nearly threw up as I saw them holding hands beneath the table.'

Toby squeezed her hand.

'Then the other man stroked Brian's thigh. I dodged out and went into a coffee bar opposite and waited till they left. It wasn't long, maybe twenty minutes. They walked very close to each other and after about half a mile they stopped at a terrace house converted into four flats. The older guy opened the door with a key. There were lights on behind three of the windows, and then the fourth came on and from across the street I could see two shadowy figures join into one. It was half past six from my watch.

'I left and went into my flat which he shared with me. Had a meal, watched a bit of telly, had a bath and went to bed. Eventually he came back about half past ten, complaining that his boss had asked him to prepare an urgent report needed in the morning.

'I asked him if it was after his drink at The Blacksmiths Arms. I told him I'd followed him there as I suspected he was having an affair. He blustered and tried to worm his way out until I accused him of being a poofter. He just broke down in tears and said he'd fallen in love and couldn't help his feelings. He just wasn't interested in women.

'I told him to pack his bags there and then and go back to his boyfriend.' She stopped breathless before saying, 'There, I'm boring you, time to go.'

'Before we do,' said Toby, 'we've got to celebrate your release from Brian,' so he ordered two glasses of champagne.

Clinking their glasses she looked steadily at him saying, 'Thank you Toby for such a good listening, I feel so good and calm now. It's a relief to get it off my chest.'

Toby looking at her, his blue eyes widened as he said 'I'd like to get it off your chest,' looking down at her breasts. She purred back 'I think I would like that too.' They finished their drink and Toby asked if she would like a coffee. She giggled back 'Your place or mine?' Toby quickly replying, 'Yours, silly, you are nearer.'

**** **** ****

He paid the young waitress, leaving her a good tip, saying 'Thank you, that was really enjoyable.' Karen slipped an arm around his waist as he led her to the Land Rover, where he half lifted her into the passenger seat. She directed him into a quiet tree-lined street of smart semis. 'That's mine number, 120,' she proudly announced. 'I used a big chunk of Mum's money when she died and I've nearly paid off the mortgage.'

'You clever girl, that's good forward planning. You are independent, well done.'

As she closed the front door she squeaked, 'Help, I've got to have a wee,' and dashed upstairs.

Toby yelled after her 'Be quick, I need one too. Funny,' he went on, 'Girls have a wee whilst we blokes have a pee. I wonder what Brian does,' to a hysterical laughter from the half-opened bathroom door.

118

After a minute or two he called, 'Karen I hope you haven't fallen asleep, if you don't come out I'll pee in the kitchen sink.' When she came out, from the bottom of the stairs he could see right up her skirt. Tom started twitching. Toby bounded up the stairs as she went into her bedroom saying she wanted to get out of her office clothes. Toby washed his hands and gargled using some of the mouthwash he found on the shelf. Peeping into the bedroom he saw she was hanging up her skirt and blouse.

She turned, blushing as she covered her shapely bra-covered breasts with one hand, and her black see through pants with the other. He went up to her, holding her face between his hands with wide-eyed anticipation.

She met his eyes as he slowly kissed her trembling lips. His tongue traced round her lips before gently probing, he found hers and gliding over it quickly plunged it deeply into her mouth, before quickly coming out to play with her tongue.

He then gently kissed her face all over, before gently, softly kissing both eyes until she was moaning softly.

He spun her around so her back was pressed against his front. His long arms reached her knees then slowly travelled up her stocking clad legs until they reached the bare flesh of her thighs, his left hand continued up her left side to caress her left breast. His thumb and forefinger gently teasing her nipple until it was proud and hard.

His right hand had cupped her mound, the fingers feeling the mass of soft hair pushing against the silk. His forefinger had traced her outer labia on either side before moving back to gently arouse her clitoris.

Now, suddenly, both his hands slipped down and with both thumbs he eased her pants down to her thighs. The long, firm finger was now stroking her hard clitoris. With a gasp she bent down and pulled her pants off before turning to face him. This time her hands were at her sides, and she had a defiant, challenging look in her eyes.

Toby stepped back, quickly shedding his slipover, shirt and trousers. He looked at her with the same challenging look as he stuck a thumb in each side of boxers and slid them down. Her defiant look turned to one of anxiety and apprehension that Toby had seen in many women when first introduced to Tom, who was at his full, throbbing best.

Silently he guided her to the bed, laying her on her back, her legs spread-eagled. Kneeling he kissed each thigh until he reached her mass of soft, black hair. His tongue traced down the outside of each lip, then back along the insides until his tongue found her hard clitoris right at the top of the arch. He softly sucked the whole into his mouth gently, playing with her clitoris with the firm tip of his tongue. She was wildly thrashing about, her satisfied moans increasing in speed and volume. He placed both her hands on Tom. She squeezed and pulled. He then pulled her up, his hands bent, holding at her pert, hard little bottom. Slowly, gently he eased Tom into her wet, gaping vagina, she gasped in pain and pleasure as she rode him harder and faster until she climaxed again and again.

She lost count at six. God, she thought, he's still hard, just as Toby rolled her over until he was on his back, Tom still inside her.

He held her hands as she rode up and down, crying 'yes', 'yes' repeatedly until she pulled out of him, as he cascaded over her.

They lay side by side both panting gently, intensely, satisfied. He reached out taking her hand in his, before putting it to his lips and kissing it. She snuggled into him, her soft hair smelling as if freshly washed as she murmured 'Thank you, thank you. I feel clean and normal again and really glad to have got rid of that wimp Brian. He made me cringe and feel worthless. I'm sad too, because you are every woman's dream and I bet you've already got a girlfriend or maybe married.' A worried frame came to her face.

Toby looking steadily at her said 'You are half right, I've only just recently met someone I'm keen on, but you never know what the future brings. I really find you attractive and lively and bloody good in bed. I hope I haven't been a shit and taken advantage when you were vulnerable. I hoped a little gentle tenderness from a stranger would get you out of the dumps.' He returned her grin saying, 'I believe in 'carpe diem'.' She playfully slapped him as she slowly said 'Seize the day'. 'You certainly do.'

'Will you promise to ring me sometime, if you can find the time in your busy schedule? Or if you get tired of your current 'dolly-bird'. I'll be here, and as promised I'll have a word with Maggie to see if we can help you. She's a good mate, but gets very lonely and we've often fantasized over a G&T, what it would be like to have a threesome with a bloke with a cock like yours.'

Toby's jaw dropped. 'Bloody hell, I thought you were prim and proper civil servant.'

'Servant, yes,' she cooed slyly, 'But not so prim!'

'Well now,' confessed Toby. 'It's always been one of our fantasies hasn't it Tom,' looking at his new erection, 'I'd be up for it, to pun a phrase, but we all three would have to make a firm promise to never, ever tell anyone else.'

'Agreed' chirped a transformed Karen. 'Look, we can't waste this,' and clambered back on to Tom.

****   ****   ****

The bookies were just closing as he scraped in, handing his betting slip to the clerk. He scanned the results board to find that the 10/1 horse had won and the other, a 7/1 had just been beaten by a head into second. He collected an each way, a win and a place, with the place double, giving a clear profit of £88. Not bad, he smiled to himself for just fucking about all afternoon.

He was soon back at the hotel, where he had a good shower before changing into a clean shirt and jumper before joining the 'gang' at the bar. Buying himself and Walter a pint, he told him that he'd dropped the forms off to Miss Williams who'd told him she was sure he'd be sent an interview invitation.

'Ah,' grunted Walter. 'Our Maggie sometimes pops in here for a drink with her boss, Major Holgate. We reckon,' he went on nodding at the boys, 'that she is having it off with the major. His wife's a real frosty, snooty old bag, with a face like a slapped bottom. From the way our Maggie eyes all the young lads up and down, maybe the major's short of lead in his pencil! Just take care lad, I reckon she could be trouble, that one!' Both Harry and Paul, who had been listening, nodded their heads. The normally quiet Paul said, 'Aye one day I'd come in ahead of the boss here,' indicating Walter. 'She were over there, sitting at that table, and she spread her legs that wide I could see her knickers. I were that embarrassed, but I couldn't stop looking, I mean she's a good looker, and her long legs, I mean it were like looking at one of them mucky mugs, but it were real!'

The others were grinning at the young lad's naivety. 'I bet you got a hard on,' said Harry as Paul turning bright red, spluttered into his beer. 'Well, I couldn't help it, and she were watching me, all smiley, and bugger me in the height if indignation, when I went to the gents to cool off.'

'Toss yourself more like,' chirped Harry, Paul now red and flustered gushed 'No, but she followed me in, she said she was sorry she'd mistaken the gents for the ladies.' Harry asked, 'Did she see it then?'

'Course she did,' replied an indignant Paul. 'You know I've got a big one, and always have to stand back from the stalls so I don't get splashed. With a hard on I were way back.' The rest of them convulsed with laughter, crashed head down onto the bar. 'Weren't that funny,' from a peevish Paul.

'No lad,' from Walter, knowing that Paul wasn't the sharpest knife in the box, patted his arm. 'No lad, we weren't laughing at you, but Miss Stuckup got more than she bargained for. I bet she were fair copped by the size of your willy.'

Paul smiled again, and happily accepted a pint from Toby. Toby went in to the dining room. After the afternoon exercise he felt a bit peckish, but to keep his weight down ordered halibut and a large glass of house white.

After briefly raising his glass to toast the Major across the room, he quickly ate in silence. As he passed reception, Bobbie was just signing in a couple for the night. She turned to him. 'Oh, Mr. Cooper, there is a letter for you,' handing him a blue envelope in Claire's handwriting.

As the guests were out of earshot, she whispered half conspiratorially, half pleading, in a little girl voice, 'Shall I come to see you tonight?' Toby was on the point of saying he was knackered and really wanted to get in an early night. He just hadn't the heart to say no. Instead he whispered back, 'I'm ready when you are,' which brought a radiant smile to her face. Incredible he thought, although she was around fifty, she now looked half her age.

As he went upstairs, he promised himself that if he ever got into a situation like hers, he would end it before it ended him! Ripping open Claire's letter he found the loathsome Peregrine had been promoted to Lieut-colonel and he was always away on courses to help him climb the slippery promotions ladder. She told Toby that she dreamed of him every night and was so frustrated she was going to buy the largest cucumber she could find in the green grocer's or one of those new electric dildo things.

Toby wrote back, telling her that he was busy, the horses doing quite well, and that he hoped to buy a couple of cottages from the local Water Board and do them up. He put on her sister's address, stamped it and popped it into the hotel's post box.

He returned to his room, stripped and climbed into bed. He'd propped his head up with two pillows. The door opened and Bobbie came in. She obviously had showered and done her hair and make-up. Standing at the foot of the bed opened her dressing gown to reveal black stockings held up by a black suspenders belt. With her 5" black

123

high-heels her legs seemed to go up to her armpits. Toby flung back the bedclothes to reveal a rampant Tom. She dropped her dressing gown to the floor, and straddling him, took Tom into her mouth, her hands softly squeezing Tom, one hand on top of the other. Holding and squeezing his balls with her left hand, and pumping him up and down with her right, she took his pulsating, hard penis in her mouth, sucking hard.

Toby groaned with pleasure. God, he thought to himself this is almost as good as this afternoon. She pulled off him and nimbly straddling his chest thrust her bottom into his face. As she carried on sucking him harder and faster he thrust his thumb into her open vagina inches his nose. He thrust and turned it till he found her G spot, bringing yelps of pleasure from her. He found her hardened clitoris with his forefinger. They both went harder and faster until they both erupted together and turning collapsed into each other's arms. Toby was soon in a deep sleep, snoring lightly. She gazed at him as had Claire, Liz, Penny and Karen. All within a few hectic weeks.

Without awakening him, she gently kissed his forehead whispering, 'Until tonight, my darling boy,' she silently left the room and returned to a snoring Freddie smelling of stale whisky. She turned on her side, gently crying herself to sleep as she knew in her heart of hearts what could never be.

Toby awoke a little later than normal, remembering the night before with equal proportions of guilt and pleasure. He felt a lot for Bobbie, but like her, realised they were not meant for each other. They were just 'ships passing in the night'.

How the hell to disengage without hurting her too much.

**** **** ****

At reception was a first class letter for him from Sylvia via Mark. He smiled inwardly as realised that for every successful bet he placed and collected the cash for, a similar amount would arrive by cheque.

He made a mental note to pop into old Farrar with the cheque and get an up-to-date statement of his account, which must be growing healthily.

All his expenses of his hotel bills, drinks, eating out, and fuel for the Land Rover were all paid for in cash from his winnings. If he could just get his hands on the cottages with some extra land, all paid for and still leave healthy balance in the bank, the first part of his plan would be achieved.

After collecting his statement he read happily that he had amassed £25400, all in a saving account giving him a 5% annual return plus the £2600 cash he kept hidden in his room.

He next drove back to Otley to the records office at the town hall to find that Miss Bateson was obviously bright and after a fistful of A levels from Bradford Girls Grammar school had gone on to gain a two-one in Architecture and Town planning at Leeds. She'd swum for the university and been a leading light in a top amateur dramatic society.

Checking on Maggie, he found that she'd gone to Harper-Adams Agricultural College to study for a degree in agriculture. Had married at twenty. The marriage lasting only one year and before taking her finals had left to look after her ageing mother, who had been the victim of a stroke. Her mother died some ten years later. Maggie had found a job in the Water Board where she had been for the last nine years.

He now realised what a tough time she'd had and how much she'd given up. He could understand her frustration and not being able to meet someone from her background, apart from the married major almost old enough to be her father.

Bemused, he drove up to Silas, where a slavering, licking Ben made him welcome at the gate. Toby gave him a couple of biscuits and headed off to the front door, which silently opened at the moment his hand was raised to knock it.

'Come on in, I thought it was you,' growled Silas standing, clutching an army tin pot. 'Brew?' he asked, adding, 'Need a bit of help?'

'I've handed in the application form and your reference letter and Miss Margaret Williams checked them out. She seemed quite impressed, telling me I was the fourth applicant and were waiting for just one more.'

'Did she, the naughty girl?' whistled Silas, handing over a steamy hot mug of strong tea. 'You must have got on her right side as it's strictly confidential as to how many they are interviewing.'

Skipping the bit of how he'd met Karen, and certainly nothing about their lunch and afternoon, he told Silas he'd also met a Miss Bateson in planning who had shown him the way to the Water Board and seemed a chum of Miss Williams.

'Oh, Bateson the Beast of planning,' grumbled Silas. 'She is a real pain in the arse to anyone putting in plans. If you could ever get on the right side of her, any planning applications you had would be a doddle and not a bloody marathon it usually is.'

Toby thought, I've been on every side, and even inside planning, so things might go his way for a change.

'I think those two are a dangerous pair,' warned Silas. 'I hear they go out to nightclubs and holiday together. Anyway, let's forget them and get on with what you came to see me for.'

'You remember the army's five P's, Silas, so I wonder if you could give me some ideas that I can put forward should I get the interview and can clinch it to make me money.'

'Right,' said Silas sitting down next to Toby at the dining table. 'It's no good buying just one, you need them both to be viable. The two have a total of 5 acres. Just a big garden,' he snorted. 'They have to look after the land running down to the reservoir. It costs them money. So you tell them you'll help them out by taking the parcel on either side of your track from the main road, including that with the cottages, right up to the water.

'I reckon that's about 50 acres. As I said before, it's poor land. Up there is worth about £100 per acre, say four grand I'd offer. The fishing rights for two rods to be included. Add 4 grand for the cottages, making a total of eight grand. You can always let them push you a bit at a time to nine, even ten is good value. When they ask why you want so much land, show them your plans.'

'Which are?' quizzed Toby.

'Well, young man, you are going to be a chicken farmer, and you need land to spread the well-rotted muck on. As a shelter belt from the wind up there, you are also going to grow Christmas trees.'

'What?' exploded Toby.

'Listen, calm down,' said Silas laying his huge hand on Toby's arm. 'It's a doddle. The buggers grow a foot a year, so every 5 years you have nearly 3000 per acre. If you plant two 5 acre strips on either side, right from the road to the water's edge, you'll get shelter and more privacy. They will grow themselves and every Christmas time you'll get a few cash-in-hand part-timers to cut them and load them for sale. Your six thousand odd trees should give you a net return of around 20p per tree or around £1200.

'Once you get the place and the land, you can do what you want. If the chicken set up costs are too much, shelve it, and let the place tick over.' Looking at the plans he pointed out that the properties had a shared well. 'That's a bonus. And if you check the water quality is fit for human consumption, get them to throw in the water extraction fees at no extra cost. That's a real plus.' confirmed Silas.

'If I get any more, they will be paying me!' stated Toby.

'That's the name of the game, boy,' growled Silas. 'They want to get rid without any hassle. You've the cash. Show them. Maybe even take a banker's draft for eight grand and slap it down. Let me know when you get the interview date and I'll give you a few wrinkles.'

Toby gave Ben a couple of biscuits and they parted.

**** **** ****

Deep in thought, Toby drove over to Walter's to collect some preliminary sketches that his architect had knocked out. As Walter was just having his tea, Toby left quickly saying he would see him at the hotel bar tonight.

Stopping at a phone box, he just caught Penny as she was locking up Hugo's shop. He told he'd got the rough plans from Walter's architect and wondered if she'd like to take a look. 'Course I would. Look, Dad wants to watch the football match tonight, so we could have a meal together at ours and spread the plans out.'

'Oh that's great Penny. The meal's on me. Can you bring back fish and chips or curry or Chinese for three, whichever you and your Dad prefer.'

'Oh,' she squealed, 'What a treat! There's a new, fantastic Indian restaurant just opened who do take-away. I've just read a glowing report today in the Yorkshire Post.'

Toby called into the hotel and told them he'd be out for dinner. Walter had just popped in for a swift pint with the boys before going home to watch the football. Toby bought a round, quickly downing his pint whilst he thanked Walter, telling him he was going to really go through the plans tonight.

Walter told him one of his mates had heard that a farmer's son they did work for had applied and just received a letter telling him to attend the interview in a week's time.

'Gee,' thought Toby. You can't beat the jungle drums in this close-knit community. He prayed that a brown envelope would soon arrive at the hotel for him.

Cheeringly waving them goodnight and saying he would see them tomorrow, he drove off to Penny's.

Colin was sitting at the table, beer in hand, the air heavy with the smell of curry. After a cuddle and quick kiss on the lips from Penny he was offered a cold beer. Penny was telling them that the poppadum and little pots of sauce were all heating up in the oven and would be ready in a couple of ticks.

Toby slipped a couple of notes into the pocket of her pinafore saying, 'That'll cover the beer too!'

'You are so kind and thoughtful. I'll give Dad his on a tray so he can watch his football. I'm just dying to see what the architect has come up with,' she said giving him an affectionate hug. 'It's so exciting!'

'Well, I need a woman's touch to help in the design. After all this is what you love and are trained in. I couldn't have it any better,' said Toby, caressing her bottom. 'Beauty and brain. I hope you don't charge too much!'

'I'll work for free and love,' giggled Penny sexily.

They downed the excellent curry, which even after an ice-cold lager left their lips tingling.

Opening the large envelope Toby extracted a large white sheet of paper folded like a map. Spreading it out on the table, they looked at each other with a mixture of excitement and awe.

Mike Mortimer, the architect had completely transformed the two adjoined cottages into a truly 'Des Res'.

Before, each unit had a sitting room, living room, tiny kitchen, downstairs bathroom and two bedrooms served by a narrow steep stairs. Mike had knocked walls down and made a wide staircase to three double en-suite bedrooms. The largest having a balcony which stretched over the downstairs kitchen extension like a wing.

Another wing on the opposite side was a large greenhouse accessed by double doors from the sitting room. He'd put this new-fangled double-glazing in dark brown hardwood frames.

The two wings now made a sheltered area which he suggested they turf and plant bedding plants in the beds along the wings. He'd even 'pencilled in' a pond in the middle. He'd left a note saying as the extensions to each cottage were within the permitted 10% extension; planning consent shouldn't be an issue.

Both Toby and Penny grinned at each other like Cheshire cats until Penny whispered, 'It's gorgeous, but I wonder how much.'

'I would guess it will double the purchase price of the cottages, so if I can get the extra land, I reckon it can cost a total of fifteen thousand. That lovely win I had at Catterick will pay for it and all the furnishings to boot.'

'Oh, it's so exciting,' squealed Penny. 'Will you let me help?'

'I've reserved all the interior painting and furnishing for you, poppet.'

'Don't you be flippant young man,' she replied tapping his nose with her finger. 'I've painted this old place for years and done work on historic houses. Just you wait my boy,' kissing and hugging him.

She shuffled a bit nervously, biting her lower lip as she'd always done self-consciously from being a little girl whenever she had to tell a lie or veer away from the truth. 'You know I'm off to an antique fair with Hugo for two nights. Well, I'll try to keep him calm and not let him get up to his old tricks,' her voice trailed off.

'Don't worry my love,' whispered back Toby. 'I've my moments, and we are not even engaged yet, which I hope to remedy with your agreement very soon. Until then, let's be free agents and never question each other about our past affairs. The future is what is important now.'

'Oh, you are a lovely, gorgeous man. I've never met anyone as understanding and generous.'

CHAPTER ELEVEN

Toby left with the plans telling Penny he was meeting Walter tomorrow to check with him and get an accurate idea of costs.

As he drove home to the hotel, a near full moon casting its soft mellow light, he yearned for his old TR and for an open roof but reflected how far he'd come in a short time.

He'd found a lovely part of the world, with honest, straightforward people. Had slept with more women in a few short weeks as he had in a year. He had found someone who he could share his life with. He was on the verge of being able to settle down in his own fantastic new-old home, which through the wonderful kindness of Liam and Kath he could pay cash for.

He then decided to put a sum aside to buy a horse from Liam for either he to train or bring over to a local Trainer and also to stop messing around if Penny accepted his hand.

He had just closed his bedroom door and about to wedge a chair under the handle when it opened and Bobbie crept in. She had been crying and had a bruise on the side of her jaw, which she explained had been done by Freddie in a drunken fit. 'Toby,' she whispered, 'I'm sorry I've got the curse so you can't touch me, but,' triumphantly opened her gown revealed her naked breasts, black stay-up stockings, high heels and thick black pants, 'I want to satisfy you.' Tom was erected and throbbing. Toby quickly undressed and stood at the foot of the bed as she bent taking Tom into her mouth. Her tongue circled round the tip of his penis deliciously making small circles back and forth.

She licked the length up and down, before pulling his foreskin right back to run her probing tongue around the base. Toby had his eyes closed, his heart beating faster and faster. She pushed him gently to the bed, where squatting between his legs she took most of his length into her throat.

Toby moaned in sheer delight and was ready to come any second. She stopped and sitting up grasped the bottom of his erection firmly with her left hand, proceeded to masturbate him with her right hand harder and faster.

She put a Dior scented hand across his mouth to stop his ecstatic cries as he exploded.

She lay down beside him, her silk stockinged left leg draped across his right leg, her scented hair on his chest. They were soon off in a deep, satisfied sleep.

Bobbie stirred first and glancing at her watch, said a hushed 'Shit,' as it was 6 o' clock and just getting light. Wrapping her dressing gown tightly around her, she crept down the corridor to her room, hoping she didn't meet any early rising guests. She felt like an intruder in her own pub.

Luckily Freddie was still flat out as she put all her clothes away. Had a quick shower and got dressed before going downstairs to start the working day.

After a night of love and a deep sleep she felt rejuvenated and wanted to do it again. Even though it might only be for a short time.

**** **** ****

Toby came down for breakfast around nine. Only three other guests were finishing off. 'You are a bit late Mr. Toby,' chirped a bubbly Lucy. 'Yes, sorry Lucy,' apologised Toby. 'I went out like a light last night. I must have been really tired.'

'I'm sure,' she murmured. 'You mustn't overdo it,' giving him an old-fashioned look.

After half a grapefruit and a buttery kipper Toby was just finishing a cup of tea when Bobbie appeared and dropped a large brown envelope on the table saying, 'This looks official, I hope it's not the revenue catching up with you.' Toby giving her a dazzling smile, said, 'If it's what I

132

hope it is, it's possibly the beginning of a new direction in my life. By the way Bobbie you look in sparkling form, you must have slept well.' he had added mischievously.

Taking the envelope into the deserted lounge he slit it open with his finger and extracted the single sheet of paper headed 'The Yorkshire Water Board' he noted that following his interest in the two properties for sale, would he attend an interview at 1400 next Friday the thirteenth.

I'd completely forgotten it was the 13th, he thought. Let's pray it's not a bad omen. He sat for a moment gathering his thoughts before going to the phone box to ring Kath, who had three runners for him.

Jotting them down, he next rang Sylvia to relay them to Mark. Then taking Karen's card from his wallet dialled her home number.

After a lengthy pause, a sleepy voice whispered. 'Hello, who is it?' to which Toby replied, 'It's the little lost boy you helped the other day.'

'Ah,' she was wide awake now and chattily asked, 'what can I do for you, or what's more important, when can you come and do me?'

'I'd be over in a flash if I could, but Karen, I've a bit on my plate today. Just wanted to tell you I've just received the interview date next Friday at 2 o'clock. What do you think?'

'Phew,' she muttered. 'That's a good time, 'cos I know there are just 5 interviews. I was chatting on the QT to Maggie. It means, my dear young man, that they'll interview at 9,10,11,12, have lunch, and then see you. They will be well fed and watered they always leave their most favoured candidate until last. They can see the others first. I'd say you are in a strong position. Maggie and I are going out to the flicks next week, so I'll do some gentle digging.

'I've got the day off next Friday, so if you come over to me after the interview I'll try to find out how you got on.'

Thanking her saying he'd pop in to see her around 4.00 next Friday, he put the phone down, saying a little prayer to himself. The week went slowly with 2 horses from Kath, which came nowhere. But as he muttered again to himself, 'That's racing,' and luckily the winning cheques from Mark arrived regularly like clockworks, so his bank balance was steadily rising, which cheered him up.

**** **** ****

Kath had told him they were waiting for something very special on Friday: the day of the interview or 'court of the star chamber' as he secretly described it to himself. Wouldn't it be bloody marvellous, he was thinking, if we could have a day approaching that bookie-busting day he'd had on the day he'd left the army!

It was on the Wednesday as he was having breakfast, looking at the Yorkshire Post propped up on the table that a pair of thin, elegant, long-nailed hands closed on his eyes from behind. 'Liz,' he exclaimed. 'I would know that scent anywhere!' She looked radiant, and was dressed in designer jeans, high heels and a pretty blue-striped frilly blouse.

'Phew,' he said. 'You look gorgeous! Dare I say being a lady of leisure, becomes you.'

'Stupid clod,' she teased. 'Firstly, can I scrounge a coffee from you, and second this is for you,' chucking across a gold embossed envelope. Pouring herself a large black coffee, she watched as Toby opened the envelope, inviting him and Penny to the wedding of Miss Elizabeth Angela Mellor and Baron Thomas Henry William Lord Middleham in one month's time.

'Liz, how super of you, I'll write my letter of acceptance of course but honestly wild horses couldn't stop us from coming. My only worry is what do we give a lord and his lady as a wedding present? Seriously, do you have a wedding list?'

'Course,' she replied, 'but knowing Penny's antique background, I feel she'll get it right. By the way it's going to be quite a bash as Harry's also getting married to Jill at the same time.

134

'You know,' she gushed, 'a double wedding, and both Tommy and Harry are going to be each other's best man. I hope it's not going to be buggers' muddle, as you know how dim Harry can be,' hugging herself and giggling like the Liz he knew so well. 'Oh, it's going to be such a hoot. Tommy and I are off to Barbados for three weeks honeymoon while some very smart London interior decorator sorts the castle out.

'Harry and Jill are buzzing off to New Zealand, looking at sheep or something. Most odd! Anyway, they are going to move into the Dower House, which is also being re-vamped. Oh, it's so exciting. Now, I'm banging on, how are you doing my dear?' squeezing his thigh.

Toby filled her in with his application for the interview to buy the cottages. 'I've got the sketches here for the work I want to do if I can get my hands on them at the right price. It will really mean I've got a home and base to work from.'

'Oh,' she giggled, looking at the plans. 'You are going to end up with quite a pad. The horses must be looking after you really well,' she winked. 'When you've got it altogether and it's all hunky-dory, what then?' she quizzed, almost wistfully at what could have been if she stayed with him.

'I'm getting on well with Penny, and getting ever closer. I think when she helps me put together my little bolt-hole, I'll know if we are a match.'

'Oh, I hope so for your sake. You deserve a good woman.'

'I thought I had one in you,' he replied gazing straight into her eyes, which moistened as she replied. 'I did too, but don't blame me for accepting Tommy. It was a once in a lifetime opportunity to have safety and be secure for the first time. I couldn't really stay here,' waving her hand around the room.

'Look love,' said Toby, 'I quite understand. I still care a lot about you, and if you ever need my help, just call on me.'

'You lovely, lovely man' she purred squeezing him again.

'Also,' whispered Toby, 'You can utterly rely on what happened between you and me stays there and will never be talked about to anyone else.'

'Thank you so much Toby. I know I could rely on you being the gentleman you are and never blowing the gaffe.'

'I see your black shadow isn't with you, how is Bess?'

'She's at the vets at the moment,' muttered Liz. 'Her back legs are giving her a bit of a gip. The vet reckons he's got some new medicine to help. It should do, it's bloody expensive.' She got up, giving him a kiss on his cheek, saying, 'Love you and leave you. I've just got an invitation for Bobbie and of course that ghastly Freddie. He will drink us dry.'

She turned and went in search of Bobbie, before Toby could warn her about Bobbie's problems. He shrugged, thinking he'd better put a quick call in to Penny at the shop to make sure she'd be free for the wedding in four weeks' time. Should allow her plenty of time to get a new outfit and come up with ideas for a wedding gift.

She was absolutely bubbling over with excitement at the prospect of being invited to what was going to be the wedding of the year, certainly, as far as Yorkshire was concerned. She reminded Toby that she would be away for the weekend with Hugo at the antique fair. 'We should be back around lunchtime on Sunday.'

'That's fine,' said Toby, 'as I've got the big interview on Friday. If all goes well, fingers crossed, I'll be chasing around like a blue-arsed fly on Saturday getting everything in place. I hope to know unofficially on the Friday and I'm told officially by letter in about a week's time.'

'It all sounds fantastically exciting,' gushed Penny. 'You are amazing. You've brought so much pleasure and buzz to so many people, I feel really honoured to be with you. You deserve all the luck in the world. I'll be praying for you on Friday. I guess my mind won't be on the job. I hope I don't drop a valuable vase or I'll be fired!'

'Not a bad move,' observed Toby drily.

**** **** ****

He suddenly felt he needed air and exercise. He done all the preparation he could, so he drove off to the local golf club which had a nine-hole course. He went into the pro's shop and paid for a round of green fees. He explained to the old boy, who was pro, head green-keeper and a committee member of decades standing, that he hadn't played for some time. He didn't have a handicap. 'Could I hire a set of clubs, and just hack round?' Toby innocently asked. 'You'll do no hacking on my precious greens, young man. I'll tell you what. Mr. Simpson, one of the committee members and a local lawyer is due out soon. As he likes a bit of company, I'll see if he'd show you round.'

A thin, sallow-faced man with a shock of white hair and the bushiest black eyebrows Toby had ever seen, seemed to pop up out of nowhere. Introducing himself as Ernest, his bushy eyebrows went into a frenzied twitching.

The pro had found Toby a pair of old discarded golf shoes, which just about fitted, and off they went.

Although Toby hadn't held a golf club since being dragged round by his father at the age of about 11, the clubs felt comfortable in his hands, and with nothing to prove or fear, he watched Ernest tee up. With his full set of shiny clubs and a spare glove hanging out of his back trouser pocket, he really looked the business.

After scraping away one or two imaginary divots, several practice swings and much shuffling, he managed to get off his first shot which went about 100 yards into the rough. Toby strode up, teed up, stood back and with a full graceful swing drove the ball straight where it bounced twice, ending up a couple of yards short of the green.

Ernest took 3 shots to get just behind Toby, who chipped onto the green, the ball almost going into the hole but swerving around the rim to end up a foot away. Ernest took two more shots before sinking his ball for a bogey five, whilst Toby took two less.

They went round the remaining eight holes like this, with Ernest getting redder, his face looking almost puce. The pro was watching the last hole, and said to Toby, 'Come off it, you've played a lot of golf for a round like that, you must be under 10 handicap. I'm damned sure Ernest was glad he hadn't got any money on!'

As they sipped a beer in the bar, Toby asked Ernest where he solicited. Slipping his business card over Ernest grinned and replied, 'Harrogate. We are one of the oldest firms and I've been there since university. By god, it's taken many years to climb the greasy pole to partnership. When my senior partner retires next year, I'll be in pole position to quote the pun.'

'I realise you're too senior, but I'm looking for a good property man as I hope to be buying soon. Can you help me?'

'Be delighted,' Ernest replied. 'I'd recommend my boy, who's been with us four or five years now and is our up and coming property expert. His name is Simon, bit older than you but please give him a ring, I'll tell him to expect you.'

After an early dinner and a swift pint with the boys, Toby told Bobbie it was his big day tomorrow and he had some work to do, before getting an early night. He promised her that if successful he'd give her a night to remember. 'Every night is a night to remember,' she murmured. 'If I don't see you before you go, all the very best of luck.'

**** **** ****

Back in his room Toby got his kit together. Silas's old boots, his oldest, well-worn cord trousers, a faded blue denim shirt and an old navy sweater with a hole in the right elbow, plus his father's old, well-used Barbour

138

jacket. He thought that wearing a red spotted handkerchief around his neck was over the top.

He had a quick shave and then the overnight stubble if left would look about right. He packed it all in his old suitcase as he couldn't leave the hotel like this, adding the plans and sketches for the 50 acres he'd got from Silas. He would change in the Land Rover near Otley. He put £100 into his wallet for the bets, leaving a balance for petrol and a bottle of wine for Karen.

Satisfied, he soon dropped into a deep sleep, awakening around 8 o'clock. He showered, dressed normally, but felt a bit strange with stubble and not clean-shaven.

He opted for a full English breakfast as he'd no plans for lunch. He rang Kath who said, 'It's looking good and all their contacts were as near 100% sure their horses were maximum bets that had been prepared for their races.'

Toby then rang Sylvia, telling her they were strong, and just for the hell of it he put through a call to Silas, who wished him luck for the interview.

To get a better price, Toby drove to Ripon and put the bets on at Wm Hill's, knowing he could collect any winnings at their Otley branch.

As usual, he made out his slip for the £5ew patent for Tamarind Grove in the 1.30 Haydock at 8/1. My Shadow at 5/1 in the 2.30, and Bay of Fire in the 3.30 at 20/1. He got the clerk to put in the prices, paid over his £70, collected his slip and was on his way back to Masham in five minutes.

He went into the bank and asked Joyce if it would be possible to have a very quick chat with Mr. Farrar. That's if he could possibly juggle it into his very busy schedule. Joyce grinned at his cheek. Millie giggled, blushed and hurriedly looked down at a ledger in which she was writing. A muffled phone call in the corner resulted in Joyce smiling at Toby. With a little wink she announced, 'Mr. Farrar indeed has a hectic schedule but could offer a ten minutes window immediately.'

As she spoke, the door opened and Harold gesturing with his hand beckoned Toby into the Holy of Holy's.

He was in a shirt, his sleeves held up by gold armbands. He was pink and sweating. Toby's jaw dropped when he saw the piles of ledgers covering his desk that looked like it could collapse any minute. 'Head-office has got their knickers in a twist as usual,' he grunted. 'I've got to check some damned false entry.'

'Oh, it's so damned good of you Harold and much appreciated.

'I'm going to an interview today to put in a bid for two cottages and I would like a bit more land. I thought it'd look better if I produced a bank letter confirming that as a cash buyer I was good for say eight thousand pounds.'

'But you've far more than that in your account' stated Harold. 'I know, but I don't want them to think I've more, or they will put the price up,' explained Toby.

'Right, I'll just get Joyce in and dictate a letter for her type up for you, so you can take it with you.'

Toby exited as Joyce entered. She returned two minutes later and busied herself at the old Imperial typewriter in the corner. She disappeared briefly into Harold's office, returning with a signed letter which she showed to Toby for his approval before slipping into a bank envelope. She handed it to Toby with a smile, wishing him luck from Mr. Farrar and herself.

**** **** ****

Glancing at his watch he saw it was time he ought to be leaving. He collected the packed case from his room, shoving it into the back of the Land Rover and set off for Otley. Going through Kirby Malzeard, Bishop Thornton and Beckwithshaw he reflected how well the fields looked in the watery sunshine.

He turned off on a little track leading to a field where the cattle had been turned out after the morning's milking.

He smiled as he saw the pile of fresh dung in the gateway. Just the job he murmured to himself. Scrambling into the back of the Land Rover he quickly dabbed the old boots into the dung. He next rubbed both hands, in particular his nails into the soft, muddy soil by the gatepost.

Wiping the surplus off, it looked as if he had the dirty fingernails and rough hands of a farmworker.

He drove into Otley finding a parking space at the rear of the Water Boards offices. Checking his watch, he was happy to see it was bang on one thirty. The interview panel would hopefully be still lunching. He announced himself to the girl at the desk. 'Oh, you are early,' she said, 'they are not back from lunch yet. Would you like to wait here?'

'Thanks,' replied Toby 'I always like to be early, rather than late, can't waste important people's time.'

Smiling back at him she asked if he would like tea or coffee. 'Just a black coffee please. I think I might need a caffeine rush to sharpen me up.'

'I'd say you look pretty sharp already,' she replied, fluttering her eyelashes.

She wiggled her rounded little bottom squeezed into a tight, black, short skirt. Returning with a large mug of steaming black coffee, she said, 'I'm popping out to the ladies, will you be ok? I'll be back in a mo'.'

She was bending down to put the coffee on a side table. Toby knew that she knew that he was looking down her wobbling ample cleavage. 'Thanks very much, see you soon,' Toby said. He took a crumpled, well-thumbed copy of the Farmers' Weekly that he had found back at the hotel.

To his surprise he found an article from a timber grower's specialist on Christmas tree growing.

Sipping the strong coffee, he soon became so absorbed in the article he nearly missed the panel coming back, led by a tall, grey-haired man in his fifties in a well-worn grey pin-striped suit wearing a gunners (Royal Artillery) tie. He was closely followed by a flushed, busy-looking Miss

Williams and a plain young girl with long, dull brown hair carrying a pile of files she could hardly look over.

Damned good, long, shapely legs, thought Toby as he finished off the coffee and sat bolt upright awaiting the call.

It was 1.55 on the large clock in reception, and bang on 2 o'clock the phone buzzed and the little girl motioned Toby to follow her, leading to a door with a nameplate announcing 'Major TCP Holgate, OBE'.

Toby had to stop the smile about to erupt as he thought how crass or cruel parents could be in naming their offspring. TCP indeed, I'll bet he was nicknamed 'Stinker' at school thought Toby.

'Mr. Cooper,' said the only other man present, gesturing Toby to sit at the sole chair facing the large, leather-topped desk. Miss Williams and the young girl with the pile of books sat either side. He introduced the girl as Miss Susan Crosby, assistant to Miss Williams. 'Well now,' began the Major clearing his throat. 'We've all read your application, which we found most interesting, and want to have a few questions answered. Would you tell us a little of your early life and education?'

'My late father,' began Toby 'Was a well-liked corn merchant in Lincolnshire, who gradually took over several smaller firms to eventually become one of the biggest malting barley merchants. He ran a small farm, growing barley which had been in the family for years. I used to spend all my free time there, helping out at hay time and then the harvest. Mainly helping my late mother with her horses.' They were all intently looking at him, nodding as he spoke. 'She was such a brilliant, gifted horsewoman, I can never understand how she was killed out exercising a young horse when I was eight,' he carried on quietly and wistfully. The major coughed and the two women blinked rapidly to clear their eyes.

'Pa said it was a terrible shock, but better for her than being paralysed for the rest of her life. She was only 30, and with Pa always busy and away on business, I missed her terribly.'

At this point, both women were openly dabbing their eyes. Toby in a lower voice, his eyes down, continued, 'Pa soon had a succession of lady friends. Although he taught me to shoot and play golf nearly as well as himself, I think my presence was a continual reminder of the loss of his beloved wife.

'He packed me off to prep school at nine. It was in the middle of the war and very cold and austere. I shone at sports, but was a bit dim academically. The Master issued a warning note called a blue paper for poor work. If you got three in one week you were automatically given 4 strokes of the cane, which happened to me weekly.'

He stole a look at the women as he spoke.

'The headmaster, it was rumoured, had been discharged from the army following a breakdown.

'I had just moved into the main school, when Pa met up with his latest, who he married in a whirlwind romance. He spent too much time with her and the business gradually slipped away. He was taken over by a rival for a mere pittance.

'Times were hard, and as they couldn't afford public school fees. I was brought home and sent to the local grammar school, which I really loved. I could get home daily and look after my pony which Ma had given me. I don't think he had the heart to sell it immediately, but I'm afraid poor old Rocket went eventually.

'I wept for days. It made me throw myself into work, sports and the combined cadet force. Whilst still at school and a staff-sergeant in the cadet, I joined the T.A. Parachute Regiment. I was awarded my wings after passing the tough P Company and the basic balloon and aircraft drops over Weston-on-the Green.

A friend and I bought a cheap Cooper 500 which we raced. I was twenty when I was called up for national service. After the basic training went to MONS Officer Cadet School. Everyone went into different regiments, and after my Para training I was luckily selected to join the Paras as one of only a handful of national service officers.'

'Remarkable,' exclaimed Major Holgate. 'What happened next?'

'Well sir,' replied Toby 'I went to 3 Para and after the training, got involved in the regiment's only active service drop since Arnhem. We took the airfield at Suez.'

'Good God,' said Holgate. 'Why on earth do you want to farm?'

'Well,' replied Toby 'I want to settle down in this part of the world. To find such a peaceful, beautiful spot with a property that I can really improve is such a find. To make the smallholding pay, I've drawn up plans which include planting Norway Spruce as windbreaks at either side.' He handed over the sketches that he and Silas had drawn.

All three huddled over the plans, whispering and pointing. 'What's that large building here,' barked the Major, jabbing his forefinger at the plans. 'That's the battery hen rearing unit. I plan to erect it when I've planted the trees and cereal crop. 'But,' retorted the Major 'You'll need more land than the 10 acres that go with the two cottages.'

'Exactly sir,' Toby swiftly followed. 'I reckon on needing an additional 40 acres. I've been in contact with one or two landowners who reckon the value of the poorish land, which will require a lot of work and expense to bring it into a good heart is worth around £80 per acre. I am prepared to put in an offer of £100 per acre for the 40 acres.

'I see you put a price of £2000 for each cottages, so I thought if I were to make you an offer of three thousand for the pair, it would save you checking out two applicants with all the time and trouble saved.'

They all stared at him in silence. It was just like farting loudly in church, Toby thought. Maggie smiled first, just before the Major who declared, 'You've certainly done your homework, and it would certainly save us time and trouble.'

'Could be the beginning of a thriving little business,' pronounced Maggie. 'That is our aim, after all, Major isn't it?'

'Indeed,' replied the Major. 'But how would you fund it?' he asked.

'A cash payment sir. I have a bank's letter here showing I'm good for seven thousand pounds,' plonking Farrar's letter in front of the Major. 'Look here,' he declared.

'This panel will have to bring the price and extra land required to the trustees when we meet in half an hour, but so far as I'm concerned, it will receive my endorsement,' to which Maggie and Susan nodded in time to the Major.

Toby noticed that Maggie's legs were open wide to reveal the briefest of skimpy, black briefs, a long expanse of white thigh with black holding up stockings.

Toby thought the Major was in for a happy hour when business was finished.

Surprisingly it was the note-taking Susan, who handed back Toby his business plans and sketches announcing that they would be writing to all applicants notifying them of their decision by mid-week.

Toby thanked them all for their time and courtesy, and left so they could get on.

**** **** ****

Outside, he glanced at his watch thinking, good, the last race had just finished so he could nip along to the bookies.

He felt that same old tension in his guts and the thrill and anticipation building up. The 1.30 was third, whilst the 5/1 and 20/1 had both won, bringing in nearly £450, which Toby shoved into the poacher's pocket in his Barbour. He nipped next door to a Peter Dominic wine shop to buy a bottle of Rose Veuve Clicquot before heading off to Karen.

He parked in an isolated spot and, diving into the back of the Land Rover quickly changed out of his farmer-boy

145

clothes into his normal wear and washed his hands in the gents.

As he reached for the doorbell, the door silently opened to reveal a dressing-gown clad Karen, smelling of bath salt and shampoo. 'Cor,' exclaimed Toby, 'You smell heavenly!'

'Just for you my dear. Oh how sweet of you,' as she took the champagne, 'I'll just pop this in the fridge, for afters,' she giggled.

'You go on up to the bedroom, and I'll be there in two ticks. I've been waiting all day for you.' Toby went up to her bedroom. Very girlie he thought, but well done. He turned round the big black panda sitting on her bed. 'Best you look the other way, old boy,' he murmured, 'Or you might be getting ideas.'

She crept up behind him, her arms around his waist. Her sweet smelling hair, released from the towel, brushed against his cheek.

Turning round, he gave her a long, deep kiss, before he broke off to say, 'you smell and look utterly gorgeous, and I feel so gungy. May I take a quick shower?'

'Yes, if I can watch,' she replied.

Leaving the bathroom door open, she returned to her bedroom which was bang opposite. Toby stood, mesmerised as he watched her drop the dressing gown to the floor, turning to face him, slipped off her black silk pants, revealing her thick black bush, which stood out against her pale, firm stomach and white thighs.

She plumped up two pillows to prop up her head as she lay on the pale satin sheet, her long nylon clad legs wide open, as she slowly started to pleasure herself with her right forefinger. Toby stood mesmerized and his eyes glued on her, and stripped off to reveal a hard, rampant Tom.

Her finger started to work faster, as Toby showered, soaping himself, but still continuing to watch. Her tongue was licking her lips, her stomach heaving as Toby quickly dried and ran to the bed.

146

Lifting up her knees, he eased Tom into her wetness. Thrusting right in, she cried out both in pain and ecstasy as he pounded into her faster and deeper. 'More, more,' she cried as she felt orgasm after orgasm.

This deep, buttock clenching wet release a woman feels. As if they are in a different place. He couldn't pull out in time, but continued to empty himself into her as she moaned like a cat purring with contentment. He rolled off her and lay on his back. Turning to admire him she took a tissue from the bedside table, and wiped the now half erected Tom, who at her soft touch, soon stood proud and ready for action.

'Hell, Toby I've never known a man with a cock like yours. Can you come all night?'

'Probably, but never really tried.'

Now she knelt between his legs and just managing to get Tom's head into her mouth. She licked and sucked until he got really hard again. With one of Toby's large balls in either hand she squeezed and released, played with her tongue until Tom once more erupted, but this time into her mouth. 'Oh, fantastic,' she cried licking her lips.

'That's the first time I've ever done that. I just can't believe it!'

'You were absolutely superb,' said Toby. 'Who would believe that brainy little Miss Prim and Proper hides such a gorgeous body, and is such a sexy undercover wildcat.'

Toby went down to the fridge to grab the chilled champagne and two tumblers, no flutes to be seen. As he was going upstairs, her phone rang and he overheard her saying 'Oh, have you had a long day?' 'But it must have had its compensations, interviewing all those fit young men.'

As Toby entered with the champagne, she put her finger to her lips as she carried on. 'Ah ha, there was only one, and he was the very last one,' still with a finger to her lips and trying not to giggle she repeated seriously. 'The panel has agreed on him and you're to write accepting his

147

offer, as we want to get the property sold ASAP. When can I meet him, Maggie?'

'Oh, don't be such a spoilsport, why should you have him first? I know you want the threesome we've always fantasised about.

By the way, I've been drinking this afternoon, felt a bit down, as were off out tonight can you pick me up here, promise my turn next. By love, see you tonight.'

Putting the phone down, she exclaimed, 'who's a clever boy then? You certainly turned Maggie on, shagged me senseless and got your deal. I'd say that was a successful day.'

'So would I,' affirmed Toby, clinking glasses. 'You know, I've never had a threesome, I must admit I'm intrigued.'

'So you are up for it then?'

'So long as I can keep it up!'

'Don't worry my love,' she cooed, 'you can keep it up more than most men. You'll have a lot on your plate for a few days, I'll leave a message at your hotel for you to give me a ring to set it up.' suggested Karen. After the second glass and as he was driving, Toby left.

**** **** ****

It seemed ages to wait, but sure enough on Wednesday a plump, brown, official-looking envelope was in Toby's pigeonhole in reception. Glancing at the stamp he saw it had been posted in Otley. He took it into the empty residents lounge, and quickly ripping it open he discovered his £7000 offer for both properties and an additional 40 acres had been accepted. He was to instruct his solicitor to contact their solicitor and send a 20% non-refundable deposit by cheque.

They would then ask him to arrange for his agent and surveyor to contact theirs to agree on the boundaries for the land sale.

148

Toby, always the optimist, had prepared what he called 'his battle plan' in the hope that he would be successful. He bounded up the stairs to fish out the old pigskin leather document case he had inherited from his father. Taking it back to the lounge, he ran through all the list of points he had to attend to in order.

With the letter, his chequebook and plan he headed off to the bank where a beaming Joyce told him, 'Mr. Farrar has just finished with his client, and having his coffee. I'll see if he can give you 10 minutes before his next appointment.'

As she went in, Toby winked at Millie, who blushed scarlet when he told her how well she looked. Joyce was back, whispering, 'He'll see you now, if you promise to be quick.' Toby put his hand on his heart saying 'honest Injun' to a giggling Joyce, who reflected how he always brightened everyone up with his humour and infectious enthusiasm. He'd be a great boss to work for, she thought.

Toby reminded Farrar about his proposed purchase, which was now on, and that he would be issuing a cheque to his solicitor for £1400, and a further one for £5600 on completion. He also thought he would need a further £3000 to knock the cottages together, get the land sorted out and stocked, making around ten thousand.

'Congratulations dear boy,' exclaimed Harold. 'You've certainly got the funds to cover it, so I'll make sure everything goes through smoothly.

If you need any further funds, I feel sure the bank would be delighted to help as you are such a good customer. I'll let you get off, as I can see you'll have a lot on your hands, and my next appointment is here. Good luck, Toby.' Quickly shaking the limp hand, Toby was off like a bat out of hell.

He nipped back to the hotel, which was quiet and deserted apart from one of the cleaners vacuuming the dining room. Quickly dialling Simon Simpson, he was put through straight away. 'Don't tell me you are ringing from jail after being hauled in for driving under the influence, or else being threatened by a jealous husband.'

'Ha, bloody ha Mr. Legal Eagle,' replied Toby. 'Now, I have a job for you, if you can stir your arse.'

'What a splendid rapport we have,' murmured Simon. 'What can I do?'

'Well, you remember I told you about my property deal? Well, were on, and I want to get cracking.'

'Brill,' exclaimed Simon. 'Look, if you want to mosey down to the bright lights and glamour of Harrogate, I'll take you out to lunch at the Drum & Monkey. Say in an hour, then we can get our feet under the table before "the ladies that lunch". By the way, bring all your bumf with you, not forgetting your cheque book, then we'll rock & roll.'

**** **** ****

Toby put the phone down, smiling at Simon who was as sharp as a razor, with a keen eye for detail instilled into him by his plodding father. The Drum was fast filling, but Simon, a regular, had pre-booked with May, the petite Irish girl who seemed to do everything from pouring the perfect pint of Guinness to serving and cleaning away, all with the blarney and a cheerful smile. They ordered half a dozen Whitstable oysters, followed by Dover Sole. Simon selected a good Sancerre to wash it down.

'No doubt I'll end up paying for this,' muttered Toby.

'No dear boy, part of our overall running expenses. We value our clients greatly and wish to retain them and keep them happy. Now, what have we got?'

Toby handed over the letter, which Simon quickly scanned and flipping it over exclaimed, 'Splendid, splendid. I thought the board used this firm in Leeds. I went to school with Anthony, who I know will be handling this.

Now, you just write me out a cheque for 20% being £1400,' which Toby did grumbling, 'I told you it would be a costly lunch.'

'Maybe, but you are in the best hands, we'll look after your best interests. May I also suggest you use Mike Mortimer, who is an old friend of my father's. Retired now, but still a brilliant surveyor.'

'Yes, he's drawn up my preliminary plans.'

'He's still qualified and likes to keep his hand in occasionally for pin money to top up his pension. Here's his card, I'll brief him so that when you get the go-ahead from the board you can meet him and go and measure up with their man, who no doubt Mike will know! Who knows, you might be able to stretch the boundaries, so to speak,' he laughed with a wink.

The Dover Sole and Sancerre went down wonderfully, a marriage made in heaven, thought Toby. Simon signed the bill and explained that the firm had an account. 'Give me a ring the day after tomorrow, and I'll tell you how we are doing!' With that, Simon was off.

CHAPTER TWELVE

Toby walked over to the Old Swan, one of Harrogate's best hotels and soon found a phone booth with a leather chair and small desk. There he went through his list, managing to get hold of Silas he asked if he would come with him and the surveyors, as he needed Silas's guide to select the best land. Walter had just arrived home to do some paperwork and on hearing the good news asked Toby to call in and have ham & eggs so they could plan in peace.

Toby rang Penny and asked if she'd like to join him for a quick coffee. 'Oh, gosh it's great news! We're not busy at the moment. I'll ask Hugo to hold fort for half an hour. Be with you soon.'

In the lounge Toby ordered a cafetiere of freshly ground coffee, which quickly appeared on a silver salver, and a selection of biscuits.

Penny, flushed from her dash around the corner, ran up to greet Toby by flinging her arms around his neck and planting a smacking kiss on his lips, much to the tut-tutting and raised eyebrows from two old biddies sipping their coffees.

Toby quickly ran over the news and explained he had been invited to Walter's for supper to go over the plans. 'You are going to be a busy boy, get yourself organised, and come and have supper with me and dad on Saturday. I've just had a brainwave, you'll have all sorts of people wanting to leave messages or try to get hold of you, so I'll have a word with dad to allow Christine to take messages for you,' she ended triumphantly.

'That's a brilliant idea Penny. I can't keep nipping into phone boxes. When I get the place I'll reconnect the phone so I'm always in contact.'

'Do you mean you are going to physically do the work?' she giggled.

'Yep, I'm to be Walter's extra 'go-for' and do all the odd jobs, whilst working alongside them. That way it will be cheaper and quicker.'

He promised Penny to ring her in the morning so he could see if it was agreed he could use Christine as his temp sec, whilst making a mental note to take a gift for Christine when he went over on Saturday.

What the hell he could take that was appropriate and involved Joe too? Then it dawned. He remembered Chris talking about the new pub restaurant just opened and calling in on his way to Walters, found a warm, friendly pub just starting to fill with eager diners.

Quickly scanning the menu whilst sipping a pint of draught Red Bass, he checked with the roly-poly landlord that he wanted to invite his girlfriend and two friends to dinner. The landlord handed over his card asking Toby, 'Give me a day or two's notice, as we are jam packed every night,' he added with a satisfied look.

**** **** ****

At Walter's, Toby gave Mrs. Walter a bunch of flowers he had picked up from a little florists shop. 'Oh, my,' she laughed. 'It's very kind of you, lad. It fair takes me back to Walter when he was courting me. Never brings them now though! With a sideway look at an un-concerned Walter. 'No love, I'm never a bad boy now,' he guffawed, looking now at Toby.

'Moving on quickly then,' said Toby. 'It's very kind of you both, me breaking up your evening.'

'Don't you worry yourself lad,' chirped in Mrs. Walter. 'It's nice to see my old man for tea, and then have him in for a bit, and not off to the pub as usual. I keep telling him he ought to buy a share in it, after all he must be one of their best customers,' she sniffed.

They sat down to a huge, succulent, smoked rasher of ham with two eggs, peas and crispy chips. She had a large mug of tea, whilst Walter poured out two frothing glasses of ale.

Toby filled them in on the progress, to many 'oh, mys' from Mrs. Walter. Toby helped clear up after their delicious meal, when Mrs. Walter said, 'I'll leave you now, I've some ironing to do.'

Walter spread the plans on the dining table and asking Toby what he wanted began sketching on a note pad. He said, 'Now you've got both cottages, you've really got a rectangular shoebox with four rooms downstairs, four upstairs. We'll get rid of one staircase, resitting the other.'

Toby admiring Walter's quick neat sketching said, 'I'll settle for two, large double bedrooms, each with its own bathroom, I think the word is en-suite. And I'll have a smaller single with a loo, basin and shower. Then we can have a decent sized, feature staircase and good sized landing with the three doors leading off.'

Walter deftly sketched away, than enquired, 'What about downstairs?'

'Let's get rid of one door, to make a good sized hall with the stairs to one side and a cloakroom, shower, loo and hand basin.

'Next we will have the utility room housing a washing machine, drier, deep freezer and all the electrics. I thought then we knock the dividing wall out so we can have a long kitchen/dining room at the front end.'

Walter sucked his pencil, muttering, 'As it's a load bearing wall, we'll have to put a bloody big RSJ in,' but then brightening up, said thoughtfully, 'I know a bloke that could clad it with a genuine old oak beam so you'd never know it was there.'

'Brill,' said Toby and enthusiastically went on, 'That's dealt with two rooms, now the other two both have chimneys, so I thought we could make two arches either side to open up the rooms and make one whopping great fire grate to heat both parts.'

Walter sketched away and triumphantly threw his pencil down. 'Bloody genius Walter! You're the

Michelangelo of the Dales. Now old friend, can you do it and what's the rough cost and time scale?'

Walter got up slowly, stretched, farted loudly and asked, 'Do you want a beer?'

Toby, hoping he hadn't offended him muttered 'Yes, please Walter,' who disappeared into the kitchen. After much banging and clinking he appeared with bottles of beer. Setting two pint pots on the table, straightened up and farted again. 'Apologies, I think I had too many peas,' confessed Walter pushing across a bottle, a pint pot and a bottle opener.

'Right,' said Walter. 'I'll charge you the daily rate to cover me and the two boys. You're welcome to work along with us and see what's going on.

'I need to pay for all materials at the end of the month, so I'll let you have all the delivery notes and invoices and you give me a cheque. I'll let you have everything at trade price. I can give you two weeks solid work on the trot, then have to pull out for a week to keep all my regulars happy.

'We'll carry on like that until the job's done, unless we have to knock off to do an emergency, which I'm sure you'll understand. I reckon four months will see it all done.

'My bill is about £50 a week so if we finish in 10 weeks, that's about £500, allow about half that again for materials. I don't think I'll be far off!'

'That's really good of you Walter. It's a deal,' said Toby shaking hands. 'If I manage a few cash wins on the gee-gees, I'll pay you cash,' to a beaming, nodding Walter.

'Just give me a week's notice, and I will crack on. Oh, I'll get these sketches drawn up properly by Mike Mortimer. Don't worry, he owes me one for helping him out of a jam, there won't be any charge.'

'Look Walter, I want you to make a profit. I always believe in striking a fair deal but always leaving a profit for the person I'm dealing with.'

'That's real good of you lad, I'm happy to have a few months' guaranteed work for me and the lads, specially under cover!

My old bones protest too much outside on a cold day. I'm not getting any younger!'

'When I know the completion day I'll ring you Walter, and then you've a week or two to organise your end. Then we can start ASAP,' continued Toby shaking hands with Walter.

He poked his head around the kitchen door to thank his missus for the splendid supper. 'When we are well on with the renovation, I hope you and Walter would care to join Penny and myself for a replay.' Laughingly she replied, 'that would be wonderful. Walter's not one for taking me out any more. It would be a right treat!'

**** **** ****

Toby rang Penny, who said, 'Dad's away on a golfing weekend. Come over and spend the night. I've a few phone messages for you.'

Toby tried to ring the hotel, but couldn't get an answer. Strange, he thought, but they were probably very busy.

Colin's house lights were on, and he could see a log fire burning merrily, the smell which made his nostrils twitch on getting out of the car. The aroma brought back lovely memories of his poor, dear mother when she cuddled him by the open fire, before tucking him into bed.

The door opened before he reached it. Penny flung her arms around him, planting a moist firm kiss, her tongue plunging in to find his. After a sensuous, lingering kiss, as they broke apart, Penny said, 'Oh, that's better. I've been missing you so much. You are such a busy boy,' she admonished with a school ma'am raised forefinger.

'I've just opened a rather good bottle of Claret and aim to seduce you and drag you off in my bed.'

'Good, oh,' replied Toby, who eyed her appreciatively, taking in her high-heeled black stiletto, her long

156

beautifully shaped stockinged legs. He knew they were stockings as he could see the slight bumps of her suspenders through the tight black pencil skirt.

His eyes travelled up to her purple, frilly shirt with a deep top revealing her splendid, full cleavage. Her face was lightly made up contrasting to the full, pink lips. Her long, fair hair flickered golden from the log fire behind her. Above all was her musky pervasive scent. By now there was no stopping Tom, who was bursting through Toby's trousers. Putting down the glass of very, very good claret, he murmured. 'A fine, 10 year old wine can wait a little longer, I can't.'

'I know my love,' she whispered. 'As you say 'Carpe diem, seize the day.'

He quickly and expertly undid her blouse before carefully draping it over the sofa beside her. Unclipping the side fastening of her skirt and slowly unzipped it before taking it off.

'My turn,' with frenzied fingers and biting her lower lip in concentration, she quickly had him in his socks and boxer.

'Bloody hell, go easy love,' exploded Toby as she pulled down his boxers, right on to rampant Tom who was now at his full height. Apologising, Penny slipped them down and gently massaged Tom. Holding her in his arms, he gently pushed her down onto the warm rug in front of the blazing fire, whipped off her tiny pants and eased Tom into position.

After twenty minutes of frenzied, noisy, passionate love making, they lay together side-by-side watching the flickering, dying logs.

It was Penny, who sat up first, saying, 'Right lover boy! You will have to start paying me for being your secretary!' She produced a list from the table, saying, 'your brief has been on, and as the Water Board want to conclude the sale quickly, will you get the balance to them ASAP. Ah, and your surveyor has agreed to meet the board's surveyor around 10 on site and he suggested you bring Silas with you.

'A Miss Bateson from planning rang and said although they were very busy, she could give the last appointment around 5.30 on Monday as they were working late.'

She was almost out of breath as she quickly gushed, 'I'm sorry but we have the antique fair starting on Tuesday. Monday night I'll stay over at the Majestic. I have to check on the stock until the ball room is locked and security takes over.'

At Toby's raised eyebrow, she hastily added. 'Don't worry. If Hugo wants to play, I'll just tell him I've got the curse. He's never disbelieved me. I must be the only living woman with around twenty menstruations a year!'

Toby grinned, but felt guilty about what he was about to do on Friday night. It was going to be dangerous, but that was the thrill, he told himself.

They turned out the lights, put the big fire-guard in front of the dying fire and with Penny clutching the wine bottle and two glasses, Toby scooped her up in his strong arms and carried her up to bed. They quickly finished the wine and were soon asleep in each other's arms.

Toby awoke to the smell of grilled bacon. He was soon up and after a quick shower was downstairs in 10 minutes. Creeping up behind an unsuspecting Penny, he nuzzled into her neck. 'Christ, you frightened me,' she squeaked. 'I nearly dropped the pan. Trust a man,' she went on. 'They come to the smell of food. It's a bit like the old story of the panda. Eats shoots and leaves.'

'Ha, ha,' replied a beaming Toby. 'What are you cooking up?'

'How about a full English?' purred Penny.

'Honestly, love I'd really like a big fat bacon butty. You know, crispy bacon, a dollop of English mustard between two pieces of brown bread. All washed down with black coffee.'

'Yes, sir' she saluted and then said, 'Seriously, I forgot to tell you. When I popped into the butcher's on the way back last night, they were all talking about the hotel.'

'What?' enquired Toby apprehensively.

'Apparently Freddie has gone too far this time. I mean, we all know he's a heavy drinker and his shouting matches with Bobbie, but this was the mother of all with shouting at each other, until he took a swipe at her giving her a terrible nose bleed.

She packed her bags and has gone. He called in an agency staff for temporary cover, and retired to his room. I do hope you can pick up any more gossip when you go back,' she chirped. 'Will do,' said Toby, thanking her for a lovely evening and the fantastic breakfast. He said he would dig out all he could. Kissing her goodbye he said, 'I'd better get my skates on as I've a lot of chasing round today.'

**** **** ****

He first went to Harrogate to give the £3000 for the balance to Simon who explained to Toby that the Board was really keen to complete the sale quickly as they were moving offices and the sum raised would cover the cost without affecting their annual budget.

He also told Toby that he'd found an old planning approval to build a small lodge house at the main gate.

'Wow,' exclaimed Toby. 'Any chance of getting the new approval?'

'I'd say there's a damned good chance, especially as there were two properties, which you are going to knock into one.

The only fly is the ointment is bloody planning. They can take forever and a day to give consent. That bloody woman Bateson is not called Karen the killer for nothing. She's given so much grief to builders and developers. I don't see you getting it this side of Christmas.'

'What price should I offer the board to secure it?'

'I should think £500 to £750 should do the trick. I think they will bite your hand off,' Simon stated.

'I'll try to get a quick appointment,' Toby replied secretly wondering at his luck in seeing Karen and Maggie later.

Kath had asked him to ring her on Friday, so he called from a telephone box at the crossroads. She was quite excited and a little out of breath. He got the feeling that something good was on. She said, 'I'm glad you rang early, cos we've got three tips from one of our best contacts. Get on as quick as you can dear, cos the prices will slide.' She gave him two at Newmarket and one at Ripon all at over 9/1. Toby thanked her profusely and he quickly rang Sylvia to pass then on to Mark. He called in at Ripon on his way to Harrogate. He put on the £5ew Patent costing £70 on at Corals, getting 9/1, 11/1 and 15/1.

He could see that the spotty-faced youngster thought he was a complete idiot. 'Just you wait, young man,' thought Toby as he pressed three fingers of each hands together in his lucky gesture that had brought him luck so far with his bets. He roughly calculated that if all three were to come in the treble alone would net around £7500. 'Steady boy,' he told himself, 'don't count your chickens!'

**** **** ****

He went to pick up Silas as arranged from his place at 10.30 so they could meet up with his surveyor Mike Mortimer.

To Toby's relief he saw Mike's old Rover parked at the entrance.

After introducing him to Silas, he told Mike that he really wanted as much frontage to the reservoir as possible, because the gently sloping fertile, south-facing land would grow good crops. Mike agreed, but pointed out that Toby would have to take the same amount of the steeper north facing land to give a square chunk. 'If they agree to you having virtually all of the frontage, we could end with about 750 yards and around 25 acres.' A good little plot they all agreed.

Toby brought up the idea to try and get the Board's approval for building the separate cottage by the gate. Both Mike and Silas exchanged a quick glance mixed with approval and admiration. Mike spoke first. 'If you could pull that one off, it would be a lovely little small holding, which in time could be worth a small fortune.'

Just at that moment the Board's surveyor, Myles Jackson drew up in a new, long-wheeled base Land Rover, into which he invited the three of them to join him.

Myles who spoke in a deep, obviously well-educated voice announced, 'by having Mike in your team, you've got the best. A wily old fox, who though retired, still knew more about his job than the youngsters coming along would ever know.'

Mike smiled with pride and the two were soon chatting nineteen to the dozen.

When they got to the cottages, Toby told Myles that Mike was now dealing with things, but if Silas and he could help they would be only too delighted. With much waving of arms and pointing, measurements were written down. They both sat down on an old table, chatting away swinging their legs like a couple of kids.

They came over showing Toby and Silas the neatly drawn sketch. 'Right,' said Myles. 'If we take the whole shore line that you see,' and turning round pointed to the left and right. 'From the edge of the wood to the bend in the road is about half a mile that way. We both reckon it's about 25 acres.

'I will certainly recommend to the Board, that will be no problem, and if you can get the required planning consent we would have no objections.

'Also, you've got a fine well by cottage number two, and I've had the purity checked. It has been certified fit for human consumption. As a matter of fact, our chief chemist says it's far better than that fancy bottled water now in the shops.'

'Get this,' he emphasised, 'you can abstract as much as you want. Free!'

'Even for watering the land?' asked Toby.

'Of course, no limit, but it's so damned wet here you'll never need to irrigate. Over there,' he pointed to a small jetty, projecting into the water, 'is your private jetty for the use of one row-boat or small dinghy. You have the fishing rights of two rods.

'I must say the Major will be a bit miffed as he has the only other rod permitted. He swears it's teaming with beautiful brown trout.'

'If I get it, please tell him I'm sure we can come to a mutually and satisfactory gentleman's agreement,' said Toby and looking at his watch realising it was past twelve, suggested they re-group at the nearest pub.

Straight away, Silas beamed happily, saying, 'The Blackamore is about 15 minutes from here and serves the best draught Red Bass for miles.'

'What are we waiting for?' cried Toby as Silas and he piled into his Land Rover; Myles shot off as he had a lot on his plate. Mike followed them.

Toby did a double take as they entered the log-beamed bar with the largest, smiling coloured chap he had seen. Silas and he slapped hands and gave each a bear hug as Silas introduced Frank who was Ex Royal Signals and been attached to the regiment in Hereford. Frank beamed, saying, 'It's bloody funny when folk come into the Blackamore and see me behind the bar. The trouble is, they think they've named the pub after me,' with a great, deep chortle.

As he skilfully pulled three beautiful, golden, frothy pints with a lovely, hoppy aroma, Silas asked him what grub he had. He looked up and with flashing white teeth announced 'Your favourite growlers, Boss' to Silas, whose face lit up as he translated to a non-pulsed Toby and Mike. 'They are my favourite, the most succulent pork pies you've ever tasted'. They settled into a corner table with three of the largest, lattice topped pork pies, onion marmalade, and a great dollop of English mustard.

They ran through this morning's events with Mike who summed it up, confiding that Myles had told him that it was all but stamped and sealed. 'The Board desperately wanted to complete ASAP and the extra 15 acres plus the reasonable offer for the plot were extra cash which would be more then welcome.

'The only hassle to them being able to complete in two weeks was getting the planning consent through. That's why Myles hot-footed it to get the Major to speed it through.'

Toby coughed and murmured, 'Well, well. All have to cross our fingers and hope that for once two government departments can pull their fingers out!'

'Righty,' exclaimed Mike, glancing at his watch. 'I'll leave you now to shoot off to the office for their meeting next Friday. I'll let you get onto the Infamous Planning Department, but I'll get the board to lean on them, telling them for once speed is of the essence.' He clasped Toby's hand in a good strong shake Toby saying, 'See you soon Mike, and please send me the bill. I'll pay it straight away.' Toby turned to Silas on the trip back and said, 'You know, I like old Mike and think I could work with him again if any big jobs come up.'

'Sound as a bell,' agreed Silas. 'Now as soon as you get any news give me a bell, and I'll get started on planning the work we'll have to do to get the farm up and running. Hopefully cash will start coming in to balance the books!'

'Do you know,' he said, 'this has just come at the right time. I have got my place running like clockwork and was getting bored. That's dangerous, 'cos that's when I can get into trouble.'

**** **** ****

Toby, dropping Silas off at his cottage thanked him again, and drove off for Otley and the planning meeting. Realising he'd plenty of time he called into the hotel to see how things were. Checking his mailbox he found two letters, both in a woman's handwriting. One he knew. The other was vaguely familiar.

As he turned, he saw Lucy dashing out of the dining room, 'Oh, Mr. Toby,' she gushed, 'you should've been here the other night. A right strop the boss was in, drunk too. It were right disgusting the way he treated our Bobbie. As he was ranting and raving, she just said, 'That's the last straw, Freddie,' and packed two right big cases, ordered a taxi, and just left. He's been up in his room since, but got on to an agency, who sent a new manageress, called Jean. She's quite nice really. Gets on with her job and gives us all ever so much help.'

'Look, Lucy, I'll not be in tonight, Saturday or Sunday. Will you tell your new boss to keep my room and I'll be in on Monday to sort things out with him.'

Nipping up to his room he had a quick shower and put on his blazer with a collar and a tie, grabbed some spare clothing and his wash kit before leaving for Ripon.

Ideal, he thought as glancing at his watch. He found he could just catch the last race at Newmarket in the bookies, with fingers well-crossed that he might have some winnings to collect. He took off his blazer and hung it in the back of the Land Rover putting on his old, worn Barbour. He didn't want to smell of old, stale tobacco all weekend.

He eased himself around the door, going up to the result board and saw with excitement that the horse had won at 10/1, which had already paid his £70 original stake back. Quickly checking the second race he found his horse was beaten into second at 11/1 which returned £16. That wasn't too bad.

The last race was in 10 minutes. An old boy in a tatty stained mac had sidled up. 'Anything you fancy in the next, mate?' he wheezed. Toby was tempted to tell him to foxtrot-oscar, but relented for some unknown reason and replied, 'Well, I just fancy that one,' jabbing his finger of his horse on the Sporting Life page pinned up on the wall.

'Nah, rubbish,' wheezed the old geezer through black teeth. 'What, at 14/1? Nah, not a cat in hells chance!' and turned away to two or three of his cronies. Much laughing and guffawing, ensured while they chunted among themselves.

Seeing he had £16 profit Toby decided to put an additional £5ew on his horse taking the 15/1. One of the old boy's mate who'd been looking over Toby's shoulder scuttled off to re-join the group to much laughing with their fingers turning into the sides of their heads.

Silence fell as the tannoy in the corner relayed the race. Toby's horse was mid field in the mile and a quarter of the race. The favourite was well out in front by 3 lengths approaching the one furlong marker. Toby's grey horse ranged up into second place and then slowly overhauling the short price favourite took the race by half a length.

The silence continued, as their laughter turned into glares of jealousy and hatred as Toby approached the counter to collect his £94. Pocketing it quickly he decided he'd better not present the valuable patent ticket. He might well by lynched. He would collect at their shop in Otley and still be in time for his appointment.

He got to an almost empty shop, where no one took any notice as he handed over his slip. The clerk hardly raised an eyebrow when he checked it, but said softly, 'If you'd wait a moment sir, I'll just pass this for the manager to check.' Toby waited as they talked together, made a telephone call, and then the manager smiling at Toby asked how he'd like the amount to be paid. 'Oh, a mixture of tens and fivers.' It was counted and re-counted before him and put into a brown manila envelope.

Toby called into the wine shop and bought a Magnum of Bollinger Rose, which he thought would go with anything. Returning to his car, he hid the envelope in the secret container he had and taking off the old Barbour replaced it with his blazer and pushed on to the planning offices.

The same young girl was at reception and rang through to Miss Bateson's office. 'They would be finished shortly, would you mind taking a seat?' After about five minutes he was ushered to Karen's office.

She was sitting at her desk, which was covered by a huge pile of manila folders, Maggie standing at the filing cabinet. They both looked really tired. Toby approached formally and shook hands, squeezing lightly, as he said, 'Good to see you again Miss Bateson,' and nodding to Maggie, 'Mrs. Williams,' before the girl quietly closed the door.

When her footsteps had receded down the passage he said, 'Sorry to beg a favour from you Miss Bateson. Before going in to explain the morning's meeting with the Board's surveyor, I wonder what the chance would be of getting planning permission for the lapsed grant for the new build.'

'Shit,' exclaimed Maggie, 'I've just had a rushed memo from Myles stating that as all is agreed, we want to ok the sale at our meeting next Friday with a quick completion the following Friday! Can you do anything to help, love?' she asked Karen, who pulled a long face, before admitting, 'Well, you're in luck because we have a planning meeting next Wednesday, and as Buggerlugs is away, I'm chairing it.'

'Buggerlugs is her boss, Cyril Fishwick,' explained Maggie.

'An absolute pillock, leaves all the work to Karen and takes all the glory,' Maggie sniffed. Karen clicked her fingers.

'Got it! I'll finish writing any other business from the last meeting and I'll stuff it in there. Saying Mr. Fishwick had realised that they had given a now-lapsed permission to build. Should the Water Board need it to affect a sale, we at planning would give it at our forthcoming meeting,' she said triumphantly. 'The girl's a genius,' cooed Maggie.

'And,' continued Karen, 'I'm in charge, and the other three old farts just come to get a good lunch.

They are just on committees to get their MBE's or whatever. Now, is that it? Have you time for us girls now?' she growled at Toby. 'Well,' stammered Toby, 'I've just a little request for Miss Williams.'

'Bloody hell, what now, and by the way call me Maggie!'

'Well,' continued Toby, 'I've been thinking that if I can build the farm cottage, I'd like to give the opportunity to a good, young lad to run his own show in partnership with me.'

They were both quiet as they looked at him. 'You said, Maggie, that I was the last of five applicants that you interviewed that day. So, I thought you might be able to let me have the names and contact numbers to see if any would want to work with me.'

'Blow me down,' exclaimed Maggie. 'What a damned good idea. Look, I'll quickly shoot over to my office before close for the weekend.'

She returned quickly and showing the list and all details to Toby said, 'You write them down quickly and then I'll get the paper back into its file.'

As Toby speedily wrote she marked the four in order. 'He would be your ideal lad. From farming stock, went to grammar school. One of four brothers, is engaged to a really good farmer's daughter.' She was away and back like a flash.

'Right,' said Karen, 'We're done, let's bugger off.' Toby stood up and thanking them both again, complimented both on how good their hair looked. 'Looks even better when it's down,' Maggie said nudging a now-lively Karen.

'Right, ladies, I'm all yours.'

'How long for?' purred Karen, squinting her eyes. Toby looking innocently at them both said slowly, 'Who is going to knock up breakfast?'

'That's my boy,' chirped Karen. 'Can't beat having a man for breakfast,' at which they both giggled like schoolgirls.

'Now Toby,' pronounced Maggie. 'I'll take Karen in my car, you follow. Do you prefer an Indian or Chinese take away?'

'Either is fine by me,' replied Toby. 'By the way I bought some pink fizz, so it'll wash anything down, and also I had a win on the gee-gees today, so let the bookies pay,' handing over a ten-pound note.

CHAPTER THIRTEEN

Toby went off on his own and sat in the Land Rover waiting until Karen and Maggie pulled away.

He followed at a discreet distance until they reached a rapidly-filling, very swish and clean-looking Chinese restaurant. He found a spot to park opposite as the pair went in arm-in arm, returning after about a quarter of an hour with a mountain of white boxes. Karen crossed the road and jumped into the Land Rover and snuggled down next to Toby.

'Are you really up for it?' she gasped. 'We are both so excited. We've never done it before. I told Maggie about our last shag, which was the best I've ever had. She was wet with excitement, she just can't find the right man after her terrible wedding and she's so frustrated. Well, so am I but you my dear man are going to put a stop to that. Even for one night it'll be worth it!'

They parked round the back of Maggie's flat which was on the top floor of a solid stone, large, detached former mill-owner's mansion, situated in a quiet, tree-lined street.

As Karen left Toby she whispered, 'Flat 6 on the top floor. Just press the intercom and she'll let you in.' She joined Maggie and, sharing out the white boxes they went in together.

Toby gave them 5 minutes, and with the Bollinger tucked into his pocket, followed them.

After two flights of wide, softly carpeted stairs he was outside No 6. A glowing Karen opened the door, her auburn, glossy hair, down to her shoulders. Kicking the door shut with her heel, she flung her arms around him.

He held her close and kissing her eagerly his tongue finding hers. 'Hey,' shouted Maggie, 'I want some of that'. Toby turned to see a transformed Maggie. Her long brown hair had been taken out of the bun she wore to work. Now, her hair cascaded down to almost cover her large, firm breasts bursting out of a white, lace bra, revealed by a sexy white see-through blouse. He tugged her to him. She smelled really good, her breasts pressed into him as he kissed her.

Tom was fully rampant and as she felt it her eyes opened wide as she gasped, 'I thought you were exaggerating Karen, but it's true, it's a whopper,' and breaking away, she was down on her knees. She feverishly undid his zip and pulled the magnificent Tom out.

Sitting back on her heels took it into both hands and squeezing hard lowered her head to cram Tom into her mouth. Karen stepped over the crouching, moaning Maggie to Toby. Suddenly Maggie collapsed onto the floor, murmuring 'God, I've come twice already,' Neatly stepping over her, Karen said 'Right, come on you, that was starters. Unless we get on with our Chinese main course, it'll be frizzled.'

**** **** ****

They sat at the round table in the kitchen-dining room came snug that Maggie had made by taking the dividing wall down to make one large room when she bought the flat.

Karen opened up the boxes to reveal half a well-done Peking duck, which she scraped from the bone and a box of still-hot flat pancakes. The two girls quickly smeared them in a dark, spicy soy sauce, piles of duck and lemon grass, and folded them into very fat cones.

Meanwhile Karen poured the other boxes of sizzling beef and black bean sauce into a pan on low heat then the rice. Toby handed over the Bollinger, which brought excited clapping from the girls. Maggie said, 'Sorry, don't run to flutes.'

An unflappable Toby returned, 'Not a problem, it'll taste good out of anything,' grabbing three tumblers he poured in the pink, fizzing champagne. 'I hate to do this,' he added putting two great lumps of ice into each glass, before putting the bottle into the fridge.

The meal was quickly guzzled, washed down by more champagne. Toby sitting between the pair of them became more aroused as he kept feeling a hand from both of them stroking his inner thigh and slowly they both feel a now rampant Tom. Their breathing became faster until Karen stood up saying 'I can't wait any longer.'

'Nor me,' gasped a flushed, giggling Maggie. She led Toby into the second of two large bedrooms overlooking the quiet garden and fields beyond.

It was simply but brightly furnished with a huge double bed. Closing the curtains with both Karen and Maggie facing him, Maggie blurted out, 'Shall we slowly strip?' As Toby unbuttoned his shirt, they both took off their blouses to reveal full, firm breasts with hard nipples pushing through their see-through bras. As Toby slipped off his trousers, they stepped out of their skirts.

Toby gathered them both to him and gently turning them round on either side of him, he pulled off his boxers.

Immediately a hand from each of them started to stroke and squeeze Tom. He ran both his hands up their thighs, feeling the soft, firm skin at the top Toby had kept Tom hard and by now was ready to burst, so he grabbed hold of Maggie tugging her over onto her back.

He knelt in front of her and lifted both of her legs up. He positioned Tom at her soaking wet open vagina. He eased half in slowly but firmly. She bit her lip and clenched both hands as Tom was soon pumping in and out ferociously. She yelled, screaming 'Yes' repeatedly, until with a final thrust Tom exploded into her.

Toby caressing both breasts, kissed her long and hard. As she wobbled off to the bathroom clutching a towel to her wet parts, Karen taking a handful of tissues cleaned Tom.

Then turning round her bottom above Toby's face she licked and kissed Tom. Toby in turn, felt her firm breasts, now hanging downwards. Parting her outer lips with both thumbs he ran his tongue up and down her lips. They both climaxed together.

171

Toby pumped up a pillow and lay flat on his back as both girls climbed in one on either side, lying on their sides, their hair piling over to cover his chest.

They slid their upper leg over his, their hands lying on his stomach, just over the sleeping Tom. With Toby's hands nestling on each soft shoulder, they all fell into a deep sleep.

The first glimmers of light were just beginning to lighten the room when Karen nudging Toby said, 'Shove over a bit dear,' as Toby squeezed right into one side as both naked girls held each other tightly, kissing each other deep and long.

Then turning round to carrying on kissing each other's bush, obviously, to excite Tom.

As Toby watched like a voyeur he saw Karen's tongue caressing Maggie's pink, plump clitoris through the mess of damp brown hair. She parted the lips of her vagina before inserting her tongue. Soon they were both moaning in an ecstatic world of their own.

With a rampant Tom and with a raw animal lust Toby cajoled, 'Girls now try the real thing, and have this one for the road.' Prising them apart, he took each in turn, in the missionary position. Determined to enjoy them both, he thrust long and deep, with such a speed, it left them both squealing with pure pleasure.

They all trooped off and managed to shower each other before dressing and staggering into the kitchen.

They both threw their arms around him begging him to 'make a day of it'.

Toby said, 'Sincerely I'd love to, but I'm absolutely knackered and I've got a chap to see at 11. Seriously ladies, it's been a fantastic night, but I think we all ought to promise it stays here, and no one must ever, ever talk about it. I've not a lot to lose, but your careers and pensions would go out of the window.' The pair, wide-eyed and alert, readily agreed and they all shook on it.

Karen said again, 'Thanks for the best night ever,' to which Maggie, shaking her head agreed saying 'Can't send a man away empty after such exercise. What can I get you?'

Toby asked if he could have a bacon butty and a strong black coffee. 'What a bloody good taste a man after my own heart.' As Toby was leaving, taking him on one side, Karen whispered, 'Call me at the office around 4.00 on Wednesday. We should have finished the meeting by then, but the old buggers can be long-winded.

Just say to the receptionist that you are Dr Marshall, and I had asked you to ring me about a forthcoming meeting. When she puts you through I'll just say 'thanks for ringing doctor' if all is well and you got your planning consent.

If for any reason, which I'm sure won't happen, and something has gone wrong, I'll say that I'll put your name down for the next meeting. Don't worry, all will be well. Sometime, if we dare, let's do it again.' Toby kissing them both, agreed before legging it to the Land Rover.

CHAPTER FOURTEEN

He stopped to ring Kath, who agreed yesterday was a good result, which could have been damned good if that second horse had just shifted its arse. She said that they had a double going at Ripon in the first and last races on the card.

He rang Sylvia who told him his latest cheque was on the way and that Mark was ever so pleased. He'd like to ask Toby and Penny to join them both for a slap up dinner wherever they chose.

Thanking her, Toby mentioned that as he would be leaving the hotel soon, would she send any other cheques to the garage, where he could collect them from Penny.

He put the two each-way bets and an each way double on in Joe Corals in Harrogate, getting; 8/1 and 6/1.

He was sitting in Simon's office, bright-eyed, bushy-tailed with a cup of hot black coffee in hand at 11.00 o'clock. Simon looking at him with an amused grim on his face said, 'You look very smug, had a good night?'

'An amazing night,' drawled Toby, 'the best news is, I managed to get a last minute meeting with Killer Bateson. Actually I thought she was rather sexy!'

'Sexy, yes,' returned Simon. 'Be very careful there, some say she's a man eater!'

'First course or dessert?' queried Toby. 'I don't think I'd really mind which.'

Simon rolling his eyes asked, 'Dare I ask what resulted in your discussion?'

'Well,' continued Toby 'She said she'd been persuaded by the board to reactivate the lapsed consent at the next planning meeting this Wednesday. As the Board want to proceed with the sale at their meeting next Friday with the aim of completing the following Friday'

'Gee,' exclaimed Simon. 'If you are able to pull that off, you must have a guardian angel looking after you.'

'Do you know' replied Toby, 'I rather think I have. No, perhaps two,' he grinned. 'Seriously though Simon, I know you lawyers are notorious for dragging your heels, and mounting up the bills, but are you all jacked up to move quickly?'

With a withering look Simon replied, 'A lot of what you say is true, but believe me we are one of the quickest out of the blocks and I would say give true value for the fees we ask.

In your case I have prepared everything, including planning permission. As soon as their legal department tell we're on, I can guarantee that there are no problems from our end and if they want to complete a week on Friday, we can!' he stated triumphantly.

'What are you doing this afternoon?' asked Toby.

'Well, I'm just about to shoot off to Masham to meet my old man. We have a regular, quick nine holes, when I can bring him up to speed with happenings in the firm.

'He was senior partner you know for twelve years,' he ended proudly. 'Why?'

'Well,' said Toby, 'I have a nag at Ripon in the last race, wondered if you would like to join me,'

'What time is the last race?' asked Simon.

'5.40,' shot back Toby. 'I'm going to try and get my fiancée-to-be, although she doesn't know that yet, to come and join me. I would just like to see if you approve,' he teased.

'I'll have to get cracking now,' said Simon. 'I'm due to meet Dad at 1.00. When we finished, we always have a pint and a sandwich. Look, I'll meet you in Ripon square at say 4.30, then we'll go in one car to the races to see your horse.'

**** **** ****

Toby thanked him again, saying he'd see him at 4.30. He then left and thought he'd call in to the antique fair to see how Penny was getting on.

175

On entering the vast ballroom, he saw a mass of people, some dressed up to the eyebrows and others like tramps, all mingling around the various stands.

He spotted Penny and Hugo at the rear with one or two seriously good pieces among many smaller items.

As he approached a fat, greasy-looking little man in a stained, creased, very old blue suit, pink shirt, pink bow tie and a dirty suede shoes, oiled his way on to the stand and stood very close to Penny. She was busy in conversation with a well-dressed white haired mature lady.

At the sight of grease ball she broke off the conversation, turning to the little man whispered in his ear, gently shoved him off the strand. As he disappeared, Toby approached. 'What the hell was all that about?'

Penny, relieved to see him explained he was another dealer pestering her to sell him the beautiful Grandma Clock at trade price. 'As soon as anyone shows any interest, he's over here and loses me the sale,' she complained.

Toby wandered over to the neat little clock saying, 'Ah, I thought it was a Graham. My old man had a beautiful one that my dear Ma had bought. It had to go with everything else to settle the debts. May I?' he asked, expertly sliding off the upper casing to reveal the workings.

He opened the front panel to check the weights and cords. Grease ball was edging closer. Toby replacing the cover asked Penny how much she wanted, pulling out his cheque book from his jacket swiftly wrote out a cheque and handed it to her saying 'Now you can put your little red sold sticker on it, and would you have your little friend here,' patting a sweaty, eye-popping grease ball on the head 'deliver it to my address, my dear lady.'

A ripple of gentle applause broke out from several adjoining stands. Penny whispered to Toby, 'It's sweet of you, but you really don't need to.'

'Oh yes, I do,' explained Toby. 'It's a lovely clock, at a fair price, which will always remind me of Mum. I am to put in prime position in the entrance hall of my, correction, our new home.'

Looking deep into her widening eyes he saw admiration and happiness. Gently taking both sides of her head he softly kissed her trembling lips to much tut-tutting from some passing old biddies.

'Any chance of you being able to get away a bit earlier today? I have a horse running in the 5.40 at Ripon and wondered if you could join me.'

After a quick word with Hugo who replied a little tetchily, 'Of course my dear, after all you were here last night, and my dear wife will be here any moment. Off you go dear and remember being the Sabbath tomorrow, I'll expect you to open up an hour later at 11.00. I'll toddle along after lunch.'

'Thanks Hugo,' chirped Penny. Grabbing her coat and handbag they wandered back down the hall to find Penny's car.

**** **** ****

'Right,' she said. 'I'll see you in Ripon square,' and flew off. Shaking his head, Toby climbed into the Land Rover and plodded after her. He found her parked up by Barclays, and finding an empty spot near her, he pulled in. As it was ten to four they decided to wander down the side street and see the beautiful cathedral. The calm, peace and quiet inside was blissful after the noise and bustle outside. 'Makes you realise,' whispered Toby 'Why people become monks and nuns.' Penny gazed up at him whispering back, 'I love the sensitive side to your character. You truly are a wonderful man!'

They sat, side by side at the back, and bowing their heads, had a moment in prayer. On their way out Toby dropped a handful of coins he had accumulated into an offertory box with a loud bang.

They retraced their steps to the square. Toby checked his watch, just twenty past he noted, then spotted Simon's

Jaguar gliding into an empty space to their right. Toby waved both arms over his head and tugging Penny, came to an out of breath halt as Simon clambered out.

'Simon, meet Penny,' gasped Toby. Simon gravely shook Penny's hand, saying, 'Where have you been hiding such a lovely lady?' to a slight blush from Penny. 'Oh, come on, get in you two, I suppose I'm the darned chauffeur again.'

'Jolly kind of you, old bean,' cried Toby busting Penny into the sumptuous, leather back seat.

'What a super smell of leather and wood,' observed Penny. 'Had her long, Simon?'

'About a month,' admitted Simon, 'Still really running her in. Dying to open her up on a quiet bit of the A1, or maybe I'll pop over to the Preston By-Pass, you know our first motorway.'

'Oh, bags I come with you Simon. Please. Please,' from Toby.

'Shut up,' growled Simon, 'You sound like a schoolboy at the tuck shop.'

'He is,' returned Penny, her hand on Toby's thigh. 'He is just like a school boy.'

After a pause Toby said 'Well, this school boy was once racing an Austin Healey 100/6 at Catterick, when a bloke called Alan who I had often chatted to, invited me to take his ex-Le Mans Jaguar D type for a spin up the A1.'

'Honestly,' queried Simon. 'You are having me on.'

'Nope,' firmly denied Toby. 'Honest Injun. I blipped the throttle out on the A1 South towards Ripon and my head was slammed back into the pommel headrest and as I was doing 140 before I knew what I was doing. Managed to turn round, and as it was quickly getting the feel for it, I gave an extra squeeze and managed 160, before burbling to the airfield gate. I think Alan was relieved I'd brought his pride and joy back in one piece.'

'I bet he was,' murmured Simon with a growing respect for his new client and for his selection in delectable girls.

As they pulled into Ripon Racecourse, a few cars were coming out, before the last race to avoid the customary gridlock and traffic jam.

The two gates to the course were open as they went in. 'Good,' said Toby checking that it was five ten. 'Still twenty minutes to go. Let's go to the pre-parade ring!' Finding a pile of un-sold race cards on a table he took one and gave one to Penny and Simon pointing out the horse 'Bolton Wanderer' number 9 on the card.

As the three of them joined the group of assorted race-goers bending over the rail surrounding a dirt-track oval walkway they could see about 10 horses lead around by a young stable lad or lass, with a number pinned to their left arm.

'Just look for number 9,' said Toby.

'Over there, look,' squeaked Penny, pointing to a smallish, dark brown mare, being lead round by a buxom blonde with large blue eyes. 'That bodes well,' thought Toby. The horse was lead into an open horsebox, where it was tacked up with head collar, reins and saddle.

'Right,' said Toby. 'You go over to the main parade ring there,' pointing to a tree-shaded patch of velvet like turf, surrounded by a smooth, hard core walk way, with a white rail around it.

'I'm just going to put a fiver on it.'

'But,' stammered Simon, 'it's 9/1.'

'I want a bet on it,' peeped up Penny. 'Here's a fiver from me.' Toby thought twice about doing it for her, remembering the old maxim of 'there's money and there's gambling money, don't mix them up!' He took the fiver, as Simon also shoved a fiver into his hand, muttering, 'Go on then, might as well be hung for a sheep as for a lamb.'

Toby, grinning, sprinted off to the Tote and put on £15 on the horse. He noticed that the Tote price was still about 9/1 and he hurried back to join them at the parade ring, handing the ticket over to Simon for safekeeping. By then all the horses were being reunited with their jockeys, who were 'legged-up' into saddles by serious-looking trainers.

They went over to the champagne bar, where Toby ordered a bottle and grabbed three flutes which he polished clean with a napkin. 'Cannot be too careful, you know,' he said. 'Especially after a busy day they tend to be a bit sloppy'.

Penny was mildly surprised, then thinking to herself it was good to see cleanliness and care in a man.

As they saw the horses going down to the start, they settled back toasting their horse and listened to the commentator over the T annoy system.

She seemed to start poorly and was in midfield. Gradually she worked her way up to fourth, coming round the last wide bend. They rose to their feet and could just make out the far blob in the distance.

The commentator's voice rose in a frenzy, as she battled up the final furlong with the 2/1 favourite and sailing past won by two lengths.

To a stunned silence from all the favourite backers, Simon exclaimed, 'Well, bugger me!'

'Not in public, old chap, shall we keep it until later,' laughed Toby to a peal of laughter from Penny, who cried, 'you did it, you did it. You clever thing.'

Toby looked at Simon, 'Oh ye of little faith, you'd better go and collect your ill-gotten gains.'

'May I?' screamed Penny, grabbing the ticket from Simon's hand and flew over to the Tote, where only two other punters were queuing. Handing over the ticket to the fat, sullen-faced woman, she was asked in a sharp voice 'How do you want it? 'Oh, in tenners, I suppose,' chirped Penny.

Sour-face reluctantly counted out £150 in tenners to Penny, who scampered back to the champagne-sipping boys. 'Look,' she gasped, 'I have never ever collected so much from a bookie.' Simon swiftly took the wad from her, counted it, and divided it into three equal piles, before dishing it out, 'Well done old man. I wish I knew how you did it! I'd give up soliciting,' he chortled, raising his glass to Toby's. 'We might as well finish our champagne and let the punters go.'

Simon dropped them off in the square, saying he'd ring Penny as soon as he had news from the board, and was away in a flash.

**** **** ****

'Bit early,' confessed Toby, 'but I feel peckish. How about I get us some fish and chips over there,' pointing at the nearest of two shops in the square. 'Mm, what good ideas you have,' and sitting on a low wall waited for him.

Toby disappeared into a small chippy where a tall, disgruntled-looking man stood behind the sizzling fryer with an overweight, sweating woman, perhaps in her fifties morosely cut the potatoes into chips on a guillotine like machine. 'Yes,' he barked to Toby, who, humouring him, politely asked for two of his Ripon whalers, one bag of chips and two pots of mushy peas.

As old sour-face dipped two large portions of white cod into the batter, Toby casually asked him if he was the proprietor. 'Who wants to know?' he snapped back.

'My name is Toby, and I just wondered how many openings you did in a week?'

'You sound like a tax man,' was the reply.

'Oh, no,' returned Toby. 'It's just that I was reading an article in the Farmer's Weekly that you could turn spent fish & chip oil into a type of lubricating or heating oil. I just wondered how much you had and what you did with it.'

'It's a right pain in the arse,' Lofty exploded, the woman nodding vigorously. 'I collect it all and have to take it down to the Tip, where they bloody charge me for it.'

'That's not good,' agreed Toby, the other two heads bobbing furiously. 'How many gallons would you have?' After scratching his thinning hair, he reckoned, 'Maybe 15 or 20 gallons.' 'Well,' said Toby, 'If after I've done a bit of homework and reckon I could use it, I'd take it off your hands saving you forking out, and also wasting your valuable time.'

Thoughtfully he added, 'I might be able to pay you.'

Wrapping Toby's fish, chips and two pots of peas in an old copy of The Yorkshire Post and taking Toby's money, he said, 'As soon as you are ready, come and see me, the sooner the better. By the way, Frank is my name, and this is my dear wife, Mabel.'

As Toby left the shop, Penny darted across the road, and linking her arm in his said, 'what was that all about? I thought you were buying the damned shop.'

'Sorry love, I'll tell you about it later. Look, I've just remembered I've got to collect from the bookies. You go home and get the oven on to crisp them up and I'll be there in two shakes of a donkey's tail.'

'It would better not be three,' scolded Penny.

Toby drove to the bookies who were just about closing. He handed his ticket over. The clerk whistled, saying, 'Just a moment, sir,' and, calling the manager over, and amid whirling biros and fingers jabbing printed tables, they both agreed. 'Just a tick, sir,' said the manager picking the phone up. After reading the ticket number and amount, he nodded and disappeared into the back office, quickly returning with a wad of twenty-pound notes.

Toby nodded in agreement at the £560 odd pounds, thanking them and apologising for being so late. Turning towards his Land Rover he caught the delicious smell of F&C coming from a very small double fronted shop which had a takeaway at one side, and a cosy little cafe with blue and white tablecloths. It was packed with very contented-looking customers. He smiled when he saw the sign 'Pete's Plaice' above the door. A round, red faced, ginger-haired man wearing a name badge with Pete on it.

During a lull in the service Toby asked the same about the used oil and got the disgruntled reply about the charges and waste of time. 'Any road,' grumbled Ginger. 'I pay enough in rates. I'd be chuffed to let you take it off my hands and if I could get a bob or two that would be grand. I reckon in the take-away and the cafe I have about 30 to 40 gallons a week.' Handing Toby his card, he said. 'Give us a ring when you are ready, lad.'

**** **** ****

Toby drove to the garage as quickly as he could. Penny cried out 'what took you so long, I thought even your old heap wasn't as slow as this. I've been here for ages!'

'Had to see a man about an oil well' grunted Toby. 'Tell you about it over supper. Must say it smells fantastic. Could I make a suggestion?' in his little boy lost voice.

Rolling her eyes Penny asked, 'What now?'

'I know it's a bit philistine, but I do really think we ought to drink a good white with it. Don't fancy a mug of tea. Do you think I could pinch one of your Pa's? I mean I'll pay him back,' taking out the bulging envelope form his pocket.

Penny's eyes widened as she exclaimed, 'God, it looks as if you've raided a bank! Go on then, but hurry up or the chips will be cremated.' He nipped down the steps to the dark, cool cellar and switching on the light saw row upon row of fine wines, Colin's long life passion.

Moving over to the neatly labelled whites, he selected a Pouilly Fuisee, murmuring to it as he retraced his steps, 'I am sorry sweetie, you were crafted for a finer occasion,' giving the bottle a little kiss, 'but you will turn an ordinary meal into something to remember'

Quickly uncorking the wine, he poured a little into Penny's glass, his left arm behind his back, like a sommelier, asked, 'I hope this is to Madam's taste.'

Playing along Penny sipped a little, swirling it round her mouth, as her father had taught her before declaring, 'that's perfect. Please fill my glass.'

Toby put the bottle in the fridge to keep chilled while they quickly and hungrily devoured the supper. Then he helped her clear away and wash up, before taking their two glasses and remains of the wine, to snuggle down with her on the large sofa.

'I've something I'd like to ask you,' he said. Putting her forefinger to his lips she softly returned, 'And I've something I'd like to ask you.'

'Ladies first,' spluttered Toby.

'Well,' began Penny, 'you know Dad is seeing a lot of Margot. They met playing golf and both love bridge. She's a widow and well-off in her own right. Her ex was a mill owner who'd only just sold out before dying from a massive heart attack on the golf course. Well,' she went on breathlessly, 'they are thinking about going on a two month bridge sight-seeing cruise and I don't want to be here alone. I know Joe and Chris are near, but I'll be lonely. Will you please come and stay?' looking pleadingly at him.

'Oh, that's all?' said Toby. I was worried that you might be wanting to get rid of me.'

'Oh, darling, darling,' she cried flinging her arms around him. 'No, please, please say yes. You are like a drug. The more I have of you, the more I need.'

Taking her hand in his and kissing her forehead he whispered, 'I feel the same about you, but only when you live with someone on a day-to-day basis do you really know if you can make it permanent. It's funny, 'cos I was wanting to ask you if you could tear yourself away from here, and join me in my humble cottage, if I get it that is.'

'Oh, you will get it. I know a deserving winner when I see one, Toby you are a good man through and through. I want to join you in the journey, if you'll have me.'

It was agreed that all went to plan and Toby got the go-ahead from the board on Friday, he would leave the hotel and move in with Penny. She said, 'Oh, and there is just one more thing. I've truly just started my curse, so I'm afraid I'm off limits for a day or so.'

'Don't worry one bit, we've hopefully a lifetime ahead, plenty of time.'

They finished the wine, Toby showered while Penny had a deep, scented bath. They were soon asleep in each other's arms.

The alarm clock shrilled; it was 9.00am. 'Far too early,' grumbled Penny, 'But I have to go and clean up the stand in Harrogate.

'Don't worry about me,' said Toby, 'I'll have a word with Joe and Chris and see if I can take them out for Sunday lunch. It's been ages since we had a good chat. You will be late back tonight, so I will stay at the hotel for the next few nights. I have a lot of planning to do.' Then kissing her, he said, 'I'll keep in touch by phone and get together when we can.'

He went over to the cottage and, seeing Joe feeding the cat by their door, asked if they would like to join him for lunch, anywhere Chris wanted. As she was pregnant with their first, she cackled with joy at a nice change. Toby said he'd be back around 12.30 as he was going for a jog.

CHAPTER FIFTEEN

When he got back to the hotel, he found the new manageress seated at reception. He received a frosty smile as he wished her good morning.

She handed over two envelopes, and glancing at them he recognised Claire's sister's handwriting on one of them. The second was a bill from the hotel. Toby opening it and checking found it was correctly up-to-date. Smiling at frosty-face, he paid her there and then from his winnings, saying, 'I'll probably be working a bit further away in possibly two weeks, so I thought I'd just keep you posted, and if I do have to move out, I'll pay you in cash up-to-date. I will be busy in the next few days, and if I miss dinner on odd occasions, that's my problem! I'll pay you in full.'

That brought a beaming smile to the sad, lined face. 'That's very kind of you sir, I do hope you have been satisfied with your time spent with us, and you have no complaints.' Toby thought to himself that if he had any complaints and dare mention them, she would have knifed him.

The major tottered out of the lounge and, seeing Toby, cried, 'Toby, good to see you again, dear boy. Must say, you've been absent on parade a few times. Been busy?'

'Well Major, as you know I've been looking for a project for a while, and maybe I might be moving on in a couple of weeks, but tell me about Freddie.'

'Hush,' as the major put his gnarled old forefinger to his lips, and steered Toby away into the lounge.

There, sitting as far from the door as possible, the major close to Toby whispered, 'Awful hoo-ha. First Bobbie left, poor girl, with her cases and a bruised cheek. Then a couple of days later Freddie packed his bags, and said he was off to visit his brother. Apparently they hadn't bought the place as they made out. They were managers working for the same group as old starchy out there,' jerking his thumb at reception. 'And,' stuttered the major, a little froth appearing at the side of his mouth, and getting alarmingly red in his face, 'The blighter was not an officer in the guards, as he pretended.

'He was a post clerk working in regimental headquarters,' he exploded. Shaking his head, he quietly muttered, 'I really don't know what's going on. We're going to the dogs.' Commiserating and excusing himself, Toby nipped up to his room, donned his old faded maroon track-suit, emblazoned with a 3 Para badge, and set off on his run out of town up to Grewelthorpe and Kirkby Malzeard before returning.

He realised from his heavy breathing how out of condition he was, and his right leg hurt so he was determined to take regular exercise to get in shape. After showering and donning dark slacks and blazer with an open necked blue-check shirt, he carefully checked his cash hidden in the room, and adding yesterday's winnings, set off to collect Christine and Joe.

He found them scrubbed up and ready to go.

**** **** ****

Wedging Christine between Joe and himself on the front seat of the Land Rover, they set off to North Stainley, to the Staveley Arms which accordingly to an excited Chris had just opened after a complete make-over.

'It's a good job you managed to book the last table,' said Joe, seeing the car park was almost chock-a-block. They found a space around the back and entered the heaving pub. The boys ordered a pint of bitter while Chris preferred an orange juice. Toby asked for three menus. The girl behind the bar handed them over, a young, plump little waitress was passing and said, 'we are really crowded out, would you like to bring your drinks through?' She led the way to a large conservatory, full of happy groups and families all talking nine-to the dozen.

The waitress asked if they wanted a starter. Toby, seeing Chris's hesitant glanced at Joe, observed, 'they look really good. Shall we all try different ones to compare?' The waitress was soon back, and after they'd all tried a sample of each other's pronounced them all really delicious. They were given a plate each explaining that they go and select whatever they wanted from a huge joint of beef, lamb, pork or chicken with all vegetables and trimmings.

'Wow,' trilled Chris as, plate in hand she attacked the mouth-watering display. Farmer-looking blokes could hardly be seen behind the mountains of food piled onto their plates as they made their way back to their tables. Seeing an excited Chris struggling with her pile, Toby took it from her, carrying it back to their table for her. She planked herself down and Toby observed, 'Well dear, it certainly looks as if you are eating for two!'

'More like three,' joined in Joe who had just returned with a selection of everything. Toby was amused to see the overflowing plates devoured right to the last pea. Patting his tum and declaring himself out, Joe left Chris at the table and went to get her a selection of pudds.

Asking Chris if all was well, after a few 'fine' and 'nice', she eventually confided that as Colin was seeing more of his lady friend, he was leaving more and more to Joe. Poor Joe was doing a lot more and having to work for longer.

He had even told her he might look for a better-paid job in Harrogate. That would mean a move and upheaval just when baby was due.

'Oh, Toby please don't let on that I have told you, 'cos Joe's so loyal to Colin who gave him his start.' Toby promised not to, just as his old friend returned.

'Just like a hunter, returning to his mate in their lair,' observed Toby, to much giggling and nudging. They ended up with coffee whilst Toby told them all about his bid for the property and the dramatic week ahead.

They both wished him all the best and hoped to see him soon. Toby settled the bill and dropped them off at the garage. As he drove back to a quiet hotel, he wondered how best to help Joe. He decided on an early night, as he wanted a full day at the little desk in his bedroom to fully prepare for the week ahead.

**** **** ****

He was up at six and pounded the side roads for an hour before showering and having a full English breakfast, so he could work till suppertime. He pulled out the foolscap size file with dividers he had bought and labelled. He added headings like Water Board, Planning, Bank, Lawyer, Surveyor, Building, Silas etc. He rapidly under each section filled in all details he had and needed to do.

He wrote a time scale on the front inner cover in pencil, so amendments could be made. He quite enjoyed it, thinking it was a bit like a battle plan for the troops in the army!

He managed to arrange times to see Walter, Silas and the bank. Taking the list of names and telephone numbers of potential farmworkers he had got from Maggie, he wrote them into the file. He checked each farm on the map of the area, circling it and labelling it with one, two or three.

Going down to a fast-filling bar and feeling pleased at his day's work, he had a pint and chat with several regulars before joining the major for dinner.

Expecting another busy day, he was in bed and asleep by ten o'clock.

After a similar start, as the day before, he was soon chugging over to see Walter, who had set the morning aside for him. Walter sat him down at the kitchen table on which was a foolscap pad, biros and the rough plans they had sketched plus the architect's plans submitted to the Board.

'Coffee?' enquired Walter from the kitchen.

'Please, Walter,' from Toby as he took out his folder, opening it up to show Walter.

'See you've been busy,' gestured Walter, setting down two large mugs of black, steaming coffee.

'Right,' opened Toby. 'I want you and your team to knock the two cottages into one,' gesturing at the plan. 'I would also like you to do the new build. Will you have the time, or have you jobs booked in? Ideally I want to be in for Christmas, and also have a tenant into the new build.'

Walter stared back, declaring, 'You've got me at a good time, I've got nought big on, and can start to shift little jobs round. There's me, Arthur my chippy cum everything, old Bert the best stonemason for miles. He taught me all I know, and young Paul who's shaping up well as a good all-rounder. Aye, I reckon there's nought much we can't do, if we set ourselves up to do it.'

'Brilliant,' cried Toby. 'Just what I wanted to hear. By the way, you've also got an un-paid 'go-for' to make your brews, clear up, go and fetch anything you want. All at no cost. Me.' Toby jabbed his thumb at himself. 'I'll be your un-paid apprentice. Walter, I want to learn all you will teach me, as I work with you. I aim to be first on site in the morning and last to leave at night. I've been farting around for a couple of months now. Long enough, I want to get my hands dirty and get stuck in.'

'Welcome aboard new apprentice,' growled Walter. 'Now you will learn what hard graft is, and being a Yorkshire man I can never resist getting summat for naught,' he grinned.

'Right,' he went on. 'What sort of tenant were you thinking about?'

'A go-ahead, grafting young farmer, Walter. One, if I pick the right one, who can join us. I'll pay his wages,' he added quickly, 'He can help build his own house, get the farming side sorted out with me and Silas and then go and run what I hope can be a profitable little mixed farm.'

'You amaze me,' laughed Walter. 'You've certainly got it all planned out. Now, if you get planning consent for the new build, I would want to get the footings in, electricity and water in first. Ideally I'd like to get walls up and roof on so we're watertight before autumn.' Seeing dismay on Toby's face, he said 'Don't worry, a lot of the work will be outside contractors, and we can still be knocking walls down at your place.'

A relieved Toby replied, 'So you still think we will achieve our Christmas target.'

'That's the plan,' muttered Walter. 'Tell you what Toby. It will be a pleasure to be involved in a new build again. It gives me a real kick, when I stand back at the finish and think I did that! Like grown out of the ground,' he stated proudly.

'I was just saying to the missus the other day that I'm not getting any younger and I don't like outside work in the cold any more. It's a young man's game. Both Bert and I have rheumatism.'

Toby gazed steadily at Walter before slowly enquiring, 'What if someone offered one good new build in summer, say May to the end of September, and then a good 2 to 3 months inside refurb job. January to end of March maybe two small inside minor refurbs.' He paused.

'I'd shake his bloody hand off,' exclaimed an excited Walter, whose turn it was, to solemnly stare at Toby. After a gulp of breath he gasped, almost pleadingly, 'Do you think you could do it lad?'

'I would bust a gut to do it; I always stand by my word. I can't see what's to stop us. Nihil Carburundum,' he shouted and, translating the crude army Latin translation to Walter, 'Don't let the buggers grind us in!' They solemnly shook hands, Walter pouring a large tot of whisky into each refilled mug of coffee before clinking pots and declaring, 'To us!'

'How will it work?' asked Walter. Toby replied slowly, feeling for the right words, 'on a new build I've been told the costs go really three ways. The cost of the plot with the planning, the actual cost of the build and the profit. Say, an equal third?'

191

'You are about right,' agreed Walter.

Toby carried on, 'Well, I'll find, buy and get planning as my cost, you do the build at your best price without compromising quality or time, and we split the profit 50/50.' He settled back, studying the other carefully, before adding, 'don't worry if my costs are greater than yours, we'll even them up as we split the profit,'

'Yes, and if I'm say two thousand dearer on the build, I'll take two grand less on the profit,' he smiled happily.

'Got another smart-arse idea,' murmured Toby. 'It's entirely up to you what you do with your cut, Walter, but your boys have been paid as they've gone along. Like normal, but do you think it would be a good idea if you paid them each a little percentage, naturally the lion's share to you, the more to Bert being the eldest, then Arthur, with the smallest to Paul the apprentice. That way, they all feel part of the team, and getting more money from the extra profit coming from fewer breakages and snagging. Gives them more pride in what is then their job. Like you said Walter.'

Walter slapped his thigh, exclaiming, 'you are bloody right, Toby. When we start, I'll bill you for work and material weekly for your spot, but for the new build, we'll give it a try. After all,' -he reflected- 'I've two pairs of hands costing me nought, we'll have it done in a jiffy.'

Toby promised to ring him on Friday when he had heard from the board.

**** **** ****

He'd arranged to meet Silas at the pub for a pint and a sandwich. As he hadn't arrived, Toby got himself a pint and took it out into the bright afternoon sun. Sitting on a bench at a wooden table he sipped the splendidly well-hopped fragrant beer, blissfully unaware of the silent figure, pint pot engulfed in his huge hand, slid down beside him.

'Good, isn't it?' Silas enquired to the startled Toby.

'God, you made me jump,' he exclaimed. Tapping his broken nose with a huge forefinger Silas went on, 'Surprise is the essence of attack, you should remember that soldier boy.'

'Didn't know I was being attacked,' retorted Toby.

'Don't suppose you are, but best be on alert at all times, you just never know,' pontificated Silas.

Toby finished his beer, and turning to Silas asked, 'Refill? And what can I get you to go with it? A ham and pickle sarnie, Toby. They do very good ones here.' Toby went off to the bar ordering and paying for two refills and two sandwiches.

'I'll bring them out to you when they are ready,' said the girl behind the bar with a cheeky smile. Toby handed over the beer to Silas with 'Happy Days', returned by Silas, who squinted at the list of names Toby had handed to him. 'Know any Silas?'

'Well,' drawled Silas, 'These two' jabbing his finger at the list Toby had written down from Maggie. 'I know they're disappointed at not having their bid for the cottage accepted. This one, I don't know, but I think he farms, malting barley in a big way with his two brothers.'

'Don't think about asking, but which of the two should I employ as the guy to run my little small holding?'

'That one! That is Barry Chambers. Young, about 20, got a pretty, steady girlfriend, a farmer's daughter called Sally. Wants to get married, can't afford the deposit for a house. Believe he was turned down by the bank. Both are the youngest kids in two big farming families. No chance of making it in farming. Young Barry worked for me off and on. Bright, takes it in, really wants to learn. Can do most jobs, very practical.

Thing is, although Barry is bright young, Sally is far brighter. Got a fistful of GCSEs, but wants to farm with Barry,' he added.

Toby said, 'Barry sounds like my man then. Could you sound him out for me, Silas?'

'Not much point, he'll jump at the job, what a bloody good turn-up for him. A new house, he can marry Sally and have twice as much land and work for a boss who wants to diversify into real income-producing ways to maximise profits. What a chance.'

The girl appeared with the sandwiches in crusty brown bread covering the large plates, with a pot of mustard and one pickle.

They wolfed them down in no time, and Toby went to refill the glasses with this golden nectar. Mustn't get pissed he told himself, but why not enjoy the simple things in life, good drink, good, simple food and good company.

Many people, he told himself, would be envious. In the sun they plotted the best way to maximise the potential to be made from the small-holding. Christmas trees growing at about a foot a year would be sourced and planted at one foot and two foot height. Contracts with local retailers and garden centres would be made during the year. Initial sales would be low, but maximised in year 3 and 4.

The front 10 acre field would be cultivated and sown with malting barley like Plumage Archer for a good, high-quality yield and price. This would give a cash return before the trees.

Then, Silas thought that two good-sized chicken houses could be used for contract rearing providing a steady income stream from minimal manpower.

Toby was keen to keep a separate shed for egg production and a few pigs for their own consumption. Sheep would be kept on the North facing steep roadside fields.

Silas ticked the rough residue off on his fingers, saying, 'There would be enough to make both families pretty well-off, and nearly self-sufficient.'

'Talking of self-sufficiency Silas,' started Toby. 'How about this for a good idea?' and went on to tell him about turning spent F&C oil into a useable lubricant. Silas was getting really interested, his dirty old pipe nearly going out. 'What I didn't let onto the fish & chip boys,' breathed

Toby slowly, 'Was that my plan is to upgrade it with a few cheap and easily sourced chemicals to turn it into diesel oil.'

'Bloody hell,' murmured Silas, 'It's a bit like the fucking philosopher's stone.'

'Quite,' went on Toby. 'If I can get several sources on board, we could be self-sufficient in diesel, with a ginormous great tank to run diesel cars, Land Rovers, all the farm machines and heat the houses in winter.

Pausing, thinking out loud, 'Maybe even heating a great greenhouse for tomatoes and out-of-season vegetables.'

Clapping his hands Silas whooped, 'Bloody genius! Can I be in?'

'Course,' replied Toby, thinking what three pints had achieved. 'They ought to be put on prescription.'

'I know,' said Silas, 'with bugger all to do at the moment, I'll collect all supplies and process it at my place. You said it's like Fort Knox, no-one's going to know what we are up to.'

'Done,' said Toby draining his glass, asking Silas to prepare and cost out the farming plan and promising to give him a ring on Friday.

**** **** ****

As it was still only 1.30 and the bank didn't close until 3.00 sharply he could just about make it. He pulled into the hotel car park and, taking his key from behind an empty reception he went to his room, locking the door, and moving out the heavy wardrobe. He lifted the carpet to reveal a cut in two floorboards, which when lifted allowed him to pull out a plastic carrier bag. Tipping the pile of bank notes onto the bed, he quickly arranged them into ten-shilling notes, pounds, fivers, tens and twenties.

It took fifteen minutes and two recounts to confirm the final total of £21,260. Replacing the boards, carpet and

195

after heaving back the heavy wardrobe, he shuffled an old duster on top of the money and went off to the bank.

Both Joyce and Millie greeted him with beaming smiles, saying Mr. Farrar would soon be free. A large, red-faced farmer was vigorously shaking the wincing Mr. Farrar by the hand, exclaiming, 'that's right grand of you Mr. Farrar. Champion, champion.'

As he strode out of the door, Toby observed to Harold 'Another happy looking customer' as he entered the holy of Holies. 'We like to please all our customers, Mr. Cooper,' chirped Harold pompously.

'Now, you are our last customer of the day and we want to be away directly,' said Harold thinking of his wife's steak and kidney pie, which would be awaiting his return.

'I've just got some cash I'd like to deposit. It's sort of built up over a few weeks and I'd be happier if it was safe with you!' Harold pressed his intercom asking Joyce and Millie 'Please lock the front door, and then come into check some money, Mr. Cooper wishes to deposit.'

The pair soon arrived and Toby moved to the end of Harold's big desk, leaving wide front part so that they both sat side by side as Toby up-ended the carrier bag.

To three pairs of ever widening eyes he said, 'Don't worry, I've not raided a bank, more like the bookies!'

'Can you explain how you came by this, this fortune?' sputtered an astounded Harold. Toby started to chuckle, then told Harold, whilst the ladies tallied it up, 'May I tell you a story, it's maybe a little risqué,' to which Harold pompously stated 'No, I'm a man of word but please don't cause any offence to my staff.'

'Well,' began Toby, 'One day on a busy Friday, a little old lady tottered into a bank--' by now both ladies' fingers had stopped counting and all three pairs of eyes were glued to Toby's as he went on. 'She demanded to see the manager as she wished to open an account and deposit a substantial cash sum. She was shown into the manager's office and deposited a carrier bag stuffed with notes. 'Do you know how much is there?' asked the manager. 'Of course young man,' she replied. '£55,610 without batting an eyelid.' The chief clerk summoned to count it, as the manager asked. 'Would you please tell me how you came by this sum of money?' 'Well,' drawled the little old lady, 'from little bets.' 'Do you mean the horses, madam?' queried the manager with a derisory sniff. 'No,' she exclaimed. 'From what I call my silly little bets.' 'Like what?' pursued the manager. There was a long pause as she looked coolly at him before saying, 'I'll have a bet with you now. I'll bet you £5000 that you have square balls!' 'Madam, really,' protested the manager, witnessed by a choking clerk. 'Will you take me up on this?' she demanded, a steely glint in her eye. The clerk coughed, saying the money was correct and he would just go and put it into the safe. The manager excused himself to the lady and quickly popped into his private loo and carefully checked himself before returning to his desk. 'So, if my testicles are normal, you'll pay me £5000?' 'Exactly,' she purred. 'I'll be in at 9.50 on Monday morning to honour me bet,' and, grabbing the receipt for her money rushed away. The Manager told his wife of the odd woman and the bet. To be doubly sure, she gave him a close examination and pronounced him normal and the money was his. We'll change the car and put in a new kitchen, she cooed. At 9.50 precisely on Monday morning, the manager rose from his desk to meet the old lady, who was accompanied by a tall, thin man without a blade of hair. He looked like a light bulb, hence his nickname 'Osram'. She waved, 'my accountant, he's here to verify the bet. Let's get on with it,' gesturing the manager and Osram to follow her into the private loo. The manager sheepishly dropped his trousers and boxer shorts, as bang on the clock striking ten o'clock she held each of the Manager's perfectly normal testicles in both her hands. 'Oh, no,' screamed Osram, banging his head on the wall. 'She's done it again!' 'What?' cried the manager, hurriedly dressing. 'She bet me £10000 that she would have the manager's balls in her hands at 10.0 precisely!'

Harold's bald head was glistening, he'd gone a dark shade of red, his lips began to tremble and his stomach heaved as he let rip of a series of loud brays like a donkey. The ladies' tears running down their cheeks and laughing like hyenas, clutched each other. Harold's eyes were closed, the braying continued. A little dog outside the half open window stopped, cocked his head and peed on the wheel of a pram. The harassed mother pushing it had also stopped at the sound. Harold coughed, saying, 'Damned funny story, must remember that for Rotary Society next meeting. Come on ladies, remember, tempus fugit, tempus fugit!' Calm was regained and Joyce handed a slip with £21,650 written on it. 'That's absolutely spot on,' confirmed Toby. 'Could you please credit my account with it, and let me have the final balance.'

'I've got your up-to date statement here. I must congratulate you in your building up such a substantial amount in the time you've banked with me. You seem to have won the same amount as we've just counted from another source paying by cheque. You've got a net worth of £52,000 after the £7000 we have transferred to your solicitor.'

**** **** ****

Toby strolled back to the hotel feeling a warm sense of accomplishment and a distinct sense of purpose. He felt tired and drained, so decided he'd have a good soak in the bath. He normally despised baths as a bit girlie. He reckoned it was just like wallowing in your own muck. Tonight was a change. He ordered a large double of his favourite malt and glass, in hand passed sour-face doing her books behind reception.

He found an empty bathroom near his room, ran a cold water in, then left the hot trickling in whilst he got his wash bag and large towel from his room. The water was just about the right temperature and half-full. As he lowered himself into the bath, he unwrapped a block of imperial Leather, his mother's favourite. He reached out, and let the 15-year-old Malt do its work as he slowly unwound.

It seemed incredible that only six weeks ago he'd left the army on a whim to go to north and meet such genuine, interesting people. From leaving Claire to meeting Liz, then his adorable Penny, the one he reckoned he was destined to be with. Oh yes, Karen and Maggie, and poor dear Bobbie. As he was recalling their faces and bodies, Tom had started to get interested. He took a large gulp of the whisky, letting it slip down.

As he put the glass down, he caught a movement in the mirror at the end of the bath. A shadow at the threshold. Eyes half shut, he pretended to drowse. Yes, there it was a movement at the keyhole. Keeping motionless, he watched mesmerised as the handle slowly turned, and sour-face's eye peeped into the room.

At his light snoring she grew bolder and stepping in, stood beside the bath gazing at Tom. Her breath grew faster, as out of the corner of his now nearly closed eyes, he could make out her fingers rubbing herself at the base of her stomach.

He opened his eyes to see her lip trembling; he slowly pushed his hand up her leg to stroke the soft inner thigh at the top of her stockings. She made to give a little yelp. Toby hoarsely whispered, 'Hush, be quiet, people might hear,' her legs opened slightly and he ran his forefinger down the front of her tight silky pants, he could feel the thick bush bursting through, threading his long firm forefinger under the side of her pants, he levered it in to stroke her erect, wet clitoris before tracing it down between her lips to push round and into her.

He quickly stood up in the bath placing both her hands around Tom, as he continued to play with her before she shuddered to a wet stop. Toby holding her face kissed her long and tenderly, before saying, 'Don't worry, it's

199

forgotten. I promise never to tell a soul. Come and join me in bed tonight,' clasping her hand to her mouth, she fled.

**** **** ****

Toby dried himself, swished the bath clean and dressed in his room. Taking a swift pint in the bar, with no regulars about, and only one or two guests dining, he had a fillet steak. Later passing reception, he asked the manageress if she could kindly have a bottle of rose champagne and two glasses delivered to his room. Her eyes lowered. She almost whispered. 'Yes, sir.'

Toby undressed, leaving the door ajar. Finding spare pillows in the wardrobe, he plumped two up on the other side of the bed. He was propped up in bed, the bedside lamp casting a dim light on the notebook that he was reading, when he heard a slight tap on the door as it slowly opened.

She was still in her uniform, and stooped to put the ice bucket, champagne and two glasses on the side table. She turned slowly and said 'I'll be back; I just have to lock up for the night. Shall I open the champagne?'

'No, I'll do it when you are back,' confirmed Toby. He noticed how tall she was, with a good figure and legs in that plain uniform.

He and Tom waited for over 15 minutes. He was almost on the point of turning the light off, when the same delicate tap came, and she was in quickly. Turning her back, she softly closed the door.

He was immediately hit by the delicate fragrance, as he could just make out black stockings and suspenders beneath the thin diaphanous silk slip. He gasped as she turned. She pulled a clip out of her hair piled on her head, and it fell down to her shoulders.

The former pinched, pale face was made up, lips painted, smiling. The top fastened at her throat with a velvet knot, opened to reveal a pair of plump, firm, well-shaped breasts with the slightest of droops, but splendid thimble size nipples already firming.

His eyes were drawn to her thick dark bush which was pushing out her skimpy pants. He flung back the bedclothes to reveal a rampant Tom. She was at the bedside and whispering a hushed 'May I?' she held Tom one slim hand over the other.

She stooped over him, her soft, fragrant newly washed hair brushing his inner thigh.

He gasped as she peeled back the foreskin with her lips to sink Tom deep into her mouth. She slowly, but firmly started to masturbate him one hand holding one of his balls whilst pumping with the other, her mouth taking the rhythm from the hand squeezing Tom.

Toby moved her downwards and more towards him. She never paused, if anything, got quicker. His left hand fondled her swelling right breast as the fingers of his right hand disappeared into her damp fur. His right thumb found the hardened pea of her wet clitoris, whilst his forefinger traced between her firming glistening labia to find her vagina. Slowly rotating his hand he inserted his finger to a small gasp from her. He pushed in, whilst slowly rotating it. With almost like a beckoning motion of his slightly bent forefinger he heard the muffled yelp as he found her G spot.

Continually working on it, to increasingly and alarmingly louder yes's he worked harder on her clitoris.

'God,' he thought, she was good. He couldn't hold on much longer. He held his hand over her mouth as she climaxed again and again.

Swiftly, but firmly, he pulled her over onto her back and kneeling with a large hand under each thigh he raised her up and Tom entered her. She held both hands over her mouth as her stomach convulsed in a series of orgasms. Tom couldn't wait any longer and filled her in a succession of great jerks.

Her hands fell to her sides, as she looked at him whispering, 'Oh, what have I done?' Toby twisted up to put a finger to her lips before kissing gently and then fiercely as she grabbed his hair, poking her tongue deeper into his throat. Tears softly rolled down her cheeks. He, wiping them away with his hand asked 'what is it love? What's the matter?' she gulped and then gazing into his eyes for any reaction, said, 'that was truly wonderful. It'd been a long time, nearly seven years. I was so pent up, so frustrated.'

He listened intently, letting her get off her chest whatever it was.

'I've had lots of offers from handsome younger men on one night stands to dirty old gits staying at all the various places I've worked at over the years.'

Sniffing, she muttered, 'Some of the old buggers have even offered money!' another sniff.

'Why me?' asked Toby.

'Was really shocked at tonight. Never, ever done it before. Then it struck me. You are so like Mike.'

'Who's Mike?' another bigger sniff. 'Mike was my ex. He was like you, big, blond and kind. A man who women just gravitate to. And he liked it. I didn't mind,' another couple of sniffs. 'He was a bloody good rugby player. Went from his university, where we first met, to playing for the county. Had on England trial, but just didn't make it. We ended up running a pub. Went very well. I did the catering. We leased two more and we were making it big time.

Instead of putting something away we travelled, had a big car, even put off having kids.

It was the tax bill that did for us. We paid up, went back to one pub. Mike started drinking heavily. One night he was guest of honour at the local rugby club. Got pissed and too proud or foolish he drove himself home. Nearly got there, only two hundred yards away at the end of a long straight he drove straight into a tree.

They reckon he must have dropped off. Doing over 100 mph. they said, he wouldn't have known a thing. The silly sod,' she beat the pillow with her trembling hands. Toby took them and kissed them before hugging her and giving her a gentle, non-passionate kiss.

Sitting up, they both sat side by side, sipping their champagne. 'Thanks,' she said.

'What for?'

'Thanks for listening to a frustrated old woman, but also thanks for the therapy. You've released me. I really feel alive and me again. I'm going to sort myself out and live again.'

Holding up her hand she said, 'I'm only ever going to get involved emotionally if I meet a man like you. That's a chance in a million.' Cheering up she refilled their glasses, and snuggling up to him asked, 'Now tell me all about you and your plans.'

It was after two o'clock when Toby finished. They both fell asleep; her back pressed Tom into Toby, who held her close. As the first rays filtered through the curtain she turned onto her back, pulling Toby onto her, saying how nice and easy does it. 'Please make it last for a long time.' Toby did as he was bid.

As they parted, they both agreed to never mention it to a soul. Jean said 'My brother is a lecturer at Leeds University, that's his number if you ever want to get in touch.' Whispering, 'I'd better get back to my room before the inmates start roaming about. Thanks for everything. You are a wonderful man. I think now I can face the future.' Toby kissed both cheeks and firmly, longer, passionately her lips.

**** **** ****

After she left, he turned on his side, away from the light and fitfully dozed until nearly nine. Quickly showering, he dressed and was in the dining room in fifteen minutes. Lucy waved an admonishing finger at him, 'Oh, you've just made it Mr. Toby. We shut shop at 9.30.'

'I know. Sorry Lucy, I just overslept. I'll have a kipper and just tea and toast, please,' and touching his head, murmured, 'Do you think you could fix me a Bloody Mary, while I wait.'

Shaking her head in disbelief she scuttled into the kitchen to give chef the order and then the bar, re-appearing with a large whiskey tumbler containing tomato juice, Worcester sauce, two large ice cubes. She whispered, 'I put a double vodka in Mr. Toby. Hope that was right.'

Waving his hand at her he nearly downed half the glass and confirmed, 'Perfect Lucy, spot on.' She retreated into the kitchen, almost immediately returning with the tray of kipper, toast and tea. She opened the door with her neat, rounded little bottom, giving Toby naughty thoughts.

After finishing, he grabbed a cup of strong, black coffee from the machine and sitting at a table in the lounge he went through all the points he wanted to cover at the meeting with Simon later in the morning.

CHAPTER SIXTEEN

Realising he had time to kill before the meeting with Simon he nipped up to his room and dug out his old swimming trunks that he had used when he swam for the army against the yanks. Hell, he'd nearly forgotten to ring Kath for a possible tip. Getting through she gasped 'I'm glad you've rung, cos I was just off to a parents meeting at the school. I'm late already. The boss says it's a poor day, with just the one running at Newmarket in the four o five'

Thanking her, he rang Sylvia and shot off to Ripon where he got 4/1 for the £10ew. He then went to the swimming bath near the Spa Hotel. He paid for a ticket to the mixed session, collecting a locker key to lock up his belongings whilst he swam.

The plump, pink-faced youth displaying a name badge with Norman on, seemed a bit out of breath and excited as Toby entered the gent's changing room.

There were clothes lockers in the middle of the room with wooden benches at either side with two large mirrors at the end. A stern notice stated 'will Gentlemen please adjust their dress before leaving'. At the end near the entrance to the pool were three, wide open showers. Two old boys were soaping themselves, chatting away to each other.

Toby found his locker and started stripping. Norman had come in with a trolley to collect the old wet towels from the hopper placed under the mirror.

As Norman went slowly about his task, his excitement at watching the two old boys and their tiny willies, grew even more at the view on the left. If he just twisted a bit, oh, this was what he waited for, why he did this poorly paid job.

There the blond man with his back to him was naked as he bent down 'Oh, God' gulped Norman, who was almost motionless, as the man turned and put his clothes into the locker.

Norman's heart nearly stopped as he looked at his huge penis, swinging. Oh, why can't I take a photo? Instead, he had to fix it in his mind for later. He started to look really busy as the man was approaching as Norman half-bent over the skip, he could just see through his fringe that the huge swinging willie was just about level with him. Oh, if only he could reach out and touch it. The man was showering. The two old boys, now towelling themselves stopped and one nudged the other glancing at Toby in the shower.

Toby put on his trunks and went out into the pool. Two old ducks, both in floral costumes, one in a frilly pink bathing cap the other in a similar purple one. Mable and Doris came with their husbands twice a week on their membership card when it was quiet.

As Toby strode to the far end, Mabel catching sight of him looked across at Doris swimming side by side in their respective lanes, as they always did. Noticing Doris's wide-open mouth, she hissed 'That's not a parcel, it's a bloody cabin trunk' Toby cleanly dived into the water performing an effortless crawl, which drew admiring glances.

It was Maurice's day off and Norman couldn't wait to tell him all about it when he got home tonight. Norman and Maurice shared a flat together, after their families had disowned both after their secret come out.

They had met at a local photographic club where each had shown over-keen interest in the nude. Maurice, preferring big-busted older females, whilst Norman liking both but rather veered preferring males.

It was a stroke of luck when the jobs advertising for swimming pool attendant and lifeguard had come up. Norman was suddenly jolted out of his daydream by five young professionals, maybe from the bank, insurance brokers who cares, were buying tickets from old Fred, his colleague. He was a retired mill worker and half-asleep all the time.

With a spring in his step Norman entered the changing room with the pretence of collecting more towels, or his favourite, pretending to clean the mirrors.

He was beside himself with glee when all five bucks stripped off and started chatting to each other giving Norman a wonderful sight of five together.

Oh, no the big blond man was back and join the last two in the shower. Norman's knees were weak. He feared he was getting what his old mother used to call the dithers.

Toby dried and dressed and left for his meeting with Simon.

**** **** ****

Sipping a black coffee in Simon's luxurious office, he ran through all the points he had listed. He told Simon that he felt pretty sure he would get the planning permission on Friday. In case he didn't, he wanted to complete a week on Friday and then wait for the next planning meeting.

'You seem confident,' Simon remarked.

'Well, what time do you leave tonight? 'Cos I might be able to give you a firm answer, hopefully around five-ish.'

'Me thinks I spy a mole,' retorted Simon.

'I couldn't possibly comment, Simon. Oh, I forgot to mention, I'm thinking of letting the house and all the land cut to a young working farmer who'll pay a reasonable rent. I'll pay him a wage, then we'll share the profits.'

'I see,' considered Simon seriously. 'Do you want me to draw up the appropriate contracts?'

'Yes, and also keep the agricultural holding number with the farm house and the 50 acres, separately the two cottages to be knocked into one with the drive. If I ever want to sell, I can sell the house and drive. The farmhouse and land could always gain road access from a now-unused road.'

'Phew,' muttered Simon. 'You certainly seem to have covered all angles. If property prices rise as much as predicted, you will be sitting on two potential great little earners. Have you thought of a name for your new address?'

'Yes, actually Penny came up with Waterside, which I think is dead brill, don't you?'

'Yep, inspirational,' replied Simon. 'Sounds a bit like a plantation house in the deep south. Tell you what, in the future to some city banker, or top law firm employee moving north it will be worth a few extra grand for the name and location alone.'

They had a quick lunch at a new trendy wine bar and left Toby promising to contact Simon around 5.00. As he had nearly three hours to kill, Toby went shopping to see what furniture was on offer, even browsing in several kitchen fitters, plumbers, bathroom show rooms and soft furnishing shops to get a handle on the ranges, quality and prices.

Passing a branch of Corals, he eased in and checking the result found to his glee that Kathy's 4/1 nag had romped home. He abstracted nearly £70 from cashier, making him almost £50 clear profit.

All grist to the mill he thought, as he made his way to Hugo's emporium. Nipping in and out of several antique dealers, he ended up at Hugo's around quarter past four.

Apparently Hugo had left early, leaving Penny to lock up. 'Lovely to see you!' she crooned, kissing him. 'Will you come and have supper and stay the night?' she asked. 'I need you in my bed tonight, and for many nights to come!'

After asking her if he could use the phone he put the call through to Karen. Penny goggle-eyed, open-mouthed, had to put her hand to her mouth to stop giggling as he spoke in such an aristocratic voice. 'Good afternoon madam. My name is Doctor Livingstone and I have a note from my secretory to telephone a Miss Bateson to check if we had attached the correct details to a planning query my department had.'

The young girl on reception was getting ready for home, and was a bit flustered as she knew the planning meeting had just finished, saying, 'One moment please doctor.' This brought more giggles from Penny.

The phone clicked as Toby heard Karen on line. 'Oh, thank you for ringing as requested doctor. The points you wanted to raise were approved and agreed. The other party (The Water Board) will be contacting you as agreed on Friday. Thank you again doctor. Good afternoon.' The phone clicked.

Toby put his phone down and punched the air, yelling a loud 'Yes'. Even the stuffed parrot on its perch seemed to wince. 'Does that mean what I think it means?' asked Penny.

'Yes, my love, I've got the deal including the new build, and they are going to let the board know tonight, for their meeting on Friday. 'How did you do it?' she quizzed.

'Best not to know, my dear. Or I'd have to kill you first,' he joked.

Shaking her head again at this lovable, amazing, mysterious man, she put the alarm on, cashed up and locked the door behind them.

Looking up at him she asked, 'Do you like liver & onions?' 'Gosh, one of my favourites. Used to hate it at school. All grey and hard like an old boot's soles.'

'Never tasted any,' she teased. 'But the way my dad and I prefer it pink, dark brown onions with mustard mash.' Rolling his eyes and crying like a wolf he retorted, 'Sounds my type of fine cuisine, yum, yum, bring it on.'

**** **** ****

Toby followed Penny home, collecting the liver from Chris who'd put it into her fridge after it was delivered. Always on a Wednesday by Bates the best butcher by far according to Penny.

Toby, drink in hand was at the fireplace examining the invites and various cards propped up, when he recognised one. It was Tommy's and Liz's wedding invitation.

Hell, it was in nearly four weeks. How time flies! He'd done nothing about a present. Asking Penny, who said, 'I will go and look at the wedding list in Casa Pupo. How much do you want to spend?'

Toby opened his arms. 'Haven't a clue.'

'Well, I think about £50 will be ok,' she replied.

During a delicious supper, as Penny was clearing away Colin took Toby on one side saying, 'I really want you to stay with Penny here in the house.

'I aim to be away a bit more, as things are going in the right direction with Margot and I. Do hope something comes of it. Been a bit lonely all these years, an old man bringing up his little girl. Talking of which, you won't let her down will you? I know you like the ladies, and as I've seen, they like you. You lucky so and so!'

'Colin, I think a lot of Penny, between you and I, I want to ask her to marry me, when I've worked on what I hope will be our future home.'

Toby went on to tell Colin and Penny his future plans, ending by saying, 'And of course the ladies usually end up by having the last word, which we mere men usually agree to,' to a clapping and agreement from father and daughter.

In bed they snuggled up together Penny directing him to use his fingers and tongue as she was frightened of creating too much noise, her father being alone and so near to them.

It delighted Toby to delight her, the only one not delighted was Tom, who was a bit miffed to be left out.

In the morning Penny rushed out, leaving Toby finishing his bacon butty and black coffee, as Colin came in. 'Sleep alright?' he shot a glance at Toby.

'Like the proverbial, and you?'

'Bit restless, need a bit more fresh air and golf' replied Colin.

'Talking of golf, Colin, I hope I'm not out of place when I ask if you remember what I was on about last night when I was talking about offering a profit sharing scheme.

I just wondered if you are away a bit more maybe the extra work would land on Joe and make him a bit resentful.'

Colin, slowly nodded his head, thoughtfully said 'Yes, I can see where you're coming from. I've been giving poor, loyal Joe more to take on with no extra staff. What would you advocate?'

'I realise Joe is a workshop manager and his Christine, just a book keeper. How about promoting Joe to general manager and Christine to be the company secretary? A decent rise in their pay and you could get together with them and Penny to arrange a profit sharing scheme. Joe could maybe take on a new apprentice, making room for Joe's protégé to be the new workshop manager.'

As Colin was still, Toby carried on, 'If I might be so bold, Joe could have your office, and you might even put his name on the door.' Toby looked intently at Colin, hoping he hadn't gone too far.

A slow smile spread over Colin's face as he said, 'Thank you my boy for saving my most treasured employee from walking and maybe even saving the business I've built up.

'By heck, it takes an outsider to spot the errors and stop the slide.' Standing up, he said simply, 'Welcome to the family. I'm just about to go and see my new general manager and then get my accountant to come round to set things up. Use the phone if you've calls to make and drop the front latch when you go.' Tapping his pocket he confirmed, 'I've got my keys' and strode off purposely to his old office.

CHAPTER SEVENTEEN

Toby rang up Harry, saying he hadn't seen him for ages and asked how his beloved old Fiona was.

'Absolutely bloody marvellous,' cried Harry. 'What are you doing today?'

'Nothing,' replied Toby.

'Now you are, you lazy sod. You can come and help me move some young pheasants for the shoot.'

'Will do,' replied Toby, adding, 'if I do, any chance of you giving me a day's shooting? You might need a good gun to keep the figures up!'

'Ok, you cheeky bugger. Get you and your wheels up here, pronto.'

'Yes my lord. Course, you are not a lord yet, just getting in some practice on me,' and he left for Middleham.

Driving up the long pebble drive, he found several cars parked haphazardly by the huge oak door which was ajar. Toby, not knowing whether to knock or ring the bell-pull, poked his head around the door, just as his lordship was crossing the hall. Tommy spun round, yelling, 'There you are, dear boy. Wondered how you were getting along. You are just the chap I need. Had a case of a good malt sent down by one of my dear Scots pal.'

'Many thanks, Tommy but I think it's a maybe a wee bit early in the day.'

'Nonsense, dear boy, puts braggots in your step, so they say. Don't actually know what a braggot is,' retorted Tommy and steered Toby by the elbow into the study.

With a gleeful shriek at spotting Toby, Liz came out of another huge door, demanding, 'Where are you taking my second bestest man after you my dear,' delivering a smacking great kiss on Toby's cheek. Following them into what she called the den of iniquity, she pronounced, 'I'll have a nice chilled dry sherry, maybe La Ligna.'

Tommy, taking a bottle from the drinks fridge quickly filled a large schooner.

'Oh, is it party time?' squealed Jill as she came in, giving Toby a big hug and even a bigger kiss.

Tommy, pouring another sherry and thrusting it into Jill's hand grumbled, 'All we need now is my son and heir and we've got a pride.'

On cue, Harry came in crying, 'Who is taking my name in vain?' Pulling a bottle from the dozen or so on the sideboard, Tommy thrust a bottle into Harry's hands. 'Might as well make yourself useful,' he barked. 'Just a finger let us have a trial sniff. We can always go back to the well later! I trust it's as good as my friend says, after all I've got twelve bottles of the stuff.'

The stuff was a fifteen-year-old Lowland malt from Auchentoshan. 'They tell me it's triple-distilled for purity before being filled into old sherry casks.'

They all eyed it, sniffed, rolled it in their mouths before Tommy declared, 'that's damned good. What a palate.' Thrusting his empty glass at Harry, barked, 'Three more, club size, please barman. Now young Toby, tell us what you've been up to. Any luck with the horses?' He enquired a little too keenly. Toby filled them in with the racing and his hopes for confirmation of his property deal this Friday.

Suddenly Liz jumped up saying, 'If I don't have anything to eat, I'm going to get quite pissed. Who is for a rare beef sandwich and horseradish?'

'Nectar from the gods,' declared Harry. 'C'mon to the cantina.' After the splendid sandwiches in small brown baguettes, Harry led Toby off to sort the pheasants out. Toby, asking how the wedding preparations were going along, was put into giggles by Jill, who he discovered was a born mimic. Jill reckoned that father and son in their joint weddings and each other's best man were just like the Marks Brothers and wistfully she said, 'If only someone could get a Yorkshire Television crew to film it, it could be a super Christmas day show.'

Harry and Toby with the head keeper soon moved a few hundred young pheasants, now growing well up into houses with larger runs up in the woods ready for their later release in the pheasant shooting season.

On their way back Harry and the keeper exchanged looks and Harry announced, 'Here we are. Let's have a few clays, shall we?' Green, the head keeper pulled a couple of over and under shotguns and a couple of boxes of cartridges and stock of clays from his battered old Land Rover and set the trap up. Toby stood beside Harry who yelled, 'Pull' to Green in his dug out ahead and to the side.

Harry missed the first two, winged the next three, and then got into the rhythm. After a succession of kills he shouted, 'Ok, Green it's Toby's turn.' Toby loaded and balanced the unfamiliar gun in his hand before his turn to cry, 'Pull'.

He hit the first fair and square before going through his cartridges without a miss. No matter how Green tried to make the shots impossible to hit, Toby smashed them.

Green came out of his butt, and walking up to Toby, hand extended said, 'Well done sir that was one of the finest bits of shooting I've come across in many a year.

The only question I would ask is, can you translate that into a live days shooting?'

'I would like to think so Mr. Green,' smiled Toby.

Harry, waving a cheery 'Bye, see you and lovely Penny at the wedding', scattered off to tell Pa what Green had said of Toby's shooting.

**** **** ****

Toby wended his way back to the hotel, where he saw a transformed Jean just handing out keys to a couple heading up the stairs. Her hair was piled up in a bouffant style with a large silver pin through it. Earrings jangled onto a perfectly made-up face, from which her eyes sparkled and a perpetual smile hovered around full, pink lips.

'Hello Mr. Cooper,' she purred, handing him his key. 'I do hope you've had a good day.' Whispering she said, 'Thank you again. I think I've just awoken from a bad dream.

'I think it's better if we don't carry on our relationship. I hope you will understand. Please contact me in the future if I can ever help you,' handing him a card.

Toby murmured his thanks and went up to his room for a quick shower and to get changed. He was relieved and thankful for Jean's positive attitude and determination to get on with her life. He wished her well and was relieved that he wouldn't be in the position of cheating on Penny, with whom he really felt he wanted to spend the rest of his life.

He was pleased to see Walter at the bar with the boys. 'You'd better get another one for Toby on me,' Walter shouted to Lucy. Toby went over and shook hands with them in turn. As a pint of Best Bitter was shoved into his hand, he raised it to them all, toasting them with 'Happy Days'.

'Aye I'll gladly drink to that,' solemnly spoke Arthur the Chippy. 'There is enough miserable buggers round here' to a 'See who's talking' from the others.

'How are you Toby?' enquired Walter, noticing that Toby's pint was disappearing fast. 'Well, I've spent the afternoon chasing young pheasants around. Damned thirsty work.' He got another round in from Lucy. Handing over a pound note he told her to keep the change.

Talking to Walter, Toby asked him if it's all right to ring him tomorrow lunchtime from his solicitors, when he hoped he would have the planning permission and the completion date. 'I have cleared the decks so we can start a week on Monday and have a flatout four weeks' work. As soon as you tell me you've got planning for the new build, I can order diggers and cement mixers so we can get the foundations in.'

Toby, saying he was just off for a bite and he would see them soon, popped into the dining room which was half-full.

It was run like clockwork by a smart, cheerful Jean. All the regulars were chuffed at being lucky to have such a good new manageress. Toby, feeling peckish after a busy day ordered a sirloin steak, which was half a crown extra to the standard fixed menu.

He took a large malt up to bed, where he ran through all his details for what he hoped would be a big day in his life. He was soon nodding and putting his empty glass down was soon away in a deep sleep, to awake around 8.30.

He had a kipper and a pot of tea before ringing Kathy who apologised on Liam's behalf, blaming the young jockey. She told him of two today, at long odds but reckoned they had been trained for today and were jumping out of their skins at home.

Toby duly thanked her, rang Sylvia and going back to his room, slipped on his old tracksuit and putting a £20 note in the pocket climbed into his Land Rover.

He was soon at Ripon where he was amazed to get 12/1 in the 1.30 and 18/1 on the 3 o'clock, with £2.50 each way on each and the same on the double he had a fiver change.

He went through Tanfield, turning right he found a small track. Ditching the Land Rover, he chugged on for about 3 miles, turning back on a loop to arrive back at his track. He had passed a pretty, working water mill, which had about 10 worker's cottages on the roadside and a further ten with a huge stone storage barn. In between was a fine, ivy-clad mullioned house, dominating to one side, obviously the mill owner's house.

As he paused to admire it, a couple of old codgers were passing. He greeted them with a cheery 'Good morning'. 'Morning,' they dourly replied. 'It's a pity, int it, bout the old mill,' said one.

'Aye,' chirped in the other. 'It's been working all them years, and now we hear tell that the boss Mr. Smith is thinking about selling up. Might be a while, like, but as his wife passed away, I reckon he's no heart in it.'

'Isn't it just a corn mill?' asked Toby.

'Oh, aye, but some the finest flour for that shop in London, Fortune and Mason or sommat, like that! Aye and for the Queen. They're real proud of their royal warint.'

Toby wishing them goodbye jogged off to find the Land Rover. After changing in the back and towelling himself off, he was soon on the road. I'm getting like ruddy gypsy, he told himself. He parked up behind Simon's office, and as it was just after 11.00, browsed round a few shops, even going into the covered markets with its many butchers and fish merchants. Stepping into Simon's office just before 12, the receptionist whisked him straight through to Simon.

'You OK?' asked Simon.

'Matter of fact, feel a bit like when you've been summoned to the headmaster's study. Feel a bit jittery. Simon old bean, you have everything in place? Got my money? No last minute cock ups, or problems we didn't expect?'

'Nope,' replied Simon. As soon as the Water Board tells me to complete, I can do it.'

The phone rang and Simon answered, Toby recognised Maggie's voice on the other end. Simon told her he had Mr. Cooper with him and asked if it would be in order to put the call on loud-speak. Having got the agreement from Mrs. Williams, he flicked a switch on his expensive-looking desk audio system and Maggie's voice filled the room. She told them that the board's meeting had just finished and she had been instructed to inform Mr. Simpson that his client, Mr. Cooper, offered to purchase both cottages, fifty acres of land and that full planning consent to erect a four bedroom, detached farm house had been granted. Could Mr. Simpson complete next Friday, and could he get Mr. Cooper to sign, include the agreed cheque from his firm, we can process it. Toby spoke, 'Mrs.

Williams, I can make time this afternoon to bring the documents to you if that would help to speed things up?'

'That would be kind, Mr. Cooper, if you can get it in this afternoon I can bank the cheque tonight and give you the receipts and deeds for Mr. Simpson.'

As Toby handed over the papers to Maggie around 2.30 she said, 'I hope you'll invite Karen and I to your housewarming ,as it is Karen you really have to thank for getting the consent through so quickly.'

'I know. I owe you both a lot. Please pass on my kindest regards to Karen,' giving her a swift kiss. He then returned to Simon with all the documents and the receipt for him, telling Simon, 'I'm turning into a bloody carrier pigeon.'

Shaking his hand Simon murmured, 'Congratulations, you've got a real bargain, but what beats me is how the hell you got planning permission so quickly. I'll have to get the firm to agree to get you a commission to speed things for us. Give me a ring next week, old boy and I will arrange to give you the keys. I suppose you want me to keep the deeds and all the correspondence?'

Agreeing, Toby left, and scuttled into the bookies to find that the 12/1 horse had just been beaten into second by a nose, whilst the 18/1 horse had led from start to finish. Pocketing the £78 odd, he reflected not bad as he had made a clear £63 profit.

He rang Walter and told him he was completing a week today, and would then have the keys. 'Right,' said Walter, 'you collect me at mine next Saturday. Say ten a clock sharp and we will have a run over and go over it all again with plans. We'll have a right set to and get everything sorted out, and our timings agreed.'

'Good man,' returned Toby. 'Look forward to seeing you then.'

**** **** ****

Back at the garage, Toby was just filling up when Joe came over, wiping his hands on an oily rag. He said with a grin, 'I suppose it's you I have to thank for this,' pointing to a shiny badge with 'General Manager' on his sand coloured overalls.

'No,' said Toby. 'It's you, you have to thank for all the hard graft you've put in over all the years.'

'Well, thanks anyway,' muttered Joe. 'Hey up, wasn't it today that you were due to hear if you'd got your offer accepted?'

'Yes, you remember well, Joe. I've just heard I complete a week today. Then I'll really have to get working. My two cottages are to be knocked into one, and a new build house, all by Christmas!'

'Oh, come on, you love being active under pressure. You'll love every minute of it!'

'I think you are right,' giving Joe a gentle nudge.

He parked round the back, going in to meet an enquiring Colin and Penny.

'Well?' queried Colin. 'Get us out of our suspense.'

'Yes, I'm on!' shouted a proud Toby. 'Next week we complete, and work starts in earnest next Monday.' Penny hugged and kissed him whilst Colin popped open a champagne bottle crying, 'Congratulations to your new home. Who knows, I might be able to get rid of the pair of you and have my house to myself,' with a large wink and pat on the back to Toby.

**** **** ****

On Sunday, Toby went to the address Maggie had given and Silas had agreed on. A large, round, pleasant farmer's wife confided she was Barry's mum and he were that put out at not getting the cottage. He'd just finished milking and he'd be down at the pub, spending all his hard earned brass, she scolded. Toby said he'd been recommended by a friend that her Barry was just the man for a job he had in mind.

219

Toby popped down to the pub and soon found Barry at the bar with a pretty girl called Sally. He introduced himself, buying a round and told them about him buying both cottages and getting planning to build a new house. 'Bloody hell,' exclaimed Barry. 'I was scratching about trying to get a mortgage on one, resentfully!'

'Also,' said Toby, 'I managed to buy another fifteen acres. That's a total of 50; makes it viable. I've plans for a chicken unit, Christmas tree growing and a few acres of malting barley.' Barry's eyes were like saucers.

'But why are you telling me all this?' a hint of rancour, almost anger starting to bubble. Sally laid her hand on his, calming him.

'Because,' said Toby 'I was hoping you'd come and join me.'

There was a stunned silence, whilst it sank into Barry. His eyes darted between Toby and Sally, who asked 'What exactly do you have in mind?'

'I would like to offer Barry the job of running the whole thing. I will put in all the dead stock and livestock, pay Barry a weekly or monthly wage. He in turn would pay to live in the new house, which I would like him to build alongside my building team. Barry would pay all his electricity, fuel used. I'll let him have my old Land Rover when I take delivery of my new one. Oh, a last point, when we do the books, and hopefully get a net profit, I'll share it with you, Barry. If you can make economies, and save, you benefit.'

Sally said in amazement 'I'm a farmer's daughter and we both know how hard, no, impossible it is to get a start.' Looking full on at Toby she said, 'I want to marry Barry, but until now, we can't. I trust you Mr. Cooper, I'm not normally wrong. I think you are a good, honest man, but maybe a dangerous one too!'

Toby looking at Barry quietly and asked, 'When can you start?'

Flushing, Barry asked, 'When do you want me to?'

They all laughed and Toby shook two hard worker's hands of Sally and Barry and said, 'I'm popping up to the place on Saturday with my girlfriend Penny and my builder around 11.00. Can you both meet up with us then? That's if you want to take the job,' hedged Toby.

'If he doesn't,' cried Sally 'I'll first break his bloody neck, and come myself!' hushing Barry as an anxious mum would to a child just about to have a tantrum. She carried on, 'Honestly Barry, it's a no-brainer. We'd have all we ever dreamed of, plus having a kind fairy godmother,' looking at Toby with her wide, blue trusting eyes. 'I don't think any lady has called me a fairy before, but I take it as a yes then.'

Flinging her arms round him and planting a soft moist kiss on his cheek, whilst blushing, all at the same time she affirmed, 'Yes, yes, yes. Thank you for a life-changing offer for which we both thank you, and promise to never let you down.'

'No, never,' chorused Barry, pumping Toby's hand, and Toby knew he'd got the right man.

Sally, with her wide, slightly moist blue eyes looked at Toby and Barry saying, 'It's funny how things work, isn't it. I mean Barry, poor lamb, was so distraught when he hadn't got the offer, but you see if you had love,' patting his arm 'You'd have had to scratch and scrimp. You couldn't really make 5 or even 10 acres pay. But now you've got the opportunity of a lifetime. Now we can get married, and have some crops of our own,' to cries of laughter all around. Barry and Sally agreed to meet up with Toby on Saturday and Barry would join the gang at the property a week on Monday to start work.

**** **** ****

The next week dragged by, but on Wednesday Simon told him to come and collect the keys lunchtime Friday, as the place would be his. The keys turned out to be four socking great brown rusty things on two plastic rings. They looked worthy of at least a castle keep, not two little cottages.

On Saturday morning, joined by an excited Penny and Walter, Toby drove back to the cottages. It seemed ages since he had last seem them, but now it was with a strange, satisfied feeling of ownership.

He and Walter weighed up where the new build would be, pacing it out and putting four stones at the corners. It looked quite big, they both agreed.

Penny, who'd never set foot in the cottage before, skipped from one cottage to the other, exploring like a little girl, while the man again paced out.

Walter measured and muttered as he wrote and sketched in his large notebook. 'They've got a definite charm and potential to make one smashing house,' declared Penny and peering over Walter's shoulder she pulled back a lock of golden hair from her face and squealed, 'Wow Walter. They are fantastic,' as she looked aghast at his neat sketches of how each room would look.

'Oh, here you've got two archways either side of a big open fire which opens onto both rooms. Very clever. A long sitting room with French doors onto the veranda, and a cosy well-lit dining room. And here,' jabbing her finger, 'you've got a farmhouse kitchen-diner with a big utility room, a rear lobby with a downstairs cloakroom and shower. I love the way you've made one wide, imposing stairway to a good sized landing which can take a small sofa. Here exactly are three double en-suite bedrooms. Absolutely spot on! Walter,' giving him a huge hug and a big kiss, 'you are an absolute genius. Oh, look at that,' as she turned and looked through the front windows,' 'that view is to die for.'

It truly was spectacular. The expanse of blue water and the gently sloping grass from the house to the water's edge. 'Waterside,' she breathed. 'What a beautiful name for such a beautiful place!'

'How do we set about it Walter?' Toby quietly asked him.

'I think,' replied Walter pensively, 'to start off, we'll split into two teams.' At that point, a loud knock on the door announced the arrival of Sally and Barry. Walter had known Barry since he was knee-high to a grass-hopper. Soon they all seemed to be happy working together.

**** **** ****

The week dragged slowly by, but at last Toby collected Barry and young Paul, and was on site at quarter to eight. A trail of vans and cars wended its way up to the cottages, led by Walter, who jumped out and introduced everyone to each other. Then introducing Toby, he asked, 'As you've volunteered to be a 'go for' and work with us as one of the lads,' he scratched his head, 'do we call you boss, gov, or what?'

'Just call me Toby. But let's get it straight from the start. I'm not snooping or checking, but both Barry and I will be living here and we want to cut costs by two pairs of extra hands and learn how our houses are built.'

At that moment Mike Mortimer clambered out of his car, carrying rolls of plans, and a sort of artist's easel stuck under his arms.

To Toby's pleasant surprise, Barry darted over to take all the equipment from a grateful Mike. Walter clapped his hands shouting, 'Cardinal sin! Come on, what's the first thing we do on site?'

'A brew,' came from all sides. Mysteriously, a gas bottle, under a large burner was set up with a huge stainless steel urn sited on top; it was filled from a Jerry can of fresh water, and was soon boiling. Tin mugs appeared from which tea bag strings dangled. A crate of bottled milk appeared from a van along with a large white sugar caddy.

As Mike set up his display board and maps, they all gathered round, piping hot, strong tea mugs in hand. Mike and Walter did a double act first, showing the new build. 'Now, what we are going to do is split into two teams.

'Bert and Toby to work on the cottages, mainly demolishing walls down, doors, stairs out, the lot. I'll show you.

'I'll take Arthur to do the shuttering for the concreting. Paul and Barry will first mark out with Mike, as the diggers will be here in an hour or two.

'I've got the cement mixers here on Wednesday. We're lucky lads, it's forecast sun for the next few weeks, so I want to get the footings in, walls up, roof on and water tight in two months, that's the end of August.'

Seeing Toby looking a bit miffed, Bert took him aside, saying 'Don't fret Toby, we'll soon have them walls down, RSJs in. I love building, but I think I like knocking stuff down as well. You haven't got to be precise like, and you can get rid of all your pent-up anger!'

Later as the pair set to follow precise marks chalked on the walls by Mike and Walter, Toby thought that Bert must have a lot of 'pent-up anger', such was the ferocity of his attack. They got along fine, virtually completing the downstairs in a day. Whenever a problem or snag crept up, so did Walter with whatever extra help they needed.

**** **** ****

Two weeks flew by and Toby realised Tommy's and Harry's wedding was upon them. Penny had hired a morning suit from Allen's in Harrogate, complete with black silk topper. That Friday evening they all enjoyed the lovely mixed grill that Penny had cooked. Colin and Margot told them how thrilled they were to being invited to his lordship's wedding.

Toby slipped out of the room, to quickly re-appear with a silly grin, and holding something behind his back, dropped onto one knee behind Penny's back as she washed up.

'Darling,' he called. She shrieked as she saw him, a tea towel in her hand and soapsuds on her cheek.

Colin and Margot stood beside each other, rooted to the spot. 'Darling,' asked Toby again, 'Will you marry me?'

The tea towel dropped, her hand went to her mouth, as Toby was up on his feet, a little box open revealing a diamond and sapphire ring, twinkling in the overhead light.

'Oh yes, yes, yes please.' Anything else was cut out as Toby's mouth found hers and gave her such a long, passionate kiss that Colin coughed, Margot felt a slight pang of jealousy, realising she was never kissed like that.

Congrats flew as did the cork from a rather rare Rose Bollinger that Colin had kept for his little girl.

CHAPTER EIGHTEEN

They set off in good time for the wedding the following morning in an open-topped Bentley that Colin had borrowed from a friend in the trade.

Joe and Chris followed behind in Colin's Jag, and as neither was invited, Chris hoped to find a spare seat and then Joe and she would drive the Bentley back.

At the church door they presented their invitations, Toby striding in with Penny and a bewildered Chris followed by Joe. Toby picked up a pile of order sheets, giving them to Chris he hissed, 'Just smile and when asked bride or groom, say bride and sit at the back. He gave them a sheet each, moving to the front with Penny. He spotted an attractive, well-dressed, middle-aged woman sitting alone in the front on the bride's side.

Stooping down he introduced Penny and himself, Margot and Colin. He learned that Hermione was Liz's mother, a former debutante, who had married a well-known bloodstock agent and racing manager. They travelled the world together buying and selling expensive horses for wealthy clients. Andy, her ex was a very serious womaniser. The marriage only lasted for two years after Elizabeth was born.

The church was packed. Well-dressed guests were cramming in like sardines. As Chris was nipped in between Penny and Colin, Toby squeezed a little nearer Hermione. This didn't seem to disturb her. With Penny crammed up tight to him, Toby was in heaven having two beautiful women on each side with expensive scent discreetly washing across him.

The choir paused. The vicar standing at the lectern smiled as people shuffled to their feet as the wedding march boomed from the huge organ.

Heads craned to catch a glimpse of Liz and her father, Jill and her farmer father John followed them down the aisle. His lordship standing by Liz, whilst on the other side

Harry closed up to Jill. The service was normal to the point of actual vows, when Harry dug into his waistcoat pocket for two rings which he placed on the Bible. After exchanging vows Tommy placed a single gold band on Liz's finger, she in turn placing the other ring on Tommy's finger. After pronouncing them man and wife, and kissing, the vicar repeated the same ceremony with Harry and Jill.

At the church door, the crowds of people who couldn't get in were waving and cheering as Tommy and Liz squeezed into a chauffeur-driven black Rolls Royce parked back to back with an identical one into which Harry and Jill took off in slowly. One car going one way, the other in the opposite direction to tour the estate before arriving at the castle.

This gave all the guests time to go directly to the castle, the ladies powder their noses, the men having a much-needed smoke or pee, or both. They all waited in a huge phalanx around the front door. The two Rolls now decanted the brides and grooms. They trooped up the wide, stone steps as Tommy's Regimental Band of the Blues struck up with the grand march from Aida, which had been played at Tommy's commissioning ceremony, those many years ago. After ten minutes, to allow both couples to freshen up, the guests entered the imposing double doors to be received by Tommy, Liz, Harry, Jill and the in-laws.

As there were over 120 guests, Tommy had told old McDonald, his butler, to whisk the buggers through. 'No chatting, that can come later. At fifteen seconds each we can get them through in half an hour.'

No one worried about a delay before the meal, as so many friends and relations had so much to catch up on. The champagne flowed like a river. Looking around Toby wondered if some of the young would stay the course at their present rate of consumption. They passed on into the huge Baronial Dining Room. Flags, pennants, shields and suits of armour glinted in the sunlight falling on the mellow stonewalls. Guests were seated at ten round tables taking twelve each, decorated in pink damask tablecloths.

Glassware and silver gleamed. It really was a worthy of a film set.

At the top table were seated both brides and grooms, their respective father and mother, plus of course the bridesmaids. The lunch was a sumptuous affair with choices of soup, fish, main, dessert and savoury courses.

The outstanding course was the two huge pink ribs of beef carved from the two trolleys. After the loyal toast, decanters of port were passed down the table from right to left, as in the army.

Waiters brought a selection of cigarettes and cigars around. McDonald, banging his dinner gong, announced there would be a fifteen minutes recess before the speeches.

He thanked the band who had played a medley of oldies, sixties music, classical, and military music throughout lunch. Everyone stood, clapping and cheering as the grateful band left for the bar. No doubt the music would be louder on their return for dancing after the speeches.

Toby approached Hermione at the top table on his way out. 'How are you doing? Do you need anything?'

'A good man would be a start,' she smiled mischievously.

'Tell you what, would you come and join our table after the speeches?'

'That's so kind of you, I'll take you up on that,' she smiled.

As people left the room, the staff moved all the tables to the outer walls, complete with their gold chairs. 'It just looks like an up-market dance hall,' observed Toby to Penny.

'I know, but just look at all the space left in the middle for dancing.'

**** **** ****

When everyone had returned, with freshly-charged glasses and blue curling cigar smoke slowly drifting to the beamed ceiling, Tommy rose and made the most fantastic speech Toby had ever heard.

The man was the most accomplished raconteur, holding the entire gathering including attending waiters and waitress in his hands as he went from laughter to pathos. 'God,' whispered Penny, 'I wish I had one of those recorder things.'

'I reckon,' whispered back Toby, 'If the BBC heard him, they'd give him a Saturday show.'

He brought in Harry, who amazingly enough, had come out of his shell. Toby wondered if the drink had contributed, but he was a chip of the old block. Just like his father. No notes or prompts. They went into a duo, reminding everyone of the Marx bros.

They brought the entire room to a standing, cheering ovation. Harry raised both hands to heaven. 'Haven't finished yet,' to cries of 'Good-o, get on with it.'

They did, Tommy telling the tale of the young chap out hunting for the first time.

Harry responded by telling how in his last term at Eton he'd been persuaded to join the Masons, and how they'd always impressed on him the need to have a good tale. One he could tell at the drop of a hat, if ever he was invited to 'sing for his supper'.

Tommy wound up with two more risqué tales he'd picked up at his club, to his sobbing eye-mopping guests, who rose as one to stamp their feet and cheered, demanding an encore. Tommy raised a hand to the band who had crept in. They were lucky to catch his last two tales, which had rendered them as helpless as everyone else. To a fantastic rendition of 'All you need is love' Tommy clutched a wide-eyed Liz to him. He was closely followed by Harry and Jill, they erupted into a great rock. Soon the floor was packed with a rocking and rolling throng. The men, ties undone, jackets off were whirling like dervishes. It became one ginormous 'excuse me' with

229

couples changing partners halfway through each new piece from the band.

Penny was whisked away by Tommy, so Toby danced for a while with Liz before Harry grabbed her and was off into the mass. Liz's father, the bloodstock agent grabbed Jill from Toby, who found himself with Hermione, who making the excuses of needing a drink returned to their empty table with Toby. The music being loud, they sat close. So close that Toby was sure he could feel the bobble of her suspender through his thin morning suit trousers.

She knew what she was doing as she wrinkled her nose telling him her story. She looked round before whispering, 'Thank you for giving Liz so much fun and love. She told me all about it. 'I,' she paused, 'envy her.' Her hand stroked his thigh and moving slowly round up found a half-rampant Tom. Huskily she confessed, 'It's been so long, since you know,' her low voice trailing off.

Everyone was still dancing, apart from a few old fossils, their backs turned to them while they huddled close together to gossip. Silently, but unseen Toby took her by the hand and slipped out of the door behind them. Unseen, apart from the beady set of eyes of Lionel 'Lino Moore'.

**** **** ****

Toby opened a door to what was a large storeroom. Putting an old chair under the handle, Toby took Hermione in his arms and kissed her hard and passionately.

She tugged the zip at the back of her dress and eased it over her shoulders to reveal two firm mounds clad in a fine black silk bra.

Toby reached behind and neatly unclipped her bra which fell down to the floor. She giggled and pulled her dress up to her waist, revealing a tight black lacy thong. Her legs were long and slender with the firm muscular thighs befitting a top horsewoman.

Toby had unzipped his trousers tugging down his boxers in one fluid movement.

For a moment they stared at each other their eyes raking each other in animal lust.

With a deft movement Toby's hand beneath her head, the other beneath her stockinged thighs, he heaved her onto the table in the middle of the room.

As he lifted her legs over his shoulders she pulled her thongs off to reveal a mass of soft black hair. As obviously she had no man to trim it for, it was naturally untrimmed which always turned Toby on. She was already wet, as he slid Tom in. It was a half moan, half anguished cry coming from her as Tom went deeper and quicker. Both of them in a hurry. This was pure raw sex with no romantic feelings. Her firm stomach arched to an even quicker rhythm, Tom plunging deeper and faster, until they both erupted in series of orgasms.

'God, that was my quickest ever,' said Toby. 'I'll be worried about premature ejaculation next.'

'Not you, dear boy. That was perfect timing. You've made an old bird extremely happy. Must admit, that's some weapon you have there, biggest I've seen this side of Suez!

Come down and visit me at my stables any time. I'm damned sure I could make a packet from charging stud fees for you from all the frustrated ladies in our neck of the woods.'

Bra fastened, she reached out to large packet of paper napkins and grabbing one, wiped herself dry. 'Want one?' she thrust one towards Toby, who taking it wiped the tired, limp Tom. Taking both napkins, she delicately dropped them into a waste bin beside the door.

Her dress smoothed, she powdered her face, fluffed out her hair. 'Is thanks too small a word?' she asked, looking at Toby. 'It was one of the best, I've known, I would love to have you for a night.'

Putting her finger to her lips and to him she whispered, 'No names,' to which Toby returned, 'No pack drill.' They

231

both giggled, fellow conspirators, that they were. Toby quietly removed the chair and sliding the door open and seeing the coast was clear, motioned her out.

She amazed him as she head held high she stalked down to the ballroom. He went the other way, turning the corner he ran into a maid wheeling a trolley full of rubbish. Pleading he was lost, she soon directed him back towards the ballroom. Grabbing a drink from a passing waiter, he strolled into the melee.

The waitress pushed the storeroom open with her trolley and stopped in her tracks, sniffing. It's perfume, she told herself, but what's that other, earthy, sweaty smell? Suddenly it hit her. It was that smell when she and her Eric had it off.

'Bloody hell,' she said to herself, that hoity-toity woman that had just passed her was sniffing of that perfume. 'Bloody hell,' she muttered again to herself as she realised Mrs. Hoity-Toity was the bride's mother, the mother of Lady Elizabeth Middleham.

Hermione, much to her irritation, had been grabbed by a balding, ferrety, pop-eyed little man who had introduced himself as Lionel Moore. He tried to impress her, as he was somewhat of a tycoon, owning six carpet, curtain and lino emporiums spread across North Yorkshire.

**** **** ****

As Toby and Penny fought their way around the crowded floor, they were constantly stopped for Penny to show off her engagement ring. Toby told Penny of a similar occasion in the army.

All too soon both brides and grooms slipped away to change, re-appearing at the top of the grand stairway. They marched one behind the other, to cheers, applause and Ribald comments before they drove off in tandem. The Lord and Lady Middleham to Barbados. An old school chum of Tommy's owned a lodge, one of some twelve at Settlers Beach for their three weeks honeymoon.

Harry and Jill were going on a Greek Islands cruise on a yacht lent to Harry from a friend, in exchange for shooting days on some of the best Grouse Moors.

It was an age before Colin and Margot, Toby and Penny set off for home. The goodbyes, huge kisses, the exchanging of telephone numbers hastily and almost illegibly scrawled into diaries took forever.

**** **** ****

As they floated through the still countryside, the sun casting a golden light, the car roof open, they could smell the leaves and wildflowers. The sun warmed up old Mother Earth for what looked like another glorious day. Penny snuggling up to Toby, gazed up at an azure blue sky and murmured, 'Let's have a late barbeque instead of Sunday lunch. We can invite Chris and Joe.'

'Agreed,' cried Colin with relish. Like many a man, he loved to show off his BBQ skills.

'Big Bwana,' Penny used to call him. They all slept the sleep of the dead, emerging to a late breakfast of bloody Marys and strong, black coffee.

Colin produced chicken thighs, sirloin steaks and plump pork sausages. The girls had chilled the Pimm's and Sancerre laying a red-and-white gingham-covered table. They rustled up a fresh fruit salad, with stilton to finish. It was dusk before they called it a day.

Toby muttered, 'I'd forgotten, I'm a working man now, have to be on site before the lads at quarter to eight.'

'Show me your lily-white hands then,' asked Joe. Toby opened up both palms to an incredulous Joe. 'They really look 10 years older! Old Walter must be working you.'

'Never been happier,' chipped back Toby. 'It's great to create something. See it rise before your eyes. Know it's all for us,' smiling and cuddling Penny.

'I'm proud of you lad,' from Colin.

'Me too,' endorsed Margot. 'You, a decorated ex-officer, working with your hands as a labourer with your builders. It takes some beating.'

'It's easy,' replied Toby. 'They are all such honest, genuine, straight forward blokes.'

After a quick cuddle Toby was soon away in the land of nod, dreaming of another day.

**** **** ****

Toby was amazed at the amount of work they had accomplished by the time Lord and Lady Middleham had returned from their nuptials.

While he and Bert had worked on Waterside, the rest of the team had all the outer walls of the new house built ready to take the new roof trusses, which would be delivered on 12th August. The glorious twelfth.

Both Tommy and Harry were busy shooting clays, to get their eye-in and also practicing changeovers with their loaders. They swapped over their guns, having taken the two shots, for a second gun just filled by their loaders.

Tommy made it looked like a ballet. The whole operation made in a fluid movement. With a covey of maybe eight grouse travelling at speed like little black dots, two cartridges would be fired, the guns swapped over and the shooter turning in a graceful arc, swinging through the fleeing birds to hopefully take another two.

After a couple of days the trusses were in place, roofing felt firmly attached and waiting for the tiling team to finish before moving on to complete Waterside.

Toby was constantly surprised at Walter who had organised and pushed his men to be just ready for the next part of the operation to take place in an uninterrupted flow. A bit like maestro conducting his orchestra, thought Toby.

Barry broke into his reverie by saying, 'I don't know about you Toby, but look at this,' he waved both outstretched arms in an arc between Waterside and his

234

house. 'It makes me real proud to feel I've helped make it happen.'

'Me too, Barry,' said Toby a lump in his throat.

They were on their own as was usual most evenings when the boys went home. Barry would stay on, unpaid to help Toby with any last minute jobs that wanted finishing or tidying the place up.

They had both agreed with a laugh, weeks ago, that builders as a breed were mucky, untidy buggers. A bit like chefs, Barry had thought. 'They all ponce about like prima donnas, wanting continued applause, and then don't clear their mess up.'

Sally had come to pick Barry up as she had to borrow the Land Rover to visit her mother in hospital. Barry proudly showed her the work to date.

Locking up at Waterside, straddling the crest of the hill, she said, 'I think it's ever such a lovely name. What should we call ours?'

Both Sally and Barry bandied various names back and forth until an exasperated Sally turned to Toby asking, 'What do you think, Toby?'

'Nothing seems quite right.' Mumbling a few names under his breath he clicked his fingers, saying 'Let's keep it simple, it's a farm and I know Sally will create a gorgeous home. There you are,' looking at Sally. 'Home Farm.' A little tear came into Sally's eye as she hugged both Toby and Barry, saying, 'There is such a lovely, warm ring to it. I'll go and buy a name plaque to go on the gate beside the cattle grid to the main road.'

When she dropped Barry off in the morning she confided how great the name was. Even dad who was a bit of a miserable old codger thought it was good.

Barry upended an old tea chest which she quickly covered with a red table cloth that she had brought with her, instantly turning it into a little table. A similar cloth covered a large object she placed under it. All the lads were pouring in and started putting tea bags and milk into their mugs.

Sally said shyly, 'Toby came up with a name for our new house last night, and I've brought a little something to toast it with,' and whipping away the table cloth covering the mound to reveal a large dark chocolate cake, with the words Home Farm.

**** **** ****

Now, first Waterside then Home Farm got the window treatment. New dark hardwood, double glazed windows were fitted by the contractor men, with the skilled 'Chippy' Arthur overseeing every fitting. He and Walter hung all the internal doors, and the solid oak external doors. Both properties were made watertight and safe whilst the electricians and plumbers, watched by an ever vigilant Walter, completing their jobs, work continued on outside.

Toby persuaded a reluctant Silas to accept a generous fee to work with Barry and prepare the land.

Christmas trees were ordered at various stages of growth from selected growers and planted.

The front field had been cleared, ploughed, and planted with winter wheat as a first crop.

After seeing many chicken units, they made a deal with a well-respected firm who would supply and erect a chicken-growing unit. They would supply day-old chicks, Barry would rear them to the size and weight required by the company, who would then take them away paying a decent net return on Barry's time and rearing costs. Barry was really enthusiastic, claiming, 'It paid better than dairy cows, and you are getting regular payments at a fixed time, better than a milk cheque!'

Penny and Toby fixed their wedding for the 2nd of December, to coincide with Penny's birthday. The aim was to get Waterside absolutely finished, painted, curtains up, carpets laid by then.

Their two-week honeymoon, which they'd selected after pouring through endless travel agents, was a Lords Bros air cruise to Spain and Morocco.

All the furniture, soft furnishings and paintings would be delivered and put in the place by Chris and Sally from the plans drawn up by Penny and Chris. They had kindly agreed to make up the beds, fill all the drawers and generally make everything ready for Toby and Penny's return on the 18th December.

Chris and Sally would learn to 'drive' the Aga, and get used to its foibles to pass on to Penny.

A family Christmas was planned for the 25th. Toby and Penny had invited Colin and Margot, Barry and Sally, Joe and Chris. 'Eight just right,' chirped Penny, who had bought a round oak dining table from Thompson, the mouse man.

They had planned a house warming party three days before for all those involved, plus family and friends.

Penny hugged herself with delight, like a little girl. 'Oh,' she said, 'It's going to be a wonderful time.'

True to his word, Walter handed over both houses fully completed and ready to move into by the end of November, and was fully paid by a grateful Toby.

**** **** ****

The wedding was a much simpler affair then his Lordship's. After a ceremony at Masham Church, they went onto have lunch at a new hotel/restaurant that had received great reviews after its chef had just gained his first Michelin Star.

Toby, at considerable expense had booked the whole hotel, which boasted a beautiful, light conservatory, which easily seating Toby's 60 guests. His Lordship and Lady Elizabeth, accompanied by Harry and Jill were chief guests.

Toby's witty but brief address was matched by Colin who was in good form. Joe as best man was short but funny, and apt from a man who had never spoken in public before. His nerves he had controlled he told Chris later, were kept under wraps because of his desire to not let Toby down. 'That was really sweet of you love,' she had said giving him a well-deserved kiss.

Toby had kept the entertainment till the last, when he asked Tommy if he would care to say a few words. There was no stopping him. He jumped up and again, without notes spoke for about half an hour. It was like a cabaret as he recounted tales no one heard before. As many of his tenants were present in addition to all locals, he brought in everyone in a much earthier, ribald humour.

The whole room rose to applaud and cheer him, the majority with tears of laughter streaming down their cheeks. Mascara was running down many a female face. The general consensus among the working fraternity was that, 'Eee, his Lordship's a right caution!

After changing, Toby and Penny bade everyone farewell as they left in Colin's Jaguar for their first night to be spent at The Old Swan in Harrogate. They would leave the next day for a lovely thatched country pub where they would leave the jag safely locked up before being collected by a chauffeur driven Daimler, provided by the tour operators to whisk them the 60 odd miles to Heathrow for the start of their two week Air Tour.

Penny said pouring through the brochure, 'I just can't believe we are going to so many exotic places! Seville, Marrakesh, Casablanca, Tenerife, Lanzarote, Bordeaux and home. Home, sweet home.'

They left on a dry, sunny day with a nip in the air to return bronzed and totally relaxed to find there had been an overnight ground frost.

The trip home seemed to go on for ever, despite them using the new section of motorway that had been built.

Penny just couldn't contain her excitement, as Chris had told her on the phone the night before that they would expect them late afternoon. Yes, everything was ready and that she and Sally had prepared a game pie for supper.

As they swept into the open gateway, the lights of Home Farm twinkled to their right. Going up their tree lined drive they glimpsed lights beckoning from the solid mass of Waterside above them.

A sharp hoot of the horn brought a beaming Chris and Sally out of the front door. Splash of warm golden light onto the pebble drive-way. After hugs and kisses all round, Toby gathered up Penny in his arms and strode over the threshold.

Standing her on her feet he kissed her, saying, 'Welcome to Waterside, Mrs. Cooper.'

After gathering their suitcases, Toby followed them into the hall. He followed a squealing Penny, who first darted into the downstairs cloakroom, before peeking into the laundry room where the two solemn eyes of the washing machine and dryer dolefully looked back at them.

The lights gleamed on the large, deep freezer. Tripping into the kitchen, even Toby stopped in his tracks.

The warm Aga seemed to greet them, as did the homely game pie aroma. The curtains that Penny had chosen fitted in so well, as did the tiles, and prints on the walls.

The soft lighting glinted on the rank of the latest kitchen gadget. The Kenwood mixer, electric toaster, microwave.

Penny loved the round oak table in the corner set for two in the Portmeirion pottery she had bought for all occasions, general and dinner parties she planned to hold.

They went hand in hand into the dining room with its twin arches either side of the central fireplace, which served both the dining and sitting room.

They could feel the warmth from the large logs burning steadily in the open fire basket.

'Sorry, it's a bit extravagant,' admitted Sally, 'but we wanted to show you it at its best. Besides,' she continued, 'it keeps this end really snug.'

The sitting room was finished in a warm, cheerful, pale yellow. The curtains to the double French doors were half open, allowing the light to show up the pale Yorkshire paving of the terrace beyond.

After running up the wide oak staircase, they checked the bedrooms and bathrooms to find that they had all been made up, towels and soap out.

On going into their room they found the twin bedside lights casting a soft glow onto the huge bed. Its top sheet turned down with a soft frilly nighty laid on one side, whilst on the other was a huge red question mark above the head.

'What?' screeched Toby, brandishing the question mark as he shot down the stairs two at a time, to discover not only Sally and Chris, but Joe, Barry, Colin and Margot.

Self-consciously holding the question mark above his head 'What do you mean by this?' to the girls. 'I hope you are not referring that I bat for the other side?' to guffaws and giggles Chris said, 'Not at all but we didn't know whether you slept in pyjama or au naturel.'

Toby gave her a playful slap on the bottom as he said, 'Pour me a stoop of ale, or flagon of wine, you cheeky wench, and all will be forgiven!'

'I have better than that to offer you sir,' cried Colin opening the large American-style fridge. On one side of the double doors were staked rows of white, rose and champagne.

'Golly,' exclaimed Toby. 'It'll take a van load to stock this lot up and a healthy bank account.' After welcoming them safely home and blessing their new home, they all left saying, 'You'll need time to be together to explore everything.'

Chris was the last to go after washing up the glasses and placing the steaming game pie, a separate dish of vegetable and a dinky little jug of piping hot gravy. 'Enjoy yourselves, and again, welcome home,' she said disappearing quickly before they could thank her.

After demolishing the superb pie, they cleared up and wandered from room to room.

'You've done a tremendous job, love,' affirmed Toby. 'Your eye for detail and colours is absolutely spot on. I love the blend of new furniture and antique. Choosing some old sofas and chairs and getting them re-upholstered in modern fabrics, is a genius. I know the whole lot came in at a fraction touch of buying from the big retailers.'

They looked up, turning out all the lights, mounted the stairs, hand in hand. Toby dimmed their bathroom light, drew a deep, warm bath into which he tipped sweet smelling salts. After slowly undressing each other, they climbed into the luxurious water at opposite ends of the bath.

After soaping and drying each other, they climbed into their new bed, making slow, passionate love until falling asleep.

CHAPTER NINETEEN

Over the next few days Toby was busy with Silas and Barry, as they finished off outside.

The Christmas trees were all planted in their degrees of height, and row of lime trees lined each side of the driveway. Now all the heavy equipment and builders had gone. Toby asphalted the concrete drive and as it was drying, scattered it with pebbles. Hopefully they would never come loose, nor need endless raking, but more importantly never allow weeds to grow.

The chicken unit was in place, feed hoppers full and ready for the first batch of birds in the New Year.

In-lamb ewes grazed the fields down to the road, waiting to be mums in spring.

Sally, who had specialised in horticulture at collage, had got the large greenhouse they had set up, absolutely crammed with fruit and veg.

Barry and Sally, Joe and Chris volunteered to help out at the housewarming, which would be absolutely packed out.

Tommy was prevailed upon to 'Say a few words' which as usual brought the house down. Tommy growled to Toby when the applause had died down. 'Any more, young man and I will have to charge you a fee!'

'Be worth every Penny of it, my Lord, but first I'll get a contract drawn up for me to be your agent, after I've successfully got you an Equity Card.'

'Cheeky young whipper-snapper,' shot back Tommy, 'but on reflection, not a bad idea,' before stomping off for a snorter.

Both Penny and Toby did the rounds, by having a quick word with everyone and thanking them for their gifts, which had piled up in a mountain in the hall.

Everyone had loosened up after the magnificent buffet of a whole poached wild salmon, slices of grouse, partridge, and pheasant. Nut roasts were available for any unlikely vegetarians. Mountains of quails eggs, salads and various mounds of home puddings were complemented by a vast cheese board.

Everyone with a glass of their favourite tipple was mingling, chatting as only a fairly tight-knit country community can do. There were obviously those who are envious or jealous, even spiteful but generally, they all knocked around together pretty well.

They have to, Toby was thinking, they each trade and rely on each other.

**** **** ****

'What a truly beautiful home you've created,' from Lino, his hands on Toby's shoulder, as he parted company from Bert's wife.

'It must have cost a bob or two,' continued Lino, sucking his teeth. 'Have you got ought left in the kitty?'

'I think I'll get by Lino. Oh, I hope you don't mind my calling you that?'

'Nay,' replied Lino, 'Every other bugger up and down the Dale does. I was wanting to have a word with you, 'cos you've obviously got a brain in your head.'

Toby listened intently as Lino carried on, 'Well tha' knows over the course of my career in the carpet trade, I've built up six shops, starting with the one at Masham.

'I inherited that when my old dad died. He was a cobbler. A damned good one, but I didn't fancy doing it. I'd just finished my national service. I'd been in the pay corps and learned a bit about business and accounts.

'I let the shop to a gents barber for a couple of years. It meant my old mum could live there and the rent kept her going. Then I heard that the first thing people would want to replace in their home after the war would be floor coverings after a lick of paint or distemper on the walls. I took a salesman's job at a carpet firm near Brighouse to learn the tricks of the trade.'

'Good thinking,' chipped in Toby.

243

'Well, they sent me on all these product and training courses. I was really taken by it. While they were concentrating on the upper end, I realised there was a lot of folk couldn't afford it, but would splash out at half the price to keep up like.

'They gave me the Dales, knowing I was from round here. Well, damned me, I was soon taking more than twice the value than those selling the top end to Bradford, Ilkley and such.

'The pay wasn't bad, but you only got more if you were promoted. And with all those old, comfortable devils above me, well it would take years.'

'A bit like dead man's shoes,' offered Toby.

'Right,' agreed Lino.

'So I handed in my notice for the month end, gave the barber one month's notice, got a new name board painted in red, a few letter-heads and some fancy business cards that copied from the big firms when I went to exhibitions. Went to see old Farrar at the bank, and took a loan on our shop to start trading.

'I picked all the firms I knew were selling well and keen to expand. To a man they all agreed payment terms to them of month after month of delivery.'

'Brilliant, you've got a sound head on your shoulders Lino,' confirmed Toby, wondering where all this was leading. 'Positive cash flow,' burst Lino. 'You can't beat it. As you know, farmers always pay in cash, smelling of milk from the old dairy churns they kept their notes in.

'More than brilliant,' he chuckled. 'I'd got the cash I didn't owe for an average of a month. That's when I started buying up shops in the right spot that had failed. Got them cheap.

'Well, to cut a long story short, a new kid on the block with, in my opinion, more brass then sense, has just offered to buy me out, lock, stock and barrel.

'He couldn't see the old Masham shop fitting into their forward projection.'

He laughed, as he said, 'Can you understand the crap these whiz kids come up with?'

'All very interesting, Lino, but if you'll excuse me I'd better circulate as there are lots of people I must thank.'

Laying a hand on Toby's arm, Lino said, 'I've kept the Masham shop, and thought as I can't deal in anything to do with carpets I would ask you if you have any ideas?'

As Lino had been rambling on, a thought suddenly clicked on like a light bulb in Toby's head. How much he enjoyed property, and doing it up. 'Estate agents always seem to do well and make good money.'

The words shot from his lips, before he'd given it thought. 'By Heck,' breathed Lino. 'I think you've got it, lad. We'll go 50/50. When do we start?'

'I'll have this lot to clear up tomorrow,' grimaced Toby. 'Let's meet at your place the day after tomorrow.' Hands were firmly shaken, but Toby wondered quite what he had let himself in for.

**** **** ****

People were gradually leaving, expressing what a fantastic party it had been. Toby noticed a gloomy-looking Farrar standing next to a thin woman with a long horsey face, her thin grey hair pinned into a bun.

As Toby approached, a half smile tried to lighten up Harold's face as he introduced his lady-wife Shirley.

'Pleased to meet you,' struggled out of pursed, thin lips, which thought Toby had never seen lipstick.

Turning to Joyce and young Millie, he complemented them both on their dresses and how well they looked. 'What's up?' he asked. 'You two normally have bigger smiles that turn many an old sheep farmer weak at the knees.'

Shirley winced and turned towards Harold. I'll bet you've never had a knee trembler you frosty old stick, thought Toby. Harold coughing and clearing his throat huskily said, 'We've had a spot of bad news,' pausing before going on, 'I'm taking early retirement, as Head Office at Park Row in Leeds, wish to send up a bright young undergraduate having passed all his banker institute exams to jolly up our sleepy little branch and increase profitability.'

'And,' interrupted Joyce to nods from Millie, 'They want us two to travel to Leeds every day. It's over an hour there and an hour back every day. Can you imagine wintertime?'

'So' chipped in Millie, 'We are going to tell them that thanks, but no thanks. It's going to be hard finding another job round here, but we wouldn't even mind going the twelve or so miles to Ripon.'

Toby said quietly, 'I may be able to help both of you. Could you both pop round to meet me at Lino's shop around two a clock the day after tomorrow? Can't promise anything, but it might just suit you. I can't answer any questions now, but will when we meet.'

'Oh, thanks ever so, Mr. Toby,' blurted out Joyce.

Toby left them all looking decidedly more cheerful. Golly, thought Toby, it's a rum old world. The final guests gone, the eight of them kicked off their shoes and toasted their toes in front of the blazing cherry-wood fire, which smelled so good.

They toasted each other and discussed the snippets of conversations whilst finishing the wine.

Colin jumped up, 'Right you lot sitting around won't make the baby a new dress,' and quickly organising a team of picker upper, a team of washers, one of driers and the final one to put away.

The house was spick and span and back to normal in no time. They split up all the food left-over, Toby remarking, 'scurrying away like little squirrels with their nuts.'

'You leave my nuts out of it' from bolder Barry, which sent them all off in peals of laughter.

When they were alone, Toby asked Penny, 'Could you invite them to join us for Christmas Day here?'

'Oh, darling that's a lovely idea. Dad and I've spent so many Christmases in hotels or with far flung relations it will make it special in our own home, with people closest to us.'

Toby pulling her up, held her tightly whilst he kissed her long and tenderly by the glowing logs.

He fished a ball of string and scissors out of a kitchen drawer saying, 'Look, before bed, I just want to measure this,' running upstairs.

'Come on love, even you don't think it's so big. Boasting again!'

Laughing, Toby said, 'No, silly. I want to measure the height from the ceiling to floor in the hall. If I hold the end of the string to the ceiling, drop the ball and you cut off the string where it touches the floor, we can measure it.' She did as he asked, cocking her head to one side and asked 'Why?'

'Well,' replied Toby, 'Old man Bates, who is supplying our Christmas trees said he would give two free trees of any size for us and Barry, to be delivered here free of charge.

'Yippee,' she cried, 'It's going to be the tallest tree, after the one in Trafalgar square.

After breakfast they unpacked their pile of wedding presents to 'whoops', 'how generous, they shouldn't have' and 'How fantastic'.

Penny carefully put the cards with each present, saying triumphantly, 'you've got enough on organising things, I'll just sit down now and write all the thank you cards. I thought I'd pop them in with the Christmas cards.'

'You are a genius, Mrs. C,' praised Toby. 'I'm glad I married a prudent wife and not a high-maintenance one.'

Whilst Penny perched at the lovely antique bureau that she had bought for the hall, she cheerfully tackled the pile of thank and Christmas cards. She hummed away as she ticked each name on her list.

Toby put a call through to Lino confirming their meeting around 11-ish, when they would discuss the idea.

Toby also said, 'Let's pop over to the Hotel for a pie and a pint, before going back to your place, as I've invited two people to join us at 2pm.'

'That sounds mysterious,' muttered Lino. 'Who are they?'

'You will just have to wait and see,' replied Toby.

'Well, I give it to you. You are quick off the mark,' returned Lino.

'Two phrases come to mind. Early birds catching worms and procrastination is the thief of time,' joked Toby.

He found Joyce's telephone number in the book and checked that both she and Millie would be able to meet him at Lino's at two tomorrow.

'Can you give me a clue what's it all about? We are both excited and would love to work with you,' the emphasis being on 'You', Toby thought. 'Sorry, Joyce, it's just an idea. Don't build your hopes up too much, it might not come off.'

**** **** ****

He was at Lino's promptly at 11. He noticed the 'Closed Till New Year' sign on the door and the lovely aroma of freshly brewing coffee.

'Will you show me around?' Toby asked Lino.

'Sure. This is the main showroom with a stockroom at the back, with a small lavy and washbasin. The missus and I live above in a lovely flat with access from the stockroom. Now, come and have a coffee and tell me about your idea, it's fair tickled me.'

'The nearest estate agency is in Ripon. Three in fact, but their business is mainly south to Harrogate and over a bit towards York. They tend to deal in big detached modern houses and semis round the army camp. I think, from here to Pateley Bridge, Bedale and Thirsk we'd have enough to go at.

248

'Just think of all the small holdings and small farms that will come up, as a lot of farmers lads don't want the life and want to work in big towns and cities.'

Lino nodding was on the edge of his seat, his beady little eyes counting pounds.

'You know this area like the back of your hand, and can quiz all your old contacts checking who's selling, who's about to turn their clogs up, barns for sale.

'Lino, your knowledge is the key. I know I've only been here a short time, but I reckon from all those you saw at the party, we could get a lots of leads.'

Lino, lost in thought, was thinking of all those 'encounters' he'd had over the years when selling his floor coverings.

He might be able to carry on, and anyway he needed some excuse to get away from the missus.

His mind was definitely made up. 'Right,' he snapped. 'How do we go about it?'

'We go into partnership,' began Toby. 'I'll get my lawyer to draw it up. We go 50/50 in sharing the profit after all costs. I propose I buy half the cost of the shop and flat. You of course, still retain your half.

'We turn the stockroom into an office for the manager, who will do all the books and paperwork required. One who can prepare our accounts ready for the accountant, quickly and cheaply. The manager with an assistant will 'man' the showroom and conduct viewing of properties by potential purchasers.

'We will have enough money in the kitty to pay their salaries for half a year, plus extensive advertising in the Ackrill group of local papers covering all our areas, plus the Yorkshire Post.'

'Blimey,' exclaimed Lino, 'you've certainly got it covered. By the way I've just bought a lovely little bungalow down by the river, which the wife has always admired.' Waving his arm at the rolls of carpet and lino half filling the store room said 'All this will be removed by the firm that bought me out.'

249

'That's good,' affirmed Toby.

'I want to put in a pair of swanky loos with all cons, a Ladies and a Gents. Nothing impresses more than clean, comfortable loos. I don't care if word gets around, and people in general, if taken short feel they can pop in. Good for the business.'

'I'll get my Penny on the case to find us good old antique partner's desk to sit in the middle of the showroom. We'll have a few cosy leather armchairs for people waiting. Let's line the walls with panels to take the photos and specs of the properties for sale, softly lit by brass picture light. You do the flooring. Oh, and we'll need a good colour printer and office equipment.'

'Come on, let's go and have that pint,' exclaimed Lino. 'I'll buy you lunch'

Toby seeing it was nearly 1.00 replied, 'Thanks Lino, but I would like to be back here before 2.00, for you to meet some people who could possibly be our new manager and assistant.'

'What about a quick snack?'

With a pint, they had a beautiful rare beef sandwich in thick, crusty brown bread, prepared by a smiling Jean, who served at their quiet corner table in the bar, with a hug and a kiss to Toby.

'I don't know how you do it,' exclaimed a slightly envious Lino. 'You have all the birds eating out of your hand. You could charm the birds from the trees you could.'

With a mouthful of sandwich, he spluttered, 'what do we call it? May old dad's name has been over the door for nearly 100 years.'

'And so it shall remain,' pronounced Toby.

'How about double barrelling it to 'Cooper-Moore Estate Agent'.' Before Lino could reply, he added. 'We could paint it in gold old English lettering on a dark chocolaty-brown background.'

'I'll find a cheap, but good Land Rover for getting around the properties. You know what winters are like, far

250

better than me. I'll get Joe to spray it in a dark brown colour and get the sign writer to letter up, identical to the shop front putting our telephone number on the sides and back.'

'Bloody hell. How do you manage to think of all that?'

'Remember the army's 6Ps,' replied Toby. 'Perfect planning prevents piss poor performance,' to a goggle-eyed open mouthed Lino, who could only lamely ask, 'When do we start?'

'Well, the world comes to a stop at Christmas and New Year. 2nd of January, and we have a fair bit to do.'

Pausing, Toby suddenly, face breaking into a big grin yelled 'Got it! The 14th February. Valentine's day. We can put big pink hearts all over the window and dish out Valentine Day cards with love from Cooper-Moore inside, and our logo and address on the back.'

'Genius,' said Lino. 'Come on, we'd better toddle back, I'm just wetting myself to see who turns up.'

'Lino, I'd like to clear up a couple of points. Firstly, with the two staff I want to us to pay them a fair monthly salary. At the end of the year, after all expenses, we'll give them a percentage share of the net profits.

'That way they will be keen to work harder, cut out waste and watch expenses, because they're share holders,' stated Toby.

'I agree, makes the job tick along and there's not bitching about pay or overtime,' returned a contented Lino.

**** **** ****

They were just brewing up a coffee, backs to the door when they heard the loud tap. As Joyce and Millie came in Lino nearly dropped his coffee, before he managed to say, 'You've got the wrong shop, bank is on the other corner.'

Toby welcomed them both in and pouring them coffee, Lino produced a box of Bourbon Cream biscuits.

'Would it be in order for us to take notes?'

251

'Of course,' replied Toby, and nodding to Lino said. 'There you are, that's just the professional approach we need to ensure success in our venture.' At a nod from Joyce, little Millie unzipped the flat leather document case she was carrying, pulling out an A4 pad, biro paused, she sat waiting.

Lino got down to telling them word for word Toby's plans, Toby nodding in agreement throughout.

When he had finished, Toby looked at them both, and said, 'we haven't discussed salaries, but we would like to match that you were both getting at the bank. Obviously, there might be times when you've worked later, but we are flexible, you can do less another time. Holidays with pay.

'I'm going to start a BUPA health scheme for all of us. Lastly, we will offer a profit sharing scheme, where we will all share in the net profit after all expenses have been paid. You two are doing the books, so you see that all is fair. I don't expect we'll do much for 4 to 5 months. We will have a proper meeting to work out the percentage later. Last but not least, Millie I think I once heard you saying you came from a big farming family.'

'That's right. I've got 4 brothers and sisters all squeezed into a four bed house with mum and dad. My elder brother Vince has the smallest to himself. Amy and I share and Dick and Pete share the other. It's a fair scrum at morning time. I wouldn't really mind but Amy's so untidy and scruffy. Me, I like to keep my things nice and tidy.'

'Lino has bought himself a new house.' Suddenly Millie grew still, her eyes widening willing Toby to go on, 'With your mum and dad's consent I'd like to offer the flat to Millie. It would save the bus ride here and back every day. You would be able to open up, and keep the place clean. Don't worry we'll make sure the rent won't be too much.'

As he stopped, she burst into tears, hugging first Toby then an embarrassed Lino, who'd nursed naughty thoughts about her pert little bosom, rounded bottom and long silky dark hair every time he went into the bank.

Toby then turned to Joyce. 'What do you think? Are we both barking mad, or do you think it's a goer?'

Joyce quickly looked at a flushed and excited Millie before saying, 'I think it's a perfectly well thought out, viable business plan with every chance of success.

Both Millie and I are thrilled at being in at the beginning of something new and exciting. We were getting bored and jaded at the same old routine at the bank. You know what they say; working for a bank is bread and butter for life. A steady job with average pay and a small pension at the end of it. We will hand in our notice to leave at the end of January.'

'I'll have a word with my solicitor to try to get contracts for me and Lino, and for Joyce and Millie before the end of December, so that if you change your minds, you can still carry on at the bank with no one knowing.'

Joyce's hand on Toby's arm declared softly, 'That's just the sort of thing you would say, and that's why we trust you and want to join you. I promise we'll both work our socks off for you.'

'I prefer black nylons,' replied Toby, rolling his eyes. 'You naughty boy,' exclaimed Joyce with a broad grin and standing up, put her arms around Toby, pecking him on both cheeks.

With a snap, Millie closed her portfolio, moved to Toby and planted a juicy kiss on his mouth, immediately blushing she confessed, 'There. I've been wanting to do that since the day I first saw you.'

I take it then that you would both like to join us and give it a go?' asked Toby.

'Oh, yes,' they both chorused. Even Lino joining in saying 'I really do look forward to something new, and think with all our joint knowledge of the local area and business we've a damned good chance of success. We'll be better than any outside Estate Agent trying to set up shop.

**** **** ****

'May I?' enquired Toby to Lino as he picked up his phone and without waiting for a reply dialled a number. As he waited, he put his hand over the receiver 'My solicitor'.

He politely asked if they were still working before the Christmas break, and was told they put the shutters up in two days, and yes, Mr. Simpson was in finishing off some work with Doreen, his secretary.

'Simon old bean, I'm really sorry to ask you a favour so near your closing time, but I've an important new project I want to discuss urgently, and if possible get some agreements out before the holidays. I'll explain all and would like to bring my partner with the manager and the new secretary to make any notes of our meeting ASAP.'

'Can you be here in 30 minutes? Doreen and I can finish what we were doing and give you an hour,' replied Simon.

'Bless you my son, we'll be with you pronto moronto. Come on Millie, you'd better come to decipher your shorthand.'

They all set off to Harrogate, Toby taking Joyce and Millie in his car.

Toby explained the idea and the ladies' position with the bank. New contracts were being produced and agreed before they took their voluntary redundancy. Contracts for him and Lino were drawn. Millie had run over all the points she had made. Doreen and Joyce typed away.

Simon taking standard employment forms personalised them. Then did the same with the partnership agreement. Toby, also told him about the separate agreement from Lino which allowed Toby to personally buy any plot or property for his own use. He would pay the partnership the agreed agency commission. At no time would Mr. Moore be involved.

Joyce and Doreen altered and inserted clauses together with Millie's help. Toby and Simon discussed the new building developing company, Toby saying it could come in January after he'd talked to Walter and his men.

The ladies rattled through, giggling and checking and by just a smidgen after five, they had the contracts ready for signing.

Joyce and Millie went over everything with Simon, and immediately signed as did Toby and Lino.

'Our really deepest thanks to you both,' said Toby. 'You've done in an hour what can take weeks of shuffling back and forth.'

'On the contrary,' returned Simon, 'Your two ladies have helped Doreen, with clear, concise agreements. We wish all our work was so easy, don't we Doreen?' who nodded.

During the trip back Joyce expressed her thanks to Toby for allowing them to be present and see everything was above board. Now they felt part of the team.

'The development idea might never happen, but just in case I could spot an opportunity to refurb a property to let out giving me rent, I'd have to move quickly. Not get involved with a partner who might dither and we miss out. In any case, it would be my money and if a loss occurred it wouldn't affect the others.'

They both nodded in agreement, Joyce saying, 'I'll do your books for you and all the costing if you like. It would obviously be in my own time and we would agree a nominated charge'

'That's good Joyce. I'll take you up on that,' enthused Toby. Wishing each other Happy Christmas Joyce promised to ring Toby in early January, when they'd handed in their notices.

CHAPTER TWENTY

What a day, thought Toby seeing it was almost 6.30 by the church clock as he crossed the cobbled square to his car. He locked the agreement safely away, before heading to the hotel bar.

He recognised veteran cars and vans parked outside. As he entered, he saw a very glam-looking Jean. When she turned, and saw him she cupped both hands around his neck, planting a kiss on his mouth.

As she pulled back he noticed the sparkling engagement ring, exclaiming, 'When did you?' to be broken off by the arrival of a thick set greying, forty-ish, smartly dressed man sporting a broken nose and a faded Para tie.

'Which battalion?' asked Toby.

'One,' was his reply.

'Ah, the immaculate one,' Toby stated. The man's eyes narrowed and his expression lost its aggression as he asked,

'How do you know that? Were you in the regiment?'

'Yes, 3 Para,' said Toby and saying, 'Ok, the gungy third,' which they both chanted together, before giving each other a big bear hug.

Peter introducing himself as the ex-CSM in Charlie Company. 'Before you get arsey-parsey about how wonderful the first is, just remember 3 Para has done the only drop in action since Arnhem,' stated Toby.

'I don't suppose you were there,' quizzed Peter.

'As a matter of fact, I was,' admitted Toby. 'I was commissioned in the Jan and still wet behind the ears when we dropped in for a cuppa with Nasser in Nov 56.'

'What was the surname sir, I didn't catch it.'

'I call myself Cooper now, as it's a bit flash round here to have a double-barrelled name. They all think you are loaded, so everything costs a bit more,' grinned Toby.

'Back then I was 2nd Lieutenant Cooper-Sneyd sergeant major.'

Jean was listening to all this as Peter struck his forehead with his hand, swearing, 'Christ, I should have cottoned on earlier. You were the talk of the whole regiment, no, the whole bloody army.

'You were the one that rescued those two lads caught up in fire. He,' jabbing his finger at Toby, 'Ran out twice under heavy fire from the Gyppos, and brought back his injured men. Saved their lives. He took a right packet in his right leg, but still carried on. They awarded him the Military Cross, though most of the senior officers thought it should have been a Victoria Cross.

'Didn't they move you out to another unit for your last year?'

'Yep, I was on a 5-year short service commission and they only wanted regular Sandhurst trained officers so I suppose my gammy leg wasn't much use in the front line. It was easier to sideways move me. I made the most of it riding and driving every vehicle known to man, riding horses and swimming in the army team against the Yanks.' Seeing Walter and the boys at the bar, Toby excused himself and joined them.

'That's some bloke,' exclaimed Peter, to which Jean could only agree.

They wouldn't allow him to buy a drink, saying what a fantastic time they'd all had at the housewarming. The other three drifted off to join a mate at the darts board.

Toby took the opportunity to run over the estate agency with Walter. Thinking that by word of mouth half of North Yorkshire would know within a week.

Going over the new development company and the idea of the annual work schedule brought a warm contented smile to Walter's craggy face. This wasn't entirely due to the double Famous Grouse which Walter had insisted buying.

'If you could bring that off Toby, it would be like heaven to us. I know the lads will jump at the chance if you get some agreements together.'

'I don't think we'll be developing much for half a year, but I hope you can get Lino's old shop sorted out for the opening in February.

'I'll find a plot for a new build to start in May. Maybe you and I can pick one up at an auction. Then we'll do just the one refurb before the year end. Don't want to rush it. Anyway, you can always do what work you want for yourself in between. Look, I'd better get going or risk being shot by my good lady. I'll drop some rough plans off for you to approve or make changes to suit yourself.'

Gripping Toby firmly by the hand, with moist eyes Walter said, 'I can't wait to tell the others. I know the missus will be well chuffed at the weight off my shoulders. We can plan holidays, have a regular wage coming in and being craftsmen with pride and not just jobbing builders.'

**** **** ****

Toby told Penny all about the plans and work ahead, after a really good fisherman's pie, washed down, rather naughtily with a fine Chablis. They stumbled up to bed, making love until falling asleep, Penny's firm breasts and soft front, firmly pressed into Toby's naked back.

Penny had left leaving a note of things to do with Toby, who was enjoying a bacon butty and strong black coffee at the kitchen table when he heard a knock at the door.

Whisking Barry in, he poured him a white coffee with two sugars, which he remembered from the building days. He asked, 'What's up?'

'Well, I was over at Dad's last night. You know he breeds the finest turkeys in the Dales and he reserved a right grand bird for you and just wanted me to measure up the Aga thing you have.' In a flash, tape measure in one hand, a grubby old envelope in the other, he took the measurements.

258

'Look Barry, I want to buy it from your dad.'

'No way,' replied Barry. 'He's that pleased that you've taken me off his hands. One less mouth to feed. I'll bring it first thing on the 24th, so your good lady can size it up for the big day.'

'That's very kind of you, and don't forget to meet us in the pub for a quicky after church, say about 12.30. Penny plans for us to sit down around 4.00.'

Toby had just settled down again to look at the day's racing, when another tap at the door nearly made him spill his coffee. He found Chris on the doorstep. 'Come in, it's chilly. Ready for a cuppa?' she poured herself one, adding milk and one sugar, and again thanking him for his kind invitation for Christmas day.

She unwrapped a brown paper parcel, which contained a roughly one foot diameter Christmas Pudding, with the top covered in glazed fruit and a similar size white Christmas cake.

'My mum bakes the best puds for miles around and sells to lots of fancy hotels and restaurants in Harrogate. She's made this extra special one for us. She says keep it in the cool larder and it'll be champion on the day.'

'I can't thank you and your mum enough. Please pass on our thanks next time you meet up.'

Chris downed her coffee, saying, 'I'd better get on, cos Joe's asked me to nip down to Masham Station to collect a part that's arrived in.' Pecking him on both cheeks, she left.

Toby sat and thought how kind it was of them both. That's Christmas lunch sorted, he thought with a smile.

Kath had told him to ring as one of last and best contacts had some really good information from an English 'over the sticks' or jumping yard. Now he could ring from the telephone in the hall, and not have to shoot around finding telephone boxes. Luxury indeed he told himself.

After chatting with Liam and the boys and exchanging seasonal good wishes, Kath passed over two horses, which she said the lad told her, were set up for their races in a good old-fashioned coup. I should pay a bumper pay-out at the yard for all their Christmases. Kath also said that they had something special for Boxing Day.

Damn, thought Toby. It's the Boxing Day shoot with Harry and his father. He wouldn't be able to visit the bookies so he'd get Mark to do it for him.

Toby checked the paper and was a bit doubtful when he saw the overnight prices of 20/1 and 25/1 in big fields. Ringing Sylvia, he found her a bit negative when she checked the prices. On impulse Toby asked her to get Mark to double the normal stake he put on for Toby as a little Christmas Box.

**** **** ****

He drove off to Ripon and passing Colin's garage pulled in to fill up. Chatting to Joe, he thanked him for the wonderful surprise of the Christmas pudding and beautiful decorative cake.

'You'd better bring some blankets to doss down Joe, I don't think any of us will be able to move.'

'Hello Colin, you are an early bird,' as paid for the diesel. 'I'd thought you'd be golfing on a crisp morning like this.'

'I was going to, but I seemed to have given my ribs a bang, can't remember when.

'Anyway, I don't think I can swing properly so I've cried off. Glad I've seen you. As a little present, I'm going to bring all the drink. Got some really good Champagne, whites and reds, gin, whisky, port, pudding wine. I've really enjoyed putting it all together.'

'There you are,' cried out Margot, coming into the office. 'One minute he's dying, next helping Joe taking out an engine. Men! Now Toby, Colin has probably told you all about the wine, well I want to tell you that I'm supplying the cheese board and bickies. Not blowing my own trumpet, but when I was in Edinburgh at the cooking

260

academy in Atholl Crescent, I knocked them for six with my canapés so I'll prepare a hot and cold selection. I'll make up a fruit basket to round it off.'

'Margot,' crooned Toby. 'That's very kind of you both. We'll make it the finest Christmas ever.'

Toby was soon in Ripon where he saw the price on the first was still 20/1 whilst the second had shortened to 30/1.

The new young clerk sniggered, obviously thinking he was dealing with lunatic as Toby put on £5 each way on both horses and a £5 ew double. As Toby handed over the thirty pounds and collecting his tickets, he overheard a whispered 'Mug Punter' pass between the two clerks.

Toby strode out thinking 'I wonder what they will say if we are lucky enough to pull it off.'

He carried on to Harrogate to collect Penny and take her to the Drum & Monkey for a lovely fishy lunch. Looking at his watch he paid the bill, taking Penny by the arm, he led her into Corals around the corner.

He showed her the price on the board and they listened to the racecourse commentary.

It was a hard uphill struggle for the three leading horses. She squeaked, 'He's there,' Toby putting a finger to his lips, as the leading horse clipped the top of the fence before crashing to the ground.

The third horse, theirs, reeled in the new leader, length by length to clear the final fence, winning by 5 lengths.

'He's won, he's won,' squealed Penny, to the disgust and envy of the regulars, who were tearing up their betting slip.

Toby handed over the 20/1 ticket to Penny, asking her to collect the money. She walked up to the glass enclosed counter nervously pushing the betting slip through the gap, the clerk dived into the till counting out £130 in fivers and tenners. They turned right and went up Parliament Street to Fattorini's the Jewellers. With a bit of dithering, Penny selected a matching necklace and earrings. Hugging him as he told her that was her Christmas present.

She said 'Can we do that again? It's so exciting.'

'It is when they win, but the bookie usually wins. In fact I want to get to Ripon, cos I've one in the last race. See you at Corals. They run in 40 minutes.'

They both arrived in their own car with 5 minutes to spare. Toby saw to his satisfaction the same young clerk was there. Blue Painter was still a 'no-hoper' at 16/1, but over the three miles in heavy going, relentlessly, moved up the field. Three out, one of leaders fell. Blue Painter was fifth, then third and quickly came alongside the second, jumping well, with one final jump ahead. The leader just struggled over the last, a length ahead of Blue Painter.

Head down, he remorselessly overtook the tired leader to win by a neck.

Penny erupted, the sour punters glared, saying that outsider would have had no chance if theirs hadn't fallen.

Toby approached the young clerk, who squinting at him trying to remember where he'd seen him. Toby slid the two tickets over, watching the youth go pale. He went into a huddle with his pal. The inevitable phone call to head office followed. The punters' piggy eyes grew envious and hostile as the clerks counted out the £70 for Blue Painter and nearly £1300 for the winning double. As the clerk handed over the money, Toby looked at him in the eye saying, 'Not too bad for a mug punter.'

The clerk flushed and looked down as Toby and Penny left the shop quickly.

Toby, holding her close, dived into the Boots two doors down, which was full of shoppers. Toby went to the back pretending to look at the toiletries where he scanned the window to see if they had been followed.

Penny whispered, 'Oh, isn't it thrilling, it's like a spy film.'

'It wouldn't be so funny if any of that lot got hold of us. It's a year or two's wage to the average bloke. No, I think we are ok, let's get a move on.'

**** **** ****

They went home in their separate cars. The lights had come on at dusk set by a timer Toby had bought. The Aga warmed the kitchen and the casserole Penny had put in before she left, gave a gorgeous cooking aroma. Toby put a match to the log fire he had laid this morning and went to the safe to deposit his winnings.

He'd just reached the hall when the phone rang. He was tempted to announce, 'who flung dung, Chinese laundry' but held back as he recognised the voice. 'Lady Middleham here, is Mr. Cooper available?'

Here I be, your ladyship, my shield in one hand, my sword in the other. Prithee my Lady what task would at thou have me to tackle?' to a peal of girlish laughter.

'Silly arse, I just wanted to see if you were both in, because Tommy has got two of those ice-cream freezer things packed with wild salmon, and Harry and I persuaded him to get the biggest and take it to that nice little man near Pateley Bridge to get it Peat Smoked.'

On she gushed, 'Well we have two socking great sides for Christmas lunch, and as we are off to Barbados after the Boxing Day shoot, I wonder if you would like the other half.'

'Liz that's absolutely fantastic of you. Do you want me to pop up to the castle to collect it in the morning?'

Noticing her slight hesitation, he asked, 'Are they with you tonight?'

'No, they are off to the shoot dinner.'

'In that case, why not bring it down now, and join us for what smells like a seriously good casserole?'

'Oh, yummy, sure Penny won't mind?'

'Not a bit. See you soon.'

Twenty minutes later Liz flew up to their front door. Toby helped her out and carried in the large half of oily, peaty-smelling smoked salmon.

Toby carefully put it into the fridge and went back to the two ladies who were chatting nineteen to the dozen.

With large glasses of claret in hand, Liz asked Toby, 'Would you mind bringing in the sack from the car boot?'

Toby staggered back with both arms clutching a large hessian sack. Dumping it by the door, he turned to Liz who said, 'It's a bag of the finest Scottish peat that the smoke house man uses. He said, 'Added to a log fire like that-' pointing to the one Toby had lit earlier, '-the smell is delicious. We've got a sack, so again we'd like to let you have the other. I know you'll appreciate it.'

Toby took a couple of the long brown turves from the sack and placed them on top of the flaming logs. As they tucked into Penny's delicious chicken casserole, a soft, sweet, almost incense-like aroma came from the fire.

'Liz, that's super, just imagine that mingling with all the other Christmas smells, it's going to be truly fantastic.' Toby went on to tell Liz how their Christmas lunch had been so generous provided by others.

'You deserve it. Both of you. You've given two young farmers a wonderful start, a team of builders regular profit sharing work, and two local loyal ladies new exciting jobs again with a chance to make more through their own hard work. I'd say you've done a damned fine job, for which a lot of people are very grateful.'

'Thank you Liz,' murmured Toby. 'You will start me blushing.' 'Not a chance,' said Liz. 'You are a gambler, who loves the thrill of living on the edge. And you know what,' to Penny 'His timing and luck usually come through!' raising her glass she toasted 'To a unique man,' which Penny chorused.

'How many have you invited for lunch?' she asked Penny, who counted on her fingers, 'we two, Barry and Sally, Dad and Margot, Joe and Chris and Silas.'

'Oh, isn't he that sour old farmer from up the Dale?' asked Liz.

'He is a damned fine farmer, divorced for years as it's nigh on impossible to stay married when you are serving in the SAS. He was decorated for some really suicidal work. He helped me and Harry no end, and as he was alone at Christmas I wanted to invite him. He's a good raconteur when he's had a few.'

'That's you my love' said Penny hugging him. 'You are always helping lame dogs over stiles.'

**** **** ****

Toby and Penny started off Christmas Day which was white from a heavy frost with a cafetiere of strong black coffee and a small balloon glass of vintage Brandy.

Whilst Penny put the bird in the oven on a slow setting, Toby lit the fire and opened the wine. They all met up in church, except Silas who stated he didn't do religion anymore and would meet them in the pub.

After a packed house and truly magical service whilst the others had coffee and mingled, Toby shot home to baste the bird and put more logs and a peat on the fire. He left all the lights on and went off to the pub.

He found Silas propping up the bar, pint in hand. He wouldn't hear of Toby buying, firmly saying, 'Now, I'm in the chair and have set up a tab for all of you whilst you're here. I feel really chuffed at you inviting Ben and me.'

'Where is Ben?' asked Toby, looking around.

'Oh, I left him in the car. He'll be like a lamb with us, but if any of the fancy London brigade up for the weekend bring in their poodles and such, he might just show his feelings and start lunch early.' The rest of the party piled in exchanging greetings and kisses.

Silas after receiving his third kiss, and about ten more from the barmaid and local farmers' wives exclaimed, 'that's the most I've had all year. I think I'm getting to like it, you'd better watch it boys, I might be on the prowl.'

The whole day passed so quickly, everything went like clockwork. Toby was a bit disgruntled to be wiped out at Monopoly by Chris and surprised when Silas won comfortably at scrabble.

It showed he still had a quick and agile brain.

Ben, having been fed lots of special treats fell asleep at Penny's feet.

The ladies whisked everything into the kitchen and soon had everything washed, dried and put away before joining the men by the fire. Story followed story, some a little sad from Toby and Silas. Army days to Penny's antique buying days and Chris's dad, a true Yorkshire farmer.

Stumps were drawn around two in the morning when Colin and Margot went to the spare room, and Toby and Penny to theirs. Joe and Chris walked arm in arm to stay with Barry and Sally. Silas turned down the offer of the spare bedroom and said, 'If it's ok with you Toby, Ben and I'll shack up here in front of this beautiful fire. We are early birds, so we'll let ourselves out, lock up and put the key back through the letterbox.'

Ben looked up, nodded and fell asleep again on his paws.

When Toby woke up, they found no trace of Silas and Ben, just the ashes from the fire which had been cleared away and a new fire laid ready to light, with a pile of logs filling the large copper log basket. A note of thanks from Silas was on the table with a brace of pheasants and a little note saying, 'Just in case you don't bag anything on your rough shoot'. They quickly downed a bacon sandwich and black coffee before driving to the castle as the rest of the guests were arriving. It was mainly family, Tommy and Liz, Harry and Jill, Mark and Felicity Woodhouse, Gerald and Miranda Woodhouse, Doctor Basil Mortimer and his wife Eunice, Hubert and Jack, one of Harry's pals, and Toby and Penny.

The eight guns and their wives climbed onto the back of a covered farm trailer with benches either side, straw on the floor and a pile of excited, slobbering Labradors at their feet.

They bounced up a muddy farm track getting out by a field gate. Belts of cartridges crossed their chests, and most carried a wide game bag hanging at the side.

They looked like desperados as they fanned out in a straight line about 2 yards apart. The wives followed behind. A couple of hares and rabbits were flushed out of the rough grass and two or three pheasant rose squawking before being brought to earth by Tommy and Harry.

They had two drives before returning to the castle for a warming lunch of cottage pie and Claret.

They managed to get one more drive in before the light began to fade.

As they all gathered around the game laid out on the ground, they were given a brace of pheasant each plus a rabbit or hare.

CHAPTER TWENTY ONE

The next day, after ringing Kath as planned, she gave him 2 horses at Wetherby, which Liam had been told were 'nailed on' to win. The prices wouldn't be brilliant so be sure to do them as a double.

Thanking her, he rang Sylvia, who seemed flustered and proudly blurted out, 'Oh, I'm glad you rang as naturally we have no contact telephone number for you. Wm Hills have a box and Mark says he will leave two tickets for you at the Owners and Trainers entrance. Will you and your wife come and have lunch? 12.00 o' clock prompt sit down. Drinks included, oh and afternoon tea.'

'Sylvia, Penny and I will be gratefully accept the tickets.' And then gave her the two horses for Mark. 'Don't look as if you know us, as no one must think there is any connections,' were her parting words.

Telling Penny to get her skates on, Toby put on his old country suit and Barbour and Penny a jumper and skirt and they were away in 20 minutes.

Picking up the A1 they were in Wetherby around 11.00. Toby nipped into a Coral betting shop and placed two £5 wins at 7/1 and 8/1 and a £5 win double costing £30.

Traffic was building up but they turned into the Owners and Trainers at 11.30 where an officious little man in too large a flat cap insisted that they show their badges.

Toby explained that they were guests of William Hill and the tickets should be in an envelope addressed to Mr. and Mrs. Cooper.

He snorted and growing red in the face turned to his colleague who began rooting about through a drawer full of envelopes.

Our man stayed firmly by Toby to prevent him going in and continually waved in cars carrying the correct window sticker. Toby said, 'You look to me as if you were a former jockey, I'm sure I would know your name, your face is familiar.' Immediately the man thawed, and mentioning some name that Toby had never heard of said, 'Go on Sir, I know if you haven't got a ticket to the Hills box, you won't get in.' 'Thanks,' said Toby. 'You might have a bob or two on Blue Angel, then on Hambleton with maybe an each way double,' and sped off to park. Hurrying through the scrum they spotted the Wm Hill chalet with two commissionaires at the door who quickly checked their list before handing over two badges and race cards before opening the door.

Mark spotted Toby and coming over with a tall, slim long legged, attractive woman, her red hair piled on her head. 'May I introduce my wife Sylvia, and I am Mark,' he added, pointing self-consciously at his shiny Wm Hill name badge.

'Now, I've put you on our table, and we're going to start lunch at 12.00. May I get you both drinks first?' stopping a passing waitress with a tray of champagne. 'Thank you so much,' Toby said taking a glass for Penny and himself.

The room was packed by faces Toby recognised from the papers. They were seated at a table of 12. Sylvia next to Toby, whilst Penny was wedged between Mark and a large, florid faced man, who Toby recognised as a famous Irish breeder.

The first course of smoked salmon and lobster was timed to be finished, so that punters could see the race on the racecourse television.

Toby took the opportunity to visit the Tote and place his bets at prices very similar to the ones he had taken.

The roast beef, served pink was magnificent. Toby was a bit alarmed at Sylvia rubbing her leg against his. She told him how Mark was always racing, arriving home too tired for anything. Yes they had no children and anyway it was too late now. If Toby would like to meet up with her one day for lunch or a chat, she'd be delighted.

Toby was gratefully relieved when dessert was served to learn that the men all move two places to the left, taking drinks with them.

Toby was seated between a horsey wife of a racecourse managing director and the glitzy giggling, peroxide blond wife of the Wm Hill betting shop manager of the year.

Now all eyes and ears were glued to the next race in which Blue Angel was running. The mare got away smartly at the start, ran along the rail and was never headed, winning by 5 lengths.

'Whoopee,' cried Penny, looking at Toby. 'One down and one to go.' Toby glancing at the Tote pay out to see that they were paying £6.00 which meant £30 to collect.

The little blonde flung her arms around Toby. 'Who is the clever boy then? At 7/1 too. Hope my Bob hasn't got too many punters on like you.'

'I've told you before Babe,' wearily from Bob. 'Mark and I make our money out of the short priced losing favourites. These odd outsiders are allowed for. Right, isn't it Mark?'

'Absolutely,' replied Mark. 'Whatever the outcome of a race, we never lose.'

'How?' demanded the horsey wife.

'Well, don't mention it outside these walls,' solemnly from Mark 'But just imagine a large firm like ours and how much money we take at all our betting shops and racecourses across the country on each race,' he paused while they imagined before he continued, 'All we make is just 2% on every race,' he opened his hands wide.

'I see,' thoughtfully from horsey. 'So like today's 6 race card you will bring in a whopping 12% of all your take.' 'Something like that,' murmured Mark. 'Now Toby, you ought to be a decent chap and let us all in on your second horse,' nodding with a slight smile to Toby.

Clapping her hands excitedly, Penny called for attention before saying, 'Look, we are twelve. Let's all put £5 in a mug and I'll go and put £60 on the horse at the Tote.'

'Great idea, what the hell,' replied Horsey. Everyone, including Mark and Bob, put a fiver into a clean pint glass. 'Right,' said Bob. 'What is the horse Toby?'

'Hambleton, in the race after this,' replied Toby. 'Bloody hell,' cried out Bob. 'He is a 9/1 no hoper, can I have my money back?'

Toby reached into the glass and handed Bob his money back. 'Anyone else not sure?' Toby asked.

'Babe, we will just lose our money, best take it back,' pleaded Bob.

'No way,' Babe replied. 'I've got instinct that this geezer,' jerking her thumb at Toby, 'Knows what time of day it is. I'm in.'

'So that's £55 I'll put on. Come on Sharon with me to check that all is above board.' The pair put on their coats and went off giggling to the Red Tote kiosk under the stairs up to the grandstand.

The crowd was thinning out as everyone watched the present race. Penny took the betting slip, carefully putting it into her bag. They found Toby at the pre-parade ring watching Hambleton, a big 16 hand chestnut with a backside like a garage door.

Toby with two, good-looking, well turned out, long legged blondes on either arm, was gazed at enviously by the motley crew of stable staff, owners, trainers and punters.

'Well, what do you think?' purred Sharon, getting a kick from all these furtive male eyes.

'I'd say he's got every chance. Do you want to go back to the Box or would you like to see it from the stand?'

Sharon wanted to stay near Toby as long as possible. She felt the warm, twitching down below which she always had just before she played with herself when Bob was tired again. Which he always was, these days.

'Let's go to the grandstand,' squeaked Sharon as Toby rolled his eyes at Penny. The open tread steps up to the grandstand were quite steep.

A few old and young men hung about underneath waiting for a cheap thrill as they looked up between the treads giving a clear view up ladies skirts.

They pondered over their race cards as men and old frumps climbed up, but you could almost hear the intake of breath as Penny and Sharon passed them and started to climb.

Their throats grew dry as they saw two perfect pairs of long nylon clad legs pass above them. Both wore suspenders, one with a tight frilly pair of pants and the other in black. No, it was hair.

Only they would know that Sharon never wore pants. Well, you never know when you'd get the chance, she'd once told her friend Michelle.

They stood side by side on the first step with a clear view of the racecourse with the finish about ten yards to the right.

It was a field of 15. Two horses jumping well lead by about 4 lengths to a group of three, Hambleton ran on the outside of the next four horses on the second circuit.

The second three had reduced the lead on the front pair who sailed over the water jump.

The inside horse just ahead of the other two spooked at an imaginary line of water and took off to the right bringing the other two horses down.

It unseated the startled jockey and carried on rider-less. Whilst the following pair carefully avoided the fallen horses and riders, Hambleton on the outside and in the clear forged ahead.

The second horse, tiring, just struggled over the second to the last, Hambleton flying past him, painfully gaining on the leader at every stride.

He was obviously a mud lover in the soft to heavy ground. He took the leader at the last to win convincingly to a hushed crowd who were to a man, nearly all on the favourite at a very short price.

'Jeepers,' shouted Sharon. 'We gone and done it,' to a glaring crowd. Toby noticed that the group of men at the bottom of the stairs had grown considerably bigger.

Sharon, delighted at seeing the upturned faces knew what was going on said to Toby, 'Hang on a mo, I've just caught my heel,' bending down and opening her legs wide, pretended to adjust her heel.

To the lucky few directly underneath, came an audible sigh, as they fixed the picture in their minds to replay again and again.

There were few people queuing at the Tote window as Penny handed over the winning ticket. She noticed it on the Tote board, that they were paying £7-20 for the win which made a grand total £396 or £36 to each of the eleven.

The sour old puss behind the Tote said, 'I haven't got that much, if you'd wait I'll get my manager to come over with it.'

'Will it take long?' asked Toby.

'Can't say, but he shouldn't be long.'

'Do you ladies want to wait while I go to the box and tell the others what's happening?' he was off in a flash to go round to the other Tote to present his two winning and a double ticket. He was also asked to wait. A worried little man in a black mac appeared saying he was the manager. He paid Toby's two single bets of £30 and £35, then from a safe under the counter paid out the £396 in 10s and fivers. Both Penny and Sharon were giggling helplessly. When Penny's back was turned, Sharon dropped her hand and squeezed a half-awake Tom, who instantly responded.

Throwing her arms around his neck, she whispered, 'I just knew you would be a big boy, but that's just brill. Ring me any time,' and went off to catch up with Penny who was striding ahead.

As they poked their noses around the door of the box, their table jumped up and cheered. The other tables all having heard of the bet clapped, one woman said what many felt when she said, 'I wish you'd been on our table.'

Penny took the wads of notes from her coat pocket saying 'There you are folks, that's £385 or £35 each. 'Now then,' whined Sharon to Bob, 'You are not as clever as you made out, Mr. Betting Shop Manager of the year. That's two weeks wages you just turned down,' to a red-faced depressed Bob.

Mark swiftly sorted out 11 little bundles of £35 which he handed out. 'It's a good feeling, taking money from a fellow bookmaker,' he grinned to Toby. 'Well done. I think I'll warn all my managers to watch out for you.'

'Pure fluke,' lied Toby.

'Oh, it's not,' retorted Penny. 'My man is a genius. Not many punters take out considerably more than they put in. He had Blue Angels as well as Hambleton and also the double on the pair,' she said triumphantly.

No one saw the imperceptible nod from Mark to Toby as he continued. 'Well, that's it. Bob, we'll have to put a countrywide ban on him. Just think if he had an accumulator. We might be out of business!'

Slapping Toby on the back he carried on. 'No, well done, long may your luck carry on.'

After another drink they all parted, joyfully wishing everyone a happy New Year.

Both Sylvia and Sharon slipped a card bearing their telephone numbers into Toby's pocket.

As they carefully drove home on all the back roads, as Toby realised he was stupid after a few drinks, Penny cuddled up closer and put the radio on.

**** **** ****

They spent the next few days walking off their Christmas excesses and giving Barry and Sally a few days break, looked after the farm.

Penny realised what hard work it was, and how tied you were with animals. They were both looking forward to the New Year's Eve buffet and dance that they had invited to at the Castle. The theme was 'The sixties and Flower Power'.

Toby had got some Teddy Boy gear together, whilst Penny was going as an American 'Bobby Soxer' complete with little skirt, white knee socks and plimsoles, her hair tied in bunches. Toby didn't really approve of her skimpy white silk pants, which would be visible when she jived.

Uniformed security staff helped them park in the overcrowded rear courtyard.

Entering the hall, they were greeted by Tommy in a Hawaiian shirt and flowers in his hair. Liz looked gorgeous in a slinky black dress, fish net stockings with similar flowers to Tommy.

There were kisses and shrieks as people met and mingled. Waiters with a seemingly endless supply of trays filled with champagne circulated.

A huge buffet was laid out in the dining room, with a stuffed boars head as a centrepiece and several whole poached and smoked salmon.

As they explored the open door to one darkened room they found it packed with guests dancing to Beatles music. In another, even darker room Procol Harum played to tightly packed gyrating bodies. In another, closely seated around a long low coffee table, people were passing rolls ups from one to another.

Toby recognised the smell of pot, and whisked Penny out. As they entered a large room, they recognised it as the sitting room. Here couples danced to Elvis. The room was lit by a strobe light, making it very night-clubbish. They met so many friends and family from the wedding and many the estate workers plus what looked like half the village.

As soon as they started to dance Penny was whisked away by Joe, whilst the postmistress, sweating, her large bosom heaving, grabbed Toby. Toby reckoned the average time you danced with a partner was about 4 minutes. Pretty good really, everyone met, had a chat, and moved on before boredom or lack of conversation set in.

Mind you, he told himself, some I'd like to hang on to for longer. Especially, some of the young, hot gang that Harry had brought from London.

Tommy and Liz appeared at the door. Tommy stood in the doorway. Hunting horn in hand, which he raised to his lips, playing 'come to the cook-house door boys'.

Silence fell as Tommy yelled, 'Come on you motley crew. Supper is served.'

Everyone spilled out of every room to join the melee clutching plates and passing down the huge table to be served be a bevy of farmers' wives bribed by Tommy.

Some plates were piled so high that they looked in danger of falling off.

Everyone sat where they could find a perch in the dining room, chairs and sofas, even up the grand staircase.

Waiters and waitresses kept circulating with trays of food and wine. It was approaching 11.45 when Tommy did his bugle act again crying out, 'Right folks, time to grab your nearest and dearest, and leave your best friend's husband or wife, and cram into the main hall.

We start the countdown to the New Year.' Quite a lot of swapping around took place as couples re-united to chant the countdown. On the last count of one, a wild pal of Harry's let off two army thunder flashes outside to an almighty explosion. Everyone kissed and then broke away to kiss as many of those who were normally unapproachable.

Hector McDonald in his Argyles & Sutherland Pipe Major uniform piped 'Auld Lang Syne' to riotous applause before. The lights were dimmed and couples peeled off to various rooms. Even the waiters and waitresses were pairing off and joining in.

Toby and Penny got separated with Toby ending up with Miranda Woodhouse, Tommy's sister. She was rather starchy and rigid.

After about 5 minutes Toby made an excuse of having to nip off to the loo, leaving her in the arms of a large estate worker. As he left the room he saw Penny and Hugo quickly going upstairs. A mixture of anger, jealousy and bitterness swept over him as he quickly and silently followed them up. He peered carefully around the corner in time to see Penny's blue dress disappearing into a bedroom.

The one next door was ajar, so he carefully went in opening the door wide to check that no-one was in before closing and locking the door.

He had seen the bed had been used and unmade, with the overpowering smell of scent and sex. He could hear muffled conversation from next door, so taking a tumbler from the bedside table, held it against the wall his ears pressed to its base. With a tight knot in his stomach he could clearly hear Penny telling Hugo how much she still loved him.

There was the rustling sound of undressing with giggles from Penny.

Then the slow, rhythmic creak from the bed, which grew faster. The only other sounds were the heavy gasps from Hugo. He'd heard enough. Replacing the tumbler he unlocked the door, his mind in turmoil. He had reached the bottom of the stairs and crossed the hall, when he saw the two shadowy figures of George Barracoush, Tommy's water baliff and general land agent skipping upstairs with the frosty Felicity, Tommy's elder sister. Toby grinned to himself, thinking how rewarding it could be if you were a potential blackmailer, to just lurk out here with a camera and a notebook!

He just squeezed into the room when he was spun around by the two long delicate arms of Miranda, the wife of Mark the merchant banker.

'You owe me that dance which we haven't finished.' She was about Toby's age and looking glamorous. A former model.

All around them couples were entwined, with hands going everywhere to low moans of pleasure. Toby felt Miranda's hand drop down and start feeling an ever-growing Tom. Her eyes widened before she kissed him.

277

He grabbed her firm little bottom in his hands, pulling her onto a now fully erect Tom. Looking at him she gasped. 'God, will you come up to town and join a few of my bored pals for lunch and a mad afternoon? You see our chaps all work in the city and are so knackered by the time they struggle home, poor lambs. They've no lead left in their pencils. We, gym-fit gals get so frustrated. We've even wondered about trying to find a personal trainer for the four of us.'

Toby, easing her slightly away slipped his hand down her tight, silk dress to feel her bush with his fingers whispering 'Let's see if a trial is up to madam's expectations.'

Slinking out of the room, they climbed the darkened stairs. Toby noticed that the bedroom door was half open. He choked slightly as he caught the aroma of Opium, Penny's favourite scent.

The bed was rumpled. He quickly turned and locked the door, before turning a quivering Miranda around. His fingers quickly pulled the zip down and pulling her around towards him slipped off the dress which she nimbly stepped out of as his fingers unclipped her bra.

She stood with her legs slightly open, her nipples pointed and hard, whilst he looked at her full black bush with her clitoris just visible.

He quickly stripped, and she put a hand to her mouth as she first saw Tom at his rampant best.

He felt savage and resentful at the thought of Penny and Hugo. He roughly raised and lowered her until she orgasmed again and again.

Laying her gently on the bed he continued this time slower and deeper until she cried, 'Please stop, you are going to kill me. You'd be fantastic in town, no wonder why there are so many happy birds here in Yorkshire if all the men are like you. Now it's my turn,' and squirming under Toby she pushed him onto his back and taking hold of a still hard Tom proceeded to take as much as she could into her mouth.

'I love your smell,' she murmured as finally Tom exploded. She leant over to the bedside table, pulling out a handful of paper wipes and cleaned both of them.

As they quickly dressed she said, 'I think it was my best shag for a long time.'

To hear her cut glass accent made Toby laugh. She popped her head out of the door, whispering, 'All clear.'

They crept downstairs to join the throng, but not before she slipped her card into his pocket. Seem to be acquiring quite a collection, he thought to himself.

Toby circled the room until he found his quarry, Carol, the plain, starchy wife of Hugo.

Sitting beside her, he offered her a glass of pink champagne he'd collected from a passing waitress. 'You look really lovely tonight, Carol. What have you done with your hair? It looks so lustrous and shiny.'

'Oh, you are teasing me' she giggled. 'I don't think I ought to have any more champagne, I'm quite squiffy already.'

When she smiled, she looked quite attractive he thought, approving of her good legs and more than ample bosom.

Taking her in his arms he did a night-club shuffle with her in a dark corner. 'You will have to hold me up,' she giggled. 'I think my legs might give away.'

He held her close and she could feel the rising Tom. 'You can't possibly like me. No one does.'

'What about Hugo?' Toby asked.

'Oh, he can't get it up properly. Anyway, it's nothing like this thing of yours.'

She went on to tell him how she had been bullied at school for being plain and had married Hugo in a sort of desperation.

'I know it sounds disloyal, but I get jealous when he's always sniffing around Penny. Oh, I shouldn't say that about your wife, please forgive me. It's just that sometimes I feel I'm getting older, and have missed out on that, you know, that side of things.'

279

Toby took her trembling hand and pressed it against Tom. With both her eyes and mouth open Toby gently and passionately kissed her. 'Would you like to see it?' whispered Toby. Numbly she croaked back, 'Yes, but how?'

Toby steered her out and realising her legs were really going, took her in his arms up the stairs.

A tousled couple he didn't recognise were coming down as he explained, 'She is a bit groggy, and wants to lie down for a while.'

All true, thought Toby, as he saw both bedrooms doors ajar, he perversely chose the one that Penny and Hugo had used. Sauce and ganders came to mind. Having locked the door, he held her to him and gently unzipped her dress. 'Oh, please don't look, I'm so shy.'

'Nothing to be shy about with a figure like yours,' gently kissing and stroking her. He pulled her slip down to reveal two large firm breasts encased in a white frilly see through bra, with matching white frilly briefs from which a tuft of soft brown hair escaped on either side, her brown stockings were held up by a white suspender belt.

As she leaned against the wall he quickly stripped off and stood naked in front of her. Both her hands grasped Tom, as he unhooked her bra to reveal two of the finest breasts he had seen.

Tom swelled even harder as with a thumb in each side of her briefs he pulled them to the floor. Her mass of shiny brown pubic hair was one of the thickest he had seen.

With half open eyes she was panting as he laid her on the bed and started by kissing her mouth, then her nipples before working down to find the hard pea of her clitoris. He slid his forefinger into her, with his thumb gently caressing her clitoris and finger going deeper and faster in circles. He had to hold his hand over her mouth to prevent the rising yelps from bringing unwelcomed attention. Her stomach rose and contracted as she experienced the most powerful of orgasms.

As he withdrew his hand he softly asked 'Would you like me to?' She nodded and gasped, 'Be gentle, I have not much experience.'

Toby raised her legs and eased the head of Tom into the moist and now widened brown thicket. With care and tenderness he slipped Tom in further stroke by slow stroke. She was soon able to take most of it before climaxing again in one almighty, shuddering orgasm.

Toby hastily pulled out a quivering Tom who discharged across her thigh. As Toby wiped away the mess, he asked her if she was ok. 'Ok? I'm shattered, but never felt so alive. I'll have to blackmail you to giving me a daily dose.'

Toby dressed quickly and asked if she wanted a hand. 'No my dear. You go down, I need a bit of time to sort myself out.' Toby blew her a kiss and went on his way downstairs.

Up and down like a fiddlers elbow in more ways than one he thought.

At the door he bumped into a worried Hugo. 'You haven't seen my wife have you? She usually sits and waits for me, never wanders off. Old Hector says he thinks he remembered seeing you dancing with her. Can't think why.'

'I advised her to maybe have a lie down as she felt squiffy.' Patting him on the shoulder, he added, 'Best of luck old chap,' and disappeared to find Penny.

They thanked their hosts and were saying them final goodbyes. They saw Hugo and Carol. 'Ah, you found her,' said Toby to a disgruntled Hugo who said 'I found her lying in bed, with no clothes on.'

'I expect she was a bit warm as well as squiffy,' replied a helpful Toby.

'Happy New Year to you both.'

'And to both of you,' from Carol. 'And thanks for the lovely dance Toby. It's nice to feel appreciated.' Hugo's piggy eyes grew smaller as he just managed a strangled 'Happy New Year'.

281

**** **** ****

Little was spoken on the journey home, as they were both lost in their own thoughts.

'A snifter?' queried Toby, as he poured himself a large Malt with just a splash of water. 'Why not,' replied Penny. 'I'll have a large G&T.'

As they kicked off their shoes and snuggled closely on the sofa to the warm glow of a large log Toby had put onto the dying fire. 'Did I ever tell you the tale of the two pompous English maltsters who went on a malt sales campaign in Scotland?' As she shook her head, he carried on.

'Well, they slowly progressed north in their chauffeur driven Bentley, visiting the main target distilleries on their list. They managed to put the backs up of most of their potential clients by telling the Scots how much more efficient the English were. Not the way to deal with the independent Highland Scots.

'The jungle drums started beating and news of the impending arrival reached the directors of one famous distiller well in advance. Warm Scottish hospitality always extended to offering a 'wee dram' before and during business negotiations.

'The production director hearing of their progress decided to have a bit of fun. Two Caithness jugs were placed on the boardroom table, along with an array of tumblers. The larger jug normally containing water was filled with pure high strength whiskey straight from the stills, before it went into the casks. The smaller one normally reserved for whisky contained pure water.

Penny sensing what was coming smiled. 'The pair, already quite merry after their fourth distillery visit of the day, thanking their hosts profusely accepted the offer of a 'wee dram'. Archie, the distillery production director, poured a tiny amount of liquid from the small jug as requested by the two 'travellers' and to their

282

encouragement added 3 or 4 time as much liquid from the large jug they assumed to be water.

'They took a large gulp, after carefully nosing the whisky which in unison they chorused 'slangevar! What fine palate' Letting the fiery peaty whiskey slip down. Their hosts responded with 'slange' and solemnly looked at their red-faced guests who gallantly tried to remember specifications and prices.

'They manfully managed the first glass, their speech getting more slurred. It would have been impolite to refuse the second glass. The two jugs were generously pushed over so they could help themselves.

'Trying to be crafty, they splashed a small finger full from the small jug into their empty glasses and topped them up with a generous amount from the large jug.

'They couldn't understand why they were getting hotter, and slightly sleepy.

'As talking became well-nigh impossible they downed their glasses, slurringly thanking their hosts and saying they would be in touch.

'Their chauffeur waiting outside put an arm around each as he decanted the staggering pair into the back seat of the Bentley, from which two little pink hands waved enthusiastically out of each windows.

'The five directors solemnly raised a glass to the departing car as they muttered 'slange' before breaking into howls of laughter as they slid into their chairs.

'"Like Bannockburn all over again,' wailed Sandy the MD. It will be a while before we see those two again."'

Both Penny and Toby spluttered into their drinks before downing them and hand in hand giggled their way up to bed.

**** **** ****

Toby had her dress off before she could protest and quickly pulling off her black thong noticed the marks on it as he dropped it to the floor.

283

Without his normal slow, gentle foreplay, he pushed her onto her back and filled her with a rampant Tom.

She was still lubricated from the encounter with Hugo, so for once he was rough and fast, she climaxed twice as Tom drove in further and faster. She tried to roll away but couldn't as her arms were pinned with his strong hands.

With one almighty drive, he exploded in her, she with her back arched and mouth wide open, he shuddering until he had finished.

As she struggled into the shower she realised it was out of some revenge and not the normal, loving Toby she knew so well. Could he have possibly found out about her and Hugo tonight? As the soothing soap and water washed over her, tears fell to be washed away.

How could she tell Toby that Hugo had raped her when she was 17 and still a student working for pin money on Saturdays. She had only experienced fumbling and sweaty kisses at college dances before. How could she explain the horrid photos that Hugo had taken of her doing disgusting things when he had got her drunk.

He'd threatened to show them to her father if she thought of leaving him. He'd done the same tonight threatening to tell Toby.

Toby came and joined her soaping her back and playing water over her, when she turned to face him, he gathered her into his arms, telling her, 'There, there baby, I don't know what happened tonight, nor do I want to, until you're ready.

'I will always support and love you and if there's anything you want to get off your magnificent bosoms, I'll be here to give you all the support I can.'

She burst into tears again, which he licked from her cheeks saying, 'they're very salty, any more and I'll dry them and go into salt production.'

Looking at the ceiling he said 'Got it! Waterside Salt. Just think of the premium for salt produced by a young girl's tears. I expect it could fetch more than gold!'

Grinning, she said, 'You, stupid man, but I love you,' and planted a soft kiss on his lips. They dried each other and climbed into bed, tightly holding each other until waking around 11 am.

Toby woke her up as he chanted 'rabbits, rabbits' as many times as he could in one breath.

'Sorry to have woken you, it's just a silly thing from school. I always do it on the first of the month. Supposed to bring you good luck and now it's New Year, it's extra special.

'I'll make us a brunch. You come and join me when you smell burnt toast.' He put on an old check shirt, joggings pants and trainers and loped off to the kitchen.

Penny dressed and quickly dabbing on a little make up followed him down, anxious in case he burnt the house down, never mind the toast.

After a long, lazy brunch they decided to 'beat their bounds'. Toby had been given a pedometer thing you clamped on your ankle and it converted strides into yards, feet and inches.

He told Penny he would love to walk around the reservoir to see the exact distance.

'We'll walk all around our land. I'm keen to check on how the trees are coming along.' Putting a finger on her nose he said, 'We'll pop into the pub for a quicky and a reward before we get stuck into that lovely game pie you stuck into the freezer.'

'Great,' she replied. 'We both have to blow away the cobwebs with a bit of fresh air.'

'Cobwebs,' retorted Toby. 'It reminds me of the bloke who named his new house cobwebs. A neighbour commented on his choice of name, to which the chap replied, 'well, it means Currently Owned By the Woolwich Equitable Building Society!

'Come on woman,' giving her a playful slap on her delightful bottom as she took the pie out of the freezer.

The air was crisp, the light frost melting in the weak sunshine. Everything looked fresh and ready for what the New Year would bring.

They were exhausted by the time they had finished their walk and done the two miles down to the pub. Penny reckoned it was a great relief to have a couple of drinks and find Barry and Sally who offered a lift home, as it was getting quite dark.

Toby couldn't wait until the 3rd of January for the planned meeting at Lino's with Joyce and Millie, to get the show on the road.

He kept reminding himself that it was five weeks until they opened and there was so much to do.

He remembered the old Officer Cadet's motto, 'If you can keep your head when all about you are losing theirs and blaming it on you, then you are not fully appreciating the seriousness of the situation!'

He firmly resolved to get a firm grip and steer this new venture to success if only for Joyce and Millie's sake. They had put so much trust in him. He wasn't going to let them down.

CHAPTER TWENTY TWO

Toby arrived 10 minutes early to find Lino sitting in his little office at the back of the shop having just got a large cafetiere ready to plunge. He had set four chairs around his old desk. An electric blow heater was on full, and the only heat source in the empty shop and flat above.

'Oh, well done Lino. And a happy New Year to you!'

'Same to you, Toby. I must say I'm a bit excited and keen to get on with the job.' At that moment the two excited ladies arrived. After the New Year greetings and kisses all round they gathered around the table in the new warm little office.

Toby got up and brought to the desk the piping hot cafetiere, 4 mugs and spoons, a bottle of milk and a bowl of white sugar lumps before asking each of the ladies how they preferred their coffee before pouring it for everyone.

Joyce was well impressed that he made coffee for them, as it was usually they who were treated like skivvies. Perhaps, this partnership thing could work, she thought smiling at Millie, who notepad in front of her, biro in hand gratefully sipped her coffee.

Lino started by welcoming the three into his little shop, where he had started 15 years ago after de-mob from the Air Force. 'I think you ladies agree, we'll let Toby give us his ideas and Millie can get everything down, if Toby is not too quick! Then we'll go over it afterwards piece by piece.'

'That's it Lino. In the Army we called it a Chinese Parliament. One person came up with a plan, which everyone kicked about, ironing out any snags or problems so that it became their joint plan which had 100% backing and support from each member of the team. That's how were going to succeed.'

They all nodded in agreement, so he continued. 'Lino and I will agree on what capital we need when we know all our costs, but I want to emphasise that there'll be more than enough to guarantee you two ladies a full year employment to ease any worries you might have.

'Lino will keep the premises and charge a rent for the offices and flat, which he assures me will be favourable.

'Millie will have the flat on a year's tenancy, again at a favourable rent. I've been thinking about names, and thought Cooper Moore sounded neat.' Three heads nodded as Millie wrote. 'I have looked at the competition from Ripon to Bedale, Harrogate to Ilkley and the majority are slick, neon lighted. Modern desks and daft looking chairs.

'I would like to go traditionally. We're in the country, where value counts and not the flash,' to nods all round, 'So I would suggest in this lovely double fronted Georgian shop with worn stone steps we have one large old partners desk with two deep leather chairs for clients and a similar chair for one of us opposite. I can see a set of deep leather club chairs at the side for people, a coffee/tea machine so people can help themselves.

'Papers and brochures on coffee tables in front of their chairs. Soft lighting. Display boards in the front windows.

'I would like two good loos for Ladies and Gentlemen to which anyone shopping can pop in off the street. They would pass through, maybe having a quick look at the brochure. It's all good for PR.

'I think our sign Cooper Moore should be in old English, say gold on green and brown.'

'Oh yes,' exclaimed Joyce. 'Gold on dark brown would look solid, country, been there for ages.'

'We would have our brochures, letter heads, envelopes and business cards all in the same,' joined in Millie. This time a smiling Lino got up and brewed some fresh coffee and produced a big box of Bourbon biscuits from a drawer.

'Oh, my favourites,' squealed a delighted Millie.

'I have ordered a new Land Rover for myself,' continued Toby 'and I'm going to get Joe to spray my old one in our colour and have his pal, a sign writer to letter it with our name, address and telephone number in gold.

'We'll pay you a little extra Millie, if you agree to keep it clean. It'll be a free advert wherever it goes, and a sparkling clean Land Rover shows to everyone our attitude to our business.'

'Hear, hear,' from Lino as he thumped the desk.

'Perhaps you ladies could choose the colour of the carpet for the showroom, with Lino's help and connections, I'm sure we'll get a good deal. Maybe we could have a carpet tile path from the front door to the loos, so that we don't ruin the good showroom carpet with muddy feet!'

'I've got something to add,' said Joyce quietly. 'Both me and Millie took our redundancy payment at the end of December, meaning we can start now.'

To a worried-looking Lino she said, 'I met Beryl Foster, what was at a WI meeting. Beryl and I went to the same school. She went on to university and joined Savills, the Estate Agents, becoming their highest paid female executive before she took early retirement this summer. The poor duck is bored and has agreed to teach Millie and me all we need to know on keeping the books, tax and legal side.

'If she can get us up to speed, she knows how we can take exams to get letters after our names.'

'Fantastic Joyce,' exclaimed Toby. 'I think I'm already redundant,' to claps and shouts of no, no from Joyce and Millie.

'I must say though,' mused Toby 'that she would be ideal cover for holidays or illness.'

'She's got a clause in her retirement that she cannot work for any other estate agent for one year. Any road, that was May, so in a few months she can!' said Joyce.

'I propose Simon Simpson as our lawyer, and perhaps Lino and Joyce could come up with our accountants. Lastly, Lino has confirmed that he only wants to be involved with the Estate Agency and has agreed that should I buy any property for myself, I may and will pay the firm any commission so that no-one loses out.

As I said before, I'm going to try and find old properties to refurbish, and even build if a plot comes up.

Again, anything which comes through Cooper-Moore will have the proper payments, made to the firm.

I'll get salary figures for you two worked out by the lawyers for you to approve or make any adjustment you feel is required.

Lino and I are both going on to the lawyers now to draw up all the docs. Can we meet in a week, to get everything signed? Walter can finish his own building work.

Millie, you can have the keys to the flat then. Let's all troop up there now. Lino left it partly furnished. You might want to paint the odd wall, but I think you could just move in.'

'Oh, it's lovely,' chirped Millie skipping around the two double bedrooms. In one Lino had left a double bed, two bedside tables and a big wardrobe with a mirror in the middle. The bathroom had a corner bath and shower.

The kitchen had been revamped by Mrs. Lino about 5 years ago, and had all the kit you'd require, even a microwave and large fridge/freezer.

Tears were streaming down Millie's cheeks as she gasped, 'It's marvellous, it's all I could ever wish for! I promise to really look after it and keep it spotless.'

'I know you will,' agreed Toby, giving her a little hug.

**** **** ****

When they met a week later, Joyce and Millie were overjoyed to find their salaries were just the same as their previous bank ones, but with the exception that they would have a good share of any net profit at the year-end.

As Toby had said, it was up to all four of them to work hard together to produce the goods.

All agreements were signed and copies taken by all. Lino handed over the keys of the flat to Millie who said she'd paint and clean it from top to bottom and she would move some furniture in which her mum had promised her.

Joyce said she'd get on well with Beryl who was really 'on the ball' and she and Millie were learning so much from her.

'As poor Beryl was so lonely in an isolated cottage after the passing of her husband Maurice, I thought it might be a good idea for her to have a little break and come and share the flat for a week or two to keep Millie company.'

'That's a great idea,' exclaimed Lino. 'Joyce can come in and they can study together, whilst we get the show on the road!' continued Lino, with a twinkle in her eye.

'She can teach Millie to be as good a cook as she is, and keep her out of mischief,' joined in Joyce.

'I'm not like that,' stammered a blushing Millie.

'No, I know love, just joking,' replied Joyce gently.

At Simon's office last week Toby had set up his property company with Walter and his three workers. They would also form a maintenance team to look after any properties he bought to let out to tenants.

He was planning to 'do up' two properties a year, then sell them, with the aim to make sufficient profit to buy a third one which he would let out.

If he could just have one free property a year, all rent would be his of course, plus any rise in the value.

He, Walter and the boys would also build one property from scratch during the summer. It would be sold via their estate agency. The agency would gain profit, whilst all the building team shared in the profit of the sale.

'Bloody marvellous if you can pull it off,' affirmed Walter. 'You are going to be a wealthy young man, but you are also making us all better off. It's what you could call a win-win situation.'

'It will take hard graft Walter, but I hope it'll be fun too. There'll be tears along the way, and things won't always go right, but so long as we stick together, we'll get there.'

The boys got cracking on Lino's shop. First they took down his little glass cubicle of an office and replaced it with what looked like a large glazed conservatory built on to the back wall of the building.

Two loos were built at the other end of the back wall which was finished in brick to look like a walled garden.

The winding, simulated brick path from the front door to the loos with their pantile roofs was surrounded by artificial grass, complete with a freshly mown stripe in a line of carpet.

The dimming ceiling lights gave the effect of sunshine on the dullest of days.

Joyce delightedly pronounced, 'It'll be like working outside in the garden, even at wintertime. It'll be the talk of the town.'

'No, talk of Yorkshire,' added Millie proudly.

Penny had found the largest old oak partners desk which sat bathed in a pool of light in front of the conservatory. She'd placed a large green leather swivel chair facing the three matching chairs.

Over to the left was a round white table with 4 solid, white, wooden chairs.

The chairs had brown and gold seat cushions to match the large 6 foot Cooper-Moore brown and gold umbrella in the table.

The walls were covered in boards detailing the properties For Sale or To Let.

As it all gradually came together, Toby admitted to Lino, 'When Penny first came up with the designs I thought it all a bit naffy, but you know now I'm really chuffed.

When you look in from the outside, especially at night, you'd think you were in the back garden of some really Des Res.'

'I totally agree,' joined Lino. 'There is certainly not another Estate Agent like this.

We'll either sink or swim and funnily enough with you and the great team you've got together, I'm putting my money on not just a swim, but swimming the bloody channel,' he chuckled.

**** **** ****

All this had taken time, but now Millie was ensconced in her flat to the envy of friends and family.

Beryl had taught Joyce and Millie all she knew and now as the grand opening by Lord and Lady Middleham was fast approaching she was preparing to leave for holiday to the Canaries with a close friend.

Millie would be so sorry to see her leave as she had been great fun, and taught her to cook and generally look after the flat.

They had all visited every estate agency in a large radius, pretending to be looking for a property for a family member too busy in the south to look for themselves, or a well off friend wanting to move back from overseas.

It gave them time to check various properties, prices and how the salesperson came across. How keen, knowledgeable and smart they were.

Toby had come across a semi-detached three floor and basement house with lovely views of the Valley Garden in Harrogate. With his developer hat on, he had arranged a viewing with Walter. The bored salesman had a smoke by the front door, leaving them to go over the empty house by themselves.

'No problem Toby,' hissed Walter. 'We can get four, 3 bedroom flats out of this.'

'Surely you mean three?' queried Toby. 'No, look there's a rear door with two steps into the rear garden. We can 'tank' or line the walls like a swimming pool in reverse. Not a drop of water will get in. They'll be as snug as a bug in a rug. We'll put in bathrooms, kitchens, double glazed windows, gas central heating, the lot,' he said with a satisfied grin.

'That's all very well, but what about the costs?' grumbled Toby.

'Well,' returned Walter 'They want five thousand for it and if we spend say £500 per flat, that's £7000 all up. I reckon we could sell the top two flats at £3000 each and the bottom two at say £2500 each, making around £4000 profit. You could rent them out for maybe £500 a year.'

Having chatted up the bored youth, Toby learned that the deceased former owner had no close heirs and the solicitors wanted a quick sale. 'For cash sale, he reckoned they would take £4500.'

Toby slipped him a twenty-pound note, saying if he knew any similar properties, could he ring him, giving the man his 'Waterside Farm' card.

They returned to the sales office where Toby put in a bid for £4500. Talking directly to the solicitor conducting the sale he mentioned Simon's name. Luckily they knew each other well. Toby was told that they would discuss his offer and let Simon know tomorrow. On their way out, the salesman buttonholed Toby saying, that he knew that the elderly couple in the next door semi-detached were keen to sell so they could move nearer their children on the East Coast.

Toby slipped him another £20 calculating that was about what the chap's weekly wage would be.

'If you can ring me with their name, and also let them know that next door was sold for £4500, I reckon we can do business!'

The lad was delighted at making such easy money and said, 'If I hear of anything that I can put your way instead of the firm, so long as you can pay me well, I will.'

Shaking hands they left him. Walter exclaimed, 'Bugger me, I've never seen such disloyalty. I'm glad he doesn't work for me.'

'If you pay peanuts, you get monkeys,' Toby observed. 'That's why I hope our team will stay loyal, because hard work will be rewarded, and we all help each other.

Anyone cheating like that only cheats themselves in our set up. If we can find one or two more like him it will make our job a lot easier. By the way, Walter if you are wondering, I'm going to go and offer the old couple the full £5000. What the solicitors miss I'll give to the old couple.'

'Just like Robin Hood,' chuckled Walter.

February the 14th, the opening day was fast approaching when some of Lino's effort by doing the rounds of his old farmer customers paid off. He found two of them, getting too old to carry on dairy farming.

With no young to carry on, they wanted to sell up and instructed Lino to put it up for sale.

On the same day, three locals who knew Joyce, wanted her to sell their cottages.

Toby heard via Walter, who had done work for a couple of yuppies, that they had been promoted and would be leaving for London. Both parties gave Toby their substantial houses to sell.

Simon pointed Toby in the direction of the Church Commissioners who were to sell two old rectories, one of them to be replaced by a new modern rectory, for which Toby would put in an application to be considered for the new building work.

Over the next ten days, five more instructions to sell were received. One of Lino's pals, Leon was a photographer who took photos of all the properties for the brochure. With a 16mm cine camera he shot them all from the outside and all the rooms as if you were walking through. He finished off with a sound track explaining and introducing each one. He turned it into a 10 minutes loop film to run on a huge screen by back projection for the opening day.

By making large photo boards of each property and hanging them on the walls, it really looked as if they had half of Yorkshire on their books.

Wire baskets were filled to the brim with brochures of the property above. The place really looked professional and business like.

Joyce had put all the property and legal books that Beryl had given her into bookends on a shelf behind her desk in the conservatory.

A large cupboard was loaded with contract forms and blank specification sheets for printing on the new high-speed machine.

Toby checked everything with each member, rehearsing them in questions and answers for the opening day. As he explained, 'We've all got to sing from the same hymn sheet!'

**** **** ****

The day arrived at last. It was dry, with none of the winds they had been experiencing. A watery sun made the day look even brighter. To be on the safe side, Toby turned the central heating up as the four of them assembled at 9 am ready for Lord and Lady Middleham to officially open them at 11.00. Joyce had borrowed two huge water heaters from the WI for tea and coffee.

Boxes and boxes of disposable cups were in place, two or three crates of milk were keeping cool by the back door and tins of biscuits almost reached door height.

Mrs. Pickles arrived around 10.30, recruited by Joyce to do the Ladies and Gents, keeping them clean, loo paper refilled as required. Mrs. Pickles did for all the important families, and was a source of knowledge as to what was going on, or as Toby put it 'who was doing who'.

After giving her a couple of her favourite chocolate biscuit and a tea with three sugars, Toby quickly found out that the doctor, Basil Mortimer was thinking of selling his practice to a larger Ripon one. They would build a new modern surgery on the field next to Basil's house if he could get planning.

'I expect he'll have a word with you today, 'cos I know he's coming,' she said with a sniff. 'Oh, and that Mr. Mark Woodhouse, you know the M.P., well I heard that he's done a deal to step down, whatever that is, and they are going to give someone his safe seat.

'What a to-do, safe seat, sounds like fireproof pants to me. Well,' she gushed on breathlessly, 'well then, they are going to make him a Lord. Fancy that! Just like his brother in law, Lord Thomas, who's a real Lord. Mind you, it'll suit her Ladyship, that snotty old cow!'

'All very interesting, Mrs. Pickles. You've certainly got your ear to the ground.'

There was quite a crowd outside now. Lino tied a ribbon of gold tape across the front door and stuck a pair of gold scissors into his top pocket.

The crowd, now some 12 to 15 deep across the bay windows parted like the Red Sea as a florid-faced Thomas and mink clad Liz approached the door.

As he rang the bell, Lino flipped over a Closed sign to Open. He opened the door, handing the gold scissors to his Lordship to cut the tape.

His deep resounding voice boomed out, 'I declare this estate agency open'

A cheer went up and the crowd surged in to, 'well, I never' 'oh, look a conservatory' 'Look at them brollies', 'It's just like a back garden'.

Flashbulbs popped as local reporters and one from the Yorkshire Post interviewed his Lordship and Lady Elizabeth, Lino and Toby.

Toby brought in Joyce and Millie, making sure that their photos would be in the paper. When people were coffee'd, tea'd, biscuits in their hands Tommy banged the glass for quiet and began.

'My wife and I are honoured to have been asked to open this Estate Agency. It's just what's wanted by us Dales folks. Being run by people we know and trust, and what's more, live here amongst us. They support our local shops and pubs. We in turn will support them.

'Mr. Moore, may I call you Lino,' a great cheer went up. 'I know your father started your flooring empire from this very shop, before you went on to expend into many of our surrounding towns, selling you floor coverings across the Dales, from isolated farm houses to small shops in Harrogate. I know we've had some in our kitchen for years. By gum, it lasts well,' to applause and cheers.

'Lino, your old dad would be proud at how you made a success of his business and are now taking on a new challenge.

'Wisely, you have joined forces with Toby, a former army officer, for whom I have the greatest respect,' to even louder clapping and cheers.

'To my sadness I've just been informed that two of longest serving tenant farmers wish to pack in, as the work is getting too hard for them. I've found them two cottages on the estate, and would like Cooper-Moore to handle the sale.'

Another cheer went up. Holding up his hand his Lordship continued. 'My brother-in-law, Mark would like to have a word.'

Like any politician given the opportunity to speak, Mark in his highly polished brogues, and in a deep, rich voice began 'Friends and constituents, I hope you don't mind my taking this opportunity, when it seems like the whole town has gathered for the opening of this truly inspirational enterprise. It will certainly put our little spot of Yorkshire on the map.' Applause broke out, even from those gathered in the street.

More flashbulbs popped as Mark continued, 'I have been honoured to represent you for the last twelve years, and won't be standing at the next election due in a year.

'I hope you will cast your votes for a younger, more with it candidate, who I know will look after you well.

'I am to take up a new challenge, and will be moving to London to be nearer to our children, who as you know both work in the city.' He paused, before adding,

'The point of all this is to say that as Felicity and I have bought a new house, I want to put our present house here 'The Grange' in the capable hands of Toby and Mr. Moore to sell for us.' More cheers and clapping broke out.

As if on cue, Basil Mortimer rose up and the crowd immediately became respectfully silent as their doctor spoke in low distinct words, 'It looks a bit like a Punch and Judy show as we pop up and down.' Gentle laughter broke out from an ever swelling crowd.

Cups of tea and coffee kept appearing and handed out in a seemingly never-ending chain.

Clearing his throat, the doctor continued, 'I'm not getting any younger, and whilst always endeavouring to be on call all the time, now find that my practice has grown like topsy. I've planned to merge with a Ripon group who wish to build a brand new up-to-date modern surgery in the field next to my house. Subject of course to your approval and the dreaded Planning Authority!' The stunned silence was broken by shouts of 'we are behind you Doctor' and 'Brilliant, a new surgery is what we need'.

Holding up his hand he said, 'I think we were all impressed with the way that Toby rebuilt two tired cottages to form Waterside, before getting planning permission to build a super new farmhouse. That has given a life-changing opportunity to a solid and deserving farming family.

I think he is the man I trust to draw up plans, with his excellent architect and apply for planning for us. He seems to have a knack! I want him to use his local builders as after all they will use the new surgery.

I will stay on for a year until the new surgery is up and running, and you are happy with your new team of doctors. Then my wife and I will retire to Dorset, where we have family. I can at last indulge in a lot more sailing.'

He sat to thunderous applause and cheering. Hoping it was the right thing to do, Toby addressed the crowd.

'On behalf of us four at Cooper-Moore, and my builders we cannot thank you all enough for the faith and generosity of His Lordship, Mr. Woodhouse and Doctor Mortimer.

What a fantastic start to our new venture. You can all rest assured that we will all give you one hundred per cent of our efforts. We all feel privileged to work for you.'

Penny popped up beside him and whispered into his ear. Toby spluttered, his mouth opening and closing like a gold fish. He looked at the doctor who gave a wink and slow smile.

Everyone was silent, wondering what was going on, until Toby said, 'My darling wife Penny has just made what was a fantastic, unbelievable day even better by telling me that she is expecting our child!' which was confirmed by a big smile and a wink from Doctor Basil.

Pandemonium broke out only stopped by his Lordship shouting 'this deserves a drink. The first round is on me!'

He followed the quickly evaporating crowd to the hotel. After kisses and hugs all round Lino kindly announced, 'I'll clear up and lock up. Away with you!'

Penny stayed religiously on orange juice in the wild party that developed, whilst Toby unashamedly got as tight as a tick on the endless supply of single malts which kept coming at him from all angles.

CHAPTER TWENTY THREE

Chris took the wheel as Toby and Joe lolled about in helpless abandon in the back.

Penny thanked Chris for the lift and asked, 'How are you keeping? I'm sorry not to have seen much of you recently.' 'Don't worry; we've been so busy at the garage that we haven't had time for anything.

Joe is so pleased at how things have turned out and your dad leaves the whole job to him. Joe just revels in it and has got a really good set of lads to help him.

Your dad reckons they are making more profit than ever, and that it's all down to Joe. It makes me feel real proud. There's only one thing that worries me a bit, it's that I've missed a period, and the next one is due around now. I just don't have the feeling, you know.'

Penny, her hand to her mouth exclaimed, 'Chris, love, that's wonderful news,' giggling, 'We'll be able to push the prams out together'

'If I have time off work, who's going to do the books? Joe relies on me.'

'Don't you worry love,' commiserated Penny, patting her arm 'I'm going to pack in my job with Hugo and help Toby.

In the meantime, you and I will share the garage. We can more than cope between us, and we can look after the babies together and be able to have a break.'

'Oh, you are always amazing, so clear thinking. I feel a lot better now. Don't say anything, I've not told Joe yet,' she paused then continued, 'Just in case it's, you know, not confirmed or something goes wrong.'

They pushed and pulled the still jabbering Joe out of the car and into the flat. 'Men,' exclaimed Penny, 'Do you know Chris, for a ghastly second I felt that the pair of the drunken bums were going to give each other a farewell kiss.'

'Men,' repeated Chris, waving as she closed the door.

Penny drove carefully home and was pleased to see Barry standing outside his front door enjoying a cigarette.

'Missus doesn't like me smoking indoors,' he confessed sheepishly. 'By gum, the boss looks as if he's seen better days.'

Peering closer, he muttered, 'He's as pissed as a newt. Well, I never thought I'd see the day. Do you want a hand with him Penny?'

'That's very kind of you Barry, I'm grateful.' Barry pulled Toby out of the car and propped him upright facing the car, he stooped and taking Toby in a fireman's lift took him into the kitchen, depositing him into a large cane-back chair. He took off his shoes and resting his legs on another chair. Penny slipped in a couple of cushions for his head, Barry took off his tie 'just in case' and turned to the door. 'I reckon he'll be safe and sound till morning.'

'Barry, that's really kind of you,' said Penny giving him a peck on the cheek as he closed the door.

Leaving a table light on and covering him with a rug, bucket in his lap, she kissed him, entreating him to be safe until the morning!

The grey, murky February light filtered into the kitchen as Toby awoke with a start at 7.0 am.

Slowly looking around him, he took in that he was in the kitchen chair with his hands around a bucket.

He wriggled his stiff legs to the floor, straightened his neck and stood up.

Last night came flooding back like a kaleidoscope. He gingerly moved around to the medicine cupboard on the wall and took two aspirin with a glass of cold water, before putting the kettle on and heaping coffee into a small cafetiere.

Nothing like hot, strong black coffee, he told himself. Clutching the hot, steaming mug he took himself to the downstairs cloakroom.

He quickly stripped and put his shirt, socks and underclothes into the nearby washing machine.

Hanging up his suit behind the door he stepped into a cold shower. The cold, powerful water was a shock to his body, but after a few minutes, he was alert and feeling on top of the world as he remembered Penny's wonderful news and all the business that had come their way.

He would have to be on the ball today and get the show on the road. He thought he heard a tapping, so wrapping a towel around his waist he padded to the back door.

Opening up he saw the little paperboy had just brought the daily papers. 'Are you ok Johnnie?' asked Toby. 'Sorry to trouble you sir, but I've got the squits and wonder if I can use the toilet. Mum says there's a bug going around, but I daren't be off sick as they might give the paper round to some other lad, but I need the money.'

'Come in, it's damned cold. What are you saving up for?'

'I want to be a doctor and need books to study. If I can get enough A levels I can go to university.'

'I was just having a shower,' said Toby. 'Follow me,' and Toby led him into the cloakroom and pointing to the loo in the far corner said 'I will finish my shower, whilst you crap over there. Try not to make too much mess.'

Turning his back to the little lad he carried on showering, the noise drowning any sounds from the corner.

Toby tried cold water then hot until normality was restored. Having soaped and shampooed, he was finished when he heard the light tapping on the cubicle door.

He stuck an arm out, grabbing a towel to cover himself before turning to face the lad who thanked him ever so much and assured Toby by saying, 'I have left everything tidy, sir.' His eyes widened as he noticed the deep scars and holes in the man's leg. Johnnie couldn't stop himself blurting out.

'Have you had a bad accident sir? Me dad fell from an iron roof, but it didn't look as bad as that.'

'Oh, it's just a spot of bother I got into in the army. They are bullet wounds and chunks of shrapnel that did it.

303

Now, let's get you on your way, otherwise folks will complain their papers are late,' as he opened the front door for him.

Toby, taking his suit, nipped up the stairs and seeing Penny was fast asleep, tiptoed to the wardrobe to find fresh clothes and had a quick shave before stealing downstairs to cook scrambled eggs and bacon. He retreated to the kitchen table where he made his 'to do' list on a pad, whilst wolfing down his breakfast.

It was only 8.15 when he took up a mug of coffee to Penny 'Look luvvie I've so much to do and get organised, that I'd be best be off. See you, when you see me,' planting a passionate kiss on her mouth.

Little did he think then that their future lives might be like that.

**** **** ****

His first port of call was to the agency, where a bleary-eyed Millie was vacuuming the grass-carpet.

'That looks weird, you should use a lawnmower,' to a giggling Millie.

Joyce bustled in five minutes later saying, 'I am so surprised to see you so early Toby. You were in quite a state last night.'

Toby grinning said, 'you know the old maxim. Work hard and play hard.'

'Talking of work,' said Joyce firmly, 'Let's get on, but where do we start?' The three had just sat at the large desk when Lino turned up.

'By God,' he said 'I didn't think I'd see you today. You must have a strong constitution.'

'Grab a seat Lino, we were just about to work out our priorities. Mind if I shoot first? Then we can bash it about to form our plan?' without waiting for an answer he started. 'Millie love, would you take notes? Right the first point is properties to sell. The two farms from Tommy, then Mark's house. Lino, could you take a camera and measuring tape to get the sales particulars? Perhaps Joyce could go with you to help after making the necessary appointments. We'll take the sale particulars for Doc's house later. I'm going down to see the dreaded planners to check how the land lays. Obviously we want to start building in, say, May. There'll be three planning meetings before May, so we'll have to get a move on.'

'When are you going?' enquired Lino.

'Soon as possible, old bean. In fact I'll ring now and see if there is the possibility of a brief chat to check on their reaction. Millie dear, do you feel you are able to hold the fort and keep any likely customers happy while the rest of us fly around like spare parts?' Seeing her unhappy look he followed on, 'Don't fret love, it's just these first few days when we're all split up to get so much done in such a short time.

'I hope we can all share meeting new clients and doing the boring showing people around.'

She cheered up at this and as the others left, she turned on all the lights and filled the coffee machine. She checked that the loos were tidy and then settled down at the big desk and started to re-read all the property leaflets they had printed.

Toby called the Planning Department and asked if Miss Bateson was available. 'I'm so sorry sir, she's not in today. I think she has a cold, but she'll be in tomorrow because it's Thursday and they have a planning meeting on Friday.'

'Thank you so much,' said Toby. 'I'll try again tomorrow,' and put the phone down relieved at not having to leave a name.

He then rang Karen's private number. It rang for ages before a sniffing, wheezing voice rasped out. 'Hello, who is it?'

'I, your favourite country estate agent.' A silence followed, before Karen's normal voice came through loud and clear. 'Is it really you? Where are you?'

'I'm just twenty minutes away and wondered if I could buy you lunch. I need a bit of advice.'

'Oh yes please, my old Mum said you must always feed a cold.'

'But you haven't got a cold,' protested Toby.

'Course not, silly, it's just that Maggie and I went out to a Valentine's Day Dinner Dance. Absolutely disaster. The only spare blokes batted for the other side and the rest were closely guarded by their wives. We just got pissed and ended up here. Maggie has just left. She'll be livid.'

Toby was secretively pleased as Karen on her own was enough! 'I'll be there in 30 minutes.'

**** **** ****

He put his old Barbour on and a little woolly hat hiding his hair and ears. With a bent back crossed the street and rang her bell.

The door opened and he was literally dragged into the hall. 'Bloody hell. You look like a bloody tramp.'

'Just to fool your neighbours into thinking that you are lowering your sights.'

'Cheeky bugger,' but as he took off his hat and coat, she flung her arms around him, passionately kissing him. 'I've booked a table at a new place near Knaresborough for 1.30. We can talk then. Right now I want you all to myself for an hour.' she replied.

Before he could say anything she led him upstairs. Tom was rapidly rising at the sight of lovely long legs on full view under her short nightie. Closing the door, she rapidly stripped him, before bending to take Tom into her mouth.

The room smelled of perfume, booze and sex. 'Maggie and I had been reading about bondage, so we tried it on each other. Dead kinky, but a dildo isn't the same as the real thing!'

She peeled off her bra and pants and handed him two black cords, saying, 'you can tie my wrists to the head with these and then blindfold me with this black, silk scarf.' Toby did as he was bid.

Tom was bursting at the sight. 'Pretend to rape me,' she softly begged. 'Be rough, cos I'm a bad, bad girl.' Toby slid both hands up her silk nightie. He knelt beside her and gently slapped her face before taking each breast in turn into his mouth, gently nibbled her hard nipples. He moved further down and parting her damp bush roughly thrust in two fingers, twisting and turning as he plunged them deeper and deeper to her animal cries.

Then lifting her by her thighs, as he had before, he thrust in the full length of Tom. He remorselessly tore into her quicker and quicker until she climaxed at each stroke.

A thin voice cried, 'That's it, I've had enough,' as he exploded all over her stomach and thigh.

Tom seemed unstoppable. He cleaned up with tissues from the bedside table and undid her blindfold, before giving her a soft, gentle lingering kiss.

Undoing her wrists he murmured. 'What would you have done if I'd just left you there and gone?' She looked wide-eyed at him. 'You wouldn't.'

'No, but some silly bugger might, just for a laugh. Be careful. I'd stick with Maggie, if I were you.'

She threw a pillow at him, saying, 'Come on, we'd better get cracking. I'm hungry after that.' Shaking his head Toby followed up with 'What a girl.'

**** **** ****

Over lunch in pub cum-bistro Toby told her all about yesterday. 'Wow, that's just incredible,' she said after knocking back half of her glass of claret. 'So really you want planning asap on the surgery.'

She smiled like a Cheshire cat as she drawled, 'Well, you are in luck you lucky boy, 'cos old Fishwick, my boss goes to Dr. Mortimer for his piles. He'll be 100 per cent behind any scheme to push ahead with a super new surgery.

'He'll want preferential treatment from the doctors, the mean old toad!

'I'll bring it up in any other business tomorrow and make sure it gets full support at our next meeting in March, when you should get the go-ahead!'

'You are a perfect angel,' replied Toby, to which she retorted,

'And you are the perfect shag, my dear. Anything else?'

'Well, yes there is,' Toby went on to tell her about the two houses in Harrogate that he wanted to convert.

'I want to sell the first development of four flats so I can use the money to buy the second one from the old couple. That, I want to keep for myself. It's like my pension, 'cos it'll continue to pay me annual rents and hopefully go up in value every year.'

'Bloody hell,' she swore. 'I'm in the wrong game,' looking at him shyly she whispered. 'I've never done it before, because any leak would cost me my job and my measly pension, but because I trust you, perhaps if you scratch my back I'll scratch yours. Can you cut me into the action?'

Toby looked at her slowly and replied, 'I tell you what Karen. For planning on the new surgery and two blocks of flats, I'll give you one of the flats. You choose, and then you can sell your present place, pocket the cash and be mortgage free.'

'Done,' she exclaimed.

'It's going to be fun and profitable for both of us.'

'I'll ring your office tomorrow,' declared Karen 'And say Mr. Fishwick has noted your application if all is ok and the deal will go through. If there's a problem, I won't ring and leave you to get in touch.'

'If you want your pad fairly quickly, can you get permission on it first? I'm buying it soon, as my boys want to get on with it in the colder weather before we move on to the new surgery in late spring, early summer.'

Helping her on with her coat, he stooped down and kissed the nape of her neck, whispering, 'Thanks a million' to which she replied 'We're going to make a million, you and I, and if every deal starts like today, I'm going to be a very wealthy girl.'

**** **** ****

After driving back to the office he found Joyce and Millie busy composing the text for her new houses and farms.

Lino had gone off to see his pal in the photographic club to get all his prints developed, so he could drop the photos and text at their printer's.

As he entered, they turned to look at him. Shaking his head slightly and looking gloomy, both their hands went up to cover their mouths.

He broke into a broad grin and confessed, 'Sorry. That was cruel of me. I managed to have a quick chat with the 'powers that be' and not only do they approve of the surgery, especially as their boss, Mr. Fishwick is a present patient of Dr Mortimer's, but also,' looking at Joyce, 'I told you that I had done the deal to buy those Harrogate flats, that we'll complete at the month's end. They must be a bit short of business at planning as they would slide those in to this month's approvals.'

'Fantastic, Toby,' enthused Joyce, thinking of the extra payments coming her way.

'It's also damned handy,' confirmed Toby. 'I can get Walter and the boys a nice warm inside job over March and April, before moving neatly on to the big surgery job over summer. Now, we can get cracking bringing in and selling as much property as we can.'

'I've been talking to Beryl,' said Joyce. 'She is really missing the busy working environment that she had. Her agreement to not to be involved for a year ends at the end of April, and I wonder if we could find a slot for her?'

'Perhaps as a consultant until then,' suggested Toby, 'and then she could be the lynchpin or a sort of spider in the middle of her web, whilst we are out and about getting on with the business.'

'Oh, I'll tell her that. She'd be so pleased. She doesn't want much salary, it's just being busy and feeling wanted. She said she really enjoyed it when she stayed with Millie.'

'And I enjoyed having her,' exclaimed Millie.

'I would love her to stay again. She taught me so much and we had a lot of giggles. I was just thinking, if she stayed here, she could move her cherished things in and let her lovely little cottage. She would have a nice little second income.'

Toby and Joyce grinned at each other. 'Now, that's a real business woman talking,' said Toby, patting Millie's shoulder. 'We will turn you into a property magnate yet, young Millie.' At this point Lino came in and proudly showed them all his photos and layouts for the various properties. Proudly, with a flourish, he brought out the proofs of each one in full, glorious colour. The full particulars measurements and agreed asking prices, all headed with the company's gold and brown logo.

'Lino, that's absolutely marvellous. What a tremendous job you've done.' Lino beamed, but couldn't help shyly saying to Toby, 'I suppose you've been fannying about all day, whilst we have been putting in some hard graft!' Toby thought to himself, you don't know how near the truth you are before telling an astounded Lino what he had achieved.

'Well, I'll go to the top of our stairs,' exclaimed Lino. 'All the builders, farmers and property men I've talked to all hate the planners and vice versa. You just seem to slip in and glide about, getting what you want.' Again, you've hit the nail on the head, thought Toby, 'but I don't know how you do it.' Continued Lino. 'Now I hope there is no bribery or ought like that going on, 'cos I'll be no part of it.'

'Nothing like that, Lino,' Toby assured him. How those words would come back to haunt him. 'No,' continued Toby. 'I find if you can find a mutual point of agreement with benefits to both parties, a deal can be done. The old principal of willing buyer, willing seller.'

Lino grunted, 'Well there's a lot to celebrate, almost as much as yesterday. Hell, we'll go over to the pub again celebrating every night if we carry on like this. I don't think my heart or my liver could stand it.'

They all laughed and nodded to each other as Lino rubbing his big hands together as he uttered, 'I don't know about you three, but I haven't felt such a buzz for years. It fair gives me a kick every morning. It's summat to look forward to.'

'Well I'll love you and leave you folks,' said Toby. 'I'd better get back to my missus before someone else does.'

'You are right there young man, you'd be best keeping an eye on our Penny.'

Toby turned Lino's words over in his mind as he went to his new Land Rover, but soon dismissed them as he drove home to tell Penny all. Well, not all, there was a part that left him uneasy and not happy with himself. He reasoned the end justified the means. Chillingly he thought, that's what Hitler thought too.

**** **** ****

The kitchen was warm and comforting, the aroma of a rich, wine filled beef casserole wafted out into the cold night air as he locked the door.

Penny wiped her hands in her apron and flicked a loose blonde wisp from her eyes as she covered him in kisses. Pouring him a large glass of Saint Emillion she said, 'How is the big hunter, back from the field?' So he filled her in with the day's goings on.

'By the way. How is your bump, and will you have to quit drinking?'

311

'Doc says, the odd glass of red now and then won't do us any harm,' she stated, patting her almost flat, model-like stomach.

'Depends how often now and then occurs. And how about a bit of nicky-nacky-noo,' asked Toby.

'I'm sure everything in moderation is fine,' she declared.

'Now, how has your day been?'

'Pretty damned good for all of us,' said Toby, helping himself to a generous glass of red wine, before going on to tell her all apart from the details of his trip to Otley.

After a warming and delicious supper, they went for a long relaxing shower together. Soaping and kissing, before drying each other and tumbling into bed, for a long night of loving and satisfying sex.

Next day Toby had arranged a full day with Walter at Mike Mortimer's. It was a bit ironic Toby thought that Mike was Basil's, the doctor's brother. He would do a good job for his brother.

'Hells bells,' chortled Mike, when Toby told him of his plans for the surgery and one house to be turned into four flats with the near certainty of a second at the end of the year. 'Nothing's agreed yet,' replied Toby, 'But Planning feels pretty sure they will all get approval.

'Mike, I don't want to muck both you and Walter about, but speed is of the essence. I need Walter to get the flats done before the end of April and be ready to do the big build on the surgery over summer. We don't have to get out of the block running, we have to come out bloody sprinting! I guarantee to pay for your work on the flats and surgery whatever the outcome of planning.'

'I know you will dear boy,' asserted Mike. 'You are a true gentleman, a dying breed! Noel Coward once said 'England's going to the dogs.'

'I'm afraid we've bloody well gone,' to an affirmative nod from Walter. 'Mike, would you mind if I put a call through to my spy after lunch?'

312

'I wish I'd had your spy over all my years, life would have been much simpler.'

Scratching his head before rattling around in an ancient metal filing cabinet Mike confessed, 'It's a bit weird but I remember one Christmas, years ago at Basil's when he was complaining about having to use his house as a surgery and consulting rooms. We sketched out his ideas for a perfect surgery on a bit of paper. I kept it somewhere here.'

After rummaging around for a few minutes, he pulled out a sheet of foolscap paper. 'Aha,' he exclaimed. 'My wife always says I'm like squirrel, and never throw anything out. Comes in handy,' as he spread the paper before them.

'Blimey,' exclaimed Toby. 'Mike, it's the real McCoy.'

'Look, it's roughly to scale with doc's house, and this is his next-door field. On the back are the front and rear elevations,' Mike pointed out. It was a large, single story, stone built building squatting nicely into the sloping field.

'What do you reckon Walter?' Toby asked.

'Be a joy to work on,' replied an enthusiastic Walter.

'I'd recommend using these new double glazed windows and frames that are made of a type of plastic that looks like wood. That way you'd never have to keep re-painting every few years.

'As you've already got mains water, gas and electricity on site it'll be a doddle.

'If we could start in early May, subject to what fancy medical kit doc might want and given reasonable weather, I reckon it could be up and running by the end of August.'

'That would be just right,' returned Toby. Mike sketched the building from all elevations and using the rest of the field produced a large car park, with raised beds and a lawn surrounded by trees.

He then produced a plan showing the consulting and treatment rooms, an office and a dispensary so that patients could collect their prescriptions on the spot to save them having to trail into the chemist in Ripon.

313

'Genius,' said Toby admiringly. 'How soon can you knock up the plans?'

'Give me a couple of hours and you can have them.'

'May I use your phone to ring my office?'

'Sure,' said Mike, waving at the phone.

He was already busy at his draughtsman's table, happily immersed, doing the thing he knew and loved best.

Toby told Joyce, that he was with Mr. Mortimer and just wondered if anyone had phoned. 'Well, we've had several enquiring about properties for sale, and three enquiries for you to market their houses.

'There has just been one woman on the line saying Mr. Fishwork is very interested in Mr. Cooper's plans which would be discussed at tomorrow's meeting, and if you had any plans it would speed things up. All very mysterious, but no doubt it makes sense to you Toby.'

'It does indeed Joyce. I'm going to Otley to drop off some plans that Mike Mortimer is finishing now. Fingers crossed they'll get them on Friday's Agenda.'

Mike's eyebrows raised, softly he said, 'Do I gather that you might get these for the planning committee on Friday? If you do, I'd say you must have the chairman in your pocket.'

'Just taking a gamble, Mike. My mole tells me they won't have much in front of them, so hopefully we can be referred to the March meeting, but that's too damned close for Walter to make a start on the Harrogate flats. Let's just see.'

Mike and Walter, heads together going over the internal photos and measurements, soon came up with sketches and elevations of the house to be knocked into four spacious flats.

'Whooped,' yelled Toby. 'One down, one to go.'

'Not so,' triumphed Mike.

'Whilst you idle pair were busy tucking in to sandwich, I got the surgery completed. So very much two down and off you go.' Toby made sure Walter had copies to work out all the materials needed so he could come up with prices for both projects.

Toby reminded him that the flats took priority, and telling Walter he would ring him tomorrow. Mike waving, cried, 'Best of luck, and anything else you need, just call.'

CHAPTER TWENTY FOUR

Toby sped off on the now familiar round to Otley. He arrived around four o'clock and going straight to reception announced he had some documents for Miss Bateson.

'I don't suppose she is still here?' he asked.

'She is still preparing for the meeting tomorrow,' replied the girl.

'Who shall I say would like to see her?'

Toby hesitated before replying, 'I don't want to disturb her, but would you please ask her if she will let you take them to her now, as she told me that she needed them for tomorrow.'

After a muffled telephone conversation she got up, grabbed the envelope and disappeared in the direction of Karen's office. She returned quickly, a smile on her face, saying, 'Miss Bateson is relieved to have them, and asked me to thank the gentleman telling him she would be in touch.'

He rang Penny from a phone box on the way home to suggest they go out to the pub and have a bite out for a change to save her cooking.

He stopped off at the office to find Joyce excited about a couple wanting a second viewing tomorrow.

'I think they are hot,' said Joyce. 'As Lino has two viewings up the Dale, can you man the office?'

'That's absolutely fine Joyce,' said Toby thankfully. He could go over timings and costs with Walter after hopefully getting good news from Karen around lunch time. 'I'll be here at 9 and will see you when you get back.'

He was nervous all morning, and Millie couldn't help but notice, as he snatched at the phone every time it rang.

He received a couple of enquiries from people interested in viewing, which he let Millie handle, and one from a woman wishing to sell her house at Kirkby

Malzeard. Apparently her dear husband for nearly 50 years had just passed away.

He couldn't help being sympathetic with the poor bewildered old girl, but nagging at the back of his mind was the worry that Karen might be trying to get through.

He made a mental note to persuade Lino that they needed two telephone lines in. As he was dictating the notes of the old lady to Millie, the telephone rang.

Karen's husky voice breathed down the line, 'who is a busy boy then? I've tried a couple of times already.'

'Sorry madam,' replied Toby, hoping Millie hadn't overheard, 'but I was just busy with a client.'

'I hope you weren't in the back screwing that young secretary of yours. Both Maggie and I need a service call late this afternoon.'

'I'm afraid Madam I won't be able to make an appointment tonight, but a late afternoon appointment would be possible, I'm sure I can manage that.'

'Ok,' she whispered. 'We'll leave early, can you make my place at 4.30?'

'That will be fine Madam, but I must leave by six, as I have an appointment near here at 6.30.'

'That'll do fine,' she chuckled. 'By the way, can you bring a little something to help us celebrate?' She paused before continuing, 'Yep, everything has gone through, and you can expect full planning on both early next week. See you soon. Bye.'

'Good news?' asked Millie raising her eyebrows. She was more confident. Dressing better, well-groomed and Toby, noticing her full little breasts peeking out of the undone cardigan felt Tom twitch. Not now old boy.

Smiling at her he replied, 'Really good news, I think we might just have the planning we want for the surgery and also possibly the flats in Harrogate.'

She darted across and kissed him. Her soft skin and sweet, clean smell, her firm breasts pushing into him caused Tom to swell and rise spectacularly. Feeling it against her, with eyes wide open, she breathed, 'I didn't

317

think you felt anything for me. I've been a good girl, and never been with a man. My mum always says wait for the right man to come along. When I first saw you in the bank I felt you were the right man! I mean you are only 6 years older than me.'

Dropping her arms and moving back she said simply, 'I'm here for you if you ever want me'

'Millie, dear, I'm very fond of you but as I'm married I'd hate to take advantage of you. Let's be really good pals. Who knows what the future holds?'

Blinking back her tears, a blushing Millie moved back, murmuring, 'That's why you are such a good man. I can wait. I'll be here for you.'

Toby pondered what she'd just said, and pursing his lips got on with his work.

Walter appeared half an hour later. Toby told him that he had just heard unofficially, that they had planning for both developments. He had to go back to see them at planning after the meeting this afternoon.

Walter whistled, 'That couldn't be better, as we'll have the flats done by the end of April. Then we can move straight on to the surgery. Tell you what; once we've got the brunt of the work done by all of us at the flats, we can leave Arthur to finish off with the plumber and decorator. The rest of us can go and get the foundations in for the surgery. Then we'll have a clear four months to get that done by the end of August. Eee, I can't wait to see you as a dad. You'll be needing a bit of time off, with all those sleepless nights.'

Millie giggled, Toby broke into a broad grin as he said, 'I'll hold you to that Walter. Millie, you are my witness.

'Now Walter, those costs, figures for the flats and the surgery should show us a good profit, whilst still making good profits for the Estate Agency side. It's truly a win-win situation for us both.'

He smiled 'I'm just nipping down to give Simon a cheque for the flats so he can complete as soon as he can.

I'll fund the costs on a weekly basis Walter to keep you afloat.

'After this, we'll put you and your team on monthly salaries and fund our company so we can carry on independently.'

'That's absolutely fine by me Toby. I know we'll all get on together, like we did when we did your place.

'It's such a relief not to be involved in the paperwork and chasing folks for money. Instead you'll find the work, and we can get on with what we do best.'

'I'm off then,' said Toby as he stuffed a cheque book in his inner pocket and set off.

Simon was pleased about the house in Harrogate to be converted into four flats. Toby told Simon he wanted to give the top flat when finished to a friend, and asked how best to do it.

'Far simpler if you give your friend a cheque to cover it, and then just buy it like the other three. No doubt Cooper-Moore will advertise for the sale, collect their fees of which you will eventually have a share, and likewise you will have the lion's share of the profit on the conversion so it shouldn't cost you a lot in the end!'

'When will we complete?' asked Toby.

'Well, the other side are talking of the last day of the month, in about ten days' time.'

'Perfect, then we can crack on and get it done in two months.'

'That's quick, you must be a hard taskmaster,' grinned Simon. Toby checked his watch and saw it was just on four o'clock.

He sped off to Otley, stopping to buy a bottle of Bollinger, arriving at Karen's just after 4.30.

**** **** ****

On pressing the button he heard Karen, 'Come on up, we are waiting for you.'

319

Glancing up he saw the curtains had been drawn. Full of curiosity and a little anxiety he mounted the stairs and tapped on the door, which was opened by Karen in a sheer black see-through slip. Her black fishnet, stockings were held up by suspenders. On her feet were black stilettos with at least 6 inches heels.

The room was warm and heavy with scent. As she led him into the bedroom, he saw Maggie who looked slimmer than last time. She was dressed identically to Karen, but in white which revealed her thick bush, causing Tom to try and burst out of his trousers.

'Thank you very much,' squeaked Karen, taking the champagne and putting it into ice bucket with three glasses beside it.

'Hope you didn't mind Toby, but as you can only spare us an hour, we want to have you for every minute. Just stand where you are. We've been talking about this for ages. Right Maggie?'

'Right,' muttered Maggie. They both moved in on him, deftly taking off his jacket, shirt and tie before unbuckling his leather belt, taking off his trousers, shoes and socks.

They gazed, mesmerised at the huge mound breaking out of the white silk boxer shorts.

'Careful, don't break it,' murmured Karen, as Maggie carefully lifted the boxers over Tom's huge, bulging head.

'Me first,' insisted Karen, who stooping, took Tom's head into her mouth. 'God, it must have grown, I can hardly get it in.'

'Move over,' ordered Maggie as she tried. Grasping Tom firmly in her tiny hands she opened wide and just managed.

'Big mouth,' chided Karen. They stood in front of him and slowly removed their bras and thongs.

Toby thought that Tom might ejaculate in any second.

Karen lay on the bed, legs akimbo and beckoned Toby to get down on his knees. Parting her mass of clean smelling pubic hair, he ran his thumbs down either side of her blood filled, enlarged lips to expose her firm clitoris.

He played with it with his tongue round and round then sucking the entire swelling clitoris into his mouth. He played with the hard little button with his tongue.

Then, licking the entire lining he encircled her vagina with his tongue, before plunging his forefinger in and going around in ever widening circles until she was wet and moaning. Looking up he saw Maggie squatting over her head, Karen's tongue outstretched caressing Maggie's open vagina. Her head was back, mouth open.

'Now,' cried Maggie as she climaxed. As if in a well-rehearsed play Maggie lay on her back, legs apart, whilst Karen turning over onto her stomach, her feet on the floor, presented her bottom to Toby.

'Now,' she cried again. 'Fuck me Toby.' Toby standing, grasping Karen's ample bosoms with each hand, eased Tom in to cries of 'More, more, harder.'

Tom responded until Karen shrieked as orgasm followed orgasm. Maggie was moaning from Karen's continued kissing of her full, wet vagina.

At a signal from Karen, they slid into reversed positions. Toby was in frenzy, frightened that Tom might erupt before he could satisfy Maggie.

She was tighter and more slippery then Karen. As Tom drove right in and out relentlessly she was crying 'Yes, yes,' until like Karen exploded in a series of orgasms.

Hastily pulling out a reluctant Tom, Toby too had several shudders as he erupted down Maggie's long, silky black-stockinged legs.

They both lay on their backs side by side, their sweaty bodies heaving as Karen said, 'That was the best shag I think I've ever had.'

'Me too,' muttered Maggie. 'I thought you were going to kill me.'

Toby cleaned himself, dressing quickly, opened the now-chilled champagne and said 'Thank you both, that was wonderful. Enjoy your champagne, you both deserve it.'

Kissing them both he said, 'Sorry to leave you, but I've really got to shoot, if you'll forgive the pun!' and was on the way home.

**** **** ****

Planning approval came through as promised, to delight from all around. Especially from the doctors' practice in Ripon, who could finalise the purchase on the field to be built on and Basil's house.

The third in the practice, a bright young doctor, John Farnell, his wife Vicky and three children were to move in once the new surgery was up and running.

Basil would stay on to ensure a smooth transition. John, a keen cricketer looked forwards to the chance of playing for Masham, who this year had won the area championship.

The next few weeks just sped by as Walter and the boys worked like Dervishes, and had done all the work they could.

They left Arthur and Paul to finish off and moved on to supervising the work on the foundations for the surgery.

Toby took the opportunity to visit the elderly couple who wished to sell their house. There and then they agreed to accept the £5000 that Toby had offered them. Simon drew up contracts for the sale in September.

From the four 'Artist's Impressions' that Mike had produced Toby had priced Karen's flat at £2500 and had a large red sold on it.

'If people think we've achieved that price, I reckon £2000 each for the other two and £1800 for the garden flat are snips.'

'Hope you're right,' sniffed Lino. 'All the more commission,' rubbing his hands. 'Tell you what though, we are doing all right. We're getting business in and managing to shift them pretty damned quick. I reckon we're onto a winner.

'The two ladies are happy as skylarks. Just yesterday, Joyce was totting up the books and reckons that if it carries on like this, she and young Millie with their salaries and profit share could almost double the salary they got at the bank.'

'Don't forget that next week, due to the good weather the boys will start building the surgery. Beryl's 'gardening leave' ends, so she will join as an advisor and secretary, moving back in with Millie to keep us on the straight and narrow.'

'Aye, I'd forgotten that. It'll free up Joyce from the bumf and let her get out conducting viewings and selling. Amazing how she and Millie have taken to it. Like ducks to water. They've right blossomed.'

The three flats were quickly sold. Toby smiled inwardly as he had not only covered the costs, plus alterations and given the boys work, but Karen's flat had been paid for!

Toby had given cash to Karen's mother, so she could buy the flat in her name and hopefully not lead a trail to Karen.

When she received the money for the sale of her Otley house, she could then show she had bought the flat with the proceeds.

As Karen was moving in, Colin proudly announced to Penny and Toby that he and Margot were to marry in June.

'We get on so well and have the same interest. I'm not getting any younger. I've been in the motor business long enough and want to retire. We're planning to move into Margot's place in Harrogate.

'I've built up a nice little nest egg, apart from the garage, and anyway, Margot's not without. Her late hubby, Paul left her a shed load of shares in their department store when he sold out to a London chain in the mid-fifties.

'Poor bloke, turned up his toes just a year after. Fancy that, working all those years, building up that wonderful store, selling out at the right price, and then not having time to enjoy it. Makes you think,' he muttered, shaking his head.

'What are you going to do with the garage?' queried Penny.

'Been giving it some thought,' he pondered. 'I'm going to put it in your name, love,' he said to Penny. 'All proper like. You'll be chairman, with Joe promoted to managing director and Chris company secretary. I'll be retained as a consultant at an annual salary we all agree on. I'm going to let the house, our old home love, to Joe and Chris on a peppercorn rent.

'Then that bright young mechanic that Joe's been bringing along can move into Joe's flat,' he ended beaming with pleasure.

'Well, you have been doing a lot of planning, and I think you've done absolutely the right thing,' said Toby shaking Colin's hand.

'So do I Daddy,' cried Penny, hugging and kissing her father. As a happy and relieved Colin, feeling a weight drop off his shoulders went off to tell the news to Joe and Chris and the rest of the team, Penny turning to Toby, tears in her eyes said, 'Oh, I'm so relieved he's going to re-marry, especially to Margot who we all get on with so well.

'Dad's been my mum too. Very difficult, but he means everything to me.'

'I do hope he'll be really happy and enjoy his well-earned retirement,' followed Toby.

'Oh, I forgot,' said Colin popping his head around the door 'Will you be my best man Toby? It'll only be a small church do, but I need someone who is unflappable and can make a good speech. Who better than my son-in-law, the man with the golden voice that can talk the birds out of the trees.'

'Colin, congratulations, and I'm honoured to have been asked,' said Toby grasping Colin's outstretched hand in both of his. 'When are you planning the big day for?'

'We've got to firm up, but we thought around the 10th of June and then honeymooning by cruising around the Greek Islands. My sister Sue and her husband both fell in love with Greece, so much so that they've given up their jobs and started a travel agency specialising in Greece. So theyve laid on the red carpet treatment throughout!

'We'll get back at the end of June with plenty of time to wait for my granddaughter,' smiled Colin.

'Grandson,' retorted Toby.

'As a matter of fact, you're both wrong,' replied Penny.

On seeing both of their jaws drop, she continued, 'I've been waiting to get you both together. Dr Basil reckons from the size and shape we might be in for twins.'

Both men gasped like gold fish, with no sound coming out of their mouths, until Toby managed a strangled 'Bloody hell'. They both hugged a tearful but happy Penny.

CHAPTER TWENTY FIVE

Work went on at a frenetic pace on the surgery, and by the time of the wedding the walls were rising daily. A bit like Jack and the Beanstalk. The wedding, no longer a little do became a big do. Margot had chatted to Lord Tommy, who had readily agreed to allow them to put up a marquee in the castle grounds for their reception.

Actually, he was intrigued as he told Harry, 'It's a damned good idea for making more revenue to keep this crumbling old pile going.

'We'll use this as a sort of blueprint. My cousin, Charlie does about 12 weddings over the summer and makes a bomb out of it. He's also talking about building rooms in an annexe to house guests and do conferences,' he said to an excited Harry.

'If we can do the same, we can maintain the fabric and décor and actually make ourselves a tidy income.'

'That's pretty damned clever Pa, I know Jill and I could throw ourselves into it and make it really work!'

The church was so full of guests and locals, that the service was relayed by speaker to the crowd waiting outside on that gloriously sunny and warm day. With Margot's military planning, closely followed by Harry and Jill, the reception went like clockwork.

Toby's witty and hilarious speech was cheered to the rafters before dancing went on until breakfast was served around 4am. Margot and Colin had left by midnight for their drive to the Majestic for the night. Their chauffeur driven Rolls took them to Manchester for the flight to Athens to start their cruise. Toby helped Penny remove the few personal possessions of Colin's which they left in Margot's large, stray-side apartment.

Joe and Chris moved in the next day to start re-decorating room by room.

Penny told them, 'Anything you don't want, sell or give to charity.'

The young mechanic was promoted to workshop manager and readily moved into Joe's now empty flat with his young wife and baby boy.

As they had been living with his widowed mum in her semi, it was a great relief all around.

As Toby watched the moves going on he looked laughingly at Penny as he said, 'You know it just reminds me of a game of musical chairs.'

**** **** ****

The three weeks flew by as Joe and the boys adjusted to their new roles and got stuck in to what was a busy and profitable summer.

As a tanned and fit Colin and his new wife swept up the hill into the village, they were amazed to see what looked a finished surgery, certainly from the outside.

Basil's substantial, detached house next door had been sandblasted to clean up the old, weathered stone to look just like the new surgery next door.

New, dark brown, double-glazed windows and doors had been fitted.

'My, someone's been busy Margot. Doesn't it look bonny? It almost makes you want to be poorly, just to go and have a butchers.'

'Well, I for one don't want you to be poorly, my love,' patting his knee. 'I'd quite forgotten what good sex was all about. You're an expert my dear. I suppose it's all that tinkering you do with cars. Makes your fingers nimble,' she ended dreamingly.

Colin couldn't help but stop at the garage on their way to Penny and Toby.

The whole place had been given a lick of paint and self-watering hanging baskets hung along the front of the showroom. The lawn to Colin's old house was beautifully striped and full of flowers. His old greenhouse had been re-glazed and painted and was crammed full of tomatoes and vegetables.

Chris came running out of the office, quickly followed by Joe and the boys.

After hugs and handshakes all around, Colin said, 'what a great job you've all done. You've given the old girl a new lease of life,' pointing at the house and garage.

'I thought you meant me,' muttered Margot to giggles and nudges.

'I'm proud to tell you, boss that with your Penny's support we've just landed the Vauxhall Agency. Look at these new models in the showroom,' waving his arm to show six shiny new cars sparkling in the spotlights overhead. 'Blow me down, Joe,' exclaimed Colin. 'You've certainly got your head screwed on.'

'And,' began Joe, 'Young Nick here right impressed the Vauxhall boys with his sales patter. They reckon he's a born salesman, so I've made him sales manager to start shifting the quota that they reckon we should easily sell in these parts.

'Toby spotted that little filling station cum garage at Tanfield that was up for sale. He sailed in, did a right good cash deal and has rented it out to us at a fair rent. Now we can move all the old part exchange cars in to re-sell.

'By hell, Toby doesn't half shift, he took on at his expense Walter's lad, who was a good, smart mechanic working at a big dealers, York way. Any-roads the lad always fancied himself in sales and wanted to move back here to family, so there you have it!'

'That son-in-law of mine,' said Colin shaking his head. 'He'll blow a fuse unless he settles down.'

As they climbed the hill and turned into Waterside , they stopped to chat with Barry, who was busy tending his large veg plot. Chickens scratched around the large wired run he'd built for them. 'They look in fine fettle,' called Colin.

'Oh, they are Mr. Parker,' enthused Barry. 'Finest eggs for miles around, Toby reckons.'

Hearing Barry's voice, Sally bustled out of the kitchen, wiping flour off one hand, whilst clutching a box of a dozen eggs in the other.

'There we are, Mr. Parker. Have these on us. Don't suppose you'll have much in the larder at the moment.'

'I don't know if it's rude or not, but how did the honeymoon go?' Colin looked at Margot, who thanking Sally for the eggs, replied, 'Well, Sally we're still married, and haven't had a cross word the whole time. We met some very interesting people who no doubt we'll meet up with again, then again some very peculiar people.'

'Aye,' said Sally, 'my mum always says there's none so queer as folk.'

'Exactly, Sally. I'm going to ask Penny and Toby, Joe and Chris, and you two to come and join us for supper in Harrogate in a few days. We can all have a chin wag, and catch up with news. Don't worry, I'll give you all plenty of time to arrange baby sitters.'

'Oh, that won't be a problem, as Beryl adores the babies, and they get on together. She can't wait until your Penny has her two little ones. She reckons it'll be like a kindergarten.'

**** **** ****

As they pulled up at Waterside, the front door swung open as a radiant, bulging Penny ran out to hug and kiss her dad. They pulled back, looking at each other up and down, at the same time both said, 'You are looking good,' before holding hands and giggling.

Toby appeared in the doorway and putting both hands on Margot's shoulders, lightly pecked her on both cheeks saying, 'You both look far more than well. You are tanned and look relaxed and happy.'

'Oh, we are,' cried Colin hugging his wife. 'Come on through to the terrace,' said Toby leading them through the kitchen, grabbing a large glass jug.

329

They went through the dining room seeing the table was laid to four, with a whole salmon and a magnum of Colin's favourite champagne, Veuve Clicquot, with its familiar yellow label. Toby settled the jug of Pimms onto the large wooden table shielded from the warm sun by a large umbrella in the green and purple stripes of Wimbledon.

'Pimms?' enquired Toby brandishing the jug and four tall glasses containing the 'fruit salad'.

'How fantastic,' said Margot. 'Absolutely perfect and just look at that view,' sweeping her arm towards the blue, shimmering water with the ripening barley stretching down towards it.

'Basil says Penny is allowed the odd glass, provided she tops up with extra lemonade. Cheers to your safe returns,' from Toby.

'We've seen a lot of beautiful places,' pronounced Colin, 'but this, that you created Toby takes a lot of beating.'

'Well,' cooed Penny, 'once we have the babies, we won't be able to get away for a bit. Anyway Toby is so busy.'

Having enjoyed their Pimms in the golden sun, they moved indoors to demolish the salmon that Silas had poached on one of his trips north of the boarder.

Penny had cooked it perfectly and when he was told of its origins, Colin said, 'you know it was literally free and wild, and it has a better flavour. It makes you feel a bit naughty, when you eat it.'

'I know what you mean,' joined Margot. 'When I take a delicious bite, I feel I want to look over my shoulder,' to chuckles all around.

They polished off two bottles of Sancerre, and as Margot and Colin were staying the night, they moved out to the warm and airy conservatory to have a coffee and a fine brandy, that Colin had brought.

They told Penny and Toby all about the cruise and places they had seen over the next hour and a half. Margot insisted on clearing everything away, washing up and with Penny's help put everything back in its proper place.

While they were busy, the boys enjoyed the brandy and a couple of Henry Clay's Cuban cigars from the box that Colin had given to Toby.

**** **** ****

Toby ran through the affairs at the estate agency, his separate building company with Walter, and his future plans. 'One bit of good news that will tickle you, Colin, is that with a bit of brass from me and scrounging by Silas is that he's now cracked it. We can convert old cooking oil into diesel that will run our tractors, plant and even our own cars.

'I'm going to fund his set up costs. He'll make his collections, process the oil and deliver to a huge tank Barry and I have set up at the farm,' he finished triumphantly.

'When they bring out that new Range Rover in diesel, I'll have one.

'Silas reckons we'll be quids in, because both Waterside and the farm use oil central heating. Just think, so long as people are eating fish and chips, fried chicken or burgers it's a bit like having our own oil well!'

'Bloody Norah,' exclaimed Colin. 'You ex-army lads ought to be running the country. Anyway, count me in. I'll buy oil from you to run our cars.'

'If you come over with me to Silas some time, we can say that you prepared it for your own personal use, as the rest of us have. There's no tax, but it's rumoured that if it catches on, the authorities might set a limit, but until then let's keep cracking away,' cheered Toby.

By early August the surgery was just about finished, with just a few tiny bits and pieces to do.

The doctors and nurses from the Ripon practice had made several visits and were delighted.

331

Basil had been paid out and the final cheque paid to Toby, Lord Middleham had been booked for the official opening. Meanwhile, Penny's bump had increased to a very large size. 'God, I hope something comes soon,' she cried to Toby. 'You are a lucky young mum to have a tip-top new surgery for later,' replied Toby.

'Where do you want to go for the delivery? Sounds a bit like a parcel,' he flipped.

'A damned precious one or two,' giggled Penny.

'I would love to have them at home, but Basil reckons that as it's two, and God forbid, but should there be complications, he reckons it'll be safer in hospital. The cottage hospital in Ripon would be fine, and it's near.

'He guarantees he'll see to me along with that young rather dishy doctor who is going to move in when Basil departs.'

'You saucy little minx,' retorted Toby. 'I'm getting jealous about my wife in the clutches of young John Farnell. Anyway, he is not that attractive, is he?' stealing a furtive glance at her.

'You silly man,' she cried. 'Anyway, you're not an angel are you my sweet?' giving him a hug and a kiss.

**** **** ****

On the 1st September she was suffering and around teatime Basil, true to his word had an ambulance there in a jiffy. Both he and Toby with two nurses were soon at the hospital. Penny was taken by stretcher to a private, light airy room overlooking a pretty garden. The room was full of strange bits of equipment.

After examining her, Basil reckoned it would be some time yet and thought there was no need to induce her. The midwife hooked her up to oxygen. Basil had one or two calls to make so Toby waited alone, holding Penny's hand. It was after midnight when the midwife called Basil. The door opened and a smiling Dr Farnell joined Basil and the midwife.

They all put on gloves and masks and the midwife started to shoo Toby out, when he said, 'Look Sister, I was in at the beginning of this, and am staying till the end,' looking at Basil who shrugged his shoulders. She then issued gloves and a mask to Toby. The water had broken and poor Penny was in agony as they stooped over her heaving and bucking body.

The first little head popped out followed by a pink, slimy little body. After cutting the cord, Basil held her upside down and she yelled and yelled.

Dr. Farnell took her, wrapped her up and handed her to a bemused Toby, who grabbed a surgeon's marker pen from the trolley and carefully wrote a letter C on the back of her little right hand. ''C' for Claire. She is the first.'

The next little head appeared, absolutely the spitting image of the first. The only difference being, Claire was almost bald, whereas the second baby, also a girl had quite a lot of darkish, matted hair, which would become blonde when washed. They called her Jenny, after Penny's late mum.

To be on the safe side, Toby repeated the operation by putting a J on her tiny hand.

She was much quieter than her bawling sister. The pain being eased, Penny was soon propped up by the midwife and handed her two little bundles. As if on autopilot, found a nipple each and started their first meal.

Penny looked peaceful and happy, as the midwife took the babies away to be cleaned up and properly tagged.

John suggested giving the exhausted Penny a mild sedative to give her a rest while the midwife would look after the two little tots. 'After all,' he confirmed, 'You'll be in for a few sleepless nights from now on.'

Toby thanked them all for their skill and kindness and kissing an already-drowsy Penny, he told her, he would be back in a few hours.

As he passed the farm, he saw all the lights were on, and Sally came dashing out, clamouring for any news. 'All three of them are fit and well. Now the hard work begins,' exclaimed Toby.

To his surprise both Barry and Chris appeared followed by Joe holding a magnum of pink champagne. To congratulations all round they raised their glasses to Penny and the two baby girls.

'You'll be famished Toby,' from Sally. 'I know you want to have a shower before you go back, but before you finish your drink I'll knock you up a nice beef sandwich with horseradish that I know you like. Uncle Albert sent us down a huge joint, and we've loads left.'

Joe, left alone with Toby said quietly, 'I never thought I'd see the day when you would be married, nor even have a pair of daughters. You know what they would say in the army, don't you?' Without waiting for a reply, continued,

'They'd congratulate you, but tell you that any damned fool can bore a hole, but it takes a real craftsman to put a spout on it.'

Toby laughed and replied, 'Well, I think that's it for the time being, at least.

By the way Joe, I'd like to ask if you and Chris would be godparents, along with Harry and Jill, who I've yet to ask. Please stay stum, until I give you the nod.'

'Of course we would be honoured. Who would have thought of it,' he pondered, 'Plain old Joe Smith sharing being a Godfather with a future Lord.'

Shaking his head he slowly smiled. 'That's just the reason, Joe, for being you. Don't ever try to change.'

Sally was back with what looked like a brick, covered in aluminium foil. Thanking her, Toby said, 'It's very kind of you Sally, I'll go and have a good soak, and wolf it down with a glass of good red.'

**** **** ****

After a few hours' sleep, he was back at the hospital, carrying a bunch of 12 white roses which the nurse put in a vase on her bedside table.

Penny looked better already. Her cheeks seemed fuller, her hair glossier and more relaxed.

The babies were brought in and placed one in each crook of arm.

Sister eased down her nighty and with a little mouth firmly clamped firmly to each swollen bosom, feeding time began.

Toby looking on softly asked, 'Will you have to start alternating them? I mean if you put the same one to the same nipple, might one end up left handed.'

'Don't be daft, you silly man,' she retorted.

Just at that moment, after a quick couple of taps on the door, Colin and Margot popped their heads in. Colin carried a beautiful white orchid, Margot a bunch of grapes.

'I hope you are not in trouble, already,' said Colin to Toby. 'No, she was just making fun of me, as usual.'

'Tell you what Colin, between us we've made the florist very happy,' waving at the plant and flowers.

At that moment a large, sweaty nurse bustled in with four more bouquets clutched to her ample bosoms. 'Gosh,' said Toby 'It looks as if the whole shop has been moved in.'

Colin was anxious as to how Penny was feeling, and couldn't resist holding each sleeping baby in turn.

They all trooped out into the waiting area as the doctor did his rounds. He suggested she stayed in for a couple of days. Toby escaped what was becoming a party by saying to Penny, 'I'll be back around teatime love. Can I bring anything that you might need?'

'No dear, but I'll make a list out for you for this evening. Stay and have a bite with me, will you?' she pleaded.

'Of course. I'm very proud of you and our two little girls.'

Lino kindly sent a mixed case of red and white wine with a note saying, 'For the guests that will keep turning up. Give them a thimble full each, mind you, or else they'll drink you out of house and home.'

Toby phoned Harry, who was delighted to be asked to become a godparent with Jill.

Overhearing the conversation, his Lordship snatching the phone from his son, shouted, 'Well done you two! You've scored a right and a left, what! Twins used to run in our family, and you'll be needing suitable transport for them. I'll get McDonald to have a shufti in the attic. I remember seeing a rather fine double pram coach, built by those splendid people over in Guiseley. It's got our family coat of arms on the front.

'Hope it won't turn their pretty little heads. I'll get McDonald to bull it up and deliver it in the morning. Bye for now, well done again,' and in a stage whisper, he continued, 'You'll have to have a word with Harry and tell him to get on with it.'

Calling in at the office on the way home Toby, was showered with congratulations from staff and clients alike.

Millie took him on one side saying, 'I've been talking to Beryl and Joyce who reckon they can manage without me for a while, so if you and Penny would like, I can come and look after Penny till she gets back to normal.'

Seeing him hesitating, she gushed, 'I could be living there and be, well, like a nanny for a bit. I know how, I've brought up my little sister and two brothers when my mum was busy on the farm. I really want to help. I'll take it as unpaid holiday if it helps.'

Toby, touched by her kindness and genuine desire to help, said, 'Thank you very much for your kind offer, Millie, I'm sure Penny will be delighted. She comes home in a couple of days. Shall I pick you up from here in the morning, show you round and how everything works. Then I'll go and collect the three of them.

'Joyce and Beryl can manage to look after the Estate Agency side.

'I'll let you do the building and development business from my house. Yep, I'll put a phone and small desk in the spare bedroom, so you can do a bit when you are able. I'll pay you as now, maybe a little extra if I'm able.'

336

She gave him a quick hug and went off giggling to tell Joyce.

Toby drove whilst Colin and Penny cuddled the two tiny babies wrapped up like two small dolls in thick, white blankets.

Toby had collected Millie with her two large suitcases, shown her around the house and got her installed in the smaller front bedroom. It overlooked the front field and reservoir. 'Oh, it's really lovely. I do feel lucky. I promised Mrs. Parker, I'll really do my best to look after you all as best as I can. You're all so kind and generous people.'

'Thank you, Millie dear. I know you will. It'll make life so much easier on Penny. You know, one baby is quite a handful, but twins must be so much more demanding.'

Toby was pleasantly surprised to see how quickly Millie picked up how everything worked and busily wrote shorthand notes of routines, meals, shopping and the myriad of little things needed to keep the house ticking over.

About an hour later Toby, Penny and Colin arrived with the two babies.

Millie took Penny up to show her how she'd organised her room and said, 'I've put the two cots here, 'cos I know you'll both want some sleep. I'll move them into your bedroom when you are ready.'

**** **** ****

She never did, as Penny, suffering from, what was to turn out to be post-natal depression was pleased to let Millie look after the girls. So it was then, when Millie became part of the family, eating with the girls, but looking after them on trips out.

Eventually, she took them to the local private pre-school.

Penny went back to work part-time for Hugo. Although she loved Toby, she kept telling herself after the pain she

337

suffered at the girls' birth she just didn't want any more children.

So whilst she cuddled up to Toby every night, she was happy to let him play with her and give her fantastic orgasms. She didn't want him to penetrate her, in case she became pregnant again.

She became expert in working Tom into frenzy and finally finishing him off by both hands and her mouth. Toby was thrilled, but naturally soon felt unfulfilled. He thought he understood her feelings and hoped that she'd get back to her normal self.

Time went on and the estate agency flourished as did the development business. Toby kept Walter and his team continually busy, very happy and getting wealthier.

Little Millie was an absolute treasure, looking after the little tots as if they were her own, with all the love and care that they deserved.

Both little girls were identical, with fair hair, blue eyes and attractive little faces. Claire the tom-boy was daddy's girl, whilst Jenny was quieter and more like her mother.

It had been after a couple of years , that Penny first announced she'd like to go back to help Hugo part time.

Toby, although feeling a bit uneasy said, 'Good idea. It'll help you feel better doing your old job and get you out and about a bit more.'

'I knew you would understand dear and the girls are so well looked after, I do feel a bit of a spare part sometimes.'

'Millie always insists she's here as long as you need her. I do think sometimes that the poor girl would like to get back to her job and see a bit of life again,' said Toby.

'I hope she doesn't,' snapped Penny. 'I really couldn't do without her. Do everything you can to keep her here,' not realising quite what she was saying.

In summer Penny mentioned to Toby, 'Hugo had taken a stand at a major antique dealer fair in Hereford and wondered if you'd allow me to go with him for four days?'

Toby felt a stab of jealousy, then slight anger. Was she carrying on with Hugo as before, he wondered. 'Sure, if you feel up to it,' replied Toby. 'I was hoping to take the girls out to see the sea for the first time. Maybe, if we get a hot day as forecast over the next month, Millie and I could take them on a day trip.'

'That sounds like a good idea to me, I'm sure they'd love it,' replied Penny.

She was due to go to the fair two weeks later. Toby had, in the meantime, run over to see Silas. Ostensibly to check on the fuel venture to see how it was going.

Over a beer or three he asked, 'Silas, the regiment (The S.A.S) is stationed in Hereford isn't it?'

'Of course, Stirling Lines, after David the founder of the Long Range Desert Group, which evolved into S.A.S of today. Why?'

Toby told him in confidence about his concern over Hugo.

'Bloody Hell mate,' replied Silas. 'She's just dropped a pair of the most gorgeous little girls. What's wrong? Can't you get it up any more?'

'No, just the reverse'

Toby went on to tell Silas about Penny acting as if she was frigid.

'Well, what do want me to do about it? Give her one?' he asked with a glint in his eye.

'You'd better bloody well not. No, I wondered if you had one of your old mates, who I'll pay, to do a bit of following and surveillance that you boys are trained for.'

'Oh, I see. Well, yes I have a mate who has just finished a body-guarding job in the Middle East. I'm sure a few notes will help to pay off his tab at his local boozer, not to mention his bookies bill.

'Give me a photo of Penny and I'll get in touch with Matt. I might have a run down to see the boys. Might even be a bit of work for an old codger like me! Don't worry, I'll sort the money side out with Matt and you can pay me when I see you.'

Toby and Millie loaded the girls into their safe car seats, Millie travelling in the back with them. Toby opened the sun roof to allow the warm sun to flood in. They stopped at the Star Inn at Harome, and sat outside in the lovely rear garden under a big umbrella, Claire and Jenny in high chairs.

Toby ordered two Lobster Thermidors for Millie and himself, whilst Millie fed the two happy little ones whose big blue eyes were solemnly taking in everything going on around them. Everyone from those lunching at adjoining tables, to people passing and even the waiters stopped to chat and gurgle at them.

After leaving the inn they went over the heather clad moors which were turning purple and dropped down to Sandsend. Surprisingly, for such a lovely day, it wasn't too busy, so they could park easily by the sea.

Toby locked the car, cradling one little one in each arm while Millie dragged their folding baby carriage, a rug, a big towel and an umbrella. They went nearly to the water's edge, before Millie laid out the rug so that Toby could deposit the babies and put up the umbrella, to shield them from the sun.

Claire looked out to the blue see on which two small yachts sailed, for all the world looking as if she was scanning the horizon, her two big blue eyes now squinting.

Jenny had crawled to the edge of the blanket, and her tiny fingers grabbed a shell, which Millie just intercepted before it went into her mouth.

'That was a near thing,' said Toby. 'Well done, Millie.'

'You've got to have eyes in the back of your head, with these two little monkeys,' giggled Millie. 'Thanks again Toby for a lovely lunch and such a lovely day. It's such a pity that Penny couldn't come. It's almost as if she can't bear to be near her babies. I've only been to the seaside twice before. We could never get away from the farm.' She said softly, 'It's wonderful being with you,' her large brown eyes fluttering as she gazed at him. 'Lovely to be with you too,' he murmured.

Toby turned up his trousers above his knees, then picked up Claire. 'Come on, you bring Jenny,' as he jogged down to the sea.

He was standing in the gently lapping waves up to his knees. The water was on the chilly side, as he lowered a squirming little Claire safely in to the water. She shrieked as her little toes met the waves, and then giggled with delight as she splashed and kicked. Millie copied Toby with Jenny, who was not as keen as Claire, and curled her legs up.

Claire, facing her took a kick like a footballer and splashed a squealing Jenny. 'That just shows how different they are, even if they are identical twins,' said Toby.

Millie nodding, replied, 'Maybe that's how they'll be all their lives. Claire's the naughty, adventurous one, like you Toby. While Jenny is quieter, more like Penny.' How right she turned out to be.

After drying off, they clambered back into the car and meandered their way home.

Millie had given the girls their milk on the way, so they were snoozing contentedly as they reached Ripon.

Toby pulled up a side street, and parked near a busy fish & chips shop. 'Shall we?' he asked jerking his thumb at the shop.

'Oh, yes please, what a treat,' thanked Millie. 'It's very kind of you, as it'll save me making a meal and washing up.' Toby was back in a few minutes with two parcels wrapped in The Ripon Gazette.

'I got two specials, chips and mushy peas. I'll pop them in the oven to warm up, while you get these two ready for bed.' With two little blonde heads safely sleeping, they attacked the deliciously well crisped fish. Toby opened a bottle of Sancerre. 'Far too good for such simple food, but we've earned it today.'

Raising his glass he toasted, 'To you, Millie, I couldn't manage without you.' Toby gave her a gentle kiss on her cheek. She blushed, saying, 'Now I won't wash my face

341

for a week. Thanks ever so, for such a lovely day. I feel really special.'

'That's because you are,' returned Toby.

'Penny is back the day after tomorrow, and I've got a fair bit on, so I'll get an early night.' He pulled her gently towards him, planting a kiss on her forehead.

He could hear her heart beating and she could feel his erection. He went into check the girls were still sleeping, then slipped into his own room. He felt excited and a growing feeling of attachment to Millie. After a quick shower he climbed into the big bed alone, and thinking of Millie, alone next door caused Tom to quickly rise.

So for the first time in many years, he seized a hot, throbbing Tom and grasping him by his huge head slowly started to masturbate.

Then holding the thick base away from his heaving flat stomach, was pumping ever faster with his right hand.

Little did he know that Millie, touching her unwashed cheek felt hot. Her breathing got quicker. She pulled up her nightie and gently feeling her left breast felt the nipple grow hard. Her right hand went down her firm stomach into her soft brown bush, her fingers parting her lips as her long, slender forefinger felt the little hard pea of her clitoris.

She moved her finger round in circles, first one way, and then the other, faster and faster, finally moving it up and down. Her stomach was bucking up and down. Her breathing became panting. Her fingers grew wet and she took the left hand from her firm, hard nipple and clamped it over her mouth to prevent the scream, she fell about to erupt. Eyes closed and imagining what Toby's huge cock would be like inside her, she climaxed in a series of orgasms like she'd never experienced before. Although kissing and playing around with one or two farmers' sons, she had felt their fingers but no more. She was still a virgin, but knew that she desperately wanted Toby to be the first.

Toby, meanwhile thinking of sweet, little Millie and wanting to take her, was aroused that he flung back the bedclothes and grabbing a large handkerchief with one hand allowed Tom to shudder and erupt into it. He wiped himself, pulling back the bedclothes fell into a deep sleep.

He was up and dressed early, but not as quick as Millie who was humming in the kitchen, as she emptied the dishwasher and laid the table for breakfast.

As she bent over, he could see the top of a black thong above her jeans. As he approached she turned and smiling said, 'You are an early bird. Caught any worms yet?'

'I think I've got one on the line, would love to reel her in,' he replied.

God, she looked great. Shiny hair, long legs, pert breasts thrusting through her top and a smiling, fresh face.

He put both hands on her shoulders, planting a quick kiss on her forehead before saying, 'I'm sorry to shoot off so early, but I've a pile of things to crack on with.'

Just at that moment the phone rang.

CHAPTER TWENTY SIX

Shrugging his shoulders and grimacing, as if to say you know what I mean, he picked it up. A broad Irish voice asking, 'You, lazy toad, are you still in bed on this glorious day? Top o' the morning Toby, it's Kath here.'

'Who could have guessed that indeed,' retorted Toby in a fine southern Irish accent. 'Kath, I'm glad you rang. I haven't wanted to disturb you when you told me that Liam wasn't feeling too good. What's the news then?'

'Oh Toby, he is ever so much better. It was a terrible, graveyard cough he had.

The doctor, a sweet little Colleen, looked just out of school. Slip of a thing she is. Well, she persuaded the old fella to give up the cigarettes. Sixty a day he's been smoking. Disgusting I call it, and damned expensive too! Says I, the old fool. You could have bought a string of racehorses from the money you've burnt over the years. Gave him such a fright, he's now stopped. Cough gone, no more wheezing. Do you know Toby, I think I've got me man back! Enough of me prattling on, he's here himself.'

The deep mellow tone of the Liam he remembered said 'Surrounded by bossy women I am, any way how's yourself Toby?'

Toby gave him a quick rundown, before asking Liam if his Trainer's Licence was through. 'That's why I'm calling you Toby. Not only is it through, but I've got a big Irish bookmaker who wants to invest in me and bring in some good horses, one of my pupils, Aidan will be my assistant trainer and his clued up wife, Rachel as secretary. A job she's done for years. Aiden has got his hands on a superb animal from a major yard that they'd spent a fortune on, but just couldn't get the best out of, so they are selling at a knock down price to move on.

'Now, you've always said that you'd come in with me when the time was right. Well, this is it. Aiden can get him for £1200, so I's like you and I to share the cost, therefore you'd only pay half the expenses. Are you in?'

'Liam, I've always told you I'd love to be involved especially if you are so keen and sharing it. I know I'm in good hands. What's his name?'

'Don't think he's got one yet,' said Liam.

'Come up with one.' Millie was listening and giggling. Toby looked at her, raising his eyebrows. She stood up and swept her arms round in circle. Toby looked puzzled, before she whispered, 'Waterside'.

Toby grinning told Liam, 'How about Waterside? I will post you off six grand Liam. Do let me know what costs will be and I'll get a standing order set up at the bank.'

'That's good news Toby. I've also got down to 5 informants, two trainers, two assistant trainers and an agent who is entrusted by the big gamblers to get their money on.

'So we are going to get one or two really serious punts in a week, and you'll be told by Kath as normal. Speak soon,' and then he was gone.

Toby wrote out a cheque and envelope saying he would post it at the office. Having drank a black coffee, a slice of toast in his hand he left, telling Millie he'd be back for the little ones bath time at six.

**** **** ****

He gave the letter to be posted to Joyce, who gave him a folder.

'It's all a bit mysterious, old man Sturdey, whose family have farmed over Thirsk way for generations, specially asked for you. I've made you an appointment today late morning, as you told me you were popping over to Silas first job.'

'Well done Joyce. Good planning. I shouldn't be long with Silas, I expect it's something to do with his diesel business.'

'All right for some,' glowered Lino, overhearing the conversation. 'Swanning in and out, while we do all the graft!'

Toby was surprised at Lino's disgruntled attitude, as he reckoned he did more that his fair share in bringing in business. I'd better just go easy a bit, he told himself. Tapping the envelope, he replied, 'Your ever efficient right-hand lady, Joyce here is just sending me off in pursuit of business for us, so what's the problem?'

'The problem is, that as I've lived round here all my life should be conducting what could be important business and not someone who's only been here five minutes,' he said to an astounded Joyce, Beryl and Toby.

'I promise I'll go gently and do my best to satisfy the unknown Mr. Sturdey. I reckon you've just seen your own arse this morning, Lino.' To splutters from the ladies, he sailed off.

Quickly getting to Silas and escorted by an excited, slobbering Ben he was greeted by a glum-looking Silas, who offered him a brew.

As they sat, Ben was wagging his tail between them. Before Toby could say a word Silas opened with, 'It's not looking good, mate. Matt followed your missus and that antique bloke. His hands were all over her and although they had adjoining bedrooms with a connecting door, Matt reckons they used one room.

'Matt knows the manager and became a temporary waiter at the Antique Fair Dinner attended by many other antique blokes and their birds. Your man was all over her during dinner, couldn't keep his hands off her.

'After they split up eventually, he saw the pair go up giggling in the lift. He gave them half an hour, before going up to the room. He could hear noise, and tapping on the door announced Room Service.

'It went quiet, then with a scuffle the door half opened to reveal the sweaty bloke with a towel round him, and your missus, clutching the duvet round her, propped up in bed.'

'Go on,' said Toby quietly.

'Matt just went in with the tray holding a bottle of fizz in the cooler and two flutes. He walked around to the bedside table nearest the bloke's bedroom.

'Settling the tray down, he could see that the other bed hadn't been slept in, and a pair of ginormous pink boxer shorts were on the floor beside the bed.

''Sent up to you sir, from one of your friends. Afraid he didn't give me a name.' After a couple of coughs yer man scuttled back to his bedroom, and thrusting a tenner into Matt's hand, he pushed him out of the door.

'So, there you have it. Sorry lad, but don't think you can trust her,' muttered Silas, shaking his head. An ashen-faced Toby replied, 'I had a feeling from the start something was going on there, but I can't understand why. I mean, just look at him.'

'Well, maybe he's got something on her, something she doesn't want out in the open. Who knows?'

'After all she's a woman Toby. Different species to us. Never can tell what's going on in their minds. Probably, best we can't.'

A sombre Toby handed over £100 in £20 notes, saying, 'I hope that'll cover it.'

'More than. I owe you some back.'

'No, Matt and you have earned it. Go out on the piss together.'

**** **** ****

He was deep in thought as he drove on to Thirsk. Pulling in to a layby, he opened Joyce's folder giving the name of Mr. Arnold Sturdey of Carlton Hall Farm. It was an arable farm, in the same family for three generations, and running to around 250 acres of prime malting barley.

He had two sons in their thirties, living and working in London. In brackets, Joyce had scrawled, 'I think someone with the same name bought some land near yours a few years ago. Happy hunting, Joyce.'

347

Good old Joyce, she brought a smile to his face for the first time since leaving Silas.

He swung into the sweeping, gravelled drive to the hall between stone pillars carrying huge wrought iron gates.

The hall sat at the end, built of Yorkshire stone, with huge slates on the roof, mullioned windows and a big, old oak studded door.

To the right, in front of the house was a large duck pond, on which a dozen ducks swam or preened themselves.

Getting out of his car, Toby dithered whether he should go around the back to the tradesmen's entrance, when the old front door creaked open and an old black Labrador chased out barking.

Toby bending on one knee scratched the old boy's head, and diving into his pocket gave him a biscuit.

'You'll be a friend for life now,' said a tall, thin man with a full head of white hair above his aquiline long nose, and the brightest pair of blue eyes Toby thought he had ever seen. Carpet slippers on his large feet, he was wearing a pair of faded, well-worn corn coloured cord trousers, blue check shirt and a navy blue cardigan with patches on the elbows, and a silk Guards cravat.

A huge hand extended to firmly shake Toby's. 'Do come in,' boomed a deep voice from such a thin frame. 'One thing I'm always keen on, is when a chap turns up, bang on time. Unlike lots of these idle buggers, who make appointments and do you the favour of turning up an hour later, with no explanations. Can't do with them. Usually kick them out.

'Now, come into my study,' ushering Toby into a large room, walled with books and a large desk, identical to the one Toby had bought for the estate agency.

Seating himself with his back to the fireplace he gestured Toby to sit down opposite him. 'I'm Arnold Sturdey, Mr. Cooper. I've heard a lot about you since you came here. Must admit, I admire how you managed to buy the two old cottages, and what a wonderful job you did in creating the one house.

'Your building, the farmhouse and getting one of the best young farmers round to run it was pure genius.

'I admire a kindred spirit like myself, but my two boys are away off in London town, one banking and the other helping run the stock exchange.'

Reaching into a filing cabinet he pulled out a bottle of twenty year old Dalmore Whisky. 'From the black Isle,' noted Toby.

'You know your whisky,' pronounced Arnold.

'Slangevar,' toasted Toby. 'Slange,' replied Arnold in a Gaelic toast that all true Scots give when rising a fine dram.

'Let's get down to business,' stated Arnold. 'I told you both of my sons are firmly established in London and my dear wife died over 5 years ago. Now, I'm rattling round here in this big house alone apart from old Kim here,' as he gestured to his faithful old lab lying at his feet, head on paws.

'Mrs. Briggs pops in daily and mucks me out, leaving my cooked supper ready to warm up. Got fed up, so I'm going to join my brother out in New Zealand.

'I've got about 250 acres of top arable land here, plus this lovely old house. Now, old Kellet, in the next farm, has always wanted this house and land, which with his 150 acres would give him a decent sized set up.

'He's an awkward old devil, with the deepest pockets and shortest arms of any man I know. We got involved in a joint scheme a while back. I paid my share, but he reneged. Never did get the money out of the blighter. Was only two thousand pounds, but I reckoned if I'd gone to court, it would have been swallowed up by the greedy lawyers. Never spoken to the man since.'

Toby waited patiently, sipping the gorgeous whisky, which Arnold generously topped up.

'Now, you'll be wondering what all this is to do with you. Well, I want you to be the middle-man and go and see

349

old Kellet and tell him, you've heard confidentially, from one of my pals that I was thinking of selling to a young city slicker in London who wanted to play farmers.

'That should get his clanger up. You can tell him that if he's interested, you'll broker the deal.'

'What price per acre are you after, Arnold?' Toby asked quietly.

'You are the agent, what do you think?'

'Land around here would fetch about £200 per acre, but for really good land like yours, I would ask £300.'

'Spot on,' exclaimed Arnold. 'And for the house?'

'You could ask £25000, I reckon you would get it.'

'You are good, my boy. I've just had an off the cuff valuation from an old friend, who is a valuer. Now, I want 350 an acre from old Kellet, which I'm sure he'll pay for the convenience and stopping anyone else getting their hands on it. Try £30,000 for the house, taking a minimum of £25,000 for it. I've come to you because I trust you, and know you'll get the maximum for me. I don't want to have to deal face to face with that little shit.'

Toby opened the file and taking out a contract form for Arnold to sign. Thanking him very much for the business, Toby got up to leave. Arnold laid a hand on his arm. 'Hold your horses, I've not finished yet,' so Toby sat back, wondering what was coming next.

'Now,' began Arnold, thumbing down tobacco into a gnarled old pipe, which he lit from a long swan match. Puffing contentedly, he looked Toby straight in the eye. 'I've told you I admired the way you got your cottages and built the farm, and employing young Barry.

'When I started after the war, his old man recommended a couple of chaps to help me. Joe retired but Geoff is still here, due to retire in two years.

'I bought land opposite you at the reservoir, running all around it to link up to the bit plus the extra you bought from the Board.' Toby sitting upright in his chair, his mouth dropped open, before he could say, 'But I thought a

Mrs. Jefferson owned it. No one seems to have met her, I don't understand.'

'No one would, dear boy,' confided Arnold, re-lighting his pipe. 'Bit of subterfuge, actually, as my dear late wife bought it in her maiden name. Bit naughty, but I don't like people knowing too much.

'When she died, it reverted to me. The total holding is about 150 acres, so I reckon it would make yours much more viable. All I ask is, we do the sale through your solicitor. He will hold the cash until I instruct him where to forward it.

'Don't put it through the estate agency. It's to benefit you and young Barry. Not keen at all on your partner, that Moore fellow. Looks a bit oily and shifty to me. You be careful, my boy, my feelings are rarely wrong! Just watch your back, that's my advice,' he concluded.

Toby stood up and with a firm handshake said, 'It's very generous of you Sir, I will respect your confidence and have a word with Simon, my solicitor today and get him to post you a sales agreement for you to sign. When would you like me to put the funds into Simon's firm and for how much?'

'Oh, wait until we've hooked old Kellet,' replied Arnold.

Toby taking the card Arnold held out for him, putting it carefully into his pocket and patting the dog goodbye, promised to keep Arnold in the picture as to how things were turning out.

**** **** ****

He drove away in a cloud of disbelief at his luck in being able to increase the farm by 150 acres of good land.

If it came off, Barry really would have a serious farm to manage, not just a large small-holding.

As Mark Twain once said, 'Land is best, they don't make it anymore'.

351

Don't dream, he told himself, you've got Kellet to buy first. He pulled into a field gate and took off his smart, polished brogues and changed into old wellington boots. He took off his tie and jacket, putting on an old Barbour, and went to find Kellet. He followed Arnold's instructions and found himself travelling up a rutted track with grass growing down the middle to what was once a smart stone double fronted house.

It had a faded name board on the wall, proclaiming Carlton Grange Herd.

A rusty metal sign depicting Friesian cow, in peeling black and white paint swung from the wall, creaking in the breeze. The whole place looked run-down and Toby wondered if this Kellet chap had the money to buy Arnold out.

He parked the Land Rover near the gate and made his way round to the back of the house to the buildings behind.

Here, all was tidy, with well-kept buildings, newish tractors and a very clean large milking parlour ready for the evening milking.

As Toby was taking all this in, a sullen, dark haired young man in a torn blue boiler suit and holed wellington boots slouched by growling, 'Can I help you?' which came out like a threat.

'I was looking for Mr. Kellet, senior,' he added.

'Who wants him?' growled back the youth. Toby hoped his 'chat-up' skills were better with the young girls at the village hop.

'My name is Cooper, and I've got a bit of good news for him, that I'm sure will make him smile,' replied Toby.

'The only thing that makes me and mi dad smile is when he kicks the arse of some slick salesman out of the yard,' snarled the youth, as he was joined by another. A taller, even more un-kept youth vigorously nodded his head.

Toby stood his ground, before advanced, right up to the first one, his fists clenched, eyes blazing.

The lads draw dropped and he shuffled backwards to his brother.

'I'm an estate agent, I've heard of some land coming up for sale, which I reckon would interest your dad. Some city slicker has already put a bid in, but if you're not interested, I'm on my way and reckon your dad will more than kick your arses to hell and back when he hears too late.'

Toby, giving them both a despairing shake of his head, turned and went slowly back to his Land Rover. It was quite a play and he hoped that he hadn't overdone it.

As he rounded the corner, a grey-haired, foxy-looking little man with a tooth missing said, 'You'd best step inside young man and explain yourself. You two come as well, and let's see what he has to say for himself.'

Toby followed them into the farm kitchen, where a small woman with hands reddened from hard work was washing up at the sink.

Dad motioned Toby to sit opposite him and the two gorillas slumped either side of him. 'Right then, what have you got to say?'

'As I said to what I presume as your sons, Mr. Kellet, I'm an estate agent from Masham way. At one of the auctions, I learned that your neighbour is thinking of selling up. One of his sons, as you probably know works in London, and I'm lead to believe has offered the house and the 250 acres to a friend who wants to be a hobby farmer.'

Both lads were upright now, casting furtive looks at dad. He was growing white, his fist clenched so hard that the knuckles were white.

Mum had stopped washing and turned round, her face horror stricken. 'The bastard,' hissed the old man. 'Why are you telling us, what's in it for you?'

'If a London bloke buys it, I don't get any commission, beside its wonderful malting barley growing land, as you know.

You are good farmers and I would hate to see some clueless part time 'Hello Henry' wrecking in a few months

353

what has taken years to build up.' There were nods of agreement all around.

Toby knew he'd caught his fish. It was just a case of reeling it in carefully and not let it slip away.

'We've not spoken in years,' muttered the old man. 'We fell out over a joint venture that went belly up. He'll sting us if he knows we interested.' The lads nodded glumly.

'Well then, I won't tell him that it's you. I can say it's someone from over my way that's heard on the grapevine,' said Toby cheerfully. 'Firstly, are you interested and have you the brass to pay for it?'

The old man indignantly puffed out his chest and exclaimed,

'I bet we've more brass tucked away in the bank than you smarmy sod.'

'Dead right, dad,' chirped the boys.

'Any road,' said the old man slyly. 'How much are we talking about?'

'I hear from my source that the London chap has agreed on £325 per acre and £27,500 for the house.' Toby finished, sat back and waited for the reaction.

Mum and the two boys silently turned to face old Kellet, who, after duly sucking his lips, announced, 'Well, we are certainly interested, but I reckon £350 is top. True it's good land but I wouldn't want to pay a Penny more than £350 and I would have thought that the house was over the top at £27,500.' Mum looked down and sighed, 'I've always wanted to live there, it's such a beautiful old house.' Old Kellet, putting his arm tenderly over her hunched, trembling, thin shoulders, suddenly said, 'You've grafted all these years, brought up these two and did the work of two men helping me build up, what is one of the finest herds in the North.

'Lads, we can't disappoint your mother. It's a golden opportunity. Ryan,' he looked at the older boy, 'you've been to college, you could take on the new arable side, and you Jake, you are the wizard on the dairy side, you could

354

take that on.' Both lads were grinning broadly, until Ryan jokingly looked at his father and said, 'And what will you be doing, sitting on your arse?' he ducked quickly to avoid the backhand aimed at him by his father.

Obviously skilled at it, thought Toby. 'Right,' said the father. 'You pop down and see him Mr. Cooper, and check that he is selling, and if so, check his price before offering him a max of £350 per acre for the land and £28,000 for the house.

For God's sake, don't say you've seen us, but give him that tale of yours as it coming from a farmer, Ripon way.'

'I'm away then,' said Toby. 'Can you give me directions, please?' This brought on an audible sigh of relief from the old man, and grins of relief from the boys. Obviously, this chap Cooper didn't know Arnold Sturdey.

**** **** ****

Toby left them, and turning right as instructed, saw a battered old Land Rover leave the farm and follow him.

Aha, he thought, they're keen to check I'm going where I said. He eventually pulled in to Arnold's drive and stopped at the door. Casually glancing over his shoulder, he saw a furtive figure moving behind the rhododendron hedge.

Arnold opened the door and quietly said to Toby, 'I see we're being watched. Hand me your card,' Toby pulled a card out of his pocket and gave it to Arnold, who read it, extended his hand and shook Toby's hand, waving him into the house.

'Well my boy,' he queried.

'We've hooked the fish, sir, now it's just about how much line we give him, before we land him.'

'Excellent,' retorted Arnold. 'What figures are we talking about?'

'I told them my contact understood you've been offered £325 per acre and £27,500 for the house.'

'Well done! And their response?'

355

'Kellet reckoned £350 was tops, and as his wife has always wanted the house, they offered £28 000 for it.'

'Right' decided Arnold. 'Tell them, I'm not a man to turn my back on a nearly done deal for a piddling amount, but tell them I'll accept £400 per acre and £30,000 for the house, including contents.

If you can get any way near these figures go ahead.'

'What I'll do Arnold, is agree with them and get them to sign on our official contract. I'll request payment direct to our solicitor's at the month end. That will assure them of their anonymity before they take possession.'

'I'll come over with our photographer next week, to take shots of the interior. Now, I'll set off back to the Glums and see what I can do.' Toby set off again.

**** **** ****

The old Land Rover pulled out of a side road and followed him in. Toby told them of Arnold's surprise at his knowledge, and reluctance to go back on the tentative offer he had received. If he could get £400 an acre and £30,000 for the house, he would do the deal with the unknown party, providing it was completed and the funds in our solicitor's account by the month end. 'And,' said Toby, 'if you agree to 30 thousand for the house, he throws in the contents.'

Mrs. Kellet jumped up with a shriek, squeaking, 'that's fantastic. The thought of buying furniture and fings was frightening me silly. We went for drinks when he was friendly-like,' darting a look at her old man. 'It were really classy, what they call tasteful. Oh,' she hugged herself.

'Right,' said her old man decidedly. 'We're on. I'll offer £380 per acre, and will take the house off your hands, including all contents for £30K.'

'I'll persuade him it's a good deal,' replied Toby. 'You drive a hard bargain, Mr. Kellet. Now if you'll sign our official contract here, and here,' said Toby.

356

He entered the title, prices and completion time. He took one copy, and left Kellet with another one, telling Mrs. Kellet that he'd get photos taken of the interiors as soon as he could and drop them off to her.

'Thank you, thank you,' she squeaked. 'It's better than all my Christmases rolled into one.'

Toby was off to Arnold's yet again, with no follower this time, but feeling a bit like shuttlecock.

Arnold greeting him like a long-lost friend rammed a full dram of his beautiful whisky into Toby's hand. He exclaimed, 'Well done indeed, my boy. You've done a splendid job,' as Toby showed him the signed contract.

'I'll get my solicitor chappie to send yours a deed of sale of my 150 acres to you personally for £100 per acre. If you can, it might as well be at the month end to co-inside with Kellet.'

'Looks as you are doing a midnight flit,' observed Toby cheekily.

'Spose it does,' laughed Arnold, 'But having made my mind up I just want to get on with it. I don't want to dither, and never make the move.' Toby asked Arnold if he could use his phone to confirm to Kellet that his bid had been accepted, and he'd get the office to send out contract.

Toby just caught Joyce at the office before she closed. She, Beryl and Lino were tidying up, and getting the post ready when Toby burst in and sat down, exhausted.

'Bloody hell,' hissed Lino, glancing at the contract and mentally calculating their commission.

'I really don't know how you do it,' said Joyce with a nod of agreement from Beryl, with a jealous glance from Lino.

'I'll get these to the solicitor tomorrow and get Leon to do some snaps ASAP.'

The telephone rang, which Beryl picked up and after a few 'Yes, Mr. Kellet, no Mr. Kellet,' replaced it. Toby looked at her warily, eyebrows raised. 'No problems, he was just confirming that all was in order and that, as his wife was so excited, she insisted he sends a ten per cent deposit to make sure it's theirs and no one will try to outbid them.

I assured them everything was in order.'

'Thanks Beryl, I was hoping they hadn't changed their minds after such a day!'

**** **** ****

He climbed back into his Land Rover and set off for home. He realised that he felt famished, as he hadn't eaten since breakfast. He also felt shattered from all the to-ing and fro-ing and diplomacy that he had used.

The benefit was that he hadn't been able to go over all that Silas had told him. Now it hit him like a sledgehammer.

He realised that his marriage to Penny was over. Perhaps it had never started! Hugo seemed to have a Svengali-like hold on her. She was always working late; many times too tired to come home. The Antique Fairs at the weekends were increasing.

He remembered that a few weeks ago, that on one of her rare visits to Waterside that she almost re-coiled from her excited twins, who fled to Millie, calling her mummy. The mummy who had replaced Penny.

'What the hell shall I do?' he cried. Then sitting bolt upright, muttering to himself I'll just do what I always done. 'Carpe Diem! I'll just seize the day.'

You can follow his progress in the second part of the trilogy:
Toby Seizes The Day

Lightning Source UK Ltd.
Milton Keynes UK
UKOW02f1254080615

253087UK00002B/14/P